REVENGE

"Vicaro, can you teach me how to become an expert marksman? How to fight a duel and kill a man?" Celeste asked.

The old bandit lowered his wineglass and stared in astonishment at her. "Women do not fight duels. No man would draw a weapon against a woman for other men would laugh and think him a coward."

"Suppose they did not know I was a woman? I could be a male cousin from Mexico City who carried a pistol and wanted revenge. I could bind my breasts flat to my chest and wear a *caballero's* jacket, trousers, and boots. I'd cut my hair short."

Vicaro appeared doubtful. "Could you truly shoot to kill a man?"

Celeste reflected on the question. Again she saw her brother lying dead with his pale face and bloody chest. And Dokken with his gloating smile. The hate she had felt then again burned in her veins.

"I could shoot Dokken for killing Ernesto if I should ever have the opportunity," Celeste said, her voice firm. "Please stay and teach me every skill and trick you possess with a pistol."

THE SEEKERS

F. M. Parker

Pinnacle Books
Kensington Publishing Corp.

http://www.pinnaclebooks.com

PINNACLE BOOKS are published by

Kensington Publishing Corp.
850 Third Avenue
New York, NY 10022

Pinnacle and the P logo Reg. U.S. Pat. & TM Off.

First Printing: March, 1998
10 9 8 7 6 5 4 3 2 1

Printed in the United States of America

Prologue
The Making Of
The Land

One colossal continent, Pangaea, held all the land of the great planet that was Earth. A mighty, restless sea miles deep covered the remainder of the world.

Composed of granite-like slag, Pangaea existed for many millions of years. This huge crustal plate was sixty miles thick and rested upon the basalt of the deeper mantle of the globe.

The Earth was already immensely old, more than four billion years, when the one huge continent existed. It was not the first supercontinent to have coalesced upon the surface of the Earth, only the last.

Two hundred million years ago the hot flows of the softened rock in the Earth's mantle, fueled and stirred by the planet's own internal heat, began to swirl upward with irresistible currents. Pangaea fractured and shattered into seven giant blocks and several smaller ones. The blocks drifted apart an inch or two each year upon the dense basalt of the ocean floor.

The island continent of Australia moved south. The North American Plate that included half of the Atlantic Ocean, moved westward to collide with a section of the Pacific floor—a mass of the planet that extended to Japan and was rafting north. At the crushing contact of these two gigantic plates, the leading edge of the North American Plate was crumpled, broken, and thrust up in mighty mountain ranges. Broad, down-faulted block valleys were formed in between these ranges.

From the hot center of the globe, mineral-rich fluids and gases were pumped into the passageways of the fractures and ruptures of the mountain rocks. As the emanations migrated upward away from the source, they found regions that were cooler and had less pressure. The minerals that could not remain in solution in the new environs differentiated and precipitated out into the fissures of the mountains. The atoms of metals began to settle out of the mineral solutions to rest along the crevices within the mountain.

Time passed, and billions more atoms of metal rose up from below to add their mass to the growing mineral deposit.

Finally the passageways through the rocks closed and the mineral-rich fluids ceased to flow. Left resting within the mountain were stringers and pods of a glorious yellow metal.

The mountains of the North American Plate cut crosswise the path of the prevailing storms that drove in from the west, forcing the moisture-laden winds to rise abruptly. The sky-brushing crown of the mountains, one day to be called the Sierra Nevada Mountains, milked the clouds, wringing stupendous quantities of water from them to fall upon the land.

The water rushed down from the rocky crags of the mountains and collected into rivulets, which grew into creeks that merged to form mighty rivers. The rivers hurried west carving wide channels across the broad valley bottoms. Near their mouth, the two streams joined their prodigious currents and charged off through a deep gorge to the ocean. For countless millennia, the ancient ancestor rivers of the Sacramento and San Juan cut and eroded the mountains. The common rocks were flushed away and the yellow metal they contained was concentrated into rich deposits in the gravels of the headwaters of the two rivers.

As the Pacific Plate continued to drive north, the land near the ocean lowered. The salty brine of the sea flooded in to fill the valleys of the Sacramento and San Juan rivers for many miles up their courses. Several hills near the river were inun-

dated until only their topmost crests poked above the water to form islands in the newly created bay.

That is the way man found the land.

He named the sunken, flooded river channels the San Francisco Bay. The deeply carved gorge leading to the sea between the peninsula headlands became the Golden Gate. The yellow metal he found in the gravels of the mountain streams, he called gold.

Chapter 1

Spring 1862
Boatswains Swamp near Gaines Mill, Eastern Virginia.

"The Goddamn Rebs are comin'," Jimmy Hathaway said, his voice tight and shaky.

"And a hell'uv a lot of them," replied Levi Coffin. He heard the rattle of metal and the muttered voices of the Confederate soldiers making their way down the steep slope on the opposite side of Boatswains Swamp. He caught the glint of sunlight from a rifle barrel, or maybe it was a bayonet, in the trees and bushes growing densely on the far shore.

Between the Rebels and the Union soldiers, the swamp was full of water from the recent rains. A few huge trees were scattered about, their black trunks rearing up out of the dead, unmoving water. The air held a thin, hazy mist that was stagnant and heavy with the odor of mud and rotting vegetation.

Levi Coffin's blue eyes narrowed as he measured the distance to the far shore. One hundred and fifty yards at the most. An easy range to hit something as large as a man with a rifle bullet. He looked down to check the extra cartridge tubes loaded and placed ready to his hand. He would need them very soon. He gripped his rifle and waited. The muffled voices of other members of his platoon of soldiers reached him from a little distance away in the trees both to the left and right. The company of Union First U.S. Sharpshooters had arrived at Boatswains Swamp only minutes before. They barely had had time enough to throw up low barricades of fallen logs to shield themselves from the guns of the advancing Confederates.

"Any minute now," Jimmy said, lifting his rifle.

Levi was watching a small brown bird that had sailed down through the limbs of the trees near the center of the swamp. The bird was skimming along a foot or so above the flat water and the floating leaves. Then abruptly the bird veered steeply upward, its wings pumping strongly, almost frantically. It darted swiftly away as if sensing the imminent beginning of the battle.

"That's what that bird must think," Levi said.

"Levi, do you think we can hold the Rebs this time?"

"Yeah," Levi said, looking at his comrade. "This time we can. This old swamp is like one of those water-filled moats they had in olden times around their castles. It'll slow the Rebs down. And there's not many trees out there for them to hide behind once they break out of the brush. They'll be easy targets."

Levi thought they might indeed stop the counterattack of the Rebels at the swamp. But he sensed that General McClellan's plan to capture Richmond, the capitol city of the Confederates, had failed. This was the afternoon of the fourth day of the battle. The general had landed his Union Army on the coast and had taken Yorktown. Then the army had marched to the west up the muddy peninsula to conquer Richmond. General Lee with his Rebels met them at Mechanicsville and threw them back. Again at Gaines Mill, Lee sent the Union Army reeling. Levi and Jimmy had been on the fringe of the fighting at Gaines Mill, and had fired only a few times at Rebel soldiers moving through woods at a distance. He didn't know whether or not they had hit any of the men.

McClellan had rushed General Porter's troops, including Colonel Berdan's Fourth Ohio Infantry and First U.S. Sharpshooters across the flooding Chickahominy River to support General

Morell's infantry division at Boatswains Swamp. The Confederate General A. H. Hill was positioning his fighting Rebels on the opposite bank.

Levi rubbed the stock of his new Spencer rifle. At eighteen years, the same age as Jimmy, he was proud to be part of Berdan's Sharpshooters. The colonel had selected five hundred of the most accurate riflemen from the Fourth Ohio, clothed them in green jackets, and named them the First U.S. Sharpshooters. They had been armed with the single shot .52-caliber Sharps rifle. Then from the five hundred, Berdan had selected a platoon of sixty-four of the very best marksmen. These men he had armed, at his own expense, with the new lever-action Spencer .52-caliber, a seven-shot repeater. The new Spencer increased the firepower of a man from ten shots per minute to more than twenty. Levi and Jimmy had made the elite platoon of sixty-four.

KRUMPH! A great explosion broke the stillness as a battery of Parrot 30-pounders fired. Immediately hundreds of other cannons joined in, 12-pound Napoleons and Whitworths, and 3-inch Ordnance rifles. The ground under Levi's feet shook with the mighty, jarring barrage of the big guns. General Hill's artillery had opened its bombardment from the west. The uproar increased as the Union's Ninth Corp on the plateau, two and one-half miles east of the swamp, began to return the fire.

"The Rebs'll be coming now," Levi shouted through the din to Jimmy.

A wave of gray-clad men, thirty strong and screaming a shrill, wild call, erupted from the woods on the far side of the swamp. They sprang into the water and charged forward. The water splashed up in muddy geysers from under the driving legs.

Levi raised his rifle. He looked down the sights at the Rebel soldiers rushing at him. He selected a large man gripping his bayoneted rifle and leaping in long bounds through the knee-deep water. Levi squeezed the trigger. The man fell as if tripped, plowing the water with his head and shoulders.

Levi chose a second target. Fired. The soldier crashed down. He shot his fine new Spencer repeating rifle across the swamp at the Rebels again and again. The rifle snapped empty. He jerked the empty cartridge tube out of the butt of the gunstock and rammed in a fully loaded one. Took aim.

The Confederate soldiers began to shoot back. Halting for a few seconds, they would throw their guns to their shoulders and fire. Then they charged on with bayonets thrust forward.

Levi felt the pounding of his heart fade away, and time seemed to slow to a crawl. He fired, levered another cartridge into the breech of the gun, and fired again. The yelling, running Rebs, now in water to their belts, went down one after another before the blazing barrel of his Spencer.

Another tube of fresh cartridges was shoved up through the stock of the rifle to the firing chamber. Shoot! Shoot! The Rebs are halfway across the swamp. Why wasn't Jimmy shooting? Levi couldn't stop them all by himself. No time to see what was wrong with Jimmy.

The wave of soldiers melted away into the swamp in front of Levi. Now there were only three left. Two. One. Then that last one fell and vanished. Only the muddy, trampled swamp water and a dense layer of gunsmoke remained to show that a battle had been fought and men had died.

Levi's breath came in huge, convulsive gulps of air. He felt the great exhilaration of the battle being won and he was still alive.

"Jimmy, we've stopped them," Levi cried. He began to laugh and pivot to look at his comrade.

Jimmy hung face down across the log barricade. His rifle was clutched in his hand. The back of his head was a mass of shattered skull bone, gray brain matter and blood where a bullet had torn free.

Levi stared, unable to believe what his eyes saw. Then his stomach heaved and foul bile came into his mouth. He struggled to breathe. Don't look at Jimmy. It's too awful. He pried his eyes loose from Jimmy's corpse.

He swallowed at the bile burning his throat and forced himself to take a breath. He focused on the layer of gunsmoke and watched it rise slowly up through the limbs of the trees. He lowered his sight to the swamp water that lay so very quietly.

The Rebels were down there someplace under the surface with their unseeing eyes washed by the bloodstained water. You got what you deserved, you bastards.

Levi raised his head and listened to the explosions of cannon fire, the Confederate batteries firing from in front of him, and the Union batteries at his rear. They sounded like the crash of distant thunderbolts. He heard the whistling flight of the big cannonballs passing overhead in both directions.

But he mustn't delay. He began to swiftly reload the cartridge tubes for his rifle. Jimmy's rifle, tubes, and full pouch of extra bullets were moved close to him. The Rebels would not be back after such a loss of men, but still it was best that he be ready.

A wild cannonball careened out of the sky behind him. It ripped down through the top of the tree above Levi's head. Fragments of broken limbs fell upon him. The iron cannonball hit the water at a low angle and burrowed onward, throwing mud and water up in a long, narrow fountain. The cannonball hit a tree, shaking it as if a giant had taken it in his hands and was thrashing it about.

Shrill, piercing yells erupted from the opposite side of the swamp. Scores of Confederate soldiers in a long line, left and right as far as Levi could see along the swamp, broke out of the woods and rushed into the water. They charged shoulder-to-shoulder toward the Union side of the swamp. Other Confederate soldiers opened up with covering fire from the top of the bank.

Levi knelt behind his small barricade of logs and lifted his rifle. He must stop those Rebels coming directly at him. Bullets whizzed past and struck with angry thuds in the trunks of the trees near him. In the woods on both sides of him, men of his platoon began to fire.

Levi's rifle bucked against his shoulder. A Rebel running hard in the lead, fell face down in the swamp. Those men behind charged directly over him as if he had been no more than a piece of wood in the water.

Levi levered in a bullet and aimed and fired; levered, aimed, fired. His accuracy with the rifle was not tested, only the swiftness with which he could kill. And he killed and killed. If he did not stop every foe from crossing the swamp, he would surely die.

He fired until the metal breech and barrel of the Spencer grew so hot that he could feel the heat in the wooden stock. He feared a shell would explode from the heat before he could completely close the breech. He dropped his gun and grabbed up Jimmy's cold one.

He flinched to the side as a bullet stung the side of his face. Damn! That was close.

The last two Rebels were close now. He could plainly see their expressions, eyes hard and determined and mouths sucking air. He shot directly into the center of the nearer man. The fellow shuddered under the impact of the lead projectile. His body suddenly became a jumble of legs and arms that splashed down to disappear under the water.

Levi quickly shot the last soldier. The man dropped his rifle, but ran blindly on. In four steps he smashed headfirst into a tree. He clung to the tree with both arms, hugging it to him, trying to stay on his feet. He moaned, a sobbing moan. His arms did not have enough strength to hold him and he slid down the trunk to sit in the water.

He started to cry in a gurgling, garbled voice. One arm rose out of the water and clutched at the wound in his chest. The crying and the gurgling sound grew louder. The Rebel began to lean to the side, and the angle increased. He moaned one last time, then slid below the surface of the bloody water. Bubbles rose and burst for a few seconds, then ceased.

Levi started to shake. His hands trembled uncontrollably. Oh, God! He hadn't joined the army to kill like this. The war was just supposed to be a pleasant romp through the fields and woods of the Rebel States, and a few minor skirmishes fought. There was not supposed to be all this shooting and dying.

His view moved over the swamp and the blood spreading in ever widening, crimson circles from the scores of places where men had fallen and died. How many men had he shot with his fine new Spencer? Forty? Fifty? He looked down at the empty cartridges scattered about on the ground. Each one of the shiny metal cylinders marked a dead man. There must be nearly a hundred empties. Horrible. Murderous.

He did not want to be alone with the dead. He cocked his ears to hear the others of his platoon of sharpshooters. There was no sound to indicate anyone was alive in the swamp except him. Was everyone silent because they too were overwhelmed by the slaughter?

Levi would leave this place of killing. He grabbed his rifle and started up the bank that lay to his rear. Then he halted and looked back at Jimmy lying across the log barricade. "Damn you, Jimmy Hathaway, why'd you get yourself killed?"

He shook his head. Jimmy had given his life to hold this little piece of muddy ground against the enemy. Levi could not give it up and run. He crept back and began to reload the cartridge tubes of the Spencers. He spoke sadly in a whisper. "Jimmy, we could've left this place. We could've gone home."

The wild, crazy Rebel yell came tearing across the swamp again. Levi lifted the deadly Spencer. Didn't these men in gray fear death as other earthly men did?

Levi shot, and shot, and shot. The body of running men melted into the dirty water.

Never afterwards could Levi remember the number of charges the Rebels made across the swamp. As the hours passed, his head rang from the great number of shots he fired, and had been fired at him. He became deaf. But his eyes functioned, watching an insane world of men running at him, running into the muzzle of his rifle. He saw the plumes of dirty gray gunsmoke lancing out at him from the exploding rifles of his enemies. After that first nick, every bullet had missed him. How strange it was that the enemy could not hit him.

Levi came to sanity again, holding his hot rifle. The swamp was empty of foes. The water lay quiet, placid, but bloody in almost every square foot. All the Rebel soldiers were dead and hidden, unseen and unseeing in their watery graves. He did not understand why he was still alive, for by all odds he should be dead.

He felt a weary sadness at what had happened this day, at what he had done. He laid his head down on the top of his little fortress. He cried for Jimmy. He cried for the dead Rebel soldiers because all his enmity for those brave, fierce warriors was forever gone.

"Anybody alive down there?"

Above the boom of the artillery banging away, Levi heard a voice call from the top of the bank behind him. He turned lethargically to look. There was no reason to hurry. He did not speak to the Union sergeant staring at him.

The sergeant came hurriedly down the bank. "How bad are you hurt?" he asked. He looked into Levi's face covered with burnt gunpowder, dirt, blood. He saw where tears had washed furrows through the grime. He glanced at the litter of spent shells on the ground, and briefly at the corpse hanging on the barricade.

"The Rebs killed my friend Jimmy," Levi said, his voice breaking. "And I shot them. I don't know how many. They are all out there under the water. But, Sergeant, this is all wrong."

"You only did your duty, soldier," the sergeant said.

"Duty? No man should kill like I did. They just ran straight into my gun like crazy men."

"It was still your duty. Now we gotta move fast. The Rebs have broke through on the north. They'll sweep south and trap us if we don't get the hell out of here damn quick. Bring your gun and shells and get your ass back across the Chickahominy."

"We just fought to hold this place. Now I must give it up and run?"

"Yes, damnit. Hurry up now."

"What about Jimmy?"

"He's dead, ain't he?"

"What the hell do you mean, is he dead?" Levi's voice rose to a screech. "Can't you see they've blowed half his head away?"

"Leave him," growled the sergeant. He hastened back up the bank and into the woods.

Levi scooped up the last of the cartridges and carrying his rifle, climbed the bank. He did not see the sergeant. But that was all right. He didn't feel the urgency that the sergeant had, only a numbing sadness. The roaring cannon was an unimportant echo on the edge of his awareness. He walked off among the trees.

He had not gone far when he saw a pool of water surrounded by large oak trees. His throat was parched with a great thirst. He crept to the water and knelt to drink. As he lowered his head, he heard the tinkling splash as a trickle of water fell. He hastily jerked up his head and looked across the pool.

A Confederate private, a middle-aged man, was on hands and knees at the base of one of the oaks on the far side of the pool. Water still dripped from his shaggy beard. Levi had not seen the man in the shadow of the tree.

The Rebel was watching Levi, and his hand was reaching for the rifle lying on the ground beside his leg.

Chapter 2

Levi's eyes locked with those of the Rebel soldier kneeling beside the pool of water. Should he try to grab his gun up and shoot the man? Could he do it more quickly than the other man could lift his weapon and fire.

"Young fellow, let's drink of this bloody water and then go on our way," the Rebel said, seeming to read Levi's thoughts. "Fighting can wait until another time."

"That's fair by me for I've killed enough men today," Levi said.

"So have I. Most of us who are alive, have killed to stay that way."

"Why do you call this bloody water?"

"Look over there," the man said and inclined his head toward the far side of the pool.

A corpse in blue uniform lay face down and nearly submerged in the water. A cloud of red water surrounded the body.

"These are damn mean times," said the Rebel.

"Yes," agreed Levi.

The Rebel watched Levi for a moment longer, his eyes prying into Levi's. Then he lowered his head and began to drink.

Levi remained on his knees, his sight shifting between the

dead Union soldier and the Confederate bent down with his bearded face in the water. He could not bring himself to drink— with the body in the water.

The Confederate raised his head every couple of seconds to check Levi, then lowered it to drink some more. The ripples made in the water by the man drinking radiated outward ever widening, sweeping across the pool to lap against the body of the dead soldier. The corpse moved slightly to undulations of the water.

The Rebel finished slaking his thirst. He picked up his rifle and started to rise.

Levi rose as the man did, gripping his rifle and primed to react to any threatening move from the man.

The Rebel spoke. "I have a son about your age out there someplace. I hope you don't kill him."

"I hope so too. And that he doesn't kill me."

The Rebel nodded. Keenly watching Levi, he backed away a few steps. Then he whirled and with his back to Levi, went with long, swift strides into the woods.

Levi, quickly putting the trunks of trees between the pool and himself, hastened away in the opposite direction.

He went east through the woods in the direction of the Union Army beyond the Chickahominy River. He had gone but a quarter mile or so when a cannonball loaded with grape shot hit the ground off on his right and exploded, flinging iron fragments and lead balls in a thousand directions. More cannonballs, mortar shells and canisters from howitzers landed in the woods around Levi, and burst, whipping the trees into shattered stems. Levi began to run.

The bombardment came from the Union batteries to the east. General Porter's artillerymen must think all their soldiers had withdrawn back across the Chickahominy and had lowered the aim of their big guns to strike east of Boatswains Swamp. The Confederate artillery was responding with an increased barrage.

Levi ran hard, weaving a crooked course over the land, seeking the most dense woods so that he would have some protection from the shells exploding in hundreds of places. He raced up and over and down a low hill. He came to a stream, hesitated, briefly casting quick looks around, and then splashed across.

He raced on. The woods thinned around him and the sun became visible, a large red disk hanging in the cloud of gun-smoke that blanketed the land. He saw a hill that seemed aflame with dozens of cannon entrenched and firing. At the top of the hill, one lone cannon and its gunners were sharply etched, pinned against the sun's red sphere. The gunners were firing to the east so they were the enemy.

A Rebel squad of six men broke from a cove of trees on Levi's left and closed on him. He sprang ahead, his legs driving, running at the limit of his strength. The Rebels knelt to shoot.

A mortar shell containing an explosive charge with a lighted fuse, and seventy-eight musket balls packed inside in sulphur arced down out of the gray sky. The fire of the lighted fuse reached into the shell. It burst with a brilliant orange flash two hundred feet above the trees between Levi and the Rebels. Musket balls, shrapnel and burning sulphur lashed down at the earth.

Levi's eyes registered the flash. His ears seemed ruptured by the explosion. A flying musket ball struck him a hard, glancing blow on the forehead. Blackness caught Levi like a thunderclap.

Levi fought up from the dark pit of unconsciousness to half life. A great sense of urgency drove him because danger threatened him, he somehow knew it. As the light seeped into his brain, a throbbing pain came to life and beat against his temples.

He laboriously pulled himself to a sitting position. He twisted his aching head and looked around in the growing gloom of night and tried to orient himself to what had hapened. Then it all came back to him, the squad of Rebels and the mortar shell.

He threw a look in the direction of the Rebels. The shell had exploded closer to those men than to Levi, and they lay sprawled in crumpled forms on the ground. Not one moved or made a sound.

Levi rested and waited for his strength to return. He caught his head in his hands and squeezed his temples hoping that would lessen the hammering pain. As the minutes passed, the fire of the Union artillery became sporadic, slowed even more, then ceased firing altogether. The guns of the Confederates trailed off to silence. The musketry of the foot soldiers of both sides faded away quickly as if they had only been waiting for a signal, any signal, to disengage from the fierce fighting.

Gradually hundreds of bivouac fires of the Union and Confederate soldiers began to flame up across a wide section of forest. As Levi watched the lights appear they reminded him of the time he had been on a dark hill above Cincinnati and watched that town light its night lamps. From the pattern of the fires of the soldiers, a distinct black strip separated them, Levi knew he was in the territory of the Rebels.

He tried to rise but his legs refused to support him. The pain in his battered head rose to a hammering crescendo. He sank back to lie on the ground. His thirst was awful. Dead soldier or not, he should have drunk at the bloody pool. He would rest a little while and then try to make it through the Rebel lines to his own outfit.

The night deepened. Overhead the cold, uncaring stars came out and shined like pin pricks in the black dome of the sky. A single rifle shot sounded far off. No more followed. He could imagine the relief of the soldiers that no battle was beginning.

An ambulance wagon, its path lit by the frail yellow light of a lantern, came through the trees. He heard the driver and the two men walking beside the vehicle talking as they passed by. He hoped they found all the wounded.

Levi made no sound, for the men would be Rebels. He closed his eyes.

Levi came awake to the sound of a bugle. He opened his eyes to find the dusk of early morning filling the woods. With his body exhausted and wounded, he had slept the night away.

Cautiously he sat up. Hardly more than a hundred yards distant, a company of Rebel soldiers were rising up from the ground and forming into ranks. They must have arrived during the night while he slept. Levi heard not one sound from the men as they took their positions. They could have been dead Rebels rising up from where they had fallen to go forward, to fight and to die again. He feared that yesterday's terrible battle had been a prelude to another struggle more ferocious and bloody today.

He watched with a bleak heart as the Rebels marched off to the east toward the Yankees beyond the Chickahominy River. He was sick to death at the uselessness of the fighting. The reason for the war had seemed so clear when he had enlisted in the Union Army in Cincinnati six months before. He had felt lighthearted when he said good-bye to his parents and younger brother and two small sisters. He had laughed and joked with the other new soldiers as they journeyed south. He had met Jimmy during the march. They had talked about the magnificent adventure that lay ahead of them as they fought to preserve the Union.

How wrong they were, for the war was not magnificent. It was an ugly, deadly thing. The two armies were locked in a battle that was self-perpetuating, an all-destroying ritual. A horrible game played between Generals Lee and McClellan. Maybe they got some thrill out of the contest between the two armies. If they did while killing thousands of men, then Goddamn them both to hell.

The preservation of the Union had no meaning to Levi if he had to kill again as he had killed yesterday. Never again did he want to see a man fall, the ranks to thin around him. The sight of his friend Jimmy lying dead across their little log fortress would forever be burned in his memory.

Levi nodded to himself. For him the battle was over. Never again would he raise his gun against another man.

He crept through the trees to the dead Rebels. Two were approximately his size, one wounded in the chest and the other in the stomach. He took the trousers from the first and the shirt from the second, and put them on as his uniform.

Moving swiftly and carrying his Spencer rifle and ammunition, he struck out to the west. Holding in deep woods, he began to work through the Confederate lines. With luck, he just might make it from the battle zone. He had no destination in mind except to go to some faraway place where there was no killing.

Levi forded the water of Boatswains Swamp at a location different from where he had fought and entered the bordering woods. A quarter hour later he broke out of the woods and Malvern Hill rose up before him. The open, grassy hillside was strewn with thousands of bodies, living and dead, Union and Confederate alike, like a ragged, gray and blue carpet covering the ground.

Most of the men were unconscious or dead, but enough moved to give the hill a crawling effect. A grievous, mind-bending sound struck Levi. The fallen boys had been left lying unattended all night and were moaning and crying for water and for someone to help them with their wounds. The sound had a palpable force that pressed against Levi.

Two ambulance wagons hurried past Levi with loads of wounded. Two vehicles were woefully inadequate for the task of carrying the multitude of wounded to the field hospitals, fifty wagons were needed, a hundred. A dead wagon hauling a bed full of corpses moved toward a long, open trench.

It would have been nearly impossible to cross the hillside without stepping on the dead or wounded so Levi veered away. He dropped down to the valley bottom and moved along the creek flowing there.

"Soldier, where're you going?" called a lieutenant marching with his platoon of soldiers along the edge of the hillside.

"Where's the field hospital?" Levi called back. "I've been hit." He pointed to his bloody head.

"Follow the ambulance wagon," the lieutenant said. He led his men on.

Levi trailed after the ambulance wagon. Traveling in that direction would get him farther away from the battlefront. Soon he should be entirely clear of both armies.

He crossed a narrow finger of woods and came out in a

grassy park of a quarter acre or so. Near the center he saw where a skirmish had been fought. He counted fourteen corpses of Rebels and Yankees lying together, literally in a heap. A young Union lieutenant had fallen while trying to rally his men. His hand was still firmly grasping his sword, and determination was visible in every line of his face.

A Confederate soldier, a mere boy, lay nearby. He had died while in the process of loading his rifle. The weapon with breech open, was clutched in his left hand, and the paper-wrapped cartridge was between thumb and forefinger of the right, and the end of the cartridge bitten and the paper still in his teeth. Then a bullet had pierced his heart and the machinery of life, all the muscles and nerves, had come to a standstill.

Levi hastened from the lieutenant and the boy, and all the other dead soldiers.

He found the Confederate hospital consisting of three long tents in a broad meadow. Hundreds of wounded lay in rows awaiting their turn at the surgeons' table. Hospital stewards had a squad of men spreading straw on the ground for the wounded to rest upon. Meager comfort, thought Levi as he studied their faces, thin and worn from marching and scant fare, and now pinched with pain from their injuries.

The sides of the tents were rolled up and tied, exposing wooden tables extending the full length of the interior. The surgeons worked bare-armed and fearfully splattered with blood. Muscular orderlies held the wounded soldiers down on the bloody, slippery operating tables as the surgeons wielded their saws and scalpels. Levi shuddered at the sight of the large mounds of severed arms and legs at every tent. A skilled surgeon could amputate an arm or a leg in ten seconds. The more quickly the operation could be performed the better for the patient for there was no anesthetic and the human body could endure the pain just so long before it died.

Levi ran a finger over his injury. The bleeding had stopped and had crusted into a scab. The pain had lessened. The wound would heal by itself. Besides it would be hours before the surgeons could be free to treat such a comparatively minor injury. He hurried past the hospital tents and entered the woods beyond.

Levi raised his pace to a trot. Frequently he saw bodies, swollen corpses darkened by the sun and giving off a frightful stench. They were the dead of the first fighting days earlier.

He broke from the woods and out into a small clearing overlooking a shallow valley. He came upon a Rebel soldier puffed and bloated in death and lying in the grass. A hundred more bodies, all Confederate soldiers, lay flung about in awkward, grotesque positions. Caught in the open by cannon firing exploding canisters, the men had been scythed down like weeds by the murderous flying metal. Flies in a black fog swarmed and droned about the corpses, gorging themselves on the rotting blood and flesh.

"Help me!" a weak voice called from a cluster of bodies. "For God's sake, help me!"

Levi spotted the source of the pain-filled plea, a soldier with his chin shot away and part of his neck gone. One of his hands was missing. The stump of the arm was tied with a crude bandanna tourniquet. He was a man who should have already died from his wounds.

Levi knelt beside the Confederate. "I can't help you. Only a surgeon at the hospital can."

"Even a surgeon can't help me. I'm a dead man. Be a buddy and load my rifle for me."

"What do you mean?"

"Load my gun. And lay it here next to me."

"I don't know," Levi said reluctantly. "Are you sure?"

The man raised his good arm in a pleading motion. "I'm sure. Hurry and do it."

"All right," Levi said and nodded with understanding. He took a cartridge from the man's bullet pouch, bit off the end of the paper wrapping, and shoved it into the breech of the man's rifle. He closed the breech and laid the weapon close to the man.

The Rebel soldier cuddled the weapon against his side. His thanks showed in his eyes that steadily watched Levi.

"Go," the soldier said. His finger sought and found the trigger of the rifle and began to caress the cold metal.

Levi whirled around and sped away. He did not want to see the man die.

Before Levi could run from the clearing, the rifle cracked. He cried out and ran faster.

He continued to travel over the battlefield of the previous fighting. He moved at a steady pace, hanging in the patches of woods as much as possible. He was always alert for bands of Confederate soldiers. In the brush thickets he saw bodies that had been missed by the dead wagon. Now and then he spotted furtive forms slipping soundless among the trees. The way the men moved meant they too were deserting, or were scavengers robbing the dead.

As Levi stole across a dirt road, a horse nickered in the woods ahead. He peered hard in among the trees. A black horse, its ears thrust questioningly forward watched him from a tangle of brush. A cavalry saddle was upon its back. A Sharps carbine was in a scabbard, and two pistols were in saddle holsters hanging over the pommel. A dispatch case hung beside the pistols.

"Hello, old fellow," Levi said to the horse. "You're just what I need."

The horse tugged at something holding its bridle reins on the ground. Then it stood with alert brown eyes watching Levi draw closer.

Levi stretched out his hand and took hold of the bridle. "Easy, fellow, easy now." Levi talked soothingly to the animal. He rubbed the horse's strong back and patted its withers. He looked down to see what held the bridle reins.

A young, dark-headed Confederate lieutenant stared up vacantly at Levi from the ground. His eyes were glazed with death. The leather reins were gripped tightly in his hand. Even in death he had not released his hold on his mount.

The lieutenant was but a little older than Levi. He would not grow any older. Levi was glad he had not been the one who had slain the man.

"Neither you nor I will fight any more battles," Levi said, humbled by yet another of the number of dead. "I don't think you would care if I borrowed your horse, and perhaps your jacket. I have no pistol, so I'll take yours. I apologize most deeply for taking your belongings."

Levi stripped off the officer's four-button field jacket with the gold insignia on the shoulders. He tugged it on. He donned the man's hat with the jaunty feather spearing up. An officer would be less likely to be questioned as to why he was leaving the battlefield, especially if he carried a dispatch pouch. He replaced the lieutenant's Sharps carbine in the scabbard with his Spencer, then climbed astride the horse.

Something held Levi there beside the dead man in the silent woods. A horrible black feeling fell upon him that he should be the one lying lifeless. But he was not dead and now every man alive, had he discovered what Levi had done and was going to do, would call him a coward and a deserter. And even worse, a scavenger who robbed the dead.

Levi believed he was different from the scavenger and the coward. He did not look for gold and silver or jewelry. And he was no coward, for strangely he had not thought of dying until this moment. Further he had killed far more than his share of the enemy. It was the killing that he thought useless that was destroying him. He could not endure more of the slaughter. But should he remain in the battle, he would be forced into situations where he would have to kill. It was better that he go swiftly from the bloody battleground.

Levi reined the horse away from its dead master, and looking keenly ahead, went up over a low ridge and down the far side. The woods were soon left behind and he picked up a dirt road leading west over farmland.

A company of fresh Confederate foot soldiers marching at the double quick and sweating heavily, came past Levi. He saluted the captain commanding the soldiers and hastened onward.

He spoke to the lieutenant's horse. The strong beast picked up a swinging lope. When the road veered north, Levi held a course due west. He would go as far as possible from the battlefields of the cruel war. All the way to the Pacific Ocean, all the way to California that he had heard so much about.

Chapter 3

San Francisco, California.

Brol Mattoon leaned on the end of the long mahogany bar and ranged his view over the Porpoise Saloon. It was a huge place with tables for two hundred patrons, a dance floor where twenty couples could swing and promenade to music without being crowded, and thirty poker tables that he rented out by the week to professional gamblers. There were rooms upstairs for the saloon girls to entertain their male customers.

It was late at night and the throng that had crowded the saloon earlier had dwindled down to one game of cards and two young men in rough miner's clothing drinking whiskey near the rear. He frequently cast a speculative look at the miners.

Mattoon was a large man, thick in chest and legs. His face was darkened by a two day's growth of coarse black beard. He was dressed all in gray, wool trousers, broadcloth shirt and a jacket. His clothing fit loosely so there was space for the .36-caliber Colt revolver in a shoulder holster, and so he could move freely and quickly.

Mattoon prized the Porpoise Saloon, located on The Embarcadero, the main street fronting San Francisco Bay, the most highly prized of all his possessions. From the Porpoise he sent out his men to collect monies for the protection of waterfront businesses. He had little concern for trouble from the police. Though San Francisco was a lusty, rapidly growing city of 150,000 people, its police force consisted of but 130 men. No more than fifty men were on duty at any one time. Rarely did one of them venture onto the waterfront at night or to the wild Barbary Coast where he had several sailors' boarding houses.

Mattoon was proud of the fact he shanghaied more seamen than any other crimp in the city. The live body of a strong man was worth several hundred dollars to a ship's captain heading out to sea on a two- or three-year whaling or sealing voyage. The pimps and their whores who plied their trade in the bawdy houses and on the streets paid Mattoon for protection. The businessmen on the waterfront, and the owners of the tugboats on the bay paid protection money, and it was a rare ship that brought cargo to San Francisco and got off again without its captain paying Mattoon's gang of collectors.

Mattoon rested his sight on the two young miners. They had arrived a couple of hours before and had been celebrating, laughing in high, good spirits and telling the bar girl who had served them of their gold strike in the high Sierra Nevada Mountains. They had tipped her with pinches of gold dust from their pokes.

He smiled without mirth knowing he would soon take the two fools' gold and send them on a voyage to the end of the earth. The schooner *Asia Voyager* had arrived in San Francisco three days before. Four seamen had jumped ship the first night and vanished among the thousands of people in the city. The ship's captain had tried to recruit replacements but with no success. He had let it be known at the right places that he needed four able-bodied seamen. No questions would be asked should they be delivered unconscious. Mattoon planned to fill the captain's order. Already he had two Chinamen chained in the storeroom below the saloon.

The card game broke up and the gamblers settled their debts with one another. The professional spoke to Mattoon as he went past with the other players to the entrance. Mattoon acknowledged the man's greeting with a small nod of his head.

Mattoon spoke to the bartender. "Fix two Mickeys for those two." He chucked a thumb at the miners. "I'll go get Marie to come and serve them."

"They must have at least five hundred dollars of gold still in their pokes," said the bartender.

"Then that's what we'll charge them for the drinks."

The bartender chuckled. "Sounds about the right price considerin' the kick they'll get out of them." He began to mix the Mickey Finns, a concoction of whiskey, brandy, and gin heavily laced with opium.

Mattoon returned from the office in the back with a tall blonde woman who was very pretty. They stopped at the bar. He nodded at the drinks and spoke to the woman. "Take these to those two men. Talk them into drinking them. They'll be flat on their backs in three minutes."

"It'll be easy, for they're hardly more than boys," Marie said, studying the youthful faces of the two miners.

"Soon as those two drink, go lock the front door," Mattoon told the bartender. "We're done for tonight."

"Right, Brol," said the bartender.

Marie picked up the drinks and walked across the room to the miners. She smiled prettily at the men and sat the drinks down in front of them. "You fellows have been good customers tonight and the owner wants to buy your last drink."

The older miner looked up at Marie, then across the room to Mattoon, and the bartender. When he turned back to Marie, there was a glint of wariness in his bleary eyes. "We've got our own whiskey," he said.

"You two are the most handsome fellows that's been in here tonight." She tousled the hair of the younger fellow. "So have a drink for a lady."

The younger man laughed and leered up at the woman. "Sure why not," he said drunkenly. He reached for a drink.

The older man caught his arm. His expression had become more alert. "Best we just drink the last of what we've bought and leave," he said.

Mattoon, watching Marie, saw the rejection of the drinks she offered. She turned away from the miners, and her smile vanished. She shrugged her shoulders as she came up to Mattoon.

"Those blokes don't want the drinks," she said. "They say they're leaving."

"Is that so? Well we'll just see about that."

Mattoon walked toward the miners. He rubbed the knuckles of his right hand on the front of his jacket as if polishing them. He halted by the table where the two men were tying their gold pokes. Without a word, Mattoon folded his thick fingers into a bony fist and slugged the older man, who was closer, in the side of the head. The man fell with a crash across the table, then slid to the floor unconscious.

"Why in hell did you do that for?" asked the second man. "He didn't do anything to you." He climbed to his feet and swayed drunkenly staring at Mattoon.

"Neither did you," Mattoon said. He reached out and grabbed the man by the shoulder and spun him sideways. Never break a man's jaw that you plan to shanghai. A man who can't eat has no value. Mattoon hit the man in the temple with a smashing blow, caught him as he collapsed, and lowered him to the floor.

Mattoon blew on his knuckles. Goddamn, how he liked to hit people, to feel his fist strike solidly, and the man's eyes go blank.

He bent and lifted the second man and draped him over his shoulder. As he did so, Marie came up and retrieved both gold pokes from the table. She flipped the dregs of whiskey from one of the shot glasses and poured it full of the glistening yellow dust.

"Is that all right for my share?" she asked.

Mattoon checked the shot glass and judged it contained at least two ounces of gold. That was far more than Marie had earned. "Sure. It wasn't your fault they wouldn't drink."

Marie managed the Porpoise for Mattoon when he was away on other business, which was most of the time. She was one of the prettiest women he had ever seen—and also the most deadly. For that reason he had never bedded her, though he knew he could if he wanted to. Best to use her kind of woman strictly for business. He knew she was skimming a substantial sum of money off the top of what the Porpoise brought in. The time would come when she stole more than her services were worth. When that happened he would shanghai her off to China. With her blonde hair and white breasts, and the white other parts of her, some rich Chinaman would pay a fortune to possess her.

"A woman could get rich working for you," Marie said.

"That's right so stick with me." For a little time more, Mattoon thought.

He caught the second man by the collar of his shirt. Then with ease, carrying one man and dragging the other, he took both through the door to the rear and down a flight of stairs to a dank, earth-floored basement.

Two Chinamen, with wads of cloth crammed in their mouths as gags, lay on the ground with both hands and feet shackled to pairs of posts anchored solidly in the dirt floor. Mattoon ignored the pleading black eyes and the movement of the men's hands signaling to be freed. He stretched the two white men between two other pairs of posts and shackled them same as the Chinamen. Roughly he gagged them to keep them from crying out should they regain consciousness. He stepped back and examined his four captives. No man once caught had never escaped from his hands.

Mattoon returned to the upper floor where Marie and the bartender waited. He spoke to the bartender. "Go tell the captain of the *Asia Voyager* that we have the four men for his crew and for him to come and get them." He turned to Marie. "The price is four hundred for each of the Chinamen for they're just half men, and eight for the others. Get payment before the captain takes the men."

"Yes, sir," said the bartender.

"You're leaving?" Marie asked.

"I've got other business to take care of."

"When will you be back?" Marie asked.

"What the hell difference does that matter?" Mattoon

snapped, instantly angry at Marie's prying question. "Just do your job."

The woman backed up a step, knowing she had overreached herself. Her eyes became hooded, and keenly alert. She had witnessed Mattoon's quick temper before, a flash of anger that was often immediately followed by a blow from his fists. The fact she was a woman would not protect her, she was sure.

Mattoon saw Marie was wary of him, but not afraid. However if she ever realized he had discovered her theft, she was vicious enough to take action to protect herself, even to try and kill him. He decided at that moment to send her on the long voyage to China in the very near future. He smiled at the thought. Marie, seeing the smile, gave a tentative smile in return. He widened his smile and watched her relax. Fool, you won't like what I have in store for you. He turned and went across the saloon and let himself out the door onto the street.

Fog had joined with the night to make The Embarcadero full of cold, damp darkness. The streetlamps, spaced every two blocks, were but small, yellow pools in the murk. Mattoon moved off without hesitation.

He reflected on the task yet to complete this night, and the payment that would follow. With pleasant anticipation, he began to whistle as he strode along.

Captain Groton, master of the clipper ship *Roamer,* matched the stride of Brol Mattoon as they went swiftly through the foggy night. The captain heard the muffled tread of the felt-shod feet of the fifty-six Chinese virgins as they hurried close behind them. Louder still came the thudding bootfalls of Mattoon's six armed guards flanking the virgins on both sides and bringing up the rear.

The time was an hour before dawn, when the government harbor officials would be asleep and the streets deserted. With luck the transfer of the girls from his ship to Chung Pak, the noted Chinese auctioneer, could be made without detection. The girls would be hidden in a secure place until their sale.

Even with Mattoon's men the captain still worried about the

Chinese tongs for he knew that they would be aware of the arrival of his ship late in the evening and the beautiful virgins hidden below decks. The tongs always knew everything that happened in the Chinese world of San Francisco. Without Mattoon it was a certainty that a band of the tong fighters would attack out of the darkness and carry off the captain's valuable cargo.

The virgins were the most prized cargo that he could have brought from the Orient. He had been very fortunate to discover the dealer in women in Canton. The man had just returned from the inland provinces with a collection of unbelievably beautiful girls. Groton had used all his money to purchase a portion of them, selecting only the most lovely. The price had been high, four hundred dollars for each girl. He had guarded them vigilantly from his female-starved crew during the long voyage from China. Now they would be quickly sold to the rich and lonely Chinese merchants in San Francisco for large sums of money. The most beautiful would bring at least three thousand dollars. He stood to make a fortune from the girls, and he did not want to lose them, not even one.

A stiff ten-minute walk ended when Mattoon halted at a large warehouse. He opened a heavy door and entered the building. The procession of girls and their guards followed him inside.

Mattoon found a lantern hanging beside the door, raised the globe and lit the wick with a match. He lifted the lantern so that its yellow light washed over the assemblage of people.

"Groton, are all your girls here?" Mattoon asked.

"I'll check," said the captain. He made a quick count of the frightened ivory faces. "They're all here," he said.

"Vetter stand watch," Mattoon ordered one of his men. "I don't expect any trouble now that we're inside but stay awake."

"Right, Brol, nobody'll get past me," Vetter replied. He closed the door and put his hand on the butt of the pistol stuck under his belt.

"Come with me," Mattoon said to Groton. He led on past huge piles of goods in boxes, crates, and barrels toward a distant, lighted corner of the warehouse.

Mattoon slowed as he approached the Chinaman sitting at a table upon which rested two brightly burning lanterns. The man was aged, and very gaunt with a sparse, gray beard. He was dressed in the most plain brown silk clothing, trousers, shirt and simple jacket with its collar turned up as if he was cold. Two wary young Chinamen, strung taut as bow strings, stood close behind the old man. Their hands were inside their loosely fitting, brocaded silk coats. One of the men wore maroon and the other black. A flat-crowned hat of matching color sat upon each man's head. Their long, braided queues hung from under the hats and reached down below their shoulders.

Mattoon halted and glanced briefly at the seated Chinaman, Chung Pak. Then his view swept over the two standing men. He knew the men represented the two strongest fighting tongs in San Francisco, the Chee Kong Tong and Kwang Duck Tong. Each man would be armed with a revolver and knife. The tongs were the only worthy competition Mattoon had. When laced with opium and their blood pumping wildly, the tong fighters were totally fearless. Men without fear were the most dangerous animals in the world.

The old Chinaman arose and bowed very low to Mattoon and then to Groton. "It is a pleasure to see you, Brol Mattoon. And you also Captain Groton."

"Hello, Chung Pak," Mattoon said. You lying, yellow bastard. Glad to see me, my ass. You and your kind are my worst enemies.

"It's my pleasure to meet you again, Chung Pak," the captain replied.

Pak focused his black eyes on Groton. "The message that your seaman brought requested that I meet you here. So I have come."

"Thank you." Groton was pleased that Pak had accepted. Through his hands passed nearly every Chinese woman that arrived in the city. The master of every fighting tong needed the assistance of the trusted auctioneer to such an extent that once the virgins were placed in his custody, they would be totally safe from being stolen. Any tong member who broke the cloak of protection given Chung Pak would be put to death in the most horrible manner. The two tong fighters with Chung Pak were there to show the protection still was in effect. They would be the strongest, and most fierce fighters the two tongs had.

"I have brought fifty-six young virgins from your land that lies so far away. They are very beautiful and should end the loneliness of some of your countrymen who now live in America. I wish that you would arrange their sale to men who will be kind to them."

"Maybe you have only fifty-five virgins to sell," Mattoon said in a coarse voice. He ran his eyes over the girls.

"Maybe so for I must pay you for your protection," Captain Groton said, trying to keep his dislike for Mattoon out of his voice. The man ruled the underworld of the waterfront, with his own motley army composed of scores of head-knockers, murderers, riffraff spawned in a dozen countries and now washed upon the San Francisco shore. Ship owners paid bounty to him to see that harm did not come to their cargo or vessels. Unlike Mattoon, the tongs of the city never directly attacked white men, though they would steal newly arrived Chinese girls from them if the opportunity presented itself.

In those first months after Mattoon's arrival in San Francisco eleven years before, a few ship captains had refused to pay his collectors when they came with hands out asking for money and promising nothing except to leave them carry on their business in safety. When denied his tribute, Mattoon never made a second request, or threatened reprisal. In the night a swarm of men would rush aboard the ship, overpower the crewmen and set fires at several locations. The landward end of the dock would always be blocked with mounds of cargo, placed there by Mattoon's men from elsewhere on the waterfront, to slow the fire engines. The ships often suffered severe damage, and one had burned to the waterline and sunk at its mooring. All during an attack, Mattoon would be in some saloon drinking with a dozen men who would be his witnesses that he had no part in the fires.

"One thousand dollars in gold, or one of the girls, wasn't

that your price?'' the captain asked, hating Mattoon and fearing which option he would choose.

"That's my price, and a damned fair one too." Mattoon chuckled at the tone of Groton's voice. Why was the man angry at the price? Mattoon had given protection as promised, guarding the girls until they could be put under the care of Chung Pak. Further, the sale of the slave girls was unlawful and carried risk beyond that which might come from the tongs.

"Which do you want, the gold or the girl?" the captain asked.

Mattoon spun around and swept his eyes over his men bunched in the edge of the lantern light. He called out to them. "What'll be your pleasure, lads, the gold to divide among you, or one of these beautiful heathen virgins to share?"

"You always take most of the gold leavin' only a little for us to divide," a stoop-shouldered Italian with a pockmarked face called back. "I'd get the same thing you get if we took a girl."

"I agree with that," said a broad faced German. "We all do, don't we fellows?"

The remainder of Mattoon's men shouted out their agreement. All were grinning with wolfishly anticipation.

"You've had your say," Mattoon replied. He turned back to Groton. "You heard the lads. Line the pretty girls up and let me look them over."

"I'll choose you one," the captain said hastily.

"No you won't," Matton said and laughed at Groton. Miserly bastard would give him the least pretty one. "I'll pick the girl. Tell them to form a circle around the lantern so I can see them good in the light."

The captain started to protest, for he knew Mattoon would select the most beautiful virgin, and therefore the most valuable. But he caught himself up short and said nothing. He could not win, so why be stupid and argue and arouse Mattoon's anger.

"I don't know how to tell them that," the captain said. "Chung Pak, will you tell them?"

Pak dreaded what he knew was about to happen, but he kept his countenance composed. The beauty of a woman was often a very great danger to her. Men such as Mattoon and his underlings did not cherish beauty as it should be cherished. God created female beauty for the enjoyment of man, and most certainly to satisfy his deepest needs and desires. So it was natural that a man should love a woman, even with some vigor, but never so roughly as to mar her loveliness. Mattoon and his band would destroy any woman Pak selected. They were nothing but dog offal.

Pak looked sorrowfully at the young girls huddled together where they had first stopped. They watched him closely staring up with frightened eyes from lowered heads. They sensed something was about to happen to them, something very bad.

"Come closer into the light, my daughters." Pak spoke in the language of the girls and motioned with his hands. Still thinking about Mattoon, Pak's voice and gestures were more brusque than he intended.

The small, young women in their loosely fitting clothing shuffled forward. They never took their eyes off Pak. I'm no protection for you, Pak thought.

"I want them in a circle around me, Pak," Mattoon said.

"Form a circle around the big ugly white man," Pak said.

The girls did as Pak said. Their eyes were turned down now and staring at the floor.

"Have them look at me," Mattoon ordered the old Chinaman. "I want to see which one has the prettiest face, and other parts."

At Mattoon's harsh, insulting tone, Chung Pak's hate for the man swelled until it almost escaped him. He heard the angry growl of his two tong fighters close beside him. They were his to command, so why shouldn't he signal and send them flying at Mattoon with their knives and pistols? They were fearless fighters and just might slay Mattoon before they were shot down. To succeed in that effort was worth the lives of the two fighters and even Pak's also. For years Mattoon had harassed and slain the Chinese men of the city, and abused the women terribly. He could do it safely, for no Chinaman could testify against a white man in an American court. How many of Pak's countrymen had Mattoon and his men destroyed? Scores surely.

None of Pak's thoughts had registered on his face. He put up his hand to silence the tong hatchetmen. He could not launch an attack on the white men now. He must discuss the intolerable situation surrounding Mattoon with Scom Lip. That tong leader would know what to do, and could organize the proper method of obliterating the enemy.

He spoke again to the virgins. "My fair, young daughters, please look at the white man."

Reluctantly but obediently, the eyes of the girls rose to the face of the giant white man with the big head.

Mattoon walked slowly around the circle of virgins, examining each face and body. Now and again he reached out and pressed the loose clothing tightly to a girl's body and felt her breast and hips. He completed the circle and started a second turn.

He halted before a slender girl, and leaned over her with his mouth open and teeth exposed like a hungry animal. She began to tremble looking up at the huge man towering above her.

Mattoon's hand snaked out and caught the front of the girl's gown at the neck. He hesitated for a moment staring into her eyes, enjoying her total fear. Then he jerked roughly, strongly downward. The girl cried out as she was yanked forward and her gown ripped down to her navel. She caught her forward movement just inches from Mattoon.

"I'll take this one," Mattoon said.

He bent and caught the tail of the torn gown and pulled upward, stripping it from the girl's body. She stood naked before him and all the men. She cried out and her hands jumped to cover her breasts, then hastily moved to cover her pubic region. Then so scared and so uncertain as to what to try and hide, her hands fluttered back and forth like crippled birds between her breasts and lower region.

Mattoon's fingernails had raked a furrow across one of the girl's small, firm teats. Now blood began to flow from the injury, coursing down and dripping from the nipple.

"My men will like her," Mattoon said to Groton and Pak. "And, Groton, thanks for bringing some real heathen beauties to choose from. Now take the others and leave." He laughed a short string of chuckles at the angry expression on Groton's face. He would like to know what Chung Pak with his unreadable face was thinking.

Groton turned away without replying. The girl no longer belonged to him. Her fate was sealed, and with Mattoon guiding, it would be a very bad ending.

Pak spoke to the remaining girls and they hurriedly pulled back from the naked one, as if she was a leper. The two tong fighters did not move. They stared at Mattoon with black, hostile eyes.

Mattoon nonchalantly looked back at the tong men. His mouth stretched into a grin as white and dead as a bleached bone. In their domain of the yellow-skinned heathen Chinese, the tong fighters were much feared. Mattoon had no fear of them. He spread his hands toward them, daring them to come at him and fight.

"Let us go," Pak said to his two guards. The odds must be better than seven to two when they did attack Mattoon.

Mattoon lowered his hands. "Leave one of the lanterns, Pak. Take the one at the outside door as your second light."

"Very well, Brol Mattoon," Pak said. He pointed at one of the lights and again spoke to his fighters. "Bring one and lead the way out of this cursed place."

The fighters glanced at each other and then questioningly at Chung Pak. He watched them stonily. Do as I told you, he willed them.

The fighter in maroon clothing made one shallow nod as if he had heard the silent command. "Yes, Honorable Pak." He took a light and went toward the outside door. Pak herded the girls after him. The second fighter came last, watching to the rear.

The girl left behind near Mattoon whirled suddenly and started to run after the last Chinaman. Mattoon grabbed her by her long, black hair and yanked her back. He spun her to face him.

He caught the girl by the waist, his long fingers completely encircling her body. She began to tremble violently as he lifted her off the floor. He brought her close, and taking most of her injured teat into his maw of a mouth, sucked long and hard on it. He liked the copper and salt taste of her warm blood, and her trembling body brought him immediate tumescence.

"Right tasty," Mattoon said, removing his mouth from the girl's teat and licking his lips. "Now for the rest of her." He folded the girl in his arms, pressing her tightly against him, and carried her to a pile of burlap sacks used to hold wheat.

The girl realized what he meant to do to her and began to strike and kick, trying to break free. Mattoon smothered her arms with is and laughed at her futile efforts. "I sure like them when they fight me," he said.

He opened his trousers with one hand, and then knelt and laid the girl down on her back on the sacks. He forced her legs apart with his knee and positioned himself. With one savage thrust, he entered her. She shuddered with the pain and screamed. God! how he liked to take the virgins. There had never been any doubt as to what he would choose for his payment. His men only thought they had made the choice. He took her completely in a flurry of deep thrusts with all his men watching.

Mattoon rose from the girl and fastened his clothing. He did not once glance down at her lying trembling on the rough burlap sacks.

Now to give the men his leavings, Mattoon thought, and at the same time bind them to him, as much as you could bind such scoundrels. He looked at Vetter who was just arriving from his station at the door of the warehouse. "Your turn's next, Vetter. But listen to me. You like to hit women when you make love to them. Don't you hit this one. Leave her face pretty for the others."

"All right," Vetter said, but showing his disappointment.

"When all the men are done having their fun, take the girl to Fat Genevive," Mattoon said. "Tell that old whore that I want one thousand dollars for this little moon-eyed Celestial. She's been used a little, but she's still worth a thousand dollars and I'll not take a penny less. You hold the money until I see you next time."

"I'll do that," Vetter said.

"See that you do." Mattoon went off through the dark warehouse with a jaunty stride and whistling.

Vetter lay down upon the ivory skinned girl. She shoved at his chest with her small hands trying to push him off. He crushed her arms against her, and entered her. She cried out with a sobbing moan.

Mattoon stepped from the warehouse onto the street. He glanced skyward through the fog and could see the night was beginning to fade and daylight not more than an hour away. He struck out walking swiftly.

He passed a section of the city containing sailors' boarding houses. He owned a block of them. A quarter mile further along, he entered a street of older one- and two-story houses. In a hurry, he did not wait until he reached the gate of a nondescript one-story house surrounded and almost completely hidden by shrubbery and trees, but stepped over the low fence and into the yard. Immediately he was lost to view by anyone watching from the street or from one of the nearby houses.

Within the house, a middle-aged Chinaman heard the heavy footsteps on the stoop. He sprang from his chair where he had sat waiting throughout the night. Never did he sleep during the dark hours, for the master might arrive at any moment—and the master demanded instant service. The Chinaman scurried across the room to the door and stopped. He bowed deeply as Mattoon shoved the door open and came inside.

"A bath and see to it that the tub's full and hot," Mattoon said, moving past the Chinaman without slowing. "Lay out my clothes."

The Chinaman held his bow until Mattoon had crossed the room and entered the bath, then he hastened to an adjoining room and to the tank of water he had kept warm by a fire beneath it. He opened the valve to allow the water to flow from the tank through a pipe in the wall and into the tub in the bathroom. He had tested the temperature of the water several times and knew it was correct.

Mattoon heard the water spilling into the tub as he undressed.

He tossed his stained clothing onto the floor, then dipped his hands into the water, wet his face, and lathered it with soap from a mug. Standing naked before the mirror, he began to shave.

"Po, come here," Mattoon ordered.

The Chinaman appeared in the doorway. "Yes, Mr. Mattoon?"

"Any visitors come here today?" Mattoon watched the man in the mirror.

"No, Mr. Mattoon." Po looked steadily back into the mud-colored eyes watching him intently from the mirror. He feared the man, but he must not show it, and he could not leave his employment until he had permission. He lowered his view to Mattoon's pale-skinned body, more than twice his size. With every motion the man made, his cord-like muscles rippled and knotted. He could and would kill without hesitation if he knew, or only guessed who Po's real master was.

"Good. Are my boots polished?"

"Certainly, Mr. Mattoon."

"Saddle my horse," Mattoon said, dismissing the man.

Mattoon had finished his bath and dressed. He wore a white silk shirt and a black, wool suit, very elegant and cut to perfectly fit his heavily muscled body. His boots shone like polished steel and a black hat sat at a rakish angle upon his head. He left by the rear door.

He moved along the tree-lined path to the stables behind the house and went inside. Po handed him the bridle reins of a black gelding. Mattoon always walked when on the waterfront, but uptown he rode wherever he went. He checked the girth, cursed loudly enough for Po to hear him, and tightened it a notch. The Chinaman never got it right.

He mounted and rode the gelding out of the stable and along the alleyway to the street. He reined the horse up the slanting street toward San Francisco's heart. He felt tremendously alive as he rode through the cool morning breeze sweeping the city. Every muscle of his body was bursting with energy, as if he had the strength of half a dozen men. He laughed at that thought, a loud laugh with no mirth, like rocks hitting. The sound sped up the man-made canyon of the street, ricocheting and echoing.

Mattoon, in his mind's eye, soared upward from the ground until all San Francisco lay spread below him. He could see the great blue bay with its scores of ships, miles of jutting piers, and the warehouses and factories lining the waterfront and The Embarcadero. Landward from the waterfront, sand hills rose covered with a multitude of office buildings and businesses, and higher still the homes of the rich. In this uptown world beneath a thin veneer of fancy clothing and polite manners, ruthless men connived against each other in cut-throat competition, took bribes, and robbed with forged documents. When all else failed, they committed murder by the ritual of the duel. A strong man who acted boldly could do whatever he wanted in this town.

Chapter 4

Celeste Beremendes shivered, and wrapped her thick wool cape more tightly around her. It was not the cold, damp wind coming off San Francisco Bay that made her tremble; fear gripped her.

The horse-drawn Phaeton buggy with Celeste in the rear seat and her brother Ernesto and his friend Lucas de Cos in the front seat, moved through the fading night down the long lumber pier extending out into San Francisco Bay. The iron-shod hooves of the horse fell with a measured drumbeat upon the wooden decking and echoed out across the dark, foggy waters of the bay. Both sides of the pier were crowded with berthed ships, four-masted coastal schooners and squat, ugly steamers used to haul lumber down from the mills along the northern California and Oregon coasts. Storm lanterns burned at the head of ships' gangways and cast a feeble light and helped the buggy find its way among the huge piles of wooden planks, beams, and boards stacked high as men could reach.

Celeste was deathly afraid for her brother. He would kill a man in a duel in the next few minutes, or he would be killed. Celeste feared it would be her brother who would feel a bullet stab through him and fall dead.

The duel was an evil thing brought about by a wicked trick played upon Ernesto. Celeste believed beyond any doubt that the incident used as the basis for the challenge to the duel had been deliberately staged to make her brother fight. John Dokken and a female friend had encountered Ernesto on the street. The woman had abruptly stepped into Ernesto's path and he had run into her before he could catch himself. Dokken had pretended it was Ernesto's fault that the woman had been struck and demanded satisfaction by a duel. Dokken was well known in San Francisco as a skilled duelist who had fought and slain many men. She had pleaded for hours with Ernesto not to accept the challenge, to apologize and let the matter pass. Lucas, Ernesto's friend since childhood and now a reluctant second for the duel, had added his strong appeal for Ernesto to refuse the challenge. Ernesto too realized the affair had been contrived to make him fight, but he had laughed their fears away.

Celeste leaned forward to look past Ernesto. Nearly a quarter mile of pier remained to be traversed and she could barely make out the end through the foggy dawn of the coming morning. A breeze rippled the thin, low-lying fog. The ships wallowed to the wind and waves and creaked and groaned as they rubbed against the wooden piling of the pier. The rickety pier swayed to the shove of the heavy ships.

Ernesto halted the buggy in the light of one of the ships' gangway lights and looked at Celeste. "Little sister, for the last time, please go back. I don't want you to see the duel."

"No," Celeste replied firmly. "I'm going with you and I will watch. You are the one that should change your mind and forget the duel. Come home with me to the *rancho* for a few days until this is forgotten."

"Celeste is correct and you should listen to her," Lucas said, turning so he could see both Ernesto and Celeste.

"I can't run away," Ernesto said. "And you, Lucas, must know that. I will go through with it and nothing you two say will change my mind."

"Not with a man such as Dokken," Celeste said. "You must stay away from him."

"I'll fight this duel," Ernesto said, his voice tight and his face drawn. "I'm not a coward."

"We both know you're not a coward," Celeste said. Men did such absurd things to show their bravery. "But I'm determined to be here with you."

Ernesto's face softened and he reached out with a hand and stroked Celeste's cheek with the tips of his fingers. "Celeste, you worry too much about me. I have my trusty pistol. I'll come through this safely."

Celeste had watched Ernesto practice. Sometimes she would fire a few shots at his target. He was quick and a skilled marksman. But he had only fired at targets. That was far removed from shooting a man.

"You're all the family I have left," Celeste said. A sob of fear for her brother almost escaped her before she could stifle it. Her father and grandfather had been killed by the Americans in 1847 when they had invaded Mexico. Her mother had died this past year.

"Yes, we're the last of the Beremendes," Ernesto said. "You should soon marry and have many children to carry on the bloodline of the family."

"I have many things to do before I marry. You are older than I am, why don't you marry one of your numerous sweethearts?"

Ernesto smiled wanly. "You're right. After this is all over, I will give that a great amount of thought."

He faced away from Celeste and spoke to the horse. The buggy moved onward down the pier.

Celeste could not but think the hollow, measured drum beat made by the hooves of the horse on the planking of the pier was like the dirge of a funeral march. She hoped fervently it wasn't an omen foretelling the outcome of the duel. She mustn't even think it for that might cause it to happen.

The fog began to roll up before the thrusting fingers of the wind and moved toward the shore. The ships at the other piers both to the left and the right became visible. Farther away ships at anchor in the bay, steamships and sleek clipper ships came out of the fog and into the light of the growing day.

The end of the pier became free of fog and Celeste saw men

standing unmoving. She recognized Dokken and the surgeon who had accompanied him. She thought a third man near them would be Dokken's second. A fourth man stood beside a horse-drawn buggy. He was the good Dr. Suazo, Ernesto's surgeon, who had already arrived. She hoped the doctor's skilled services would not be needed.

A fifth man stood off by himself. He was the judge of duels. He was a *gringo*, old and gray with age. He wore a long cape and stood very erect. He had once been a duelist who fought other men's enemies for pay. For the past several years he had taught the use of pistol and sword at his academy, and sometimes officiated at the duels of others. Celeste had heard he was a fair man with allegiance to none of the forces striving for power in San Francisco. The duels the man judged were said to strictly follow the Code Duello.

Ernesto brought the buggy to a stop near the judge. The three climbed out.

The judge of duels glanced at the newly arrived men, and the woman. What was she doing here? Should he try to send her away? No, let it be. He checked his watch and then looked at the eastern sky. The heavens above the hills on the distant mainland across the bay were rapidly changing from gray to blue. The hour for the contest was at hand. He hoped there would be no killing. A strange thought for someone like him to have, but he had seen far too many men die for little reason.

"It is time to begin," the judge called to the adversaries and their seconds.

The duelists and their seconds moved toward the judge. The surgeons with their satchels of scapels and tourniquets and other medical paraphernalia drew together near the edge of the pier and out of the probable line of fire. Celeste went to stand beside Dr. Suazo.

Dokken and Ernesto removed their coats and hats and handed them to their seconds. Both men wore thin silk shirts so that should a bullet strike them, it would not carry pieces of wool or cotton into the wound and thus be more likely to cause infection.

The judge spoke to the two duelists. "Is there any argument that I can make to persuade you to forego this?"

"No," Dokken responded quickly.

"Then I must also say no," Ernesto said. He felt a slight quiver run through his body and the wind seemed suddenly colder.

The judge looked from the confident face of Dokken to the strained countenance of the young Mexican. This was not a fair match. Dokken had fought eight duels that the judge knew about, and he was still hale and hearty. Beremendes had never fought a duel. Still, the judge thought Beremendes must have considerable skill or he would not have accepted the challenge. Who of the two was the quickest and most accurate marksman would soon be known. Chance sometimes intervened and one man's weapon would misfire, and then even the least experienced might win.

"Allow me to see both weapons," said the judge.

Lucas de Cos and Dokken's second removed Navy Colt revolvers from the wooden cases they carried and presented them to the judge.

"Will one loaded cylinder in each weapon suffice?" the judge asked the duelists. "In that way if a man misses his opponent, there shall be no second shot at him."

Dokken chuckled. "One bullet is all I have and all that I'll need."

"One is enough," Ernesto said.

Celeste felt the throb of her heart in the temples of her head as Ernesto and Dokken responded to the judge. The haggard face of her brother was terrible to see. She should have done something, anything to prevent this crazy duel. Oh, God, it was now too late.

The judge checked the cylinders of both revolvers and examined the firing caps. "They are satisfactory." He handed the pistols to the duelists. "As agreed to by your seconds, the distance will be ten paces by each of you. I will call fire when the duel is to begin. Is that understood?"

"Right," Dokken said. "Let's get on with it."

Ernesto nodded in the affirmative. He tightened his grip on the cold butt of the pistol.

"Then stand before me and face in opposite directions. Go ten paces, then halt and turn. Stand ready, guns pointed at the ground. I caution you, don't raise your weapon to fire until I give the command."

The judge paused and glanced at the faces of the two men. "Go ten paces," he directed.

The duelists paced out over the pier. Their seconds backed away to stand beside the surgeons.

Celeste watched Ernesto and Dokken finish their last stride and pivot a quarter turn to present the thin side of their bodies as targets. They stood motionless staring at their opponents. A deep hush held sway over San Francisco Bay.

The raucous call of a hunting seabird ravaged the early morning stillness. Celeste jumped, startled by the sudden sound. The gray bird sailed past, its head turned downward and its black eyes examining the gathering of humans on the end of the pier.

Celeste concentrated on the judge, listening for his signal as if she, as well as Ernesto, stood poised to jerk up a pistol and fight the duel.

"Fire!" the judge's command came sharply.

Celeste saw Ernesto raise his revolver with a swift lift of his hand. Then he staggered backward. At the same instant, Celeste heard the explosion of Dokken's heavily charged pistol.

Ernesto leaned forward at the waist. His grip loosened on the pistol and it clattered down on the planking. He tottered on his feet, then steadied himself with a supreme effort. He turned his head and looked at Celeste, his eyes wide with pain. He tried to speak but no sound came from his lips. He reached out with his hand as if trying to support himself on the air. He crumpled and fell face down on the pier.

For a moment Celeste was frozen by the shock of seeing the ghastly expression on Ernesto's face and him falling so lifelessly. She screamed a wild, animal scream of pain and fear and bound forward. She screamed out again as she sprang across the last of the space separating her from Ernesto.

She choked off her cries and dropped to her knees beside her brother. His white shirt was quickly becoming soaked by the blood streaming from a hole in his side directly in line with his heart. She lifted his head and stared into the slack face and the brown eyes swiftly glazing with death.

"Oh, merciful God. No! No! Ernesto you can't be dead. Please speak to me." Her voice rose to a shrill command. "Brother mine, speak to me!"

Dr. Suazo, Lucas and the dueling judge hurried up. The surgeon knelt and hastily began to examine the still body. Dokken strutted up with a pleased expression on his face and swinging his pistol by his side.

"Ernesto is dead, Celeste," the doctor said sadly.

"He can't be!" Celeste's voice was brittle with anguish.

"I'm afraid he is, Celeste," the doctor said and put his hand on her shoulder.

She angrily knocked the doctor's hand away. "This affair from the very beginning was all a trick to kill my brother." Her hot eyes swung up to lock on Dokken. "You murdering bastard. I know your reason for challenging him to a duel. But you won't win. Never! Never!"

She lowered her view back down to her brother. She saw his cocked pistol laying beside his shoulder. Her boiling anger surged. Swiftly and without warning, she snatched up the pistol and swung it up to point at Dokken smirking down at her. She squeezed the trigger.

Chapter 5

The judge of duels turned from the dead man to the young woman vehemently cursing Dokken as a murderer. Her angry eyes were hard with the urge to do murder herself. The judge agreed with her it had been an execution rather than a duel.

He was caught by surprise when the woman suddenly grabbed the unfired pistol from the pier. With unsuspected swiftness, she pointed it at Dokken. The judge could not let her kill the unarmed man. He thrust out his hand and knocked Celeste's pistol to the side.

The bullet zipped past Dokken, stinging the side of his face. He dodged to the side. By instinct as he moved, he jerked up his gun to point at Celeste and pulled the trigger. The hammer snapped on an empty cylinder.

Dokken was startled at the pistol failing to fire. Remembering his gun was unloaded, he lunged toward Celeste drawing the pistol back to hit her. "You Mexican bitch, I'll knock your head off," he bellowed fiercely.

"Stop!" the judge shouted at Dokken, and stepped in front of the rushing man.

Dokken continued to bear down on the judge, intending to shove him out of the way. He halted as the judge's hand disappeared inside his cape. The man was old, but he was not one you could insult by laying a hand on him. And Dokken's pistol was unloaded. He stared threateningly past the judge at Celeste. "She Goddamned near shot me."

"She just saw her brother killed," said the judge. "She doesn't know what she's doing."

"She knows all right. See the look on her face."

Celeste watched Dokken closely. How wonderful it would be if there was another round in Ernesto's pistol she still held. The judge now had his back to her and there was no one else close enough to stop her from shooting Dokken.

"If you were a man, I'd kill you," Dokken growled.

"You're going to be the one that dies," Celeste said, her voice controlled, and eyes cold, black spheres of obsidian. "I can't do it now, but soon someone will put a bullet through your heart."

Dokken laughed disdainfully at Celeste. "No Mexican can beat me with a pistol. You and your kind are finished in this city." He took a white handkerchief from his pocket and dabbed at the thin trickle of blood from the bullet burn on his face. He held the handkerchief out to show Celeste the blood. "That's as close as you'll ever come to shooting Dokken."

He glanced at his second and the surgeon who had accompanied him. "Let's go, there's nothing here worth wasting time on." He took his coat and hat from his second, and pivoting on a heel, strode off along the pier toward the shore.

Celeste's face was taut with hate as she watched Dokken's retreating back. She felt a deep sense of helplessness for she feared the man might be correctly forecasting the Mexican people's fate in California. They had come into a wilderness more than a century before and through bitter toil and hardship made California a pleasant land to live in. Now they were being ruthlessly robbed and killed by the conquering Americans. Celeste's head lifted defiantly. The years since the American victory in 1848 had been horrible, and now her brother was dead, but she would not surrender easily.

She bent over the corpse lying so still on the pier and spoke in a whisper. "Ernesto, my brother, you have my solemn vow that Dokken will soon join you in death."

"Celeste, what do you want done?" Lucas asked.

"I'll take Ernesto to the *rancho* and bury him in the family cemetery," Celeste replied. She took her brother's coat and hat from Lucas, and laid them and his pistol on the seat of the vehicle. "Dr. Suazo, will you please help Lucas put Ernesto in the buggy?"

Celeste spread her long cloak on the floor of the vehicle, and Lucas and the doctor placed Ernesto's body upon it. She climbed up into the buggy and seated herself. She laid the pistol in her lap and it felt comforting to her. She picked up the reins.

"Do you want me to go with you to help, Celeste?" Lucas asked.

"No. I can take care of what must be done. The burial will be at the *rancho* in three days. Ernesto would want for you to be there."

"I'll be there, you can be sure of that."

"Thank you, Lucas, and you too, Dr. Suazo, for your help," Celeste said. She tapped the reins on the rump of the horse and the buggy moved off.

Celeste looked down at the face of her brother and his blood soaked chest. "Dokken will die," she promised again, her voice like brittle ice breaking.

Half dazed with her grief, Celeste guided the carriage around the piles of lumber and toward the shore. In her deep sadness, she did not hear the iron-rimmed wheels rumbling on the wooden planking of the pier. Nor did she see the stevedores and sailors coming along the pier and staring at her and the body at her feet as she passed.

The fog was lifting on the shore and San Francisco was coming into view. Normally she would have delighted in the sight of the beautiful and fabulous city built on the hills above the great blue bay. Now her eyes never rose above the horse's ears.

She reached the end of the pier and reined the horse onto The Embarcadero, the main way fronting the bay. She unconsciously avoided the other vehicles on the street. Three blocks later, she turned left onto Mission Street and climbed steadily up through the city.

Celeste halted the buggy in the driveway of her *hacienda*. The building was single story, long and rambling, and made of adobe with a tile roof, the tile had long ago faded from red to a rust brown. The windows were small; at the time of construction, glass had been very expensive. The house was nearly three-quarters of a century old, one of the most ancient in the city. It sat in the center of ten acres of wooded, rolling land overlooking the city. Her grandfather had purchased the land and built his home outside the town for privacy. Now the town had grown into a city and expanded to press against the borders of the land. Celeste noticed the worn appearance of the house. Repairs and new paint were needed but she had no money to spare for something that was not an immediate necessity.

The two Mexican servants, a man and woman, both old, had been waiting for Ernesto's and her return and now had come out of the house and into the courtyard at the sound of the carriage. They halted when they saw Celeste driving the buggy and the body of Ernesto lying motionless on the floor of the vehicle.

"Come and help me," Celeste called, climbing down from the vehicle.

The woman began to cry as she and the man drew near. The man turned his face away from the scene.

"Stop that," Celeste ordered. "It is done. Ernesto is dead. Now we have tasks to perform. Come and help me carry him inside. Then I have something very important for Ignacio to do."

The three tenderly clasped Ernesto's body and lifted it from the floor of the buggy. They carried it through the wide entry door and into the big *sala* of the *hacienda*.

"Elosia," Celese said to the woman, "you took care of Ernesto when he was a child. Now for the last time bath and cleanse him and dress him in his very best clothing. When that is done, we will take him on the ferry up the river to the *rancho*. Tomorrow the ceremony for the dead shall begin with all his friends around him.''

Celeste motioned for Ignacio to follow her and led him outside.

''Who's the most brave and skilled *pistolero* of all our people?'' she asked the old man.

''The great man, Vicaro Zaragosa, *señorita*,'' Ignacio replied, surprised at the question. ''I've heard many tales of his fights with the Americans, and also Mexicans. He always wins for nobody can beat him shooting a pistol.''

''I agree. My father often spoke of him and said he was a friend. When I was a girl, I saw him at the *rancho*. Saddle a horse and go find Vicaro. Tell him the last of the Beremendes needs his help.''

''The Americans call him a bandit. It would be dangerous for him to come to San Francisco.''

''I know. Tell him to come to the *rancho*.''

''Perhaps I'll not be able to find him for he does not stay in one place for long but travels through the tall mountains. What then?''

''Leave word with trusted people who might know his whereabouts. He'll hear and come.''

''Should I find him, he will ask why you need him. What shall I say?''

''Tell him he will learn that from me.''

''Very well, *señorita*. I'll search for the famous man. I hope he'll let me find him.''

''Ride swiftly, Ignacio, for I have made a vow that I must keep.''

Ignacio hastened into the *hacienda* and dressed in garments suited for riding, with spurs for his boots. He was old and was very pleased the *señorita* felt he could accomplish such a search. In the stables behind the *hacienda,* he saddled a horse and mounted. The strong *caballo* carried him through San Francisco at a gallop. The bay ferry transported man and horse across to the mainland. Ignacio rolled his big spurs over the animal's

ribs. They raced east into the foothills leading up to the Diablo
Mountains.

"Beremendes is dead," Dokken said.

"Since I see you're still alive, I would think so," Mattoon
replied. "Did you have any trouble?"

"Yeah, from that Beremendes woman. She was at the duel.
After I'd killed her brother, she grabbed up his pistol and came
damn close to shooting me." Dokken touched the bullet burn
on the side of his face.

Mattoon's sight flicked to the slight injury and then away.
"Just one of the hazards of a duel, the unexpected. I believe
we agreed on a price of a thousand dollars."

"That's right," Dokken said. He had not been asked to sit
down and stood before Mattoon, who was seated behind his
big mahogany desk and watching him with his strangely colored
eyes—snake eyes Dokken always thought. The two men were
in Mattoon's office on the third and top floor of his bank. The
office was large and richly appointed with oak paneled walls
and thick wool carpet.

Mattoon reached into a drawer of his desk and extracted a
packet of bills. "Here is your pay." He tossed the money as
if it was of no significance.

Dokken snatched the money from the air and slid it into his
inside jacket pocket. Mattoon was wealthy and could easily
afford to pay a high price for the services he desired. However,
he did not accept failure. "Thanks," Dokken said.

Mattoon rose from his desk and walked past Dokken to the
window overlooking Market Street lying below. He clasped
his hands behind his back and tilted his head to stare down on
the mounted riders and horse drawn vehicles moving on the
street and the pedestrians on the sidewalk. Several prosperous
businessmen he knew entered the bank. They would be making
large deposits, as were many others, deposits amounting to
millions of dollars. The reason for all their good fortune, and
Mattoon's, was war. The Civil War in the East between the
Northern and Southern states was causing tremendous destruc-

tion. That war, at least the destructive part, had not touched California. It never would, Mattoon thought. But due to that same war, orders for the material needed to fight battles, cannon, all manners of small arms and ammunition, clothing, food, and hundreds of other items, was making the merchants and bankers of San Francisco rich.

Mattoon spun around and fastened his sight upon Dokken. "The Beremendes case doesn't come up until the middle of September. I have no intention of waiting that long to get possession of the land."

"The commission's calendar is full with all the land-grant cases it's hearing, and they won't be hurried." Mattoon, even with all his influence, hadn't been able to obtain preference with the Federal Land Commissioners.

"I've waited ten years for the stubborn Beremendes to cave in. I'll wait no longer with them retaining possession of the land until the case is finally settled." Mattoon didn't need the Beremendes land to be wealthy. He desired the magnificent stretch of mountain and valley land for itself alone. He craved the land as he had never craved anything before.

"We've gotten rid of the brother, so now let's destroy this last obstacle. The woman."

Dokken knew he was not being asked for his opinion on anything Mattoon said, and he remained silent. All of the legal documents that had been filed before the Land Commission showed Dokken as the opponent of the Beremendes, but he was only fronting for Mattoon. The man laid out the strategy for gaining possession of the land and provided the money to carry it out.

"The Beremendes must be nearly bankrupt. No bank will lend them money on the *rancho* since the title is being contested. Both the brother and the sister have even been here to get my bank to loan them funds. I turned them down. With great sorrow, of course."

Mattoon laughed coarsely as he moved back past Dokken and reseated himself behind his desk. "We must keep her lawyers busy so that their fees will keep mounting. Have your lawyers file motions before the commission that will keep the

Mexican woman busy responding. We must make her spend money faster than she can make it.''

''I'll see to it this morning.''

''I know what she'll do next to obtain money,'' Mattoon said. ''Here is how we'll stop her and make several thousand dollars doing it.''

In the little, whitewashed chapel beside the *hacienda* on the Beremendes' *rancho* on Mount Mocho, the priest from Sacramento spoke praise for Ernesto and delivered his soul to the diety. The pallbearers rose from their seats and carried the casket to the family cemetery on the bluff looking down on the San Joaquin Valley.

Celeste did not cry during the eulogy or the burial. Ernesto would not have wanted that. She could hear his spirit calling for revenge. She would give him his revenge. Dokken's life was forfeit for the death of Ernesto.

The large gathering of Mexican friends and the few that were Americans, departed, winding down the long curving road from the *hacienda* to the valley floor. Most turned north on the main road to Sacramento while some went off in other directions to adjoining *ranchos.* Celeste watched the people and their vehicles grow ever smaller with distance and finally disappear.

Restless with many things on her mind, she returned to the *hacienda* and changed into riding clothes, boots, leather trousers and a cotton shirt. Emerging once again, she went to the corral and saddled her favorite mount, a silver-gray mare. She swung astride.

For a moment she sat upon the mare and surveyed the buildings of the *rancho* constructed on a wide bench on the side of Mount Mocho. She had spent most of her life here, staying in San Francisco only a few months each year to attend school. The main structure, the *hacienda,* was a large U-shaped house with a flat roof and walls of two-foot-thick adobe. The inside was cool in the hot summer and the three fireplaces kept it warm in the winter. Nearby was the weaver's hut containing looms and wheels to make thread and a rack to weave the thread into cloth. A blacksmith's shop was to the left of the weaver's hut. Beyond that, at a hundred yards or less, was the *matanzas,* the place for slaughtering cattle and sheep. Farther away still, some one-eighth mile, were the small adobe homes of the nine *vaqueros* that helped the Beremendes operate the *rancho.* In reality, she had more *vaqueros* than she needed to manage the small number of livestock. However the riders were men from families that had been with the Beremendes three generations. She could not tell them to leave.

A large vegetable garden lay between the weaver's hut and the *matanzas.* An *acequia,* irrigation ditch, wound around the slope of the hill from a nearby spring and carried water to the garden. Ignacio's oldest son, a man with his own family, was plowing the garden with a yoke of snow-white oxen. Celeste wasn't certain whether Ignacio prized the son or the oxen most highly.

The *rancho,* worked diligently by the Mexican families, was nearly self-sufficient in its production of food and clothing. However, large expenses were being incurred in the courts in San Francisco. Celeste did not know how she would meet those costs. She had less than a thousand dollars in cash. She owned one hundred and fifty thousand acres of land, but with the title to that land being challenged, no bank would lend her money on it.

Her grandfather had acquired the land of the *rancho* in 1800 for service as a major in the Spanish Army against the Indians in southern California. The King of Spain had granted him thirty-three square leagues, 228 square miles, a huge expanse of land lying partly on the east flank of Mount Mocho in the Diablo Mountain Range and partly in the San Joaquin Valley.

When she was very small, her grandfather would show her the *diseño,* the map of the land grant, and describe the directions and distance of the boundaries. When she was older, they would ride and he showed her the rock cairns that marked the corners and side lines.

The Americans conquered Mexico in 1847. The Treaty of Guadalupe Hidalgo was signed in 1848. All California and Arizona and New Mexico and much other territory was taken by the Americans. Her grandfather died that year. She often thought it was because of the shame of defeat. Her father had been wounded in the battle for Mexico City. He had made his way painfully home to California. His injuries did not heal and after languishing for months, he too had died.

Celeste's mother, the Señora Beremendes, had managed the *rancho* for ten years, until Ernesto had become a man and began to help her. Her mother and brother had continued to run cattle and sheep, even on the valley bottom with its rich soil. Several of the other ranchers cleared the bottom land of brush and grew wheat, a grain not only golden in color but worth much gold for export. The wheat, hardened in the dry, warm air, kept wholesome for months and was shipped all over the world for a high profit. In 1861, the ships that brought coal and iron from Liverpool, England, to San Francisco carried three million bushels of wheat back on their return voyage across the ocean.

Under the Treaty of Guadalupe Hidalgo, the United States government was bound to honor all legitimate titles to land in the areas ceded by Mexico. In 1851, the Americans established a Federal Land Commission in San Francisco to hear Mexican claims for land. The Beremendes filed their grant documents with the Americans for the land that had been in their family for more than half a century.

That was when their trouble to clear title began. A strange American, John Dokken, appeared with documents proclaiming the land the Beremendes claimed was in reality part of the Armendarez Land Grant that he had purchased from Carlo Armendarez. Lieutenant Armendarez had been under the command of her grandfather in the battle with the Indians, and had bravely helped rout the foe. On Major Beremendes's recommendation, the King had given Armendarez a land grant of fifty thousand acres immediately adjacent to the Beremendes Land Grant. Carlo Armendarez had returned to Spain and never saw his grant. Over the years, he had leased the land to various ranchers. Upon Armendarez's death at an old age in Spain, Dokken appeared in San Francisco in possession of the grant. Strangely, the land described in the Armendarez Grant included the Beremendes land. Dokken's lawyers argued that the Beremendes Grant documents and map were fraudulent, and further, that the description of the grant did not conform to the markers on the ground. That latter claim was true, for the boundaries of the grant had been laid out without the benefit of survey instruments. Until now those discrepancies had meant nothing because everyone respected the old rock cairns as the true boundary markers. In a court of law, the lack of conformity between the written description and the ground markers had become very significant.

Celeste was certain the land description in the Armendarez Grant had been altered. She had had several experts examine the Armendarez document, but they had arrived at conflicting opinions as to whether or not the document had been modified. She was still attempting to find the copies of the grants that should be in the official records in Spain, for a copy was kept of all the King's grants. To date and after much searching, the copies had not been discovered. She wondered if it was possible that Dokken had somehow reached out from America and destroyed the grant copies. Still she had a strong claim on the land, that of possession, for the Beremendes had used the land for more than half a century without a protest from Armendarez. This would, when the case was finally heard, substantially strengthen her case before the Land Commission.

All the legal arguments and maneuvering to defend the Beremendes's title for eleven years had nearly destroyed the family fortune, but she would somehow hold on. She knew that should she win before the Land Commission, that would be only the first step for her enemies would appeal the decision to a higher court, even to the Supreme Court. Dokken seemed to have unlimited funds to do that.

Celeste felt the full weight of the task of managing the *rancho* now that Ernesto was dead. Riding always helped soothe her when she had problems so she spoke to the mare. The willing animal left the corral at a trot. Celeste rode south over grass covered hills studded with patches of brush and short oak trees. When she reached a wide shelf of the mountain where the land was more smooth, she raised the mare to a gallop. The sweep of air past Celeste's face and the feel of the mare's back between her legs lessened the turmoil and worry in her mind. She reached out and petted the mare on the side of the neck. "We'll make it, girl, somehow."

Celeste shifted her attention to the immediate needs of the *rancho* and began to evaluate the condition of the cattle and sheep she passed by. Only a few hundred cattle and perhaps 6,000 sheep remained of the vast herds that once grazed the Beremendes's land. Most had been sold for funds to pay for defense of the land title. To make matters worse, two years past in 1860, the bottom had fallen out of the livestock market. Prices had plummeted to a third of what they had been. The price of wool had remained firm and that kept the *rancho* going.

Celeste rode down from the mountain and into the San Joaquin Valley, the great oval depression some four hundred miles north to south and fifty miles east to west and lying between the Coast Range and the Sierra Nevada Mountains. Table flat, the valley's fertile soil was now producing a tremendous quantity of wheat for the Union Army fighting a civil war in the east.

She halted at the border of her land. Lying before her mile after mile for as far as she could see to the north, east, and south, there was nothing except a plain of wheat turning from green to gold, maturing swiftly under the warm, yellow sun. The owners of that wheat would reap a fortune in a few days.

The Beremendes's *rancho* extended down from high on Mount Mocho and encompassed forty thousand acres of the bottom land. She must without fail have a substantial portion of that land cleared of brush, leveled, and ready to sow with the seed of wheat in time for next year's crop. There must be a way to accomplish that large task. But how?

Chapter 6

The lone horseman held his weary mount at a gallop as the shadows grew and darkened in the hollows. He had been riding for two days, not following any road but moving cross-country through the brush studded land. For the past three hours, he had been upon the Beremendes's *rancho*. He topped a ridge and halted to stare warily ahead.

Celeste stood in the patio of the *hacienda* and watched the evening dusk settle upon Mount Mocho, the tallest peak of the Diablo Mountains. She was disappointed and unsettled for another day was ending, the sixth since she had sent Ignacio off to hunt Vicaro Zaragoza. Ignacio had returned on the fourth day unable to find Vicaro, but he had left messages with trusted people as she had directed.

She was about to turn and enter the *hacienda* when she saw the rider appear on the ridgetop beyond a shallow valley. He reined his long-legged *caballo* to a stop and sat in his saddle looking in the direction of the *hacienda*. She knew with certainty the man was Vicaro Zaragoza, the *pistolero* and bandit— but a bandit only to the Americans. He was a hero to her people and she felt proud of him.

He was a cautious man, Celeste thought as she left the patio and walked out to where she could be seen. She lifted an arm in greeting. A sense of pleasant anticipation came over her at once upon seeing the man again.

The rider spurred his mount and the horse instantly broke into a run. The animal swooped down into the valley with its rider and then up the slope to Celeste. The horse, a magnificent roan, came to a prancing stop in front of Celeste, its rider so firm in the saddle that he seemed to be part of the animal.

The man wore a broad-brimmed, black *sombrero* and closely fitting, black trousers and vest over a dark red shirt. The buttons on the jacket were of silver, and much needlework with silver thread decorated the front and back of the garment. Now his clothing was dust covered from his long ride. A large pistol hung in a holster on the man's hip.

The man watched Celeste from the deep shadow beneath the broad brim of his *sombrero*. She stared up trying to make out the features of the half hidden face.

The horseman swung down from his mount. He swept off his *sombrero* and bowed from the waist with a graceful movement. Then he straightened and looked at Celeste with piercing eyes.

Celeste was shocked at the aged man that stood before her. Every strand of his thick hair was white. A web of wrinkles creased his face, with deep ones coalescing at the corners of his eyes where he had squinted against the sun for more than a half century.

"*Señorita*, I'm Vicaro Zaragoza."

"I know you, Señor Zaragoza," Celeste said and stepped forward extending her hand. "I am Celeste Beremendes. I remember you from long ago."

Vicaro took Celeste's hand, pressed the soft, warm flesh, and then released it. "You were very young the last time we met. It does me honor that you remember. The years have made you a very beautiful woman. But even when you were a girl, the image of the lovely woman you would become was already in your face."

Those twelve years since last she had seen the *pistolero* had also wrought great changes in Vicaro. She thought she saw the hand tremble that held his *sombrero*.

"I'm pleased that Ignacio's message reached you and that you came so quickly."

"Your father was a friend. Once he gave me his favorite *caballo* to out-race the *gringos* that chased me. They would surely have caught and hung me. He put himself in danger that day to help me, and I never forget a friend."

Celeste smiled. "Nor an enemy."

Vicaro returned her smile but said nothing. The truth of the statement was in his black eyes.

"Come inside and have some wine and food with me," Celeste said. "I know you must be hungry."

"I would like that for I have come a long ways." Vicaro led his horse to a tie post and secured its reins to the iron ring.

Celeste guided the way into the house and to the rear to the big kitchen. There were ample remains of the evening meal and she placed them upon the long wooden table. She selected a bottle of dark, strong wine. There were serious matters to discuss.

Vicaro began to fill his plate. His hands did indeed tremble, Celeste saw it clearly now. She was very disheartened. He was now an old man who had once been very strong, and brave, and skilled with weapons. He would no longer be the greatest *pistolero* in all California.

Vicaro looked intently at Celeste. He smiled knowingly. "Yes, Vicaro Zaragoza has grown old."

Celeste jerked, startled at the words of the man. He had read her thoughts exactly.

"I'm no longer a *pistolero* that all other men fear. My hand shakes a little, and my eyes are not now sharp like those of a hawk. I do not search for fights. But I'm still better than most men with a pistol."

"You knew my thoughts," Celeste said in amazement.

"A man such as myself who for years lived by fighting, must be able to know what another person is thinking, especially an enemy, then act before he does. Your thoughts were not difficult to know. Ernesto has been killed. You send for Vicaro the fast *pistolero*. Then you see a man with white hair. It is all very clear to me. I regret that I disappoint you, but no man should be ashamed of growing old. There are worse things, like being dead."

"I didn't mean to insult you with my thoughts."

A pleasant smile came upon Vicaro's seamed face. "No offense was taken." The smile vanished. "I only wish I could kill your enemy the *gringo,* John Dokken. But he is an expert *pistolero* and I could only kill him from hiding, without facing him as a man. That I would never do."

"I understand. Please eat and then we will talk about old times."

Vicaro finished eating. He refilled his wineglass and sipping at the amber liquid, talked with Celeste of events long past. He smiled often as he described California when it was ruled by the distant government in Mexico City and life was serene and slow-paced—before the Americans marched in and conquered California and changed everything for all time, and before Vicaro became a bandit.

The old man ceased speaking and quietly watched Celeste. He sensed the worry in the young woman. "How goes the battle in the American courts to clear the title to your *rancho?*" he asked.

"Slow and very costly. The man Dokken has very good lawyers, and also forgers. I admit he has produced some very authentic-looking documents. But I believe we will win before the American Land Commission."

"Is the death of Ernesto part of the *gringo's* plot to take your land?"

"I'm certain it is. If Dokken can't win legally, he will kill the Beremendeses."

"Do you fear for your own safety?"

"If the Land Commission rules in my favor, then I will be. I think Dokken murdered Ernesto to scare me, perhaps also with the idea that without him I could not raise enough money to continue the legal fight."

"Could your riders keep you safe should enemies come to the *rancho* to harm you?"

"They are all good men and skilled at hunting the wolf and coyote that kill our sheep, but they would have little chance to beat men like Dokken. They would surely try and I know how to shoot.''

A thought burst brightly in Celeste's mind. Her eyes opened quite wide as she leaned forward, tense and excited.

''Vicaro, can you teach me how to become an expert marksman? How to fight a duel and kill a man?''

The old bandit lowered his wineglass and stared in astonishment at Celeste. ''Women do not fight duels. No man would draw a weapon against a woman for other men would laugh and think him a coward.''

''Suppose they did now know I was a woman. I could become a Beremendes's cousin from Mexico City or from Santa Fe, a male cousin who carried a pistol and wanted revenge.''

Vicaro studied Celeste. His eyes dropped down over her ample bosom, down her arms to settle on her wrists and hands. ''You appear strong for a woman, maybe even strong enough to handle a pistol.''

''I've worked with the men for years in riding, branding and shearing. I'm really stronger than I look. Also, I'm taller than most Mexican women.''

''Still you're a woman and shaped like one, though not to an extreme.''

''I could bind my breasts flat to my chest, and I could wear a *caballero's* jacket and trousers and boots. I'd cut my hair short.''

Vicaro appeared doubtful. ''Could you truly shoot to kill a man?''

Celeste reflected upon the question, probing the inner, most secret recesses in her mind. She again saw Ernesto lying dead with his pale face and bloody chest . . . and Dokken with his gloating smile. She had almost been successful in shooting him that time. The hate she had felt then again burned through her veins.

''I could shoot Dokken for killing Ernesto if I should ever have the opportunity,'' Celeste said, her voice firm. She realized slaying Dokken might be only the first use of the skill as a *pistolero*. She might have to kill other enemies to hold her *rancho.* "Will you please stay here at the *rancho* and teach me every skill and trick that you possess with a pistol?"

"I would do that for a Beremendes, but would your father approve?"

"My father would surely approve and my grandfather would urge you to teach me."

Vicaro evaluated Celeste with a skeptical expression. Then he relented and grinned wolfishly. "I believe they would. Let us begin now with the lessons. All the practice you must do will take a very long time. Surely months, perhaps years, will be needed before you can hope to survive a duel, or a gunfight in some dark street."

"I can't wait years, not even months. I can hardly wait weeks. I'll get Ernesto's pistol."

Celeste hurried away and a moment later returned. She handed the Colt revolver in its holster to Vicaro.

The aged bandit pulled the Colt Model 1851 Navy and lovingly held it in his hand. He ran his fingers down the cold iron of the barrel. "This is a fine weapon, and has been well taken care of. I used one for years. Now I carry the Colt Army Pistol." He touched the butt of his holstered revolver.

"Should I use the same type of gun that you do?"

"No. Your pistol is .36 caliber. The new Army Colt is .44 caliber and has a louder explosion and stronger recoil. You will be less likely to flinch when you fire this lower-charged gun. The ball from a .36-caliber pistol is powerful enough to kill a man if the person firing it is a marksman. Which you must be before you hunt Dokken."

"How do we begin?"

"Buckle on the pistol and stand in front of me," Vicaro directed. "Let's see if you have the makings of a *pistolero.* You may not possess the strength to swiftly lift the weapon, or you may be clumsy. Stand closer. I want to test something. Closer still so that I can touch you. That's about right. Now give me your pistol."

Vicaro removed the caps from the nipples over the six cylinders and handed the revolver back to Celeste. "Put it in your holster, loose yet snug."

He extended his right index finger and pressed it against the center of Celeste's chest. "Put your hand on the butt of your pistol and get ready to draw. When you feel me take my finger away, draw as fast as you can and point the pistol straight at the center of me. Don't waste time trying to cock it for now. Look me in the eye. That's right. Get set."

Vicaro's finger released its pressure. Celeste snatched at her pistol.

A hard object jammed her in the stomach. She looked down to see Vicaro's loaded gun, the hammer eared all the way back, buried in the front of her shirt. She gasped, shocked.

"I don't believe it. You moved your hand down, pulled the pistol and brought it back up before I could hardly think."

"You are very slow."

"Let's try it again. Now I know what it's all about."

"All right. Get ready."

The result of the second contest was little different. Celeste barely had hold of her pistol before she felt the iron barrel of Vicaro's gun against her stomach.

"You had better forget about drawing a weapon to fight. Learn to shoot more accurately than your enemies. That's all an honest man, or woman, needs."

"At least show me how the draw is done correctly."

"The movement is simple. I'll do it extra slow. First catch hold of the butt, wrap your smaller fingers around it. Start lifting it up. Your first finger goes in through the trigger guard. Your thumb begins to cock the hammer while the gun is in about this position. Here the gun is level, just forward and above the holster, finger on the trigger and gun fully cocked.

"You can shoot from this position, but accuracy will be poor. So shove the gun out toward the target. Aim it better as it moves out. Fire here, while there's still a little bend in the elbow. Now try to do it exactly the same way. Do it slowly."

Two hours later Vicaro nodded. "That's getting close to the right way to draw a pistol. Speed will come much later, if ever."

"What do I do next?"

"Practice every day for about ten years. Draw the gun while

on horseback, sitting down, falling left and right. In the darkness, bright sunlight, in the rain. There's no end to practice, but you should give up the idea of starting a fight with the pistol in your holster. Have it in your hand when danger threatens. Use all your time practicing to hit a target, but do the practicing from all the positions I just mentioned. Few fights are done as duels, most occur suddenly when least expected.''

Vicaro saw the determined cast to the young woman's countenance. What a dreadful shame it would be for one so beautiful to die with a bullet through her heart. But fate would take her where it willed and there was absolutely nothing Vicaro could do to alter that. He could only prepare her as best he could.

"Ammunition will cost many dollars. Even if you get very good, there will always be somebody who is better. And there are accidents. One of your loaded chambers may not fire, yet those in your enemy's pistol will.''

"I'm going to learn, Vicaro. I must, so please understand and help me.''

"I will stay here at the *rancho* and teach you all that I know. But only you can develop the skill to be an expert *pistolero*. Practice ten thousand times, a hundred thousand times, until callouses grow thick, the gun is a feather in your hand, and the barrel finds the target like a magnet is drawn to iron.''

"I will learn—you'll see.''

Vicaro replaced the caps on the nipples of Celeste's pistol. He handed the weapon back. She was brave enough to be a fighter. Still he had grave doubts that she would ever be fast and accurate enough to kill such a man as Dokken.

"When you can shoot the swift dove from the air, then we shall know that you are becoming one with your pistol. You must, if you are to live and your enemy die.''

Chapter 7

Levi Coffin awoke with the southern Ohio moon casting pale silver rays down through the big oak tree above his head. He arose at once and rolled his blanket. Without eating, he saddled his horse and led it out from the woods to the dirt road he had followed the day before. He climbed astride and rode through the predawn darkness of the forested hill country.

He had fought the Rebels at Boatswains Swamp nine days before, and had traveled steadily northwest ever since. The evening just past, he had crossed the Ohio River on a ferry boat at a village named Portsmouth. Darkness had caught him shortly thereafter and he made a fireless camp beside the road.

The passage of time since the battle should have lessened the awful memories he had of the screaming Confederate soldiers charging at him across the water filled swamp and the shooting and killing he had done to stop them. But the horror was not diminished. He shuddered as scenes of the battle with men falling flashed before his eyes. He saw them as if looking over the iron sights of his Spencer rifle. When would he be allowed to sleep without nightmares or spend a day without recalling the slaughter?

He felt the bullet wound on his forehead, running his finger along the slight concavity in the flesh. The wound had healed quickly and cleanly, as injuries most often did on young, healthy animals. The scab had peeled away the day before and, unknown to Levi since he had no mirror, had left a bright pink scar on the dark tan of his face. He did not need a permanent reminder of Boatswains Swamp, but he had one.

He focused his attention on the way ahead. The dawn was breaking and he could see along the rutted dirt road for nearly half a mile. The forest of oak, poplar, chestnut, and other trees crowded close on both sides. In this early hour of the day, he journeyed alone.

Levi rode slumped in the saddle and let the horse set its own pace. Overhead the fiery orb of the July sun climbed above the horizon and inexorably mounted its high sky path. He felt the heat through his shirt and trousers, civilian clothes of homespun cotton for he had discarded the Confederate military uniform days before.

He entered a dense woods and was glad for the shade. He almost grabbed for his rifle when a flock of crows exploded up in a mass from a big gum tree. The black gang drove off cawing to each other. A squirrel on the limb of an oak extending out over the road chattered angrily complaining at Levi's passing. He rode on, the squirrel scampering back along the limb and watching with alert brown eyes from the far side of the trunk of the oak.

A buggy drawn by a single horse came into view. A man drove and a woman sat on the spring seat beside him.

The man and woman warily watched Levi approach. The man lifted the rifle that stood between his legs and held it in his hands.

Levi nodded at the couple. He understood the cause for the man's caution. With so many men gone from their homes and far away in the army of the north or south, outlaws and renegade bands of deserters roamed the countryside raiding and killing.

Shortly the dirt road joined with a much used highway and he began to meet many travelers. A stagecoach pulled by six trotting horses passed him with a jolting rattle. He overtook a drove of hogs being driven along the road by a man and boy. Going to market, Levi figured.

The forest gave way to farms, cleared areas of various sizes with houses and barns and fields. As he continued on westward the size of the farms and the houses became larger, showing obvious prosperity. He knew Cincinnati could not be far away. His excitement mounted.

Levi rode his horse into the dark woods along the creek, dismounted and tied it. The animal would be well hidden until he returned. He moved off among the trees. The sky was heavily overcast and the night dark, yet that slowed him not at all. He could have found his way blindfolded from here to his destination.

He reached the edge of the woods and looked across the wide hayfield to the two-story farmhouse. Though only the lighted window in the side of the house where the kitchen was located could be seen, in his mind's eye he could see every detail of the house.

As he drew near the border of the field, a light appeared in the living room of the house. That told him the family routine was proceeding as usual. He let himself through the iron gate set in the fence that kept the cows out of the yard and the garden.

Quietly he crept to the kitchen window, half open to let in the cool evening breeze. His mother was moving back and forth between the table and sink clearing away the dishes of the evening meal. The delightful aroma of vegetable soup and cornbread and cinnamon apple pie reached him and his empty stomach growled.

He studied the loved face of his mother as the lamplight illuminated it at varying angles when she turned about. She had a lovely open face with blue eyes, and skin tanned from tending her garden in the sun. Her long brown hair was done up in a tight bun at the back of her head, as it was every day except Sunday, so it would not get in her way as she worked at her many tasks. She was beautiful. He recognized that as a son and a man. No wonder his father had chosen her as his wife.

However the most-loved thing about her was her understanding. He knew he could walk in through the screen door and she would welcome him with all her heart, even though he might be a killer and an army deserter.

He leaned his cheek against the glass windowpane. Oh, how he wanted to speak to her, to take her in his arms and hug her to him one last time. For just a moment the smoothness of the glass felt like the cool smooth skin of her hand that he remembered so well.

She was turning in his direction with a questioning expression on her face. Did she sense his presence? Levi pulled hastily back out of the light. She must not know he was here. "Goodbye, Mom," he whispered.

Levi stole along the side of the house and stopped at the window of the living room. His brother and sister were lying side by side on the floor and discussing something in an open catalogue. His father, a broad man with a rugged face, sat in a chair reading a newspaper. He kept up with the news and would know about the battle in Virginia. He could never know how terrible the fighting and dying had been. Should Levi tell him about his hatred for killing, he would understand. But he would not agree that Levi had the right to run away from the fight and desert the army.

Levi could never return home and face his father for the shame would be too great. He was now an outcast. Better that it be thought that he had been killed in the war and his body never found. He looked up at the second floor and the window of the bedroom where he had slept nearly every night of his life. He would never again hear the rain rattling against the glass, or the cold winter wind whistling around the eave trough while he lay snug and warm under the quilts made by his mother's hands.

He turned and ran across the yard.

* * *

Levi followed the railroad tracks that ran through the center of Cincinnati. The people on the street looked at the gaunt young man on the black horse. When they saw the fresh scar upon his forehead, their expression softened. Sometimes they spoke a greeting to him. Levi, not understanding the cause of the friendliness, was surprised at the townsfolk's actions.

He reached the railroad station, a long, yellow building close to the tracks, and entered. The agent, a stoop-shouldered old man, was seated at a desk and listening to a chattering telegraph key. He wrote swiftly on a piece of paper. When the key stopped its coded talking, he tapped it a few coded signals of his own. He turned.

Levi noted the same quick appraisal of his face that others had given him. Then the railroad agent smiled good-naturedly. "What can I do for you, young fellow?" he asked.

"The railroad goes all the way to St. Joe on the Missouri, isn't that so?" Levi questioned.

"Yep. With a lot of stops in between here and there. You want to go that far, do you?"

"Yes, and take my horse. That's if I have enough money," Levi said. He had found three twenty-dollar gold pieces in the breast pocket of the lieutenant's jacket. Those coins taken together with what he had found on the private and his own funds now gave him nearly one hundred and thirty dollars.

The agent checked his rate book for a moment and then informed Levi of the cost of a ticket and transportation for the horse. He added, "You've got to supply your own horse feed and water."

"When is the train due to leave?"

"Six o'clock this evening, give or take a few hours. The war has made the schedule of all trains a matter of waiting for it to get here."

"I'll take a ticket for me and my horse."

"All right. Going west there's almost always plenty of room. Going east the military takes up nearly all the passenger cars as well as the box and flatbed cars."

Levi counted out the required money and took his ticket. "Where can I get a good meal at a cheap price?"

"Two blocks west along the street and on the right, a place called Marvin's," replied the agent. He looked up at Levi's head. He seemed on the verge of saying something.

"Thanks," Levi said quickly before the man could speak. He pivoted and hastened with a quick step from the station. He wanted no questions from the railroad agent.

Levi ate a large meal, the first decent food he'd had in days. Then feeling somewhat more at peace with himself, he went shopping and bought a second pair of trousers and another shirt. He examined the healed wound on his forehead in the mirror in the clothing store. He was surprised at the vivid color of the new flesh. To hide the scar, he purchased a hat, a wide-brimmed, flat-crowned one of a gray color.

He found a bath house and for the price of a dime bathed. After finishing, he put on his new garments and washed his dirty clothing in the bath water. With the wet clothing hanging over an arm, and leading his horse, he returned to the railroad tracks.

The horse was staked out to graze. The wet garments were hung to dry on the limb of a big chestnut tree. Levi lay in the grass and leaned against the bole of the tree. Now and again he dozed as the sun crossed over its zenith and inched down the heavens.

The couplings holding the cars of the railroad train together rattled and clanked and the speeding iron wheels emitted an endless series of rapid click-clacks as they crossed the joints of the rails. Levi liked the sounds for they measured the ever increasing distance he was being taken from the Union and Confederate armies locked in their deadly battles in the East.

When the train stopped at towns to unload and pick up passengers, he sometimes made hurried trips to stores located along the nearby streets to purchase food for himself and to livery stables for grain to feed his horse. There was a bucket in the box car, and water for his horse was easily obtained from the overhead tanks that supplied the boilers of the locomotive. He slept in his seat. At night, when the passengers were few in number, he would spread his blanket in the aisle of the car and sleep stretched out full length. On the third day as darkness settled upon the swaying cars, the train swept out of Illinois and entered Missouri.

Levi awoke in the morning to a world lashed with rain and wind. Lightning, bright as exploding suns, flashed in the gray dawn. The burst of thunder could be heard easily above the noise of the train. Every stream Levi could see from the train window was a rushing torrent of brown water.

In midmorning the storm began to slacken. Within an hour, the wind and rain ceased, only the heavy clouds remained behind.

Levi started to settle back for a nap, when abruptly the train began to slow. The big wheels of the cars screeched as they ground on the iron rails. The train came to a shuddering, jerking stop.

Levi went to the door and climbed down to the ground with the two dozen or so other passengers. Men and women from the remaining cars were also unloading. Levi, wondering why the train had stopped, joined with several men moving toward the locomotive.

He stopped in front of the steam engine and looked down into a flood-swollen creek. The middle supports of the railroad trestle were gone, washed away. The two rails still attached to their wooden crossties, hung in a sagging loop between the stone abutments on each bank of the creek.

"Damn lucky that I saw the bridge was washed out," said the engineer as he nervously wiped his sweating face with a red bandanna. "Telegraph lines are gone too." He pointed at the broken wires hanging from poles on both sides of the creek.

"What do we do now?" asked a passenger.

"We must get a message to the station manager in St. Joe," the engineer replied. "That's about twenty miles ahead. There's horses on board the train. Where're the riders?"

"I'm one of them," Levi said.

The engineer turned to Levi. "The creek's falling fast so

you can ford it on horseback. Will you ride to the station manager in St. Joe with a message?''

"Sure." Levi wanted to hurry on to St. Joe, and far beyond that town.

"Good. Tell him what's happened here and to stop the east-bound train. We sure don't want it to wreck by running into that." He gestured at the deep channel of the creek. "The washout is bad so he'll need to send a big work crew to repair the track and trestle."

"You'd better write down what you want so the agent will know I'm telling the truth."

"I'll do that while you saddle up."

Levi hurried back to his car. He packed his belongings and went to the box car. Shortly he had saddled, unloaded his horse from the box car, and returned to the locomotive.

"Move that horse along," the engineer said, handing Levi a folded piece of paper. "That east-bound's got to be stopped and the agent in St. Joe can do that."

"Twenty miles won't take long," Levi said.

He rode down the slanting bank and forded the creek. The engineer was correct, the water was falling fast. The horse scampered up the far bank and broke into a run along the tree-lined railroad tracks.

A mile later a muddy road angled out of the woods and ran parallel to the railroad tracks. Levi swung onto the road. He saw not one person. He hurried on, splashing through the puddles of water that lay like dull pools of lead on the dirt road.

Levi held his mount to a gallop as the woods that crowded the road gave way on the right to a farmstead, a cleared area of about five acres. A moderate-sized log house sat up a short lane from the road and in the center of the clearing. Behind the house a field of shoulder high corn was beginning to tassel.

Levi saw a boy of twelve or thirteen years kneeling beside some object lying in the grass of the front yard of the house. At the sound of Levi's horse, the boy leapt to his feet and whirled around. He leaned forward, seemingly on the verge of springing away. Even at the distance, Levi saw the strained, fear-filled face of the youngster.

The boy hesitated, poised, his eyes sweeping over the strange rider on the road. Then he straightened and began to wave both arms frantically above his head. "Mister, please come and help me," he cried, his voice shrill, hysterical. "They've killed both of them. My mother! My sister!"

Levi reined his black off the road and ran him up the lane to the house. As he drew closer, he saw the body of a girl perhaps eleven or twelve years old lying at the feet of the boy. She had that still, slack look of the dead. Levi knew that posture very well.

Tears filled the boy's eyes and his jaws trembled. He wiped at the tears with the back of his hand. "Look what they've done to my sister," he sobbed. He pointed at the body of the girl, but did not look.

The girl lay on her back. Her thin cotton dress had been ripped apart and pulled aside exposing her young body just starting to bud to womanhood. There were bad bruises on her pretty face with blood on her mouth and Levi knew she had bravely fought her attacker. A gaping knife wound penetrated her chest into her heart.

Levi was certain the girl was dead, still he knelt and placed his ear close to the bloody mouth. There was not one whisper of breath. He arose shaking his head and feeling his own deep sadness at the awful crime.

"She's dead," Levi said.

"I know," sobbed the boy. "They did the same thing to my mom. She's on the porch."

"What happened? Where's your dad?"

"He's off in the army somewhere fighting the Yankees. He should've been here taking care of us." The boy became racked with sobs. With an effort, he controlled himself.

"Three men came riding out of the trees over there." The boy pointed. "One of them ran Sis down. Two of them caught Mom. They did those awful things to them and then killed them."

"Why didn't they catch you?"

"I stayed overnight with my grandpa and grandma who live over the hill about a mile away. I was almost home when I saw the men come out of the woods riding fast toward the house. I hid. I saw what they did." The boy again broke into heavy sobs.

"I'm sorry this happened to your family," Levi said.

The boy stifled his crying, his wet eyes fastened on Levi. "Mister, I see you've got a rifle. Go after them and shoot them. They've only been gone a little while. I can show you their tracks. If you hurry you can catch them easy. One's riding a skinny mule that I bet can't run very fast."

Levi shook his head in the negative. "Better you go tell your grandpa what happened. He can get some neighbors and they can catch the men. Or you can ride with me to St. Joe and get the sheriff."

"That'd take time and the killers would be long gone. Are you afraid?"

"No. I'm just telling you what you should do."

"You're afraid. You're a coward." The boy's voice was full of contempt. "Just give me your gun and horse. They took all of ours. I'll catch them. I'm not a coward."

"You've had a bad loss so I'll overlook you calling me a coward. Do you want me to help you take your sister's body into the house?"

"I don't want your help for anything," the boy exclaimed angrily. "I'll take her in the house. You just go away and let us alone."

The boy knelt and pulled the torn dress over his sister's violated body. He lifted her limp form up in his arms and started toward the house.

He halted and his anguished face turned back to Levi. "Get the hell off our property, you Goddamn coward."

Chapter 8

Levi mounted his horse and rode across the clearing in the direction the boy had pointed. He quickly found three sets of hoofprints in the damp earth and followed them to where they entered the woods. One set of tracks was considerably smaller than the other two and more rounded in shape. Those would be the ones of the mule.

He turned aside from the trail, for he would not pursue the raiders, and went to the road. He would notify the sheriff in St. Joe of the attack on the farmstead. The town was not more than ten to twelve miles distant and the law officials could ride back to the farm before dark and pick up the trail.

Levi raised the horse to a swift gallop toward St. Joe. The clouds were lowering and threatening more rain. The forest closed in tightly and the limbs of the giant trees, every leaf hanging motionless, arched out to span the road. In among the trees of the damp woods, tendrils of fog were rising up from the ground like gray spirits. To Levi it seemed he rode down a dank, murky tunnel watched by ghosts.

The way climbed a hill and then descended a long grade into a valley. There it wound a course through a downfall of twisted and broken timber where a tornado had touched down.

As Levi came round a bend, three riders broke from the woods and rode into the road some one hundred yards in front of him.

The horsemen were facing in the opposite direction, toward St. Joe, and did not see Levi in the gloomy woods, or hear his horse's hooves on the soft earth. Then one of the men looked to the rear and spotted Levi. He called a sharp warning to the other two men and jerked his mount around.

Levi pulled the black to a halt. His eyes locked on the men on the road. By their sudden reaction to one lone rider and the way they now evaluated him, he judged them rogues and scoundrels.

The man who had first seen Levi began to speak swiftly to his two cohorts. The two nodded agreement and all three moved, fanning out to completely block the narrow road.

A lump of ice formed in Levi's gut, for as the men separated, he saw one sat upon a tall, skinny mule. The image of the ravaged and mutilated body of the young girl at the farm flashed in Levi's brain. He felt the tingle and slither of his anger and hatred swell like the uncoiling of a great snake in his stomach.

He must get past the raiders and speed on to St. Joe and inform the sheriff of what these men had done and where their sign could be found. The thought died as quickly as it was born. The three men were walking their mounts toward him. They were not going to allow him to pass. Their desire to prey upon those weaker than themselves was not satisfied. He was alone and they planned to make him their next victim.

He glanced at the dense woods, close by and dark under the heavy overcast. With two jumps of the black, he could be into that protective tangle of tree trunks and brush. He had an excellent chance to elude the men there, but he didn't kick his horse and run. Instead he was remembering the boy kneeling over the body of his dead sister. She had lain so very still, so innocent and undeserving of the horrible crime committed upon her. He seemed to hear a young girl's frightened, pain-filled cry for help. Levi was startled by the clarity of the voice for he knew it was entirely within his head. Crimes did not die silently with their victims.

The raiders were now within eighty yards and moved steadily

closer. Two of the raiders were reaching for their pistols. Fools, the distance is still rifle work, thought Levi. The man who had spoken to the others drew his rifle from its boot.

Levi yanked his Spencer from its scabbard, swung a leg over the neck of his horse, and slid to the ground. He stepped quickly away from the horse. He needed the animal and it must not be injured by any return shots.

He raised the Spencer and pointed the black eye of the barrel at the man with the rifle, who seemed to be the leader. He must be killed first.

Levi fired his rifle, and instantly levered another cartridge into the breech of the gun. He swung the weapon onto a second rider before the first one had fallen from his horse.

The remaining two raiders were taken by surprise by the speed with which Levi had dismounted and fired and killed one of their group. They were men who survived by stealth and trickery, and then only against the weak. They had not expected one man to bravely attack three.

Levi's rifle bucked against his shoulder a second time. The man on the mule was slammed backward onto the rump of his animal. The pistol he had started to lift fell from his lifeless hand. The mule bolted, dumping the rider's body.

The third man spun his horse on its hind legs and hit it a savage blow across the ribs with his pistol. The horse plunged away from Levi and along the road. Never had the raider seen a man move so fast and shoot with such accuracy. The frightened man struck his horse again with the heavy iron pistol driving it away from that hazardous place.

When Levi had first touched his rifle, he was determined to shoot all three of the men who had raped and killed the girl. Even if they had given him a mortal wound, he would not fall until he had finished what he had set out to do. The effort of the last raider to escape him was as useless an action as trying to bring the girl back to life. For Levi knew, with the assurance that only truly competent men ever know, that he could send a bullet to hit the raider at any place he chose.

Levi shot the man through the center of his back, shattering his spine. The man tumbled from his running horse. He bounced and rolled with a jumble of legs and arms upon the soggy ground. The frightened horse raced on along the road.

Levi gripped the Spencer and stared at the crumpled forms of the three men. Two of them lay so close together that they were touching each other. The third man was but a short distance away. Levi sucked a burning breath into his lungs and then cried out. "To hell with every one of you!"

He clamped his jaws shut. Words had no importance. His wildly beating heart slowed as he stood in the gloomy forest and looked at the corpses, and the blood that had raced so hot through his veins became chilled. His hands trembled as he began to insert fresh ammunition in the cartridge tube of the Spencer. Even killing murderers was a fearful thing to do. A deep, dark melancholy fell upon him.

He caught the mule and securely tied it to the belt of its dead master. The mule would identify the men as one of the murderers once the boy at the farm described the attackers. Perhaps the boy would know who had taken the full measure of revenge on the slayers of his family, and that Levi was no coward. Levi hoped he would for somehow that was important to him.

The horse of the leader was an excellent animal, strongly built and clear-eyed. It would make a good packhorse for Levi's long trip across the plains and through the mountains to California. He tied a rope around the beast's neck. With the animal in tow, Levi set a fast pace for St. Joe.

The ferry gave a shrill blast of its steam whistle, spun its big, side, paddle wheels and pulled away from its berth at the wharf in St. Joseph. Once clear of the wharf, the paddle wheels bit more swiftly into the water. The ferry swung to settle on a course west across the Missouri River.

Levi stood with his horses near the bow of the vessel. The craft was single-decked and broad, with a single smokestack spouting smoke. It was crowded with men, women, and children, and buggies, wagons, and horses. All manner of freight in boxes, barrels, and crates were jammed into every inch of spare space.

Levi, upon his arrival in St. Joe, had immediately delivered his message to the railroad agent. He had also informed the sheriff of the attack upon the farm family, but said nothing about his own battle with the raiders. Surely should he have done that, the sheriff would have detained him in St. Joe for days, possibly weeks, while an investigation was conducted. That was the last thing Levi wanted for he was driven to hurry on to California.

There was a second reason Levi wanted to speedily leave St. Joe. Missouri was a Confederate state. As he had talked with the sheriff, a company of Confederate artillerymen, with their cannon and howitzers drawn by sweating horses, came rumbling into St. Joe. They had gone directly to the bluffs overlooking the river and begun to construct emplacements for the big guns. The artillery captain told the citizens that a full company of infantry was but two days behind. The Rebels meant to hold St. Joe with its railroad and to prevent the Union Army from using the Missouri River to transport military supplies. The war was traveling swiftly west. Levi hoped it had not reached California.

He had traded the slain raider's saddle for a pack saddle. Then searching quickly through the stores of the town, he had bought food, a section of waterproof tarpaulin, and other items sufficient to round out an outfit that would get him to the Pacific Ocean. Once he had finished, he had less than ten dollars left for the nearly two thousand miles yet to travel.

Levi looked about the ferry and noted that there were none of the big covered wagons that immigrants used to haul their possessions overland to California or Oregon. The season of the year was already too late to begin a trip to such far away places. The people on the ferry were returning to their farms located west of the river on the Nebraska plains.

Once he was beyond the rim of the outlying settlements, he would have to journey alone. He had acquired a map of the overland trail to California. The way had been heavily traveled for years and was deeply worn and littered with discarded furniture, broken wagons, the bones of horses and oxen, and the graves of those immigrants who had not survived the difficult miles. He would have no trouble finding his way.

He removed his hat and faced the bow of the ferry to let the breeze created by the movement of the vessel cool his warm face. To his surprise, a group of men, all strangers, were looking at him and talking among themselves. Levi counted six in the party, and the way they stared bothered him. Did they somehow know he was an army deserter?

One of the group, a big man with a long brushy beard, left his comrades and pushed through the crowd of people and vehicles on the ferry deck toward Levi. The man halted and his eyes, black and penetrating, inspected Levi from head to toe, hesitating for a brief moment on the scar on his forehead. He glanced at Levi's two horses, the army saddle on the black and the rifle in its scabbard.

Levi placed his hat back on his head to hide the scar, and waited for the man to show his intentions.

"Is that a Spencer rifle in that boot?" asked the man.

"Yes," Levi replied.

"I thought so from the shape of the stock. Best rifle made today. My name's Ottoson, Ralph Ottoson." The man extended his hand.

"I'm Levi Coffin," Levi replied, wondering what the man wanted. He shook the offered hand.

"My friends and me," Ottoson nodded in the direction of his comrades, "are going to California. We heard there's been a new gold strike out there in the Sierra Nevadas. Where might you be heading?"

"The same place."

"We were kind of hoping that was the case," Ottoson said. He nodded at Levi's rifle. "Do you know how to use that Spencer, or is it just an ornament?"

"I'm too poor to own something that I can't use."

Ottoson grinned at the answer. "Are you traveling alone?" he asked.

"Nope, I'm planning to take these two horses with me."

Ottoson broke into a smile. "You're a smartalecky young

fellow, but I think underneath that you're all right. If you can hold up your end of the work and stand with us in any fighting we get into with Indians, I'd like to give you an invite to travel with us.''

Levi ranged his sight to check the men and their equipment. They had saddle horses, and heavily loaded packhorses. There was a rifle in a scabbard on every mount, and the men wore pistols, as did Ottoson. They appeared well prepared for a long journey.

When Levi looked back at Ottoson, the man was closely regarding him. ''Have you ever been in a gunfight and killed men?'' Ottoson asked.

An expression of deep sadness came over Levi's face. Then he lifted a hand and swept it across his eyes as if brushing away the cobwebs of the memories the question had awakened. His mouth tightened, he wasn't going to answer such a question.

''I gather that you have,'' Ottoson said. ''Was it a fair fight?''

Levi bore Ottoson's stare without looking away. He knew it would be safer to travel the long distance through Indian country to California with other men rather than try it alone. Why not with these men who appeared to be honest and their offer a straightforward proposition?

''Yes, fair, if you mean did they have guns and an equal chance to kill me.''

Ottoson studied Levi for a few seconds more, then he spoke. ''We can use another gun. I'll gamble that you are a man who'll stand tough in a fight.''

''Since you'll take a chance on a stranger, I'll take a chance on all of you.''

Ottoson threw back his head and laughed. ''Good. We'll ride like hell and be in California before all the gold is dug.''

Chapter 9

Celeste swung the pistol up, cocking it as it rose, shoved it out and pressed the trigger. Just the way Vicaro had drilled into her. The pistol cracked. She heard the thud of the lead ball striking the half hundred balls already embedded in the post.

The wooden post was six feet tall, half a foot in diameter, and an old straw hat sat upon its top. The bark had been cut away to expose a section of white wood the size of a hand approximately eighteen inches below the hat. This was the second post in the past month that had sat on this very same spot in the gully north of the Beremendes's *hacienda*. The first one had been shot to pieces.

"Are you ready for the second shot?" Vicaro Zaragoza asked.

"Ready," Celeste replied. The Colt revolver rested lightly in her hand hanging by her leg.

"Fire." Vicaro's voice was sharp.

Celeste fired again. The bullet slammed the post, ricocheting off the compacted mass of lead and sending splinters flying.

"Excellente," Vicaro called. "You do it exactly right. However your hand was slower with the second shot. Your hand must be stronger so it can lift *la pistola* more quickly."

Celeste studied the post. For the first three days of practice, Vicaro had her firing at large paper targets. The spread of the pattern of her shots had gradually tightened until her hand could cover them. One morning when she went to meet with him, he had led her to the gully and showed her a post with a hat.

"Since you plan to kill a man, you should practice shooting at a target that somewhat looks like one," Vicaro said.

"From now on until you fight Dokken, this will be your target. Now send a bullet into the heart of that God-cursed man standing ready to shoot you."

Celeste had fired day after day at the post until the part that represented the heart was shattered. Vicaro cut another post and planted it in the ground. The practice continued under the critical eye of the old *pistolero*.

Vicaro called out again and Celeste fired twice more. Her pistol was now empty and Vicaro handed her another loaded one. She had purchased a second gun exactly like Ernesto's so that once the practice started Vicaro could reload the empty weapon while she shot and thus speed her practice.

Celeste fretted at the delay in seeking out Dokken. Yet at the same time she worried. She had the desire to kill but she doubted that she had the courage. Violence was foreign to her nature, and she had never observed the killing of a human until that dreadful day when Ernesto had been shot to death.

She did not want to die, for life was too grand for that, even with all her troubles; therefore, she must not falter at the crucial moment in the fight with Dokken, for surely he would then kill her. Courage and strength, those two things she must acquire. Vicaro could not teach her those things as he had taught her to shoot. Only she could take herself the rest of the way to being a brave *pistolero* and duelist.

"Vicaro, is there anything more that you can teach me to increase my skill with a pistol?"

"No, Señorita Celeste. You know all the movements to shoot swiftly and accurately. Now you must practice until you are more skilled than any man you might fight."

"I want to fight only Dokken."

"There may be others who wish to harm you that you do not yet know about."

"I hope there is only Dokken."

"Do you want to shoot some more?"

"No. I must be alone for a while. We have a cabin on the south end of the *rancho*. I will go there and think about what I plan to do."

"I understand," the old man said. "There are times in a person's life when he must look inside himself and find the truth of what he is. When will you go?"

"Just as soon as I can get ready. We have plenty of powder and caps for my practice. Please help me mold a supply of bullets."

"I'll melt the lead right away," Vicaro said. He walked off toward the blacksmith shop.

Celeste worked with Vicaro through the remainder of the morning and the middle of the day. Again and again lead was melted to a liquid in the hot forge and poured into the bullet molds. To cool them they were immersed in a bucket of cold water. The teats that always remained at the pour hole and the raised rims where the two sides of the mold came together were carefully shaved away from each bullet with a sharp knife. Celeste filled a sack with several pounds of lead balls.

"That should be enough," she told Vicaro.

"By the time you have shot all of them you will be a much better *pistolero*."

"I won't waste any," Celeste replied.

"I'll saddle your mare and rope you a packhorse while you gather your food and clothing."

"Be sure to put the straw hat in one of the pack saddles."

"Yes, the hat must go with you."

"Would you stay at the *rancho* while I'm gone? The cattle and sheep are on good pasture. Now I'm going to start the men preparing the bottom land for growing wheat. You could help Ignacio keep them at the task."

"How long will you be gone?" Vicaro asked.

"I don't know. Maybe a month. Perhaps even longer, until I feel ready. But don't worry about me for I'll be safe."

Vicaro looked into the lovely face of the young woman. He feared for her and yet at the same time was proud that she wanted revenge for her brother's death. "I'll stay and help Ignacio as long as I can. Until the *gringos* discover I'm here."

"Thank you. Thank you for all your help."

"Always keep your pistol with you," Vicaro warned her.

"I will." Celeste hurried into the *hacienda*.

Celeste packed her bedroll and enough food to last several days. She carried the items from the *hacienda* and stowed them in the pack saddle on the horse that Vicaro had brought to the front with her mare.

She turned to Ignacio and Vicaro who stood watching her. "We must plant wheat this year," she said to Ignacio. "To do that the land of the valley bottom must be cleared of the brush patches and leveled."

Celeste saw the expression of dislike for the task on Ignacio's face, but she continued on. "Take our *vaqueros* and begin. Start where there is the least vegetation and the land is most flat. You will need many tools. Go to Sacramento and get them. Our friends who own the hardware stores will give you credit in my name. Ignacio, listen to me for this is very important. Hundreds of acres must be ready when planting time arrives in the fall."

"I hear you, *señorita,* but the men will not want to do that kind of work. They work hard when they are upon their *caballos.* On their feet, they do not work so well. And it will be very hot down there in the valley."

"If they do not clear the land, there will not be a *rancho* to ride upon for the *gringos* will own it," Celeste said, aggravated at Ignacio but knowing he spoke the truth. "Vicaro will help you convince the men to work very hard."

Ignacio looked at the old bandit, and then smiled crookedly. "*Señorita,* with Vicaro watching, the men will work very hard."

"Then see that it's done," Celeste said, her voice firm.

* * *

Celeste rode into the yard of the cabin with evening dusk falling. She removed the saddle from the mare and the pack saddle and provisions from the second horse. Both animals were hobbled and turned loose to graze.

She surveyed the one-room cabin that was made of stone, and had a flat earthen roof. It sat high above the San Joaquin Valley on the east flank of Mount Mocho. A long ledge of sandstone outcropped from the mountain side just above the cabin. A spring welled up at the base of the ledge. Many years ago her grandfather had walled the spring. She went straight to it and lay down and drank from its cold water.

Celeste arose and looked both ways across the mountainside with its broad grassy meadows and patches of brush. She turned to gaze down at the great, flat bottomed valley. Purple shadows had filled the broad chasm while to the east the far mountains were still partially lit by the sun's rays. She had always loved this lonely, isolated place. She was glad she had left the *hacienda* with all its people and activity. Here a person could truly search her soul.

She returned to the cabin and carried her provisions inside to set up her camp. Darkness was falling swiftly and Celeste dug out her candles. The bottom end of one was melted with a match and then placed on the table top and held until the wax hardened. She walked into the yard. The noise of the night insects was building. A slow wind came alive and began to fall into the cooling valley. The stone walls of the cabin emitted low clicking sounds as they cooled. She saw the outlines of the horses nearby and heard them cropping the wild mountain grass.

She folded her arms across her breast and leaned against the cabin wall. If there was one place on earth where she could prepare herself to kill, or perhaps be killed, it would be here. She forced her mind away from those dismal thoughts. Tonight she would think only of the happy times when Ernesto and she had played here as children.

Chapter 10

The male golden eagle rode the blustery wind, kiting north on his eight-foot wings along the eastern flank of Mount Mocho. The aerial hunter had prowled this land for thirty years, an extremely long life for an eagle. He knew every hilltop, every gully, every tree. Today he would first inspect the place where the white animal with the sweet meat sometimes gathered.

The eagle saw the small house where the humans stayed. His telescopic eyes had already told him that no sheep were there, but the lone human on the slope above the cabin drew the hunting bird. He would go a little closer. He set his wings and began to descend in a long glide.

An explosion erupted from the ground, sending shock waves jarring the air. Then another, and another, until six gunshots had rapidly been fired in a rolling volley that was almost one continuous sound. The eagle was frightened by the noise and he flared his strong wings, halting his descent. He pumped hard climbing away on the soft ladder of air.

Celeste watched the fist-sized rocks that she had placed upon the top of the boulder shatter into hundreds of pieces and go zinging away. She holstered the empty pistol. She pivoted left, drawing a second pistol from the waistband of her leather pants.

She shot at the knot on the post that she had set in the ground, and upon which the straw hat rested.

Splinters flew from the post at her intended point of aim. She nodded with satisfaction. Already she was better with a pistol than Ernesto had been. That was very unexpected, but so necessary.

All morning she had practiced, shooting at her targets from the hillside above, from the slope below, with the sun in her face, and at her back. She felt the familiarity, the immense ease with which she handled the pistol. She was very near to being ready to challenge Dokken. That thought sent a chill through her body.

She walked to the cabin, entered, and sat down at the crude table and reloaded the two weapons. Holstering one and leaving the second on the table, she went to the pole-framed bunk and lay down. After a short rest, the strenuous work of the day would start.

Celeste squatted beside the slab of sandstone and gripped the two ends. She grunted as she hoisted upward and came erect with the heavy load. What would her mother have said at such an unladylike sound. How shocked that gentle woman would have been to know her daughter planned to kill a man.

Celeste brought the block of stone in against her body and carried it to a new stone wall rising from the earth. She placed the slab so that it overlapped the ends of the two below and thus would bind them together and strengthen the wall. She remembered from long ago when she had heard her father give instructions to his workmen, that the correct way to lay a wall was to place one stone on two and two on one.

Cattle and sheep were held in the vicinity of the cabin during periods of the year when grass was available. A corral to hold the mounts of the *vaqueros* had been needed for a long time, but somehow had never gotten built. Celeste was constructing the walls of the corral.

The sun burned down like a fireball. Sweat dripped from her face and trickled down between her breasts. Her shirt was soaked. She halted to catch her breath and check what she had built in a month.

The corral was square and some sixty feet on a side. Already the wall was nearly three feet tall. She wondered how many tons of rock she had carried and lain. The task was becoming more difficult, for the closer supply of stones had all been used up and now transporting additional ones from a greater distance was a true test of strength and determination. She had brought no gloves and at first the rough stones had badly bruised her hands. That period was now past and thick callouses had formed on palms and fingers.

Her body had grown lean and hard. She could see the muscles in her arms and hands, and feel the strength in her shoulders and back. The two-pound-and-ten-ounce Colt pistol seemed to have lessened to but a fraction of its actual weight. She could now hold the gun out horizontal and aimed at a target for many seconds before her arms would start to tremble.

Her hands and face were burned to a deep brown. The sun had also roughened her normally smooth skin. That was good because now she would appear more masculine. She often talked to the mare, and at those times, she practiced speaking in a deep male tone.

There were other female characteristics that she recognized and was working to change. Women touched their hair from time to time. Men rarely did. Also she must look men directly in the eyes. That would be difficult, for from the very earliest age, little girls are taught not to look beyond a glance at a strange man.

She reached up and touched the grime on her forehead. The sweat had dried quickly in the warm, dry air, crusting into a thin film of white salt crystals on her skin. In the evening she would bathe at the spring.

Feeling restless, she decided that enough stone work had been done for the day. She whistled for the mare. The faithful steed never drifted beyond Celeste's call. The packhorse was now also let loose but it dragged a long thirty-foot *riata* so it could be easily caught.

The mare stopped grazing in the meadow below the cabin

and raised its head to listen. Celeste whistled again. The horse came at a run, tossing its head and watching the woman with its intelligent brown eyes.

Celeste saddled and swung astride. The mare left the yard at a rocking chair gallop. Celeste spoke to the mare and petted the satin smooth shoulder of the horse. She felt better already.

Celeste awoke in the dark. She was troubled by the passage of time. Dokken still lived and her oath to her brother Ernesto went unfilled. She also felt frustrated because the increase in her skill with the pistol had stalled. For the past week try as she might, there had been no further improvement. Something was blocking the perfect coordination she must have between eye, brain, and hand.

She climbed from her bed and stood on the dirt floor of the cabin. The passage of time worried her for another reason. How many acres of valley bottom land had Ignacio and the other men prepared for the planting of wheat? She should be working with her *vaqueros,* encouraging their efforts, and adding her strength to accomplish the task. But that must wait for now. Dokken's death came first.

She dressed, picked up her pistol from beside her bunk and strapped it around her waist. She left the cabin, and from the stone stoop looked about in the darkness. The night was totally silent. The grass and the scattered trees around the cabin were bathed in light from the half moon. Farther away to the east, the San Joaquin Valley was a great pool of blackness.

The mare watched her from under the nearby oak. The horse nickered and came up to the stoop and nuzzled the front of Celeste's shirt. It raised its head and sniffed at her face.

"You are spoiled but you are my only companion," Celeste told the mare. She petted the long bony jaw, and the muscular neck. "Now go away for I have something to do."

Celeste climbed the familiar path up the slope to the spring at the base of the rock outcrop. She bathed her face in the cold water and drank several handfuls. Lifting her shirttail, she dried her face.

She leaned against a huge block of stone that had fallen down from above. Around her the night lay quietly, the wind motionless, and all the animals of the darkness, the large and the small, were mute as if voiceless. She listened to the silence and waited in the cool morning hours for daylight to arrive and the long hours of practice to begin anew.

In a bush on the mountain side above the spring, two small brown wrens stirred as light brightened the darkness of night. They rose from a squatting position on their roost. Thin legs straightened, and strong tendons relaxed to unclamp clutching claws from twigs that had held the three-ounce bodies safely all night. Fine feathered wings stretched and sharp eyes examined the set of each feather to insure they were aligned for best flight.

The tiny cock cast a flicker of a one-eyed glance at the even smaller hen and launched himself from his perch. She was instantly at his side, then ahead of him, pressing down on the cool buoyant air to stay aloft. The first drink of morning was only seconds away.

The birds flew directly at Celeste standing by the spring. The brown wings beat a few strokes, then stiffened for a short glide and repeated to produce a flight of rises and falls. The birds drew within a hundred yards of the woman, fifty yards, and nearer. They sighted the strange form that should not have been there by the water. Wary of the unknown animal, the wrens zoomed up at a steep angle, their strong little wings swiftly stroking the air.

Shoot! cried Celeste's mind. She shoved away from the boulder. Her hand dipped down and came up with her revolver. Two shots blended into one rolling explosion.

The small bodies burst into blossoms of feathers that drifted downward lazily on the quiet air. Celeste spun left. She triggered the gun at a white pebble on the ground. It vanished in a puff of pulverized rock.

The plumage of the birds had not yet settled to the earth. Celeste's eye picked one single, oscillating feather, and pointed the barrel of her weapon. She fired and the feather vanished.

Celeste's blood rushed in exaltation at the unexpected triumph. The gun was, as Vicaro had said it must be, one with her hand. More than that, the accuracy had been enormously better than ever before. Some new, perfect link between hand and eye had been forged. As if two red-hot lengths of iron had been pressed together and struck with a hammer to make two one. When one end moved, so too did the opposite end at that exact same fraction of time. The eye saw, the mind thought, and the hand moved, all instantaneously.

One feather had caught in the seed head of wild rye grass. The delicate down of the end of the feather that had been next to the warm, live body of the bird was startlingly white. It glowed a little beacon in the dusk of the morning.

Sorrow for the death of the wrens rose in Celeste and hot tears gushed up from their little salt springs and streamed down her cheeks. She wiped the tears away, but the sorrow remained. She would kill no more innocent things. She would kill only the murderer Dokken who had no innocence. It was now time to challenge him to a duel.

Celeste rode north along the foothills that separated the San Joaquin Valley from the Diablo Mountain Range. The gray mare, towing the packhorse, moved at a swift gallop, her long legs swinging easily. She sensed they were heading home and she needed no urging to hurry her pace.

The rider and horses passed Crow Canyon and onward under the high looming shoulder of Copper Mountain. The steep, stony maw of Del Puerto Canyon slid by.

Celeste climbed the mare up a rocky ridge that extended out into the valley. From the top she could see miniature forms of her *vaqueros* on the flat bottomland about half a mile ahead. A wave of dismay struck her. Even from this distance she could see that little land had been cleared of the scattered brush, or leveled, or raked with a harrow to kill the wild grass.

She spoke sharply to her two horses and sent them in a run straight for the men lying in the shade under a leafy oak tree.

Celeste pulled the horses to a halt and sat looking down

upon the men who had sprung to their feet at her fast approach. They held their *sombreros* in their hands and watched her with expressions of concern.

Trying to control her anger, Celeste swung her hand out at the land that had been cleared, thirty acres she judged. She locked her gaze on Ignacio. "Why is such a small amount of land ready for the planting of wheat?"

Ignacio's eyes were full of remorse. "We try, Señorita Celeste. You catch us resting in the shade, but we seldom stop. We know that we must grow wheat."

Celeste examined the men more closely. She saw their weary faces and their shirts were sweat soaked.

"Then what has gone wrong? Nine men should have cleared ten times that much land."

"I agree," replied Ignacio. "If we had the proper tools to work with. We have only those poor, worn out things to use." He gestured with his hand at the tools lying on the ground.

Celeste cast a look at the few old mattocks, garden hoes, and axes. "I told you to go to Sacramento and get hand tools and the big harrows that you needed."

"I did go, *señorita*. But I had no money and none of the merchants there would trust me to take the things and pay him later. They all say that you must pay cash for everything. I believe they think you will lose the *rancho*."

"They'll be correct if we don't get a good wheat crop grown this year. The seed grain must be in the ground by November. Keep working. Do the best that you can. Where is Vicaro?"

"He left. The *gringos* came to arrest him and he rode away very fast."

"All right. I'll buy tools and also hire more men." She had badly misjudged the amount of effort required to prepare the land. "We will need not only harrows but big scrapers to level some of the rougher land and teams of mules to pull them."

She reined the mare toward the *hacienda* on the mountainside above her. While she had been practicing with a gun to kill a man, her *rancho* had been slipping out of her hands.

* * *

"We can't work for you, Señorita Beremendes," said
Ricardo, a strongly muscled Mexican. "We must be paid as
we work. If we waited a year for our money, how would we
feed our little ones?"

Celeste had come to the Mexican section of Sacramento,
several square blocks of small adobe houses along the river,
and asked Ricardo to gather men for her to speak to. He had
quickly agreed, for the Beremendes name was known and well
respected. In only a short time he had assembled this group.

"I can't pay now," Celeste said. "But I must have workers."

"I'm truly sorry that we can't help you," Ricardo replied.
"But there are many jobs for us now and we are paid at the
end of every week. If we were rich men, then we would come
and help you for you are one of us."

"I'll get money to pay you," Celeste said.

She stepped up into her buggy and drove away from the
men. She could not blame them for refusing to work for her.
Their children must eat.

Shortly Celeste came upon a crowd of people gathered on
the top of the bluff above the Sacramento River. Most were
men, still there were also women and children. Some of the
men carried pistols and rifles. A section of land was being
roped off, surrounding a machine that flung targets into the air
for marksmen to shoot at. One of the shooting contests frequently held in Sacramento was soon to begin.

She was about to drive her buggy on when she spotted
Dokken arriving mounted upon a spirited roan horse. The man
did not see Celeste. He tied his horse to one of the several
hitching rails and went into the crowd.

Celeste's jaw hardened and she veered aside. She fastened
her buggy horse beside Dokken's mount and climbed down.
She would watch her adversary and perhaps learn something
about him that could help her in the coming duel.

Chapter II

At Placerville in the western Sierra Nevada Mountains, Levi Coffin said good-bye to Ottoson and the five other men who had crossed the plains and the high Rockies with him. Leading his packhorse, he rode steadily on to the west, feeling more driven than ever to reach San Francisco and the Pacific Ocean.

The land fell away before him and the cool ponderosa pine forest was left behind. He traveled through a land of low rolling hills covered with wild grass tall as a horse's knees and studded with short oak trees. He saw herds of brown cattle and white sheep and riders on good-looking horses.

In the edge of night he encountered the southwest flowing American River. He stepped down from his mount and squatted by the edge of the river as the horses drank. He grumbled to himself. The water was tan in color from being full of the fine silt washed downstream by the gold placer mining in the mountains. He lay down and drank beside the horses. On the tree-lined bank, he made his camp.

Levi arose with the arrival of daylight and continued on beside the meandering body of the river. By midmorning he could see the buildings of a small city. He decided that this must be Sacramento on the river by the same name. He was within easy striking distance of the goal he had journeyed three thousand miles to reach. He would arrive totally broke for he had spent his last coin in Placerville.

As he approached the outskirts of Sacramento, he saw a gathering of people in a large open field overlooking the Sacramento River. He estimated their number to be at least three hundred. Now and again a pistol or a rifle fired on the fringe of the crowd. Levi decided to investigate and guided his horses to ride closer.

He saw that a shooting contest was being organized. His hand moved to rub the stock of the Spencer rifle in its boot beneath his leg. Maybe he had found a way to earn some money in a short space of time.

He dismounted and tied his horses among others at one of the several hitching rails. Carrying his rifle in the crook of his arm, he moved through the crowd toward half a hundred men standing, talking and examining their guns in a roped-off zone near the river.

Just outside the enclosed area, Levi stopped beside a man sitting at a table containing an open ledger and a cash box. "Good day," he said to the man.

"Hello," the man replied. "Do you want to sign up for the rifle or the pistol shootoff?"

"I'd like to try the rifle match. What's the charge?"

"Fifty dollars and you supply your own cartridges."

"How much is the prize money for the winner?"

"That depends on how many shooters sign up and pay the entry fee. Of course, I get my cut for setting up the match. Are you going to enter?"

"I'd like to but I must raise the entry money somehow. Do you want to buy a good horse?"

"I've no use for another horse, but look over there." The man pointed. "That man in gray clothing is George Louden. He's the Wells Fargo agent for California. He's always looking for a good riding horse, or harness horse. And men good with guns. Go talk to him about your animal."

"Thanks, I'll do that. Who's the big fellow in the city suit with him?"

"That's Brol Mattoon, a businessman from San Francisco. He sometimes shoots in the pistol contest. Always wins when he does. If you're going to enter the rifle contest you'd better hurry. I'm going to close the register in ten minutes."

Levi moved through the people to Louden and Mattoon. As he came close, the Wells Fargo man cast an eye at him.

"Something I can do for you?" Louden asked, sweeping Levi with a quick glance noting the youthful, wispy beard, and the long brown hair tied back with a length of rawhide. The fellow's clothing was faded and showed rough usage, and his hat was battered and sweat stained. He had made a very long journey.

"Are you Mr. Louden?"

"I'm Louden."

"My name's Levi Coffin. I'd like to enter the rifle shoot, but I need to sell a horse to raise the entry fee. I've got a good one and thought maybe you would be interested in him."

"Louden, you don't have time to look at a horse now," Mattoon said. "Let's make a bet on the rifle match."

"In a minute," Louden said. He looked at the rifle on Levi's arm. "We don't see many Spencers out here in California," he said.

Mattoon spoke. "Louden, this fellow is just another man who came West to escape fighting in the war back East. Now he wants a handout. There's hundreds like him in San Francisco."

Levi felt his face harden at Mattoon's words. He looked at the man. Mattoon stared back, his mud-colored eyes full of challenge. Levi held back the sharp retort that came to his lips.

"Maybe so, but they don't carry Spencers," Louden said. He had heard of the sharpshooter companies being formed and armed with Spencers in the Union Army.

"What difference does it make what kind of rifle he carries?" asked Mattoon.

Louden spoke to Levi. "Are you good with that rifle?"

"I hit what I aim at," Levi replied.

Louden thoughtfully rubbed his chin. "Come with me, Coffin," he said.

Levi went with the man inside the roped-off area. Mattoon strode along beside them.

Louden pointed at a small catapult with a side-swinging arm, and then at several boxes containing round glass spheres. "How many of those balls could you hit without missing one?"

Levi took hold of the arm of the catapult, swung it to compress the spring, and then let it loose, measuring the speed of its return. Next he picked up one of the glass spheres some four inches in diameter, and hefted it in his hand estimating its weight. He judged half its volume was hollow.

"How many could you hit?" Louden asked again.

"I don't rightly know. But I plan to hit more of them than any other rifleman here," Levi said.

"Should I bet on you to win the contest?" Louden said.

"That's the way I'll bet if you buy my horse," Levi said.

Louden fell silent looking at Levi. The fellow was hardly more than a boy, yet the eyes that stared back at him were those of a confident animal.

"I bet this Coffin, if that's his name, doesn't win," Mattoon said.

"Who would you put your money on?" Louden asked.

"On Lasch. He's won the last three rifle matches."

"I think he'll lose today," Louden said. He spoke to Levi. "I'll buy your horse unseen. Here's fifty dollars for the entry fee. If you win there's another one hundred dollars in it for you."

"I'll win."

"I bet you don't," Mattoon said in a rough voice.

Levi turned toward Mattoon. He could not understand why the man had taken such an instant dislike for him. "What have I done to bother you?" he asked.

"Go sign up with Baker the shootmaster," Louden quickly interjected. He gave Levi a light shove on the arm. The young man must not get into a fight with Mattoon for that would be suicide. "You're almost out of time."

"All right," Levi said. He gave Mattoon one last look and turned away.

Levi heard Mattoon's voice behind him. "Louden, that fellow is a deserter from one of the armies back East. The horse you just bought is stolen, and the rifle probably is too. I'll give you two-for-one odds and bet a thousand dollars the deserter loses to Lasch.''

"You're covered," Louden replied. Was his instinct about Coffin wrong?

Baker, the organizer of the shooting contests, walked out in front of the crowd. He whistled shrilly through his teeth and raised both of his arms above his head. The hubbub of the crowd dwindled.

"Ladies and gentlemen, we are ready to begin the shooting contests. We have eighteen marksmen for the pistol match and twenty-two for the rifle. The pistol shoot-off will be first. The winner's purse will be five hundred dollars. Each elimination round will be five shots for each contestant. They will shoot in the order I call their names." The man began to read from the register.

Levi moved to a vantage point to observe the pistol shooting. A young, very pretty Mexican woman took a position beside him. She did not look at Levi. Her attention was focused entirely upon the shooters.

Celeste watched the contestants as one after another stepped into the firing box, a square space marked off with chalk on the ground. As the men fired at the glass balls flung out by the swinging arm of the catapult, she evaluated how they handled their weapons, cocked them, aimed, fired. Her attention focused even more intensely and her pulse hammered when Dokken came forward for his turn to shoot.

The catapult hurled the first glass sphere and it sailed past Dokken. He lifted his pistol with a smooth motion. His revolver cracked. The ball shattered. The following four balls were just as easily disposed of. Dokken had survived the first elimination round. So had five others.

The catapult was moved back ten yards to a pre-marked location and turned several degrees so that it would throw the glass spheres past the contestants at a steeper angle.

As the glass balls zipped out from the catapult, Celeste thought of the two birds she had shot. Though she still felt sorrow at killing the wrens, their deaths had told her the level of her skill. Soon she would know how good Dokken was, while he would not know about her. She was pleased at that.

The second elimination round ended with three shooters remaining. Each had a perfect score. Dokken had survived.

The range was increased another ten yards and the catapult turned so that the target would pass almost directly across in front of the shooters.

The initial marksman of the third round missed three of his five targets. He mouthed something that Celeste could not hear but thought must be a curse and stalked off.

Dokken and a large man dressed in elegant clothing were left. The larger man said something to Dokken and laughed. Celeste noted a strange momentary expression came upon Dokken's face. Was it fear? Why would that be? Then the expression was gone and no one who had not been watching Dokken as intently as Celeste could have caught it.

Dokken's bullets struck his targets one after another, until the fifth. The glass globe sailed serenely on after the pistol fired.

To Celeste's amazement, the big man standing off to Dokken's side raised his pistol to point in the direction of the fast-disappearing glass target. He fired, the burnt gunpowder smoke stabbing out of the black iron barrel. By some unearthly wizardry, the bullet struck the glass ball as it arched down toward the ground far away. The glass exploded and the multitude of glass shards caught the sunlight and gleamed in a brilliant silver shower for a brief instant.

The man immediately turned his revolver upward to the sky and fired four rapid shots to round out the required five. Laughing he slid the weapon into a holster inside his immaculately tailored coat.

The crowd of people was totally silent. Then the meaning of the man's action was understood. He had proved he was the champion, then had deliberately wasted his shots into the air, thus allowing Dokken to win. The people roared their approval of the man's deed.

"That fellow just threw away five hundred dollars," Levi said.

"Yes, he did," Celeste said, turning to look at the person who had spoken to her. A raggedy, blue-eyed *gringo* man, more a boy, was looking at her. She saw the rifle in the crook of his arm. "Are you going to compete in the rifle contest?"

"I'm going to try my luck at hitting some of those glass balls." Levi smiled into the black eyes watching him so earnestly. The woman was one of the prettiest he had ever seen.

Celeste smiled back at Levi. "I wish I could stay and watch you shoot, but I must hurry off to San Francisco."

"That's too bad."

"Good-bye and I hope you win," Celeste replied.

"Thanks," Levi replied.

Celeste cut a look at Dokken standing talking to the contest organizer. Then she left the crowd and went to her buggy.

Louden came to Levi. "I've bet Mattoon five hundred dollars that you beat Lasch."

Levi was shocked that Louden had bet such a large sum on him. "What odds did you get?"

"Mattoon gave me two to one that Lasch wins."

"Who is this Lasch?"

"I've often wondered that myself. He began coming to the shoots about two years ago. He always has money and bets heavily on himself."

"Does he often win?"

"Yes. He's won every time I've been to a match and saw him shoot."

"Sounds like my work is cut out for me."

"That it is, and a big job." Louden's features were somber. "I'd sure enjoy taking Mattoon's money."

"I'll do my best to help you," Levi said. He sensed a rivalry between the two men. Was it a friendly one? He gestured with his thumb at Mattoon who stood with another man, quite tall, rail thin and with a long bony face. "Is that second man Lasch?"

Louden looked in the same direction. "Yes, that's Lasch. He's an arrogant bastard. Mattoon is probably telling him about the bet he has made with me. Watch yourself for Mattoon doesn't like losing and Lasch may try a trick on you."

The shootmaster called from inside the roped-off shooting area. "Ladies and gentlemen, it is now time for the rifle match. The purse is six hundred dollars. Winner takes all. That's a lot of money and I expect you'll see some fine shooting to win it. Will the contestants come on this side of the rope?"

"I'll see you later," Levi told Louden.

"Good luck. Beat Lasch."

"I'd better. If I don't, I'll be flat broke and you will'uv lost a lot of money," Levi replied. He stepped over the rope. Knowing he had been the last man to sign the register, he took a position at the far side of the gathering of shooters. Baker began to call out names.

Lasch, trailing his rifle, walked toward Levi. His thick-lipped mouth was stretched in a smirkish grin. He halted, and set his feet in a pugnacious stance. "Mattoon just told me there was an army deserter at this match and that you could point him out to me."

Levi tensed at the word deserter. He remembered Louden's warning. Mattoon and Lasch didn't know anything for sure and were playing a game to rattle him and hamper his shooting. Their words were a very real threat for he was a deserter from the army. Union officials would be glad to arrest him and ship him back East for court martial. Or there could be a closer danger. California was a Union state. An army post of some sort might exist in Sacramento and he could be imprisoned there.

Levi locked eyes with Lasch. He must show no concern, no fear at the man's statement. As he started to reply, the first shooter of the elimination round fired his rifle.

"We'll have to wait to talk," Levi said. "See me after the match." He turned his back to Lasch.

Levi expected Lasch to say something more to him or even grab hold of him for turning his back, but neither happened. After a moment of tense waiting, he heard Lasch move away.

One marksman after the other fired his five rounds. Lasch shot, earning a perfect score. Then Levi stood in the shooter's box.

He thought of Mattoon with his thousand-dollar bet against him and believing him an army deserter. Then there was Louden betting he would win. And his own desperate need for money. He took a breath, let part out, and nodded to the man working the catapult.

The glass globe whizzed out, rising in the first part of its swift trajectory. Levi lifted the Spencer. The gun came so familiarly to his shoulder. His cheek met the stock, rested against it. His eye looked down the sights, moved the rifle barrel to track the silhouette of the target rushing across the sky. The path of the globe was almost directly away, an easy angle to hit. He pressed the trigger as the flying sphere of glass reached the top of its trajectory. The glass exploded.

The catapult man tripped the arm again. The Spencer roared out. The glass shattered.

Levi fired his five rounds at targets and missed not one of them.

Only eight contestants remained for the second elimination round. Levi had known most of the original riflemen would fail. Though many men were skilled at hitting stationary targets, a small fast-moving one was an entirely different matter.

He looked at Louden, and the man nodded. Levi was glad for the approval, but they were easy targets.

The catapult was carried out twenty yards and positioned so that it would throw the target to cross more steeply in front of the contestants.

The first shooter failed in two of his five attempts to hit the speeding targets. Lasch was the second marksman. His rifle swung easily to track the glass ball whipping across from right to left. He broke all five and turned to glance at Levi.

"It'll start getting hard after this round," Lasch said.

"I expect so," Levi replied.

Each of the next five men failed to hit one or more of the targets thrown past them. Then Levi stepped forward and stood waiting, his ears cocked to hear the metallic snap of the arm of the catapult, and his eyes to spot the speeding target. From the very first time his father had placed a rifle in his hands, Levi had had an uncanny knack of hitting moving targets. He felt that here today in the strange land of California his skill would be tested to the limit by the man called Lasch.

Levi exploded all five of his glass targets and stepped out of the shooter's position. He extracted the cartridge tube from the stock of the Spencer and began to shove fresh shells into it.

At an order from Baker, the catapult man picked up his machine and carried it to a new location twenty yards more distant. The angle with which the target would cross in front of the contestants was increased further still. Lasch stepped up to shoot.

The arm of the machine was tripped. The glass ball was almost invisible as it drove through the air. Yet Lasch's bullet broke it. And then four more. He laughed out loud.

Levi stepped to the shooter's position. Only Lasch and he remained of the contestants. Should Levi win, he would have made two enemies, and he believed they would be tough, unforgiving enemies. His breath was coming swiftly and his muscles were much too tight for accurate shooting. A slight tremor was in his hands.

Damn it, he mustn't let their threat unnerve him and cause him to miss a target. He had to have the prize money. Perhaps, should he win, he would have made one friend, Louden the Wells Fargo agent. He wasn't sure what help that could be. But he owed the man to do his best.

Just shoot, he told himself. That's the only thing you can do for you've come too far to stop. Let your rifle answer Mattoon and Lasch. He raised the Spencer and spoke to the catapult man. "Ready."

The glass ball came hurtling out from the catapult. Levi shot and the target vanished. Number two went the same way, and three, four, and five.

The match organizer spoke to Levi and Lasch. "Gentlemen, you have shown what men can do with rifles. The people have been truly entertained. Still the decision as to which of you is the better marksman has not been made. If I move the targets farther away, I doubt they can be seen to hit. Do you have any suggestions as to how to resolve this?"

"Base the final round on quickness," Levi said. "Let both of us shoot at the same target. The man who shoots first and breaks the glass would win."

"How many targets?" asked Baker.

"One or three," Levi said.

"What do you say, Lasch?" Baker asked.

"That way is okay with me. Use three balls."

"Then move up and stand beside Coffin. Both of you face the catapult."

Baker spoke to the catapult man. "Tie a long string on the trip lever so you can get back out of danger. Then launch the first target."

Levi focused every sense on the metal arm of the machine and the feet of space just in front of it. So focused was his concentration it seemed he could see the particles of air, could hear the tension being put on the trip string.

The metal arm swung. The glass globe leapt into space.

Levi fired. The glass shattered to powder. Lasch did not shoot.

A murmur, almost a gasp rose from the crowd of people. The catapult man looked shaken.

Louden, who stood behind the rope area near Levi, spoke out loud in wonderment. "Coffin burst the ball the second it left the machine. It's impossible to be that quick. Yet I saw it."

"Throw another," Lasch called out in a hoarse, angry voice. "That was only luck."

The catapult man cocked the launching arm and placed a glass sphere on it. He backed away and worriedly picked up his string. He crouched, and without pausing, tripped the catapult arm.

Levi never afterward could remember raising the Spencer or touching the trigger. But he would always remember the explosion of glass fragments just in front of the catapult.

And Louden's yell of astonishment, and pleasure.

Chapter 12

Levi turned from the target catapult to Lasch standing beside him in the shooter's box. The man was gripping his rifle and staring at him with a fierce expression. Levi thought the beaten man was going to strike him with the rifle. But Lasch pivoted away, stepped over the rope marking off the shooter's area, and pushed roughly into the crowd of spectators.

Levi watched after Lasch until he merged into the people drifting off toward their horses and vehicles. He sighed with relief at the man's leaving before there was any trouble with him. To his surprise he found his own rifle was held tightly and his finger on the trigger.

"Well done, Levi," Louden said, drawing near. "And you're right to watch Lasch. I believe he's a man who'll not forget that you showed him up today as a second-rate rifleman and will try to get back at you."

"He's sure not second-rate."

"Compared to you he is."

"I had to win. I was flat broke."

"And I sure wanted to take Mattoon's money. Here he comes now and he doesn't look happy."

"George, you made a lucky bet, and I'm here to pay off," Mattoon called out as he approached.

Louden chuckled. "Coffin said he'd win and he did just that. So cross my palm with gold."

"No gold. How about paper money?"

"As long as it's Union money."

"That's what it is." Mattoon pulled a large roll of bills from his pocket and began to count.

"One thousand dollars and you're paid in full," Mattoon said, laying the last bill on the Wells Fargo man's hand.

"You'll probably get it all back next time we bet."

"Not if Coffin shoots."

Mattoon turned and studied Levi's face, and then ran his sight up and down the young man's lanky body. After a moment and without a sour expression, he focused back on Louden. "I'll see you later, George. First time you come to San Francisco, let me know and plan to come to my home for dinner."

"I'll do that. So long."

Louden, staring after Mattoon, spoke to Levi. "He's a sharp businessman and has financial interests throughout California. Some of his businesses I don't approve of and he's fought and killed some men in duels that I thought were unnecessary. But he's got friends in high places. He could one day be mayor of San Francisco, or maybe governor of the state."

"He didn't act like he wanted to be my friend," Levi said. "And now after losing a thousand dollars, he sure won't be."

"Mattoon's quite changeable, and difficult to understand. One day hard and sharp-tongued, and the next day just the opposite."

"This must have been his bad day."

"Yes, I'd say so. Levi, I want you to come to work for Wells Fargo. The pay will be five dollars a day. That's the best pay an honest, working man can earn in California."

"What would be my duties?"

"Ride rifle guard on the gold shipments Wells Fargo brings down from the mountains. We transport nearly three-quarters of the gold from the mining camps and the towns such as Placerville and Dutch Flat. We guarantee safe delivery to the

U.S. Mint in San Francisco. Outlaws are hurting us damn bad, holding up the stages and wagons and making off with the gold.''

''I don't want a job that would mean shooting somebody.''

''But I need a man like you, a man better than anyone else with a rifle. I'll make your pay six dollars a day.''

''It's not the pay. It's the shooting that I might have to do. I don't want to be responsible for someone dying.''

''But you would only be fighting robbers who'd kill you for a dollar.''

''There's little likelihood of that if I'm not riding guard on one of your gold wagons. I thank you for the offer, but I've got to turn it down.''

''I'm down right sorry to hear that,'' Louden said. ''However the job is always open for you to take at any time. If you change your mind look me up. I'm in the Wells Fargo office in Sacramento part of the time, but mostly in San Francisco.''

''I'll do that,'' Levi replied. He put out his hand. ''Thank you for your trust, and your job offer.''

''I hope we meet again.''

''So do I.''

''Keep your horse. You've earned it.''

''Thanks, Mr. Louden. I've got to likin' that old horse.''

Levi entered Sacramento, found the riverfront, and purchased passage for himself and his mount on the river steamboat *Whipple* bound for San Francisco. There were nearly a hundred other passengers, city people, miners from the gold fields of the Sierra Nevada Mountains, loggers from the lumber camps, and farmers who tended the thousands of acres of crop land in the inland valley. A few of the passengers were like Levi, new people from the far regions of the east.

A few minutes later the *Whipple*, its boilers hot, smoke streaming from its twin smokestacks, and pistons beating like some giant heart deep within the wooden body, pulled away from the pier and plowed downriver. To Levi's surprise, the

Whipple towed a huge barge that was pressed low in the water by thousands of sacks of wheat piled high upon its deck.

He climbed to the second deck so that he could see over the manmade levees. Several chairs were lined up beside the deck house. Levi seated himself and settled back to enjoy the trip, some four hours long he had been informed by the ticket agent. He felt pleased with the money in his pocket, but he regretted making enemies of Mattoon and Lasch.

Sacramento fell away behind and the river became tree lined. Beyond the trees, were broad fields with every square foot covered with golden wheat stubble, or shocks of bundled wheat not yet run through the thrashing machine. Levi smiled with pleasure. The farmers had reaped a large harvest. He had found a rich and generous land.

The Sacramento River wound its course to the west across the wide flat land of the San Joaquin Valley. Many steamboats passed heading up river. Nearly everyone towed a barge behind, some of them empty. Levi judged the empty barges were going to Sacramento to pick up a load of grain.

Levi grew restless and walked forward to the railing to watch ahead. He could hear the bow of the boat slicing the water and the splash of the two huge rotating paddle wheels. The wind created by the movement of the boat smelled of wetness and mud. It was pleasantly cool as it fanned his face.

The riverboat *Whipple,* its paddle wheels spinning and smokestacks pumping smoke, passed Point San Pablo and entered the salt water of San Francisco Bay. To Levi, from his position on the upper deck of the riverboat, the full sweep of the bay came into his view. The water of the harbor had a silver sheen from the glancing rays of the sun that had fallen halfway down from the top of the sky. He counted forty-six ships, both sail and steam, at anchor and motionless on the silver water.

The captain sounded a blast on the steam whistle to announce his imminent arrival at the docks of the city. The spin of the paddle wheels slowed.

"Damn the captain," said the man standing by the rail of the boat near Levi. "He blows that whistle every time he comes into the docks. Bursts my ears when he does that. Plumb unnecessary for everybody can see the boat is coming."

"A loud whistle all right," Levi agreed. The man was old with a seamed face and a black hat set upon his white head. "You live here in San Francisco?"

"Yes. For more than fifteen years. Even before the gold rush days of '49."

"What's the city like?"

"Frisco is what the harbor and the gold from the mountains have made it."

"What's that?"

"A wicked city, and a rich city, and will probably always be so. It has one of the best natural harbors in the world. Ships sail from here to every major seaport in all the faraway continents. The last census counted 150,000 people. Twenty-five thousand of that number are Chinamen. Of course, many other nationalities have come here. The town's growing rapidly. There's plenty of lumber for building material, brought down by ship from the forests on the north California and the Oregon coast."

"A man should be able to find work here," Levi said.

"All except Chinamen and the free blacks. Both groups have a hard road to go to find someone to hire them. The white men don't like them competing for their jobs. They hate the Chinamen worst of all. They'll work for a dime when the white man wants a dollar. The blacks are almost as cheap. The Chinamen sometimes get beat up awfully bad. The law officers don't do much about that. They're all white men."

The old man pointed ahead where the current swirled around a multitude of canting masts and spars sticking up above the water of the bay. "There's hundreds of dead ships on the bottom. In '49, '50 and even '51 the crews of many ships went gold crazy and abandoned their vessels. Seven hundred in '50 alone, they rotted and sank right at their anchorages. Now they've been forgotten, and the men too. The port officials have made passageways through the wrecks by dragging some aside.''

The man fell silent watching ahead as the captain slowed the riverboat and steered a course through the forest of timbers projecting from the water.

Levi could make out long, rickety-looking, wooden piers jutting out from the waterfront quay of the city. Ships were tied up to every foot of dock space. A host of men and vehicles were scurrying about moving a huge tonnage of cargo to and from the ships. Beyond the piers the waterfront was crowded with warehouses and factories. The hills rising up from the bay were covered with buildings of every description. He had reached famous San Francisco.

The riverboat slowed as two tugboats steamed out from the docks. The captain waved at them as they chugged past toward the wheat barge he towed. The tugs secured themselves to the barge, one on each side. One of the riverboat crewmen, at a signal from his captain, cut the barge free.

The riverboat continued slowing as it drew near its berth. The rotation of the paddle wheels reversed, the water boiled and the boat gently bumped the wooden piling of the pier. Lines were tossed from the vessel to men on the pier and they were made fast to cleats on the dock.

''All passengers disembark,'' called the deck steward. He moved to help two deck hands swinging out the top deck gangway and lower it to rest one end on the pier. A strong ramp was run out from the lower deck to accommodate the several dozen wagons and buggies and saddle horses that had been transported.

''Good luck to you in San Francisco, young fellow,'' said the old man.

''Thank you, sir.''

The old man walked toward the gangway. Levi went down to the lower deck and stood beside his black horse and watched the other passengers. He patiently waited, enjoying his arrival at his final destination.

The passengers hastened down the gangway, but Levi hung back until he was the last to leave the riverboat. Leading his horse, he walked leisurely along the dock that was jammed with heavily laden drays, wagons, and carts. Stevedores carried huge loads up and down the gangways of the ships. Seamen, ship officers, craftsmen, and travelers bustled about speaking a Babble tongue of languages. A thumping, steam-driven pile driver was hammering long timbers into the bottom of the bay to lengthen the pier. A huffing steam paddy added its hiss and clank as it scooped sand from along the pier to deepen the water so the larger ships could come close in to land. He stopped for a minute to watch a steam-powered winch hoisting a cargo of freight from the hold of a ship and swinging it onto the dock. Most of the workers on the dock were burly white men. However at one vessel a line of small brown Chinamen, carrying loads on their backs larger than they were, labored up and down the gangway.

Levi approached a man bossing a group of workers. "What's the shortest route to the Pacific Ocean?" Levi asked.

A surprised expression passed over the man's face. "Just straight west through town and up and over Mount Sutro. The ocean's not more than four miles away. Why do you ask?"

Levi grinned sheepishly and replied, "I promised myself that the very first thing I'd do when I reached San Francisco was to go for a swim in the ocean."

"You'll find it damn cold," the man said with a chuckle.

"Then I'll know when I'm in it."

"That you will."

Levi mounted and rode from the busy docks and through the blocks of large warehouses.

He turned up Market Street and soon passed the Harpenning Block and the four-story Grand Hotel with its four hundred rooms. A tiny steam locomotive pulling a loaded passenger coach rattled by down the center of the street.

All the thoroughfares he passed were lined with big buildings and the sidewalks crowded with people and the street with horse drawn wagons, surreys and buggies. There was a constant rumble of noise all around him from the iron-rimmed wheels of the conveyances and shod hooves of the horses passing on the wooden planking that surfaced the street.

He wondered about the great quantity of lumber needed to cover the numerous streets until he recalled the old man telling him of the huge forests on the coasts of northern California and Oregon. With water transportation, timbers could be brought cheaply to San Francisco.

Levi stopped at a restaurant and had a beef sandwich, a wedge of cheese and a slice of cake packed for a lunch. Now he was prepared to spend the night on the ocean shore. He spoke to the black and it went at a gallop up the sloping street between the rows of buildings.

Three miles later, he reined the horse to a halt amid the brush and oak trees on the top of Mount Sutro. Before him, a mile distant, spread the mighty rolling waters of the Pacific. He breathed deeply. Even from a mile away the west breeze brought the smell of the ocean salt water to him.

He sat in his saddle for a time and looked at the ocean, watching the waves roll in, never ending. The sun, hanging low over the water, was a crimson ball. A tall-masted schooner with brilliant white sails was pinned against the darkening water. The ship, racing swiftly on the wind, was heading directly for the land. North of him and closer, a steamship came out between the headlands of the Golden Gate and drove away into the sea.

The horse caught its wind and began to nibble at the wild grass. Levi pulled its head up.

"None of that now," he told the horse. He touched its flanks with his heels and began the descent to the ocean shore.

Reaching the beach, Levi removed the saddle from the black and slapped the animal away to graze. He spread his blankets on a patch of beach grass between two boulders above high tide. He pulled off his clothing while all the time watching the waves sweep in to stroke the narrow beach. With a rushing charge, he rushed barefoot and naked across the beach and plunged into the breakers.

The cold water enclosed him and instantly robbed him of all warmth. Still he swam onward beneath the surface, exulting in the coldness. Finally he surfaced, spraying salt water from his mouth and flinging his head to throw the long wet hair from his face. He swam back to shallow water. Shivering, he hastily finished bathing and walked back to his bedroll. He dried on a corner of a blanket and slid into his clothing.

Idly he laid out his supper and ate watching the sailing ship and listening to the break of the sea on the rock and sand of the shore. A flock of shorebirds skimmed in to find their roost in the bushes nearby before the night fell. They landed, uttering little chirping calls to each other, then fell silent.

Levi watched the ocean drown the sun. As the daylight crept away to the west and dusk fell, the sailing ship dropped its sails and became stationary on the dark swell of the deep. Levi wondered why the ship hadn't set course for the Golden Gate instead of to an anchorage off the coast.

With the sun gone, a cold wind began to blow off the water and Levi wrapped one of his blankets around his shoulders. The long journey had been safely completed and he should be pleased, but strangely a gloomy melancholy fell over him as the wet twilight settled on the ocean. He had much to try to forget.

The stars came out. A yellow half moon rose over Mount Sutro and began to eye the earth. Levi crawled into his bedroll, propped his head on the saddle and watched the stars begin their nightlong whirling turn across the ebony heavens.

He lay for a long time awake, pondering his future. He heard the tide's inexorable invasion of the land. Late in the night he slept.

Chapter 13

The schooner *Dolly* ran eastward with her sails full and hard with a stiff wind. She was returning to San Francisco after two years hunting seals in the cold south Pacific and Antarctic Oceans. She had survived the terrifying storms that came directly from the South Pole, and the attempted mutiny to take over the ship, and the murder of the first mate. Still, the voyage had been successful and her hold was full of valuable sealskins.

Errin Scanlan saw the land of America rise up out of the heaving Pacific waters. From a hazy, gray smudge on the horizon, the coastal mountain range of the continent had grown steadily until now the land stretched north and south as far as he could see. He felt his heart beating happily. A new life without the heavy iron shackles around his ankles and without the cutting lash of the cat-o'-nine-tails upon his back was about to begin for him.

Errin was on the *Dolly* by the smallest of chances. He was a convicted highwayman of England who had been transported halfway around the world to serve a life term in the English penal colony of Australia for robbery and for killing two "thief-takers"—bounty hunters. After four years of hard labor and the most cruel and inhuman beatings with the cat-o'-nine-tails, he had escaped with Tim Swallow, another convict, by stealing a small fishing boat in Sydney and sailing out into the winter storms on the Pacific Ocean. Swallow had died of hunger and cold during that terrible ordeal.

Nearly dead himself, Errin had come upon the *Dolly* moving under reduced sail. No one responded to his calls for help. He managed to climb aboard on a rope hanging over the side. Captain Griffith lay wrapped in furs on the main deck and, the crew, who had tried to mutiny, he had locked below decks. Errin helped the captain kill four of the mutineers and subdue the remainder. The captain agreed to take Errin with him to the ship's home port, San Francisco.

Errin had learned seamanship during the long voyage to Australia on the prison ship. The captain, seeing his skill, and judging him a man to trust, made him first mate replacing the mate who had been killed. Errin moved into the mate's cabin, and exchanged his convict clothing for the mate's.

Errin had been off duty all afternoon and had sat leaning against the crank windlass used to raise the big anchor. He watched ahead. Tad the cabin boy came and talked with him for a time, and then left to go about his duties. When the day grew old and the sun slanted in steeply, Captain Griffith came to the rail of the ship near Errin. He spread his legs to brace against the pitch of the ship and gazed as did Errin toward the land.

"Scanlan, it might be dangerous for you if we ran straight into San Francisco. Some of the crew might be holding a grudge on you for killing Walloghan, and inform the American officials that you are an escaped English convict. The Americans might ignore that, but then again they could arrest you and notify the English of your capture. The English have a consulate here in San Francisco. I think it best we put you ashore by small boat somewhere away from the city."

"I appreciate that," Errin said. "I'd not like to trade a prison in Australia for one here in America."

"All right then. We'll drift-anchor off the coast tonight. In the morning just before daylight, Karcher will row you ashore.

San Francisco is a large city and you can easily disappear in it.''

An hour later the land was hardly two miles distant and fog could be seen forming like smoke in the harbor entrance between the headlands of the Golden Gate. Griffith ordered the sails lowered and halted the voyage of the *Dolly*.

A sea anchor, a large funnel-shaped canvas object, nine feet at its greatest diameter, was lowered from the bow of the ship and into the water at the end of two hundred feet of stout cable. The sea anchor would sink into the deep still water and hold the schooner against the push of the wind. The vessel would drift not more than a mile during the night.

With the anchorage made, Captain Griffith called to Errin, ''Scanlan, come below with me.''

''Aye, Captain.''

Griffith led the way down the ladder and along the narrow passageway to his cabin. He closed the door and lit the brass gimbaled oil lamp on the table.

''Sit down,'' said the captain.

Errin seated himself. The captain took the second chair and faced Errin.

''You've become an excellent seaman and have been a lot of help in sailing the ship,'' the captain said. ''We'll not talk about your help in the mutiny. You know how I feel about that. You're developing into a good first mate, though you need more salt water to pass under your keel. Would you like to sail on my next voyage?''

''No, Captain, I'm a landsman. I'll take my chances on shore.''

''I thought that would be your answer. Now I want to pay your wages.'' Griffith extracted a leather pouch from a drawer in his navigation table and counted out several gold coins into his hand. ''Here's two hundred dollars. You surely earned all of it.'' He handed the coins to Errin.

''Also Karcher is bringing you up a bundle of sealskins from the hold. You can sell them at the California Fur and Hide Company on Market Street. They're located three or four blocks up from the waterfront. Can't miss it. I judge one big bundle of skins should bring you about another two hundred dollars."

"Thanks, Captain, for all you've done for me."

"You've done as much or more for me."

A knock sounded on the cabin door and Karcher's voice came from the passageway. "Captain, the skins have been brought up and are stowed near the Jacob's ladder."

"Very well, Karcher. You're relieved of duty until an hour before daylight in the morning."

"Aye, aye, Captain." Karcher's footsteps sounded drawing away.

"One warning for you," Griffith said. "San Francisco is a rough city, especially the Barbary Coast—that's a section of town on Pacific, Kearney and Broadway—so keep the Colt pistol. You may have need for it. Watch out for crimps on The Embarcadero. They'll shanghai you. They'll bust your head or slip you a Mickey Finn and you'll wake up out at sea and bound for a three-year voyage to nowhere."

"I know about the tricks crimps play. They're plentiful in London too." He touched the pistol. He had practiced many hours shooting at targets Tad tossed onto the waves. The skill he had possessed before being arrested had quickly returned.

Scanlan woke to a light rapping on his cabin door. Tad's muffled voice reached him. "Mr. Scanlan, Mr. Karcher said I should tell you the longboat's in the water and ready to take you ashore."

"Very well, Tad. Tell Karcher I'll be there shortly."

Errin arose from his bunk, lit a candle, and dressed in the dead mate's clothing. As he packed a supply of powder and shot for his pistol, he wondered if the mate had a wife and children in San Francisco. He left the cabin, went forward along the passageway, and climbed to the main deck.

A light on-shore wind blew. Overhead, the heavens were full of bright stars. The land lying to the east was invisible in the darkness, but the land of America was there and waiting for him. He was a free man in a great new country. Looking past the main mast, he could make out three men near the starboard quarter of the ship. He walked forward to join the captain, Karcher, and little Tad.

"The boat's ready, Mr. Scanlan," Karcher said.

Errin spoke to Griffith. "Good-bye, Captain." He held out his hand. "Thanks again for everything."

"Good luck to you, Scanlan," the captain replied. He shook Errin's hand.

"Karcher, I'll hang a lantern in the riggin' so you can find your way back to the ship."

"Thanks, Captain."

Tad stepped forward. "Captain, may I go ashore with Mr. Karcher?"

"Sure, lad. Use a second set of oars and practice your rowing."

Karcher motioned at the cabin boy. "In the boat you go."

Tad went nimbly down the Jacob's ladder and into the boat.

Errin followed the boy. Once in the boat, he braced his leg against the gunwale and called up to Karcher, "Hand the skins down."

"Coming down," Karcher said.

A moment later Karcher scrambled down the ladders. He dropped his oars in the oarlocks, and with Tad trying to match his strokes, pulled the boat into the darkness lying on the water.

Chapter Fourteen

Levi pulled his rifle from its scabbard and watched the row-boat draw closer to the shore. In the moonlight, he could make out two men at the oars, one of them small, and a third man sitting in the bow of the craft. The third man was looking at the beach. He said something to the oarsmen and they stopped rowing.

Levi had awakened early and had been waiting for the sunrise when the boat had become visible on the ocean. It had approached from the direction of the sailing ship that had anchored the evening before, so he judged it one of that vessel's small crafts. As he watched, the boat ground on the beach some thirty yards along the beach from him.

He remained motionless to blend into the boulders that flanked his camp. With that, and the distance the rowboat had landed from his camp, the sailors should not readily detect his presence.

The sailor in the bow of the boat stepped out onto the land. "Thanks for rowing me ashore," he said.

"Here's your skins," one of the men in the boat said. He passed a large bundle to the man on the shore.

"Watch out for crimps," the smaller figure said in a boy's voice.

"I'll do that. Take care of yourself, Tad."

"Yes, sir."

The man on the shore dropped his load and taking hold of the boat shoved it out into the water. The oarsmen swung their craft around and pulled into the night.

Levi saw the sailor pack his skins a few feet back from the water and seat himself upon them. He sat facing the ocean.

A smuggler, thought Levi. Why else would he leave his ship and come ashore in the darkness?

Errin stared at the ocean that was strangely marked with alternating bars of silver and blackness. The moon, lying low against the wet horizon was casting a shimmering white frost upon the crest of the waves while leaving the sides turned toward him in total darkness. Through those patches of light and shadow, the boat carrying Karcher and Tad crept away like some alien water creature.

As Errin watched, the moon sank behind the curve of the earth and all the heaving water turned black. The craft transporting his two shipmates vanished. He felt a pang of sadness at their going.

The wind blew cold off the water and he folded his arms putting his hands inside his jacket. The coldness reminded him of past days and he drifted backward through his bleak memories. He recalled mining the coral rock from under the icy water of the sea off Van Diemen's Land, and for rebelling against the prison rules, of being locked in the frigid, solitary dumb cell for days, and standing naked under the brutal lash. He shivered as he again saw Swallow's dead, pinched face staring up at him as the corpse slid under the waves. He had been a good friend.

But those were yesterday's memories and he pulled back from them. He had arrived in a bright, new land that held much gold. He began to sing, a raunchy street song about a highwayman and what he stole from the pretty misses. He jumped to his feet and singing lustily, started to dance, stomping the ground joyously and whirling wildly about on the beach and in the shallow waves. His voice rose, flinging the song into the wind. He felt his life running strong and vital.

Levi watched the singing, dancing sailor. In the half light and with his long black hair, and shaggy beard, he seemed a crazed spirit, a marionette gone out of control. Yet he sang with a happy tone. The fellow started a second song, bellowing it out even more boisterously than he had the first one. The sailor was having a grand time. If he was a smuggler, then he seemed to have little fear of being caught.

The sailor stopped his dancing. He finished his song, and seating himself once again on his packet of furs, stared silently into the night blanketing the ocean. Slowly and without sound, Levi climbed to his feet. He leaned on the boulder and waited. Dawn was near and he wanted to be ready for whatever the sailor might do when daylight came and he saw Levi.

The dawn broke through the darkness and Errin roused himself. He stood erect and looked to the right along the stony, wave lapped beach, then to his left. He saw Levi and instantly moved his hand to rest on the butt of the pistol in his belt.

"Do you plan to rob me?" Errin asked, glancing at the rifle in Levi's hands.

"I want nothing a smuggler has," Levi replied. He braced himself to respond to any threat from the fierce looking sailor. The man had shown no fear at seeing Levi, only a tightening of his body, square built and muscular, in preparation to fight.

"A smuggler?"

"That's my guess."

Errin threw back his head and laughed. "You're wrong. I'm worse than a smuggler." Errin realized that someone spying him coming ashore in the dark with his sealskins could easily draw the conclusion that he was indeed a smuggler.

"Then what are you?" Levi asked.

"I'm a bloodthirsty pirate."

"You're joshing me."

"Maybe." Errin grinned at the serious young man. He didn't want trouble and he had observed the easy familiarity with which the fellow held the rifle. "No, I'm not a pirate. Just a man newly arrived in California." He nodded his head along the shore at Levi's horse. "Is that your mount?"

"He's mine."

"I'd like to get these sealskins to San Francisco. It'd be easiest if the horse carried them there. I'd pay you."

"I'd not take them if they're smuggled."

"Now why would I smuggle such a small lot of skins?"

"I've been wondering that myself."

"They're not stolen or smuggled."

"Then I guess I can help you. What's your name?"

"Errin Scanlan. What's yours?"

"Levi Coffin. Give me a minute to roll up my blankets and I'll be ready to go."

"I'm in no hurry," Errin said, shouldering his skins and walking toward the American.

Levi whistled for the black. The animal came at a trot, its ears pricked forward and alert brown eyes studying the stranger.

"Good-looking horse," Errin said.

"He'll do."

Levi finished saddling the horse and spoke to the Englishman. "Put your skins on the seat and I'll tie them so that they won't fall off."

Errin did as directed. Levi, with a few deft hitches of a length of rope, fastened the large bundle of skins to the saddle.

"How far to San Francisco?" Errin asked.

"About an hour's walk just to the east over Mount Sutro."

Levi picked up the reins. Errin fell in beside him and they turned their backs to the ocean.

The men said nothing to each other as they climbed up through the brush and boulders on the flank of Mount Sutro. At the top they halted, looking down upon San Francisco.

"It's a small city compared to London," Errin said.

"Big enough for me," Levi replied.

"And me too." Errin looked beyond the city. "That's a fine sheltered harbor." The water of San Francisco bay was brilliant blue in the morning sun and pleasing to his eye. The bay was some three miles wide straight across to the mainland, and several miles long north and south. A multitude of ships were docked at long piers, many others hung at anchor. He counted six ships departing, and three arriving coming around the headland to the north. He thought one of the sailing ships was the *Dolly*.

"It's the only harbor I've ever seen so I'll take your word for that," Levi said.

"I've seen a few in my travels."

"Been to sea long?"

"For a while," Errin replied shortly. He started down the slope of the hill.

They walked together, feeling the awkardness of strangers. Neither made an effort to start a conversation. Half an hour later they entered the outskirts of the city, and continued on through a residential area of large, expensive houses and came to the business district near the waterfront.

Errin halted in front of a tobacconist's shop. Levi stopped also and cast an inquiring look at Errin.

"Wait for me a minute, if you would," Errin said. He stepped up on the sidewalk and entered the open doorway of the shop. A minute later he emerged with a cigar in his hand. He ran the roll of tobacco under his nose and breathed deeply of the pungent aroma. In the penal colony of Australia to be caught with tobacco in your mouth, or in your possession meant fifty lashes. "Ah!" he said. He stuck the cigar in his mouth, and puffed it into life from a lighted match.

As Errin savored the smoke, he gazed around at the congestion and hustle and bustle of men and vehicles on the street. The variety of businesses here was as great as in London. Immediately around him were a bank on the corner, a newspaper office next to it, a photo studio, a laundry, and an apothecary—the largest he had ever seen, with its huge front windows crammed with its mysterious bottles and jars. Farther away down hill toward the bay, he could see a harness factory, an iron foundry, a wheelwright shop, and several other businesses and offices.

"I see the California Fur and Hide Company just down there," Errin said and gestured with his free hand. "That's where I'll sell my skins."

They halted in front of the establishment and Errin untied his bundle of sealskins. "If you'll wait for me, I'll buy you a meal for your help."

"I'll wait." Levi knew no one in the city and the sailor seemed like a good enough sort with whom to eat a meal.

"This shouldn't take me long," Errin said.

Errin ate slowly and said not a word. He had ordered two full meals, one with beef as the main course and the second with fish. There were three kinds of fresh vegetables, two desserts, a cup of custard and a wedge of apple pie. Both milk and tea sat near his plate. He intended to eat every tiny crumb. He had been robbed of a hell of a lot of eating.

Levi was amazed at the sailor's appetite, and the small bites he took and the thorough chewing of every mouthful. Now and again, the man brushed at his long, black beard to remove a stray piece of food.

Errin laid down his fork. He cast an amused look at Levi. He had observed the American watching him with great curiosity.

"I've missed several meals over the years," he said in explanation. Never would he tell Levi of being an escaped convict from Australia.

"That was a good start on catching up," Levi said with a smile.

Errin broke out in laughter. "How long have you been in San Francisco?" he asked.

"Since yesterday. Spent my first night on the beach."

"Then we're both strangers here. Do you want to throw in with me, at least temporary? We can learn the town together. If you need some money, I can loan you some."

Levi glanced down at his much worn clothing. The Englishman must think him broke. "I've got money. Enough to last me a few weeks."

"Enough to buy some clothes?"

"Yes."

"Then let's dress like gentlemen before we get arrested for looking like beggars." Errin wanted to dispose of the sailor outfit as soon as possible.

"All right, but first a bath, a shave, and then a haircut."

"You're right. Then we'll see all the sights San Francisco has to offer."

Errin lay relaxed as the barber lathered his face and stropped a straight razor. The keen blade slid along his face removing the tough beard. With short hair, no beard, and dressed in a city man's suit, no one from the ship would know him. At least he hoped that would be so.

The barber tipped the chair and sat Errin upright. He glanced at Levi in the next chair. For the first time, he saw the scar on the American's forehead. There must be a story there, but Errin would never ask. Questions brought return questions. He wanted none of those.

At a men's clothing store, they pursuaded the tailor to sell them two wool suits he had on display to show the quality of his work. Neither Levi nor Errin wanted to wait for new suits to be made. While the tailor made some alterations in the suits to provide a better fit, they bought white cotton shirts and ties, and additonal outfits of denim pants and sturdy shirts that could be used for riding and working.

Later, dressed in their city suits, and after telling the tailor they would return for their purchases, Levi and Errin left and walked along the street.

"I haven't had a brew in years," Errin said. "Let's stop in this saloon and have one."

"I'll drink one with you," Levi said.

"Good. I'm still buying."

"All right."

They shoved open the door and went inside.

Errin's first pull at his mug of beer was cold and tangy and he let it trickle slowly and deliciously down his throat. "Bartender, how do you get the beer so cold?" he asked.

"With ice. There's a shipping company here in San Francisco that hauls shiploads of ice down from the fields of icebergs off the coast of Alaska."

"Great idea. I salute them." Errin took another drink of beer and turned to Levi. "I like cold beer," he said.

"What other kind is there?"

"Warm of course. Shipping ice as a business seems odd, but then, if a man could start a business that no one else was in, he might make a lot of money." He looked steadily at Levi. "How are you going to make your fortune?"

"I hadn't thought about making a fortune. But I've been offered a job. Louden, the boss of the Wells Fargo Company has asked me to take one at six dollars a day to guard their gold shipments."

"Gold shipments? From where to where?"

"Wells Fargo picks up the gold that's mined in the Sierra Nevada Mountains at towns like Placerville, and guaranteeing safe delivery, hauls it to the mint here in San Francisco."

"I'd think highwaymen would rob them."

"Outlaws do take some of the gold. That's why Louden wanted me to hire on."

"Why you?"

"I'm a fair shot with a rifle."

"You must be more than fair." Errin drank some more beer and evaluated his new comrade. "How did he know you could shoot a rifle?"

"I stopped off in Sacramento on my way here and entered a shooting match. Louden bet on me and made some good money."

"I'd like to see some of that kind of shooting," Errin said. He called out to the bartender. "Two more beers." He turned back to Levi. "I've got a feeling that I'm going to get rich in this town."

"How are you going to do that?"

"There are ways, many ways. Working for a daily wage isn't one of them. All men who become rich do it by having other men working for them."

Levi reflected upon the Englishman's words. "You're right. They're surely not farmers. They're men who own factories, or companies that make and sell things by the thousands."

"Or mine gold, or own banks."

"It's been several years since the first gold was discovered. I would think most of the easy gold has been found."

Errin grinned. "I wasn't thinking about prospecting."

"What then?"

"I haven't got it figured out. But then I just got here."

The bartender arrived with the fresh beers and sat them before the two young men. Errin picked his up and held it out to Levi. "Here's to becoming rich."

Levi clinked his mug against Errin's. "To money and lots of it."

They drank, grinning across their beers at each other.

Errin sat his mug down with a thud on the bar top. "Levi, you seem like a fellow I could get along with. Why don't you and I become partners in getting rich. We sure as hell don't know each other and it'd be a gamble on both our parts. But a man can use a friend in a strange city. We'd share everything equally. We could do it temporary-like with either one of us calling it quits at any time with no hard feelings."

Levi turned away and looked out the window at the people passing on the sidewalk. Would Errin have suggested they become partners if he knew that Levi had deserted the Union Army and robbed dead soldiers of their clothing, and money? That the horse that had carried his skins, was stolen?

"There's something that you might want to know about me before you make that offer."

Errin looked into the strained face of the American. "I'm not interested in what you've done in the past. We've both come to a new land, and a new land gives a man a fresh start with all the old deeds cut off and left behind."

"Are you sure you don't want to know?"

"I'm damn sure." Errin's answer was quick and hard. He didn't want to tell his new friend that he had once been an English highwayman, and a killer, though he didn't think killing bounty hunters was much of a crime. "I'll judge you on what you do from here on. Just as you'll judge me."

"All right then, I'm willing to give a partnership a try," Levi said. "But I don't think money is going to come easy."

"Maybe it will. It just depends on how good our plan is. Drink up and let's go see what this fine city of San Francisco offers two strong, handsome men."

"Handsome?"

"Handsome enough to get by."

They laughed together and drank deeply of the beer cooled by ice from Alaska.

The two men sauntered down Market Street passing among the well-dressed hurrying businessmen, the laborers, the street vendors hawking their wares, and a few women and some noisy children. Errin also recognized the drifters, rogues, and the chancers, so familiar to him in his native London. San Francisco would very nicely substitute for his native city so far away.

As they passed one of the few small parks, a young woman in a bright blue dress came running up to them. Her pretty, fresh face broke into a wide smile. "Sammy," she cried, rushing up to Levi and throwing her arms around his neck. "Oh, I'm so glad to see you again." She pressed her face to his chest.

Startled, Levi took her by her shoulders and tried to push her back. Her arms dropped to his waist and she clung tightly to him.

"I don't know you," Levi said, applying more effort and extracting himself from the girl's arms.

"But I'm Helen. Don't you remember me, Sammy?"

"My name's not Sammy."

"Aren't you Sammy Holbert?" the girl questioned, gazing up with wide brown eyes into Levi's face.

"No, miss, I'm not."

The girl pulled loose from Levi's grip. She pressed her hands to her sides and began to back away.

"Then I'm terribly sorry. I've made an awful fool of myself. Please forgive me." She hastily turned away.

Errin stepped quickly forward and his long right arm encircled the girl and pulled her to him. "Not so fast, girlie," he said.

The girl was instantly fighting him, her hands reaching up to scratch at his face. He captured her hands and yanked her hard against him, driving her breath out with a swoosh.

"Check your wallet," Errin called to Levi.

"What?"

"Check your damn wallet!"

Levi felt his hip pocket. "It's gone," he said.

"Just as I thought," Errin said. He tapped the struggling girl on the head with his knuckles. "Now stand still while I search you."

Errin had seen the girl's hands, as she had pulled away from Levi, go into the folds of her dress. He slid his hands down her body. Levi's wallet was tucked into a pocket sewn into her dress at the thigh. He withdrew the wallet and spun the girl around. "You're not a very good pickpocket."

With an abrupt jerk she pulled free and started to dash away. But Errin with one swift step, recaptured her. He held her, feeling her soft and rounded body pressed to him.

"How did you know she took my wallet?" Levi asked.

"I've known a few pickpockets in my time."

"Please don't turn me over to the Fearless Charlies," the girl begged.

"Fearless Charlies, what are they?" Errin asked.

"The Charlies. The law."

Before Errin could reply, a harsh voice shouted from behind him. "Turn her loose."

Both Errin and Levi turned to look. A large, heavily built man was hurrying swiftly toward them. His beefy head was thrust belligerently forward.

"Well, well, the guardian," Errin said. He had seen the same combination of a pretty girl and a tough man teaming up to pick pockets in England.

"I said turn her loose," bellowed the man advancing upon Errin.

"Why should I do that? She's just a little thief and should be locked up."

"If you don't get your hands off her, I'm going to break your head."

Levi glanced at Errin. A look of wildness had come into his eyes, yet a calculated, controlled wildness. Levi would come to know that expression. It was a warning to the man if only he could read it. Levi checked the girl held snugly against Errin by his arm. Her white teeth were bared like she was a young animal caught in a trap. As he watched, her expression changed from that of pleading to one of anticipation of being freed from Errin's hold.

"You're not man enough to break my head," Errin said, his words like pieces of iron hitting together.

"Like hell I'm not," the guardian said. He grinned wickedly. "I've broken the heads of men a hell of a lot bigger than you." He moved forward, his eyes squinted almost shut in his broad face.

"Hold her." Errin flung the girl to Levi.

Errin growled, a guttural sound deep in his chest. He leapt at the man, his body moving with unnatural speed and formidable strength. His fist lashed out, a ferocious blow to the man's face. The guardian halted dead in his tracks. Almost too fast to see, Errin struck again, and again, left and right. The man crumpled to the sidewalk.

Errin, rubbing his bruised knuckles on the front of his jacket, turned back to Levi and the girl. "Now, Miss Pickpockets, we'll see about you."

The girl, her arm held by Levi, raised her eyes from the man on the ground to Errin's face. Her eyes were hard with surprise and disappointment. "I don't want to go to jail. They do awful things to girls in there. Isn't there some way I can pay you to let me go?"

"What did you have in mind?" Errin asked.

"I could give you and your friend some loving." She caught Errin by the hand and held it tenderly.

"Levi, what do you say to that? Does some loving sound good to you?"

"I don't think I want any part of it."

"She's pretty and it was your wallet."

"I'll pass."

"We're partners and agreed to share everything." There was a smile behind Errin's eyes. His new friend was even more innocent than he looked.

"Not girls. That doesn't seem right. Are you going to take her up on her offer?"

"Maybe you've had a girl recently. I haven't had one in a very long time."

The girl's eyes fastened on Errin. "How long has it been for you?"

"Almost five years." The scent of her perfume and her hand clasping his were tantalizing promises that had awakened all the memories of the pleasure a woman's soft body could give a man.

The girl sensed Errin's desire for her and she smiled and her eyes flashed. "I'll give you the best time you've ever had. Both of you, if you like."

Errin ran his fingers along the girl's cheek. "I'll surely take some of that. But first." He bent, lifted the unconscious man, and carried him to a nearby park bench. He laid the man so that it appeared he was sleeping.

He returned and took the girl by the arm. He spoke to Levi. "Are you certain you don't want some of this pretty little thing? She's willing to take both of us on and promises a good time."

"You go ahead by yourself. I'll wait for you." Levi was looking at the girl and she seemed disappointed at his refusal to join with Errin.

"All right if that's the way you want it. Hang around here close somewhere so I can find you when I'm finished. Could be a little while for I've a lot to catch up on." He pulled the girl close and walked off with her.

The man on the bench began to moan. Levi moved hastily away. He didn't want to be close when the man became fully conscious, or a policeman appeared and began to ask questions.

Levi looked along the street at the girl in the blue dress

hanging on the arm of the well-dressed Englishman and smiling up into his face. The pair could be taken for lovers.

Errin had proved himself a fierce fighter, but what kind of a business partner would he make? Would he also become a friend? Don't worry about that now, Levi told himself, for the arrangement was most probably only temporary.

Chapter Fifteen

"I know men in England who became rich by working kids, working thousands of them," Errin said. "Some of the kids were only six, seven years old. They got only a few pennies a day for twelve hours of the meanest kind of jobs. Orphans got no pay at all, only a little food, damn poor food, and a roof over their heads."

"I'd never work kids," Levi said.

"It's nothing but slavery and pure hell for the kids." Errin remembered becoming aware of the existence of the world about him in the parish orphanage on Turnmill Street in London. He had questioned the overseer about his parents. The man had answered not one query, either not knowing or deciding not to respond. At six years of age, Errin had been shipped away from the orphanage, along with fourteen other boys of like age to the industrial center of Derbyshire, and into the cotton mill that would be his home and place of labor. Twelve hours every day he worked, from cold dawn to weary night with his lungs full of cotton dust. He had proved rebellious from the first day onward. Punishment came immediately and each time it became more severe. He had borne scars long before the King's prison engulfed him and the cat-o'-nine-tails had cut its signature on his back. For refusing to feed the billy bobbin on the weaving machine in the mill, the foreman had whipped him with a leather strap, cutting his tender, young flesh. Then the foreman screwed two iron vises of a pound weight each to his ears. The iron had hung on Errin until he agreed to work. He still had scars from the vises. But that first interval of submission was short lived. Again he refused to work and was stripped of his clothing and hung by a rope around his wrists on a cross-beam above the weaving machinery. After hanging for hours, he had caved in and gone back to work. That was the very last time he had ever surrendered to punishment. Errin remembered his final day as a child slave in the cotton mill. He had fallen asleep in the late part of the shift. He awoke to find his hands still going through the motion of feeding the bobbin with the machinery stopped and all the other children gone. The foreman had made his head count and finding his number short by one, had come back into the mill with his strap. As the man drew back the strap to strike, Errin dove past him and into the day and the world beyond the walls of the cotton mill. The people on the street watched the raggedy, skinny urchin dart past. He vanished into a warren of shacks, raced onward past decaying tenements, running along narrow, tangled alleys choked with garbage and offal.

Levi heard the sadness and anger in Errin's voice. Was he once one of the orphans? Perhaps one day Errin would tell him more about his early life.

Levi and Errin had left the lodging house where they had spent the night and were moving along the sidewalk toward the waterfront. They had talked late into the night about what type of enterprise they should undertake to make their fortune. They had arrived at no plan worth pursuing. They were continuing the discussion as they walked along.

On the sidewalk ahead, a tall, gangly black man leaned against the side of a building and looked at the people as they passed. He saw Errin and Levi approaching, and noting the quality of their clothing, drew himself up straight. When they were a few feet away, he stepped out into the middle of the sidewalk and whipped off his hat.

"Good day, sirs, would you gentlemen be needin' any work done today? I'd work real cheap." The black man's words had come in a rush.

Errin and Levi halted at the man's sudden movement into their path and his rapid gunshot of words. "What's that you want?" Errin asked.

"Work. A job. I need a job."

"We don't have any work for you," Levi said, surprised at the man's request.

Errin saw the disappointment come into the man's black eyes. "Where's your master?" he asked. "Does he know what you're up to?"

"I'm a free man," the Negro said, his eyes direct and proud. "I've got no master." Then he smiled wistfully. "Except the master of hunger which is drivin' me hard right now."

"I thought all blacks were slaves in America," Errin said to Levi.

"There's a sizeable number of free blacks in the North. Some even in the Southern states. All of them here will be free since California voted against slavery and supports the Union cause."

"What wage would you take for a day's work?" Errin asked the black man.

"A carpenter or a bricklayer would make three dollars a day. I'd work for half of that."

"How many black men do you know of who are looking for work?" Errin asked. A thought was jelling in his mind.

"Hundreds. Most white bosses won't hire us because their white workers pick fights with us. But we got to work to eat same as white men."

Errin spoke to Levi. "Hundreds of men who'll work cheap. Levi, that gives me an idea."

"What's that?"

"We find work for them." Errin pointed at a crew of men passing with a wagonload of wooden planks. "The timbers of the streets must always be breaking and need replacing. That's a lot of work." He gestured in the opposite direction. "There are many new houses being built on the hills. More work."

Levi joined in. "I saw a big warehouse and a new pier under construction on the waterfront, and two new steamships being built for the Union Navy at the shipyards."

"Right. And the foundries, factories, and weaving mills are all busy. We should be able to find work for a hundred men."

"Two hundred," Levi said.

Errin spoke to the black man. "Meet us here in say three hours. Just maybe we'll have a job for you."

"I'll be here, unless I find one myself."

"What's your name?" Errin asked.

"Isaiah Green."

"All right, Isaiah Green, wish us luck."

"I sure do," Isaiah said.

"I think we're onto something good," Levi said.

"Yeah, we can take a cut of every man's wage that we find a job for. Let's try the foundries first. That's some of the hardest work to be found and should be the easiest place to contract out some workers."

"Stoking the furnaces and pouring the hot iron are the meanest jobs," said the foundry owner as he studied the two neatly dressed young men. "The workers don't like the hellish heat and the fumes. The men don't last long before they quit."

"We've got men that'll last," Errin said. "They're black and they're hungry." He was looking past the man and through the inner office door into the foundry with its strong wooden benches laden with large molds and castings. Twenty or so men were hard at work. The furnaces were at the far end of the foundry. Still he could smell them and feel the heat coming through the open door.

"I don't hire blacks. They bring trouble."

"They'll work cheaper than the white men," Errin said.

"That doesn't make any difference. I still don't want them. My white workers would leave."

"Maybe there's a way to get them accepted by the rest of your crew," Levi said. "I saw it work in Cincinnati. Tell your white workers that you've decided white men shouldn't have to work at the furnaces. That those jobs are suited only for blacks. Whites should always have the better jobs.''

The foundry owner looked sharply at Levi. "The whites might buy that. How cheap will your blacks work?''

Levi and Errin looked questioningly at each other. "You decide for I don't know your wages here,'' Errin said.

"What's your usual pay?'' Levi asked.

"Two dollars seventy-five for a twelve-hour day.''

"How many furnace men do you work?''

"Four.''

"We can supply four men who'll work for two dollars.''

"One seventy-five,'' quickly countered the foundry owner.

"One-ninety,'' Levi said.

"Done. When can they start?''

"Tomorrow morning.''

"What guarantee do I have that your blacks will stay?'' If my white workers buy my story about the job at the furnaces being fit only for blacks, they'll not want to go back to them.''

Levi looked inquiringly at Errin. "How can we guarantee they'll stay?''

Errin held out his hand to the foundry owner. "You have our word that if the blacks don't stay, Levi and I will work the furnace for a week. We'll bring two white men with us. That should show whites are not too good to do the work.''

The foundry owner shook Errin's hand and then Levi's. "Then we have a bargain. Work begins at six in the morning and ends at six in the evening.''

"All right,'' Errin said. "You pay us and we'll pay our men,'' Errin said.

"What are the blacks really working for?'' asked the foundry man.

"One dollar and ninety cents,'' Errin replied. "We receive a few pennies for finding them jobs and guaranteeing their work.''

"Fair enough. I'll see you and your blacks tomorrow morning at six sharp.''

Errin and Levi left the foundry. Once clear of the door, Errin clasped Levi by the shoulder and playfully shook him.

"Well done, partner. That was our first test and we passed. Was that the truth about the workers in Cincinnati?"

"I was told that by a friend, so I'm sure it's so."

"Let's find Isaiah Green and have him get us the men we need."

"Then we'll find more jobs to fill."

"Some of them should be for white men," Errin said. "We can catch the new arrivals coming fresh off the ships. In a new country I believe they would want us to help them find jobs." He smiled. "Don't tell any of them we just got here, too."

"We're honest-to-God businessmen," Levi said proudly.

"We need an office. You rent us one, and a house. I'll start rounding up workers and finding jobs for them."

"Right," Levi said.

Errin smiled inwardly. This was the very first time he had made an honest penny since he was a child. After running away from the weaving mills of Liverpool, he stole to survive. A daring lad, he became a sneak-thief, a "snow gatherer," stealing clean clothes from off the hedges where they were hung to dry. Used clothes had value and could be easily sold. He drifted back to London where he became a "star glazer" cutting the valuable panes of glass from shop windows in the night. There were fences always willing to pay for the expensive, hard-to-obtain glass. As his size and courage increased, he became a "snoozer" sleeping at railway hotels and decamping with some passenger's luggage that happened to be left unguarded for a moment. For several years he earned his food, good food, and stylish clothing in this manner. Then a grand opportunity opened for Errin. In one set of rich luggage stolen from the Hellspont Hotel, he found a brace of silver-inlaid pistols. He had held the beautiful single-shot, cap-and-ball pistols in his hands and marveled at them, and what they could mean to him. The top of the heap of thieves was the highwayman. He would become one of the elite class. He went often into the countryside and practiced with his pistols. His hands seemed to have a natural aptitude for the weapons. When he was satisfied with his skill, he traveled to Birmingham and stole a beautiful gray horse. He became a "two pops and a galloper,'' a mounted highwayman with two pistols prowling the King's highways and ''bailing up,''—waylaying—the rattling coachmen.

"Levi, raise your end of the sign about two inches," Errin called. He stood in the edge of the street sighting at the large wooden sign Levi and Isaiah Green had hoisted above the door. The sign read "Scanlan and Coffin, Skilled Craftsmen."

"How's that?" Levi replied.

"That's level," Errin said. "Make it fast."

The two men, balancing themselves on short ladders, began to nail the sign in place.

Levi and Errin had rented a three-room office on Pacific Street just off the waterfront. The front room was used by Levi who kept the records and paid the workers. He also maintained an open office to sign up any walk-in worker or businessman needing employees. A second room directly behind Levi's was used by Errin when he was not out in the city rounding up workers and drumming up contracts. The thrid room was off to the left side and much larger than the other two. The workers were assembled there and briefed on their jobs.

Errin noticed that some of the many vehicles going past on the street were slowing and the occupants watching the installation of the sign. The people moving on the sidewalk looked up to read the words. There was something satisfying about being in an occupation where a man did not have to hide his actions. He was proud of what Levi and he had accomplished in but two weeks.

He had met every ship arriving at the docks and talked with the most skilled workers, many being immigrants from foreign countries. A majority of them had signed up with him, agreeing to pay him a portion of their wages should he quickly find employment for them. Then with his roster of craftsmen, he had gone from one business to another contracting out his workers. Errin's job was made easier by the enthusiasm and quality of work that Levi had applied to his portion of running the company.

On the street a buggy stopped and George Louden sat observing the hanging of the sign. As Levi climbed down from his ladder, Louden stepped out of his vehicle and came toward him.

"Levi, are you in business already?" Louden asked.

"Hello, Mr. Louden," Levi replied. "Yes. I've got a new business, and a new partner."

"What kind is it?"

"We find skilled workers and contract them out."

"Not a bad idea. An organized labor pool."

Levi called out to Errin. "Come and meet Mr. Louden."

Errin approached the two men. "My name is Errin Scanlan," he said and extended his hand.

"I'm George Louden." He shook the offered hand.

"Mr. Louden is with Wells Fargo," Levi said. "He's their California manager."

"Levi has told me about you," Errin said.

"He won me a lot of money with his rifle," Louden said. "Damn fine shooting. The best part was taking Brol Mattoon's money. That was the first time I ever saw him lose at anything."

"I've never seen Levi shoot," Errin said.

"It's something to see," Louden replied. "How's the new business doing?"

Levi and Errin broke into smiles. They looked at each other and their smiles broadened.

Louden noted the pleased expressions of the two young men. "As good as that?" he said with a chuckle.

"It's extra good," Levi said. "We've already got over a hundred men contracted out. And I've got a hell of a fine partner."

Errin wished Levi hadn't told how many men they had working. He had learned long ago that a man must keep most things secret.

"I like to see young men succeed," Louden said. "Maybe some day Wells Fargo can do business with you."

"Why not today?" Errin said. "Do you need any skilled craftsmen?"

"Not today. Unless you have someone who can stop the men robbing my gold shipments. I'd pay a lot for their scalps."

"Any idea who's behind them?" Errin asked.

"I've got Pinkerton detectives working on the robberies. I may have some solid evidence soon."

Louden looked at the two young men. "Since you fellows are new in San Francisco, maybe there's some things you haven't found out yet. First off, you're near the waterfront, the meanest part of San Francisco. You can't expect the law to give you any protection. In this large and rapidly growing city, there are only thirty-five policemen. They are called Fearless Charlies. And they are indeed brave men."

"We've met some of the Fearless Charlies," Levi said.

Louden nodded. "They can do little to investigate crimes. They are barely able to keep the frequent gang battles in the alleys and off the main streets. There are dozens of small armies. The Chinese tongs have their fighters, the brothel owners their enforcers, and the saloon keepers association their paid guards. The tongs with their *boo hao doy*, hatchetmen, are the most secretive. They are tough and vicious as any white gang. Fortunately they almost always fight among themselves for territory to extort protection money from the Chinese merchants, to sell opium, and control the Chinese whores. The worst of the tongs is the Chee Kong run by Scom Lip. He's ruthless, but damn intelligent. If you ever have dealings with him don't underestimate him.

"The bankers have joined together in a protective association. On the waterfront, the thugs rule. They force protection money from both the white and Chinese businessmen. The Chinese pay twice, once to their own kind, the tongs, and then to the thugs. Damn sad situation all the way round. All of these groups will kill to protect their property, or to keep other thieves or pimps out of the area they consider their territory."

"And you have your Pinkerton detectives," Errin said.

"Yes. I have my own little squad of men. I must keep them or my company would be robbed blind."

Louden sighed. "San Francisco has many murderous thugs, pimps, charlatans, and men who are half honest. But she also has many truly honest men. Someday they will rule San Francisco, but not yet.''

"Thanks for your warning," Levi said. "So far we haven't had any trouble."

Louden climbed up into his buggy. "I wish both of you continued good fortune in your new business. Keep your guard up."

Levi gestured past Louden to the opposite side of the street. "There's that fellow, Mattoon, you bet against at the shooting match."

Louden twisted to look. He raised his hand and called. "Brol, come and meet two new businessmen."

"All right," Mattoon said. He stepped down from his buggy. As he crossed the street, he looked up at the sign. "Skilled craftsmen, eh. To my knowledge, there's no other business like it in town."

He turned to Levi. "Is it profitable?"

"Nothing to brag about," Levi said shortly. He didn't like the man.

Louden spoke. "This fellow is Errin Scanlan."

Mattoon fastened his sight on Errin. "I'm Brol Mattoon."

"Hello," Errin said. He had observed Levi's reaction to the man. Anybody Levi didn't like, Errin would carefully watch. And if the man tried to cause trouble for Levi, then he would have to deal with Errin.

Mattoon, showing little interest in Errin, spoke to Louden. "George, I'm glad to run into you. Later today I was going to come by and see you. I've got some business for your company."

"I'm always ready to talk business," Louden said. "Let's go to my office." To Errin and Levi he said, "Don't forget what I told you about the city."

Chapter Sixteen

Dust lay four inches thick on the well-traveled road Errin followed toward the Sierra Nevada Mountains. Each hoof fall of his horse sent a yellow geyser spouting up. The fine dust hung in the quiet air behind him for minutes before it settled back to the road.

Levi had told Errin about the golden treasure of the Sierra Nevada Mountains, and the testing of the golden metal made into coins at the U.S. Mint in San Francisco. Errin had decided he must see the gold fields. He borrowed Levi's horse, obtained a map of the surrounding country, and caught the riverboat to Sacramento. Immediately he had struck out for the mountains on the main road to Placerville.

He peered out from under the broad brim of his hat at the yellow sun hanging in the vast opal bowl of the hot sky. Its rays scorched him and hammered his eyes down to a squint. How could this be the same sun that had shone on green, cool England?

He lowered his eyes to look ahead through the heat that lay on the land. The air shimmered and danced, distorting visions and distance. Visible beyond and above the field of heat, and miles away, the Sierra Nevada Mountains soared into the sky.

There in the mountains and hidden from him was the South Fork of the American River, and the gold-rich town of Placerville upon its banks.

The road had been slowly climbing ever since it had left Sacramento. Now it turned up more steeply and led into a long narrow valley between low, brush-studded hills. A slow wind birthed small dust devils that picked the dirt up from the road and played with it in tall, spinning columns. Now and again Errin was caught by one of the dust devils; however, that bothered him little. He was a free man going where he wanted and doing what pleased him. Nothing could dampen his joy of simply being free.

A low lying cloud of dust came into view ahead. The cloud moved, extending, and gradually a Concord coach drawn by three teams of trotting horses could be seen. Errin rode to the side of the road and waited for the vehicle to reach him and pass.

The coach drew parallel to Errin, its wheels rumbling and trace chains rattling. The pounding hooves of the six horses stirred up the dust in a thick yellow pall. The trailing coach was nearly hidden in the lung-clogging dirt. He caught a quick glimpse of the dusty faces of the passengers in the open windows. He did not understand how they could breathe. Four other passengers rode on the high swaying top of the coach. The dust there was only a little thinner than that inside the coach.

The vehicle swept by, the driver lashing out with his long twenty foot whip and the popper cracking over the heads of the straining teams of horses.

To be free of the dust, Errin left the valley and rode up to the crest of the ridge of hills that paralleled the road. He went on to the east with the elevation steadily increasing, his view open for miles.

He halted on a high point to survey the land and let the horse catch its wind. North of him some six miles beyond the foothills of the Sierra Nevada Mountains was the junction of the South Fork with the Middle Fork of the American River. To the south, the foothills extended for forty or fifty miles, until they vanished into the far hazy distance.

He twisted about and looked backward to see how the land would appear when he returned traveling west. The wide San Joaquin Valley, its broad flatness made wavery with rising heat columns, seemed to stretch away forever. He thought he could make out some green that could be farms, and the town of Sacramento, a dark area at the junction of the valleys of the American River and the Sacramento River. He felt awe at the immensity of this land of California. And it had gold. His pulse speeded at the thought.

As he prepared to move on, he heard a noise coming from his left. He rode cautiously over the crown of the hill to see.

The road to Placerville came into sight two hundred yards away and below him. A pair of men, one with a pick and the second with a shovel were digging in the road. They worked hurriedly, their heads often turning to stare first one way and then the other along the road. The dust stirred up by their tools rose thickly about them.

Errin drew back out of sight. He dismounted, tied his horse, and crept back to watch from behind concealing bushes. The men worked on, mostly hidden in their own dust. The dirt they dug was flung aside and scattered about so that it could not be easily detected. Errin knew a trap was being set. But for what? And were there other gang members hidden about?

He settled down to watch. As the men worked steadily on, a trench some two feet deep and of equal width began to stretch across the road. Frequently one or the other of the men would walk away from the dust and look carefully both ways along the road.

Errin glanced in the same direction. He could see at least a mile to the east and nearly that far west before the road curved out of sight behind hills. The road lay empty.

The trench had grown to a length of fifteen feet and almost completely spanned the road when one of the men, who had stepped out to scan to the east, called out sharply to his comrade. Errin had spotted the same thing. A blinking light, sunlight off a mirror he judged, was flashing from the point of a hill to the east.

The men ceased digging and spread a piece of canvas over the excavation. Shovels full of dirt were placed along the edges of the canvas to anchor it. More dirt was lightly sprinkled onto the remaining surface. The men grabbed up their tools and hurried into the brush beside the road.

A volley of shots erupted up the road. Seconds later, a wagon carrying two men and drawn by a team of running horses raced around the base of the hill and into view. A horseman led the wagon and a second followed close behind. Further back a quarter mile, five riders chased after the wagon and its accompanying horsemen.

Errin watched the trap close upon the gold wagon, for he knew it could be nothing else. The men in the rear fired rifles and pistols again and again at the wagon. Though they were mounted and could have overtaken the wagon, they made no effort to do so. They wanted only to drive it to its destruction.

Errin wanted to warn the men with the gold wagon, but knew that was impossible. The wagon would reach the trench before he could run down the hill to the road. Further he was within rifle range of the men in the bushes beside the road. There was nothing he could do but watch as the wagon and its two mounted guards sped ever closer to their ruin.

The lead guard reached the trench. The front hooves of his horse stepped upon the canvas stretched across the excavation. The animal plunged down. Errin heard the cracks of the horse's legs breaking. The rider was flung forward, crashing down and tumbling with flailing arms and legs. The momentum of the horse carried it on, sent it cartwheeling to fall upon its rider.

The team of horses pulling the wagon struck the ditch. The lead horses fell, their legs buckling under them and bones breaking. Hooked to the wagon tongue by their breast chains, the rest of the team was dragged ahead. Immediately, the front wheels of the wagon slammed down into the ditch. The vehicle stopped with gut-tearing abruptness and the rear end flipped into the air.

The tail end of the wagon continued to rise, pressing down

on its oak tongue and flipping forward. The tongue snapped just in front of the bed of the wagon. The vehicle and the men and three heavy wooden crates fell upon the team of horses.

The trailing guard saw the now exposed trench, and jumped his horse over it. His frightened mount ran on a hundred feet before he could drag it to a halt. He spun it around toward the wrecked wagon. As the horse turned, a rifle cracked in the bushes beside the road. The guard tumbled from his saddle.

One of the men who had been on the wagon slowly and laboriously climbed to his feet. He stood swaying and clutching his ribs. The rifle in the brush fired again. The man fell boneless as a cloth doll.

The crippled teams of horses, bound in a tangle of harness, trace chains, and a length of tongue, struggled to rise on shattered legs. Their terrible screams of pain and fear made Errin shiver. Not one horse made it to its feet.

The five mounted outlaws rushed up and sprang down from their horses. A tall, thin man with a long face threw back his head and yelled out in a stentorian voice. "Yahoo! Wells Fargo has just given us a fortune."

"Let's quick take a look at it," a second man shouted.

"Check the guards first, Toll," the first man ordered. "Shoot anyone that's still breathin'."

The two men who had dug the trench came out of the brush leading their mounts and two packhorses.

The tall man shouted at them. "Hurry your asses. Get the gold transferred to the pack saddles. I want to be out of here in two minutes."

"One of the guards is still alive, Lasch," Toll called. A pistol fired. "Now he's not."

"Put the horses out of their misery too," Lasch said.

The pistol fired several more times.

Six of the men worked speedily, breaking open the wooden crates and loading the pouches and bars of gold into the leather satchels of the pack saddles. Lasch stood watching his men and checking the road.

With the bandits intent upon their task, Errin stole down through the bushes. He halted above them on the hillside.

"Lasch, why can't we divvy up a pouch of these nuggets," Toll asked. "Nobody can trace nuggets."

"Let me have one of those," Lasch said. "Now everybody hold out your hand."

Lasch opened the throat of the pouch and dribbled nuggets into each man's outstretched palm. "That's for a little spending money until we get the gold exchanged for paper money we can use without worrying someone might guess where it came from. Now get on with your work."

"There's more gold here than we thought there'd be," Toll said. "The horses are going to be loaded damn heavy, I'd guess nearly three hundred pounds each."

"They can carry it for a spell and we have fresh horses half-way along. We'll be at the Sacramento River and the boat before dawn."

Errin lay in the bushes and watched the men separate into groups. The men called Lasch and Toll led the packhorses off due south. Three men rode east toward the high country. The last two men went north along the foothills. Any pursuing lawmen wouldn't know which group had the gold, and would have to divide their officers to chase all the highwaymen.

Errin felt the strangeness of the twist of fate that had brought him upon the highwaymen committing the robbery. He was sorry for the dead guards and the horses so callously mutilated and slain. The robbery had been savage. He had always carried out his robberies without injuring man or a horse. How very different these bandits were. As the thieves faded away into the land, Errin thought of Levi's friend the Wells Fargo agent. The man's company had suffered a severe loss. A plan came to Errin, a very dangerous plan.

Chapter Seventeen

Errin followed the tracks of the highwaymen south with the Sierra Nevada Mountains rearing up on his left and the wide San Joaquin Valley below him on the right. He approached every ridge top warily, and stopped often to scrutinize the land ahead to check the ravines, the boulder fields, and brush thickets where the thieves could hide and spring a trap on him.

As he trailed the bandits, the sun had passed overhead and the shadows swung around to point long, dark fingers to the east. The fields of brush had dwindled to but patches, and the dry, wild grass threw a brown blanket over the land. The terrain had become ever rougher with dry watercourses separating long steep ridges that ran down into the valley. The serrated land looked as if some giant lion had clawed the flank of the mountain.

He climbed his horse up a sharp, rocky ridge and looked over. He ducked quickly, for the robbers were in the valley less than a quarter mile distant. The two men had transferred the pack saddles to fresh horses. Now they were reloading the last of the bars and pouches of gold, from where they had been temporarily stacked on the ground, back into the leather pouches of the pack saddles. Without delay the thieves swung astride their mounts, and leading the packhorses, headed due west down the narrow valley.

Errin pulled out his map and studied it, comparing the features shown there with the land spread before him. He had heard the robbers mention reaching the Sacramento River before daylight. First they had traveled south some twenty miles. Now on their westerly heading they would pass well clear of the town of Sacramento and strike the river some ten miles downstream from the town. Errin had heard them say that a boat would be waiting, and once away, they would leave no trail for a lawman to follow. The robbers and the gold would disappear.

He reined his horse around and hurried it down into the creek valley behind him. That valley ran west paralleling the one the thieves traveled. He raised his black to a gallop along the gravelly creek bottom.

Half an hour later and five miles farther along, the ridge that separated Errin from the route he thought the bandits would take had shrunk to a third of its original size. He rode up to the top and stopped in a patch of oak brush to look down into the valley beyond.

Nothing moved in the narrow creek bottom below him. Could he have made a mistake in his reasoning of what the men would do? Perhaps they were riding more slowly than he had anticipated. He would wait a little while, and if they did not show, he would be forced to go looking for them.

Errin's blood began to strum through his veins for at the bend of the creek upstream, two riders leading packhorses had come into view. His quarry was in sight and now he would take the stolen gold from the thieves for himself. From the way the packhorses moved under heavy loads, the gold must be worth a fortune. He leaned forward low on the neck of his mount and went down through the brush into the valley ahead of the riders.

* * *

Lasch reined his horse to a stop. With a worried expression, he twisted around and cast a sharp look behind, and then up at the tops of the ridges both left and right.

"What's botherin' you?" Toll asked.

"Something's wrong. Don't you feel it?"

"Nope. There's no way anybody could know where we're at."

Lasch continued to scan the land around him. He stared ahead at the patches of brush bordering the gravelly creek bed. Everything lay quiet and unmoving except where the slow wind stirred the brush on the hilltop. Yet some warning gnawed at him.

"I feel someone or something's watching us," he said.

"Deer or wolf, that's all it could be. No sheriff could be close to us."

"Could be a cowhand or sheep herder. We wouldn't want them to see us."

"I haven't seen either sheep or cows. Let's get onto the river. It'll soon be dark."

"All right," Lasch said reluctantly. He kicked his mount ahead.

Errin, hidden in a dense clump of bushes, remained motionless as the men halted and sat their mounts. He heard them talking. The man Lasch was a wary animal. Then they came on, each man and horse drawing a long dark shadow behind.

The clank of iron hooves on the stones of the creek bottom grew loud as the robbers drew close to Errin. He watched them through the bushes, measuring them. Lasch was a narrow, high-shouldered man. He looked wiry. He would be very quick. The second man was square built with a large round head. Errin hoped the men would surrender their gold without a fight for he didn't want to have to shoot them.

The men were close enough. Errin pulled his pistol and cocked it. He leapt out from the brush and into a position where he could see both riders. "Halt!" he shouted, pointing his pistol.

Lasch's horse, startled by Errin's sudden appearance, reared high, its hooves pawing the air. The robber jerked the reins tightly to hold the horse up on its hind legs. He shifted in the saddle to be shielded from Errin's pistol by the brute's thick body. In the same instant, he grabbed his pistol and fired down at the man on the ground.

Errin sprang aside as the horse reared and the outlaw's gun crashed. He felt the wind from the passing bullet on the side of his face.

He quickly shot up at the rider. His bullet drove in under Lasch's ribs, plowed upward at an angle and tore free at the shoulder. Lasch tumbled from the saddle.

Errin swung the barrel of his revolver to the second robber, hoping fervently the man wouldn't fight. The outlaw, his face hard and determined, had drawn his pistol and was lifting it to point at Errin.

Errin fired quickly at the broad chest of the man. The outlaw shuddered at the impact of the bullet. He rocked backward. His feet came loose of the stirrups and he rolled to the ground.

Breathing hard, Errin stared at the corpses of the two highwaymen. It had been a futile wish to think they would give up the gold without a fight. He shouldn't take their deaths too seriously for they were killers. He bent and went through their pockets and took their wallets.

He stripped the saddle and bridle from both riding horses and slapped the animals away to fend for themselves. Leading the packhorses carrying the gold, Errin returned to the black. He rode toward the sullen red orb of the sun lying on the peaks of the California Coast Range. The mountains seemed to bleed.

The hours stretched long and weary as Errin traveled through the shadow-filled night. His eyes probed ahead in the dim light of the three-quarter moon. He had left the foothills of the Sierra

Nevadas far behind and now journeyed across the wide wheat fields on the bottom of the San Joaquin Valley.

Lasch had talked about the Sacramento River and a boat to transport the gold to a safe place. Errin had no boat waiting. He must climb over the Coast Range to the town of Oakland. There he could catch a ferry across the bay to San Francisco.

He stepped down to walk and take the load off his tired mount. There was nothing he could do to ease the burden of the heavily laden packhorses. Nor would he stop, for he must be off the flat valley bottom and in the mountains before daylight caught him. The farmers would be coming early into the fields and must not see him.

The moon dropped behind the mountains and heavy darkness blanketed the land. Errin saw a star lose its mooring in the black heavens and fall streaking to the north where it disappeared in a final winking flash. He stopped and stared at the spot where the light had vanished. The exhausted animals halted and stood motionless around him. An eerie calm settled around him as if the whole elaborate clockwork of the universe had ceased ticking.

A bleak, disquieting emotion welled up within Errin. He had killed two men, and even though they were murderers, he hadn't been able to shake the weight of their deaths. Worse still was the fact that he had fallen so very easily back into his old ways of being a "two pops and a galloper," a highwayman. It had been only a few days past when he had told Levi that they were in a new land and could start a new life. Should he continue on with being a robber, he might one day kill an innocent man. He never wanted to make that grievous error. He felt the ghost of the end that awaited him hanging on the gallows.

His thoughts focused on Levi. The younger man had proved to be a good comrade and partner. What would he think should he discover Errin had Wells Fargo's stolen gold? Errin knew one thing for certain, he didn't want to lose Levi as a friend.

He shook himself. He was damn tired and that was what

was causing his gloomy thoughts. Exasperated at himself, he tugged on the horse's bridle reins. "Let's get on."

The murky shadows of the night died slowly upon the Diablo Mountains. The first frail light of the coming morning dawn caught Errin above the floor of the San Joaquin Valley and halfway up the flank of Mount Mocho. He had found the perfect hiding place for his gold, a field of boulders a few yards distant from an outcrop of lava rock protruding from the mountainside. He could return and easily find this exact spot again. Now to get the task done before daylight came.

No one must observe what he was about to do. He pivoted about, his eyes straining to pierce the gloomy dusk. The mountainside to the north lay empty. Behind him, the land sloping down into the valley was void of life. He faced south. He jerked, startled at what he saw. A rider sat his mount not a hundred yards distant and watching him.

Errin was jolted at the totally unexpected presence of the steed and rider and their complete stillness. How had they drawn so close without him seeing them? The horse was of a light gray color and, even in the gloom, seemed to catch light from somewhere and glow with a silver aura. At the same time the slender rider, garbed in some manner of dark clothing, blended almost perfectly into the mountain behind him. As Errin peered through the dim light, the rider seemed to fade in and out, to be there astride his motionless mount one moment and then the next to disappear, like a transparent rider upon a supernatural steed.

Damn weird, thought Errin as he raised his hand acknowledging the silent rider's presence. Where did this fellow come from, and why now just at the precise moment Errin was preparing to stash the gold? It was strange that he would be out riding at an hour much too dark for a working cowboy to be about. A feeling came over Errin that the appearance of the rider had some significance. Was he an omen? And if so, an omen of what?

The man made no response to Errin's greeting. He simply

sat upon his mount facing Errin, and watching him, at least Errin thought so but could not tell for the man's features were not discernible because of the lighting and distance.

Errin leaned forward, concentrating on the slender rider. He was flesh and blood, but whether man or woman, Errin could not be certain one way or the other. Was he, or she, the owner of the land where he had selected a place to hide his gold? Regardless of that, the rider had seen Errin with loaded pack-horses at an hour when men should not be traveling. Errin's plan was spoiled.

He turned away from the silent rider upon his luminous mount. Leading his horse, Errin went up the mountainside. He must rethink what he would do.

Errin caught the last ferry of the day from Oakland just before it cast off for the trip across the bay to San Francisco. Two rough-looking men, leading their saddle horses, followed him on board the ferry.

The men, both armed with pistols, had been waiting for the ferry as he came down through the town to the docks. Errin recognized them as part of the gang. They were the two who had dug the trench across the road, that had attacked the Wells Fargo gold shipment. Now they were eyeing the weary pack-horses that were obviously heavily loaded but with something of small bulk.

Errin turned his back to the men. Upon leaving the strange horseman on the side of Mount Mocho, he had never again considered hiding the gold and later recovering it. For some reason he could not explain even to himself, he took the unexpected appearance of the rider as a sign that he should not keep the stolen gold.

He had considered the fact that news of the robbery and the death of the four guards would be widely known and because of that he was running a large risk in openingly bringing the gold to San Francisco. Should someone discover what he carried, they could notify the law and he would be arrested as a thief. But never had he thought that he would encounter some members of the gang of robbers who had stolen the gold. Should the men identify the packhorses, they would most likely jump Errin at the first opportunity.

Night was falling on San Francisco when the ferry docked. Errin mounted his weary black and towing the exhausted packhorses left the ferry and went onto the waterfront. He checked behind for the robbers and saw them go off along The Embarcadero. Much relieved that the men were not following him, he climbed into the darkening city toward Sansome Street and the Wells Fargo Office.

A few minutes later Errin was approaching Louden's office. From half a block distant, he saw the windows of the office were bright with yellow lamplight. Now if Louden was only there.

In front of the building, he dismounted stiff and weary and tied the horses to the hitching rail. When Errin shoved open the door and entered, Louden was at his desk with three armed men.

"Hello, Errin," Louden said. He noted the dusty, exhausted condition of the man. What did the fellow want at this late hour?

"These your men?" Errin asked.

"Yes," Louden replied. "Why?"

"I got something outside that belongs to you."

"What's that?"

"About five to six hundred pounds of gold."

Louden sprang to his feet. "Gold! You've got the gold?"

"Yep. Brought it to you. Better get it off the street and locked up someplace safe."

"Go bring it in," Louden ordered the men. He spoke to Errin. "Sit down, you look worn out. How come you've got the gold?"

"I happened to see the robbery, but couldn't stop it. There were too many thieves. So I followed the two that went off with the gold. They decided to fight when I wanted the gold and I had to shoot them. Maybe you know who they were." He took the wallets from his pocket and tossed them onto the desk in front of Louden.

Louden studied Errin's grim face. The Englishman was more than he appeared. Louden picked up the wallets. "Lasch, by God. So that sonofabitch was one of them."

"He acted like he was the leader. You'll see that other man was named Toll."

Louden looked inside the second wallet. "Yes, I see. I don't know him. How many other men were with Lasch?"

"Five. They went off in different directions. I saw two of them on the ferry when I crossed from Oakland."

"That's good news. You give the Pinkerton agents a description and they'll go looking for them."

The men came inside carrying the leather pouches from the pack saddles. They piled them on Louden's desk.

"You'll find some of the nuggets missing," Errin said. "Lasch gave them to his men to spend. He told them they'd get the rest of their share when the gold bars had been exchanged for paper money."

"Did he say how he would make the trade for paper?"

"No. He acted like it would be easy to do."

"I wish I knew who would make the exchange. Do you know the value of the gold?" Louden asked.

"Haven't any idea," Errin said.

"Not considering part of the nuggets are missing, fifty-eight thousand dollars."

"I knew it had to be a fortune," Errin said. He felt a tinge of highwayman's regret at having given up the gold.

Louden studied Errin. "Have you been in town since the robbery?"

"Nope. Just followed the robbers and then came overland to Oakland to catch the ferry."

"Well there's something you should know. After I heard of the robbery and the death of my men, I posted a reward for the return of the gold. Ten percent of whatever was recovered. That comes to five thousand and eight hundred dollars. I also promised a reward of five hundred dollars for each and every thief. I owe you a sizeable amount of money."

"Well, I'll be damned," exclaimed Errin. "I didn't expect any reward."

"You're an honest man. Come by my office in the morning and I'll have a bank draft ready for you."

Maybe I'm becoming too honest, Errin thought. Oh, well, it's too late now. "I'll be here bright and early. But you'd better make the draft out to both Levi and me. We're partners and have agreed to share everything half and half. Except for women."

Chapter Eighteen

"The Germans are damn fine workers," the construction foreman told Levi.

"Glad to hear that," Levi replied as he watched the score of men fasten the strong bracing beams to the pilings that had been sunk deeply into the floor of San Francisco Bay by a steam piledriver. In a few more days the five-hundred-foot extension of the pier would be completed, and Errin, or he, would have to find new employment for the men. "Don't forget us when your next job comes up."

"I'll give you first chance to bid."

"Thanks," Levi said. He moved off along the pier toward the shore. With Errin gone to the gold fields, Levi had posted Green in the office while he took on Errin's task of visiting the workplaces of their contract craftsmen. He enjoyed being outside in the city rather than performing office duties regardless how important they were.

He came to a tall-masted sailing ship tied up to the pier. A puffing steam engine was hoisting a cargo net full of long, narrow crates aboard the ship. Curious as to what might be the contents of the containers, Levi spoke to the seaman standing nearby and watching the loading. "What's in those crates?" Levi asked.

"Coffins. Each one has a dead Chinaman in it all ready for burial back in their country."

"That's a long way to go to be buried," Levi said as the cargo net swung down into the hold of the ship.

"Every Chinaman that has money when he dies is shipped home to be buried with his ancestors. The *Flying Cloud* will carry two hundred of them back. That French steamship just there," the seaman pointed at the ship next along the pier, "is carrying three hundred and twenty corpses. Those Chinamen who are poor have just their bones sent home. The *Pacific* took seven hundred sets of bones last week. It was in all the newspapers. That was the biggest number ever on one ship."

Levi checked four other jobs scattered about the city, and at the end of that time found the day ending. He felt restless and decided to explore the city and take in some entertainment. Errin, from his search for employment for their contract workers, knew the city quite well. Levi on the other hand, had much to see for the first time.

Hungry as only young men can be, he ate a huge meal at a German *Wirtschaft* on The Embarcadero. Then he walked uptown to the Bella Union Theatre and caught a troupe of Boston actors performing a three-act comedy play, one he found enjoyable. At the conclusion of the play, he left the theater with the laughing, happy patrons.

Levi, with no particular destination in mind, drifted through the city. He watched the night fall, filling the narrow streets and cramped alleyways. A cold sea breeze carrying fog crept up from the bay and stole in among the buildings. He smelled the fog and his tongue tasted it, tangy and heavy with salt.

A lamplighter came into sight on the cross street ahead of Levi. The man reached up with his flaming torch to touch off the gas jets of the streetlamp at the intersection. The light cast by the impure gas distilled from asphaltum made only a dim yellow pool in the growing darkness.

The sound of a flute and cymbals playing an alien, Chinese piece began on a balcony above the street. Levi saw two Chinese men with the instruments. With the men was an old woman wrapped in a shawl. She started to wail a Cantonese lament of sadness and to rock to and fro. Levi stopped to watch and listen. The homesickness of these people in a foreign land so far from home must be even deeper than Levi's. He breathed in the multitude of pungent smells of San Francisco. He liked the city's location on the ocean and the bustling waterfront, the mix of races of peoples, and the thriving businesses. Best of all, he appreciated the opportunities the city had given him for a new and interesting life.

He left Chinatown and walked three squares along Church Street and came out on Jackson Street. He passed a brightly lighted house with a sign naming the bottom floor half sunken in the ground as Blind Annie's Cellar. He had been told of the place, that it was an opium den. He saw a man leave the street and go down the steps and into the cellar.

The fog had become more dense, forming droplets on Levi's eyebrows. His cheeks were wet with moisture. He tried to brush it away with his hand. Never had he experienced a fog so thick and clinging. Maybe the drippy, foggy night should be left to the people who better knew their way around the city.

He came to the streetlight haloed with the wet sea vapor and halted to get his bearings.

Chun Quang trembled with uncertainty. Was this the moment for her to try to escape?

The inside of the swaying carriage was totally dark for it was night and all the leather curtains had been pulled down over the windows and fastened securely. Chun and the other twelve Chinese girls sat jammed hip to hip on the four seats of the horse-drawn vehicle. She had deliberately hung back during the loading and climbed aboard last so that she would be nearest to the door.

The Americans had closed the door of the carriage and tied

it shut with a length of rope. However if she was given the right opportunity, that would not hold her captive. She drew the sharp, two-edged knife from its sheath inside her clothing and held it against her leg.

A short time earlier, Chun and the other forty-eight girls had been brought from the cabin of the steamship that had just arrived from Canton, China, and ordered into the four carriages that had been waiting on the pier. Several Americans, giant men to Chun, now escorted them through the streets of San Francisco. She must escape before their destination was reached and she would be locked away behind strong walls.

She began to saw on the coarse hemp rope with the knife, making her movements slow and short, so the girl next to her would not become aware of what she was doing. The strands of the rope parted one by one and then the door was freed.

She shoved the door partway open and looked outside. The shadowy figure of one of the Americans paced beside the front wheel of the carriage. No one was visible to the rear. She took a deep breath and jumped down to the ground. Immediately she hiked the tail of her long dress to her knees and darted away into the night.

The guard near the front of the carriage heard Chun's feet striking the pavement. He whirled and caught a fleeting glance of her, fast disappearing into the darkness. He shouted, "Cranson, one of the little bitches is getting away. Help me catch her."

Chun heard the shouted warning and ran faster. They must not catch her. Never slowing, she sought the deepest shadows, hugged the walls. Always there were the echoes of racing feet behind her in the foggy darkness. She began to try the doors in the sides of the buildings facing the street. She hoped desperately to find one that was unlocked so she could get off the street. But no door was open and she was being slowed by her search.

She sprinted ahead fearing she would fail to elude the men

for they would know this foreign city while she had not one whit of knowledge of which direction to run to escape.

She ran on and on at the top of her strength with her breath coming hot and scalding in her lungs. She knew the long-legged Americans would soon catch her unless she found a place to hide. She plunged headlong into the black mouth of an alley and prayed it wasn't deadended. She must not be caught and sold to be a slave of some man in America.

The alley ended and Chun veered off along a narrow street. She went but a short distance when she broke out into a lighted intersection. From the opposite corner of the street, a man pivoted to look directly at her. She slid to a stop with a moan of despair. How had one of her pursuers gotten ahead of her? But no, she had never seen this man before.

Levi saw the Chinese girl run out of the side street and stop in the light of the streetlamp. She was a slender, elfin figure with long, black hair hanging wild and loose down over her shoulders. The tail of a red dress was pulled up in her hands to free her legs for faster running. She flung a look behind her and then twisted to stare through the fog at him.

"Please, sir, help me," Chun called. She must trust the man, and hope he would come to her aid. "I'm being chased by men who will hurt me."

The girl was breathing heavily and her words were accented—still Levi understood them. She was exceedingly lovely even with the frightened expression on her face. He looked into the darkness from which she had sprung. He heard the thud of rapidly approaching footsteps.

"Who are they?" Levi asked.

"They want to sell me to be a slave," she replied hastily. The man asks questions when we should be running, thought Chun.

"Come with me," Levi said. "Maybe we can get away from them."

Chun hurried close. Levi took the Chinese girl by the arm.

Just as he started to hurry off with her, two men erupted from the darkness and into the intersection.

Chun cried out at the appearance of the guards. She gripped her knife and held it hidden and ready in a fold of her dress.

"There she is, Cranson," one of the men said.

"It's a damn good thing we caught her," Cranson replied. "If she'd gotten away from us, the boss would've broke our necks."

The men moved toward Levi and Chun. "Come here you little moon-eyed bitch," Cranson said.

Chun moved partly behind Levi. "Don't let them take me," she begged.

"She doesn't want to go with you," Levi told the men.

"This ain't any of your business," Cranson said. "She's bought and paid for."

"That's not true," Chun cried out and gripped Levi's arm. "No one bought me. They forced me onto a ship in Canton and brought me here."

"She says she's not been bought," Levi said. "And anyway, one man can't own another."

"That's where you're wrong," Cranson said. "Get out of the way."

"I can't do that."

"Then you're going to get the worst beating a white man ever had," Cranson said.

Levi's spine turned cold. He could not whip both of the men, maybe not even one of them. But he would try. He pushed the girl out of the way against the wall of the building abutting the street.

The men attacked more swiftly than Levi had anticipated and were already within striking range when he turned back. Cranson was closer and his big fist lashed out and walloped Levi in the mouth.

The smashing fist sent pain ricocheting around inside Levi's skull. The taste of blood was suddenly salt and copper in his mouth. He stepped toward the man, taking a hard blow to the body as he pounded aside his defense. Then Levi was inside and he struck Cranson fiercely with a left and right. Cranson backed up, shaking his head.

The second man lunged in and hit Levi a solid blow to the side of the head, spinning him part way around. Then both men were upon Levi, pummeling him savagely in the ribs and back.

Levi fell, the breath knocked out of him. He rolled away from the men. He must get to his feet before the two kicked the life out of him lying unprotected on the ground. His empty lungs sucked starvingly at the air as he struggled to his knees and on up to his feet.

His head spun. His mouth was full of blood. He spewed it out in a spray of red. He was no match for the men. He was going to get the beating they had promised him.

Errin was extremely tired as he walked along The Embarcadero. But he couldn't rest for he was worried about his young friend Levi. He had been searching for him since shortly after nightfall. He hoped Levi hadn't been shanghaied. Errin was familiar with crimps. They were plentiful in London where they plied their vicious trade. San Francisco was said to be worse than London. A man's body was a valuable piece of merchandise, and it was free for the taking. He had seen whaling ships, and ships that hunted seals, and others that hauled cargo at anchor in the harbor. More than likely several of those ships' captains were waiting for crewmen, shanghaied or not, to work their vessels. Captain Griffith of the *Dolly* could be one of them for he had many disgruntled seamen.

After leaving Louden at the Wells Fargo place of business, Errin had gone to his office to tell Levi about the gold and the promised reward. Isaiah Green informed him that he had not seen Levi since early morning. Nor did Errin find Levi at their rented house when he went there. He had set out to search for Levi.

He turned and climbed away from the waterfront. He soon found himself on the Barbary Coast. He checked several saloons, gaming parlors, and billiards halls and still no sight of Levi.

Errin entered a street several blocks long crowded with older buildings. An unusual number of windows and doorways opened onto the sidewalk. A low musical chant of the voices of women filled the dark canyon of the street. Though the litany was an announcement of bodies and sensual delight for sale, he heard a mournful, unhappy core to it. The place could only be the "Street of Slave Girls" that he had heard about. It was one of the infamous crib areas and the place of the cheapest whores. Each Chinese woman had a window where she sat to display herself to the men passing on the street. The Chinese men called the women Chinoise, "daughters of joy," and the white men "singsong girls." Their life expectancy was short, five years or less. Death usually came from disease or by their own hands. Several men lounged about with guns and knives in their belts. They were the protectors who kept the drunks and cruel men from beating the women, but they also forced the women to stay and sell themselves. Errin quickened his pace, the meanness and the human sadness of the place driving him away.

He felt his deep exhaustion and knew he must give up his search. The city was large, and with the streets steeped in fog and darkness, it would be nearly impossible to find Levi.

As he made his decision to return to his house, he saw three men fighting with swinging fists under a street lamp a block distant. It seemed that two of the men were pounding the third. That poor soul resembled Levi. Errin broke into a swift run. If the man was Levi, he was taking a hellish beating.

Errin shouted a shrill cry to try to stop the fight. No one paid him any attention. As he raced closer, he saw a young Chinese girl huddled against the wall of the building near the battling men. Was she the cause of the fight?

Closer now, Errin saw it was Levi being beaten by the other two. He shouted at the top of his lungs, a cry full of anger and challenge. The three men heard him and whirled to look.

Levi recovered quickly, and using the break in the attack, backed away from the two men. The figure of a man was rushing along the street through the darkness at them. Now there was three of them, Levi thought.

Errin ran into the light under the streetlamp and stopped beside Levi. He threw a fierce look at Levi's opponents and then reached out and took his friend by the shoulder. "You still got all your teeth, partner?" he asked Levi.

"Just barely. I think some have been knocked loose."

"We'll make them pay for that," Errin said. He faced the two men and coldly measured them. "Now it's an even fight, two against two. Let's see how you like that."

He sprang at the larger of the men, Cranson, and hit him a hard blow to the chin. Cranson struck back and faded to the side and came in at Errin from the right. Errin twisted to meet him and they traded a flurry of blows. Errin felt the jarring impacts of his fists crashing against the man's body and that was damn fine. Cranson covered himself with his arms and back-pedaled away. From that first tangle, Errin knew he was the stronger. Cranson knew it too. His arms dropped and a hand went to the knife in his belt. He leapt at Errin and his arm swung.

Errin whipped his head back as the knife blade swished past his neck. He blocked Cranson's reverse swing of the knife with his left hand and drew his pistol. He slammed Cranson's hand with the gun barrel, and felt the bones break. The knife fell with a ring of steel on the street.

"Go to sleep," Errin said. With a backhanded swing, he cracked the man on the head with the pistol.

Cranson sagged to hands and knees. To Errin's amazement, Cranson shook his head and coiled upward on a knee.

"Hard-headed bastard," Errin said. He didn't want to hit the man again with his pistol and risk damaging the weapon. He drew back his booted foot and kicked the man powerfully in the face, knocking him down flat on his back. Cranson lay crumpled and still.

Errin spun quickly to go to the aid of Levi, but then stopped. Levi was holding his own with the second man and Errin decided to only watch. Now was a good time to discover what kind of man he had taken on as a partner. How brave and how tough was Levi?

"Help him," Chun shouted at Errin.

Errin only shook his head and continued to observe the fight.

"Please help him," Chun pleaded and clutched at Errin's arm.

"No," Errin replied and pulled free of her hold. He fully believed she was the cause of the fight. If he hadn't happened upon them, Levi could have been badly hurt, or even killed.

Chun hesitated but a second more. She brought up her knife and stole toward the struggling fighters.

Errin came up behind Chun and grabbed her by the shoulders. She twisted in his grasp and stabbed out viciously at him with the knife. Errin almost failed to catch her arm as the knife drove at his throat.

"Damnit, girl," Errin growled, and roughly wrenched the knife from her grip. The Chinese girl was as dangerous as the men.

"Let me go," Chun said angrily. "I will cut the man."

"I believe you would. But Levi's winning. Stay clear of them." Chun started to struggle and Errin shook her once to emphasize his order. "Stop it!"

Levi pressed his opponent, blocking a blow, and sending another glancing away. Now his adversary was open. Levi waded into the man, hammering him in the gut, then raised his aim and slugged him on the chin. The man collapsed unconscious.

"There, see, the fight's over," Errin said to Chun and released her.

Levi breathing hard and smiling victoriously through the blood on his lips, called out. "Errin, damn glad you showed up."

Errin nodded. "So am I. Let's get out of here before one of the Fearless Charlies comes along. I don't want to try to explain this to them." He pointed to Chun. "What's the story with her?"

Levi finished wiping the blood from his mouth on the sleeve of his shirt. "All I know is she came running out of that street with those two chasing her. They said she had been bought, but she said that was a lie. She asked for help and I tried to keep the men from taking her.'' Levi saw the girl edging away from Errin and him. She seemed almost as much afraid of them as she had been of the other men.

He spoke to Chun. ''What's your name?''

''Chun Quang,'' she said and stopped moving away and stood still.

''Well, Chun, my name's Levi Coffin and that's Errin Scanlan. Do you need a place to stay tonight?''

''No. I will be all right now.''

''Let her go on her way,'' Errin said. ''I think she'll be nothing but trouble.''

''I don't believe she has any place to go.''

''Oh hell, Levi, do what you want, just do it quick.''

''Miss, for the last time, do you want a place to stay? You'll be safe with us, I promise.''

Chun looked searchingly into Levi's face. Yes, she could trust him, she thought. She sensed something much different about the second American who watched her icily. Without the slightest expression of caring, he had only watched as his friend fought desperately against a very strong opponent. And he would not allow her to go to his friend's aid. Errin was one of those hard men.

''I will go with you until it is daylight. Then I will leave.''

''All right,'' Levi agreed.

''That's finally settled so let's go,'' Errin said. He led off into the night.

Levi fell in beside Errin. Chun took a position away from Errin on the opposite side of Levi. She walked two steps behind the men.

''Tell us the complete story how you were brought to San Francisco,'' Levi said to the Chinese girl. She was seated facing Errin and him with her slender, fine-boned body tense and erect, and her jet black eyes watching them warily, suspiciously. She seemed so vulnerable that he wanted to take her in his arms and tell her she was completely safe with him.

Chun gripped her hands nervously together and prepared

herself to reply. She was with the men in the house they had reached after a long walk along dark streets. Both were staring at her. The gray eyes and the blue eyes of the white men—looking out from their long, bony faces, so different from her people—seemed cold and uncaring. The man called Errin was the worst. His lips were stretched into a thin smile as if he wasn't prepared to believe anything she said. She focused on Levi and wondered how she should begin.

She took a deep breath. "I never thought of coming to America. It happened because of the buyer of girls on The Street of Merchants near the waterfront in Canton. He had bought many pretty girls that would be taken to America to become the wives of Chinamen who had become wealthy here. Fathers can sell their daughters, you understand, and it is often done. Among the girls, there were several that had been sold against their will. As the group was being taken to the ship that would transport them, some of the girls broke away and ran. The buyer's men ran after them and easily caught them. I happened to be on the waterfront and they also grabbed me and forced me onto the ship. The buyer did not believe me when I told him I was not one he had purchased. Or he acted as if he did not. I was locked aboard the ship with the others and brought over the sea to your country.

"I did not want to be owned by some man who would beat me, but there was nothing I could do until we arrived here. When they loaded us into carriages to be taken to be sold, I knew I had to escape. I cut the rope that held the door closed and ran." Her eyes fastened upon Levi and softened, became almost worshipping. "You bravely helped me when those men would have captured me. Somehow I must repay you."

"She was kidnapped plain and simple," Levi said, saddened by the wretched manner in which the girl had been treated.

"So she tells us," Errin said with a skeptical expression.

"You don't believe her?"

"What else could she say to get help to escape?" Errin still chafed at the girl's action that had gotten Levi into a fight with men who could have killed him.

"Well like I told those two fellows who were chasing her, one person can't own another."

"In China they can. Can't they, miss?"

"Yes. But I'm telling you the truth. The buyer did not purchase me, and I was forced to come to America."

"I believe you," Levi said.

"If as you say you were forced to come to America, how is it you speak English?" Errin asked brusquely. "It takes more time than crossing the ocean to learn a foreign language."

Chun looked steadily at the doubting Errin. This man must be convinced she spoke the truth. "My family was very poor, as are many families in China. Worse still, all my father's six children were girls, and girls have little value. All parents want sons so they can care for them when they get old." She looked from Errin to Levi wanting them to understand her plight. "To help my father and mother, I went to the American Baptist Missionaries who had an orphanage in Canton. I worked there at the orphanage taking care of the children. The missionaries taught me English so I could understand their Bible and explain it to the children."

"Well what do you think now?" Levi said to Errin.

"All right, Levi, I'll go along with you and her. But she's trouble. She's very pretty and must be worth several thousand dollars to some lonely Chinaman who has struck it rich here in America."

She is pretty, thought Levi, as his heart pounded away. "Chun, you've got to watch out for the ship's captain for he'll be looking for you."

"Yes, I know for he was responsible for delivering me safely here to be sold."

"I will help you get passage money back to China," Levi said.

To Levi's surprise, the Chinese girl began to vigorously shake her head *no*. "Now that I am in your land of the Gum Shan, the Mountains of Gold, I will stay and work very hard and become rich. Then I will return home."

"Everybody wants to get rich here," Levi said.

"It'll be a damn sight harder for her to do it than us," Errin said.

"I would imagine so," Levi replied. "Now, Errin, just because she's staying the night with us, doesn't mean you can treat her like you did the pickpocket."

Chun glanced from Levi to Errin and back. What did that mean?

"She's yours, Levi, not mine. You decide what you want to do with her."

"She belongs to nobody. She's free to go where she wants and do what she wants."

"You're wrong about that. A young Chinese girl like her wouldn't be safe on the street for ten minutes. One of the Chinese tongs would make her a prisoner and sell her, or a pimp would grab her and make her a whore."

"She can stay here until she finds a safe place with her own people in Chinatown."

Errin shrugged his shoulders. "Like I said, she's yours to do with as you please."

"Chun, you're welcome to stay here until you find a safe place to live," Levi said. "I'll get you some blankets, and you can make a pallet to sleep on in this room."

Chun arose from her chair. "Thank you. I will be no trouble to you." She bowed to Levi. Then to Errin but not nearly so low. "May I have my knife, please," she said to Errin.

"Just don't cut my throat with it while I sleep," Errin said and gave her the knife.

Chun pulled the blanket Levi had given her close about her. She was safe for the night, if the men had told the truth and didn't want her.

But the immensity of being all alone in America lay heavily upon her. She had no concept of the risks and perils she had fallen into. She must be very careful. The captain of the ship that had transported her over the ocean would surely be searching for her. And what of the pimps and the tongs Errin had said were on the streets and would take her captive and make her a slave?

How was she to survive in this foreign land of America where danger seemed to be everywhere? How could she become rich when just staying alive and free might not be possible? She had spoken so bravely to the two men, so why was she now trembling?

Chapter 19

"What should we do with Chun?" Levi asked. "Do you think it's safe for her to be seen on the street?"

"The first thing you should do is take the China girl to bed and put a smile on her face," Errin said.

"Her name's Chun, and don't talk about her that way," Levi retorted.

The two men were in their office, with Errin by the door and ready to leave and Levi behind his desk covered with rosters of men and invoices.

"Well, she hasn't smiled even once that I ever saw," Errin said, amused at Levi's reply. He hadn't been joking with his suggestion. He had observed how the China girl often looked at Levi, her dark eyes lingering lovingly upon him. Levi had seemed embarrassed by her obvious interest. If Levi ever overcame his bashfulness, then perhaps Chun would not be leaving their house.

"She's just a girl, Levi, prettier than most, but still just a girl and wanting some man to show he cares about her. In this case that's you. She wants that more than anything else right now, certainly more than you putting her someplace else to live."

"You're wrong, she just feels grateful toward me. I don't want to take advantage of her. I'll find a proper place for her and that'll end it."

"She's feeling more than grateful."

"I don't see it, so that must make me a fool."

"No partner of mine could be a fool. But the next time you're alone with her, reach out for her and see what she does."

"I'll not do that. Just stay out of my private business."

"All right." Errin saw Levi was taking his remarks in the wrong way. Not wanting to argue with his comrade, he left the office. He mounted the black horse and reined it off along the street.

He checked on half-a-dozen jobs that were in progress, and collected on a completed contract, that of painting a Union warship, a steam frigate. He cashed the government bank draft and withdrew additional money so he would have funds to make the weekly payroll of his men. He stored the funds in one of the saddlebags on the horse.

The neighborhood of smaller homes fell behind as Errin climbed the horse up Market Street. Near the top of the broad hill, he came to an area of handsome two- and three-story residences, both brick and frame. Many of the homes were quite old and, with their large fenced yards, resembled the country homes of the rich outside London. He stopped at times to view the well-tended yards with their spacious expanses of grass, neatly trimmed hedges, and large swathes of brilliantly blooming flowers. The delightful fragrance of the flowers wafted to him on the slow wind.

The people of those grand homes lived in luxury. He could also have such a life for he was no longer a prisoner in chains. He was free and was growing wealthy. With the profit from Levi's and his business and the reward paid by Wells Fargo, he and Levi had now accumulated a substantial amount of money.

The sense of good fortune and well-being came from having returned the stolen gold to Wells Fargo and receiving the unexpected reward for his honesty. As a highwayman in England, the taking of other men's valuables had not bothered him. Here in America, that way was forsaken and never again would he surrender to the temptation of pulling his pistol to steal another man's money.

A carriage driven by a Chinaman outfitted in maroon livery and perched on a seat in front, went by. A pretty young woman in a full-length dress of a bright yellow color sat in the passenger seat. A man on horseback rode beside the buggy. An ugly brown bulldog with a huge head trailed at the horse's heels.

The woman looked at Errin as she passed him. He smiled at her and touched the brim of his hat in greeting. She smiled back at him, her rouged lips curving up in a very friendly way.

The rider saw the woman's flirtatious response and he scowled at Errin. He looked down at his bulldog, then back at Errin in a belligerent and calculating manner.

Errin shook his head in the negative and moved the flap of his jacket aside to show the pistol in a shoulder holster. The man didn't seemed impressed by the gun. Errin grinned with an expression daring him to loose his animal. The man rode on with no word to his bulldog.

The women are friendly and the men are not, thought Errin. I must remember that.

Half a mile further along, the hill became less steep with large trees widely scattered about. There were only a few houses, most appearing quite old, and separated from each other by broad open areas of two to several acres. Beneath one of the trees, several vehicles were parked and a score of men had gathered.

Errin brought his horse to the edge of the crowd, and from his saddle, looked over the heads of the men to see what drew their interest. A low wooden platform was being removed from the rear of one of the carriages by a portly, gray-headed man. He placed the platform on the ground and stepped upon it.

"Gentlemen," the man called, "may I please have your attention. As most of you know, I am Albert Talbot, broker and auctioneer. I have been commissioned by Señorita Beremendes to sell three acres of her land in one acre parcels. You now stand on one of those parcels. They have been surveyed and the corners well marked. If you look around you can see those markers.'' Talbot pointed at each of the four corner stakes.

"This is a lovely location for a home. It overlooks the city and our beautiful San Francisco Bay. The land is free and clear of any mortgage. A warranty deed shall be issued to the fortunate high bidder.''

Errin dismounted as Talbot went on with his introductory spiel for the auction. He moved to stand beside an elderly gentleman.

"What is an acre of land worth here on the hill top?'' Errin asked the man.

"Fifteen hundred dollars to two thousand,'' the man replied. He smiled wryly. "But the Beremendes woman won't get half what its true value is.'' He gestured at a woman and an old Mexican man sitting in a buggy nearby and watching the proceedings. "That's Celeste Beremendes there.''

The woman wore a black flowing dress with many pleats. A matching black mantilla was upon her dark hair. She was leisurely fanning herself with a small fan. Errin judged her young, but could not make out her features because the fluttering fan obscured his view.

"Why won't the land bring the proper price?'' Errin asked.

The man fastened his old eyes upon Errin. "You're new in San Francisco?''

"Yes. I arrived not long ago.''

"Well I've been here several years and have seen this sort of thing before.''

"What about the land value?''

"There'll be few bids by white men for Mexican property. Just three or four to make it look legal. The Mexicans lost the war of '47 and many Americans think all the land claimed by Mexicans should belong to Americans. You can bet that a scheme has been hatched to steal these three acres of prime land from the Beremendes woman.''

"So the bidding is rigged,'' Errin said, evaluating what the information might mean to him. He had every intention of remaining in San Francisco and someday would want a home. This location was indeed a choice site with the big trees and the view to the east at the beautiful bay and beyond that the coast mountains.

"I would like to own this land," Errin said.

"I'd like to have a home up here myself. This acre of land is one of the most desirable properties in all the city. It's been in the Beremendes family for a hundred years. I imagine she hates selling it."

The auctioneer called out, "The bidding shall start at four hundred dollars. Bids then shall increase in one-hundred-dollar increments. Now who'll bid first?"

"I think I'll bid," Errin said.

"Then watch yourself," the old man said.

"Why?"

"You'll find out."

Celeste watched the Americans and hoped the auction went well with spirited bidding. Her attorney had examined previous sales in the area and told her to expect some amount near seven thousand dollars for the three parcels. It was a sad thing to sell part of the original homesite, but she had no choice. She would sacrifice these acres to save the *rancho.*

Dokken was present and talking with another man. *Madre de Dios,* how she hated the man. What was he doing here? Surely he would not buy her property and thus put money into her hands with which to fight him.

"I bid four hundred dollars," a man shouted.

"Five," a second called.

"Six hundred," Dokken called.

Celeste was surprised that Dokken had bid. What was his scheme? She knew he must have one. She waited for the next bid.

The auctioneer called to the group of men. "Come, come, gentlemen, the land is worth several times six hundred dollars. What am I bid?"

He stomped his foot upon his platform. "I have six hundred. Who'll make it seven hundred?"

The crowd of men remained silent. A few lowered their heads and stared at the ground. Dokken slowly began to smile.

"Who'll bid seven hundred?" the auctioneer repeated in a wheedling tone.

Celeste felt her heart hammering in her bosom. The land was valuable and the Americans must see that and bid for it. What was wrong with them? Then her blood ran cold as she realized what was happening. The Americans had banded together against her and were about to steal her land.

"I bid a thousand dollars," Errin called. Damn the crooked band of men. He took a step forward and held up his hand to identify himself to the auctioneer.

Talbot smiled. "I have a thousand dollars. Who'll make it eleven hundred?"

Dokken twisted quickly to look at Errin. An expression of surprise, that swiftly changed to anger, washed across his face. He glanced at a big, blond-headed man near the edge of the gathering, and nodded.

Dokken turned back to the auctioneer. "I bid eleven hundred."

"Twelve." Errin's voice was loud and firm. He had seen the bidder's signal to the other man.

"Thirteen hundred," Dokken said.

"Fourteen hundred." As Errin spoke, the blond man came up on his left side. The man jostled Errin with his shoulder.

Errin stepped away. The man immediately moved to stand with his shoulder touching Errin's.

Dokken bid again. Errin raised it by a hundred dollars.

"Damn, you, stop crowding me," the blond man snarled. He jabbed Errin roughly in the ribs with his elbow.

Errin's anger came so hot it seemed to burn him. The man had deliberately elbowed him. Errin knew the game was to force him out of the bidding, and if he did not stop competing, this man near him would start a fight.

Errin folded his fist into a bony hammer. The fight must be over quickly. He whirled around and rammed his fist into the man's stomach. The man folded over Errin's driving fist, and his breath left him with an explosion of air. Errin struck a savage blow to the back of the man's neck. The man crashed face down unconscious on the ground.

Errin stalked toward Dokken. He stopped barely two paces away. "I know that man was yours. He wasn't much of a fighter. Now let's you and me finish this game you've started."

Dokken began to slide his hand toward the pistol inside his jacket, but then halted. The men around him knew he was challenging the Beremendeses in court for the big Mexican Land Grant on Mount Mocho. They would prefer that he win, rather than the Mexican woman. That was the reason they had made only token bids against him. However the presence of this well-dressed stranger and the ease with which he had taken Dokken's man out, may have destroyed the clannish agreement the Americans had made against the Mexican. Most likely they would not back Dokken in a fight with another American.

"He isn't mine," Dokken said.

"That's damn odd, for he was trying to stop me from bidding against you so you could steal the lady's land."

"I told you he isn't my man. I don't know him."

Errin knew the man was lying, but it was time to let the matter end. He called out to the auctioneer. "Let the bidding start again. I bid two thousand dollars."

"Make him show his money," Dokken said to the auctioneer. "He's got to have half the amount he bids."

"Mr. Dokken is correct," the auctioneer said. "Let me see your money."

Errin went to his horse and took a sheaf of bills from the saddlebag. He returned to Talbot and held the money out to him. "There's enough here to pay cash for half, and I can have the other half soon as I get to the bank. Now, Dokken, show us your money."

"I'm not bidding any more," Dokken growled.

Errin laughed at the hostility in the man. He turned to Talbot. "Announce my bid and see if I have any competition."

"I have a bid of two thousand dollars. Do I hear twenty-one hundred dollars?" The auctioneer ran his gaze over the gathering of men. No voice rose to bid.

"Going once for two thousand dollars. Going twice. Three

times. Sold. The land is yours, young fellow. Step forward and give me your name.''

"Now the rest of you, don't go away. There are two more excellent one-acre tracts of land to be sold. The bidding for them will commence in a moment.''

Errin glanced at the Mexican woman as he gave his name to Talbot. She was watching him steadily over the top of her now motionless fan. All he could see were her large brown eyes.

He counted out a thousand dollars and handed it to Talbot, who in turn gave him a receipt for the money. "Mr. Scanlan, a deed will be prepared shortly and delivered to you,'' Talbot said.

Errin turned from the auctioneer and walked to the woman in the carriage. He stopped and looked at her steadily, and was pleased when she lowered her fan to look directly at him. He was struck by the intelligence that shone in her dark eyes, and the penetrating intensity with which she evaluated him. Then she smiled and a surge of pleasure washed over Errin. With her fine, smooth skin tanned by the sun, and the exquisitely sculptured planes and curves of her brow and cheeks and delicate nose and mouth, the Almighty had fashioned an altogether beautiful face.

"Is the price satisfactory?'' Errin asked. "If not, then I'm willing to discuss what you consider is fair.''

"Your bid is acceptable,'' Celeste replied.

"Then I'm pleased.'' He bowed to the woman. Perhaps it was a foolish gesture, but one that seemed proper at that moment. She acknowledged his bow by inclining her head, and her eyes widening a little in surprise.

Errin went to his horse and mounted. He sat astride the animal until he heard active bidding from several of the men present. They had obviously decided not to allow Dokken to steal the land. Errin made one last pleasant appraisal of the woman as he left.

Chapter 20

Celeste rode out of the burning sun with Ignacio and into the shade of the oak tree. She dismounted from her mare and took down the damp water gourd from where it hung on a limb. She drank deeply of the cool water as she surveyed her crew of men and mules working the rich bottom land of the San Joaquin Valley.

Dust rose in dense clouds from several moving machines. Four metal scrapers pulled by teams of mules were scooping up the higher ridges of dirt and depositing it into low places. Other mule teams were pulling plows. Iron-spiked harrows were dragged to break up the clods left by the plows. Men with axes were chopping brush.

The hired men had been working for five days. If she could keep them at the task until the middle of November, more than a thousand acres would be ready for planting in time to catch the winter rains to germinate the seed wheat. Then in the early summer, she would harvest her first golden crop of grain. The *rancho* could yet be saved.

She thought of the man who had fought Dokken's accomplice and bought the first parcel of land at the auction. That act of his had started the bidding by others and provided her with money to pay the workers. "Thank you, Errin Scanlan," she said to the wind. She wondered if the deed she had signed to the land had yet been delivered to him.

"Ignacio, come with me," Celeste ordered brusquely. "We're going to San Francisco."

Ignacio hurried toward his mistress. Never before had she spoken in such a tone to him. He knew why she was so abrupt, and he was afraid for her.

Celeste pulled herself astride the mare with one strong yank of her arms. Without waiting for Ignacio, she spurred the mare and sent her racing up the mountain road to the *hacienda*.

Celeste bathed in the cool water in the big tub in the bathhouse. She moved slowly, leisurely. This might be the last time she would ever see the old, the dear familiar things she had grown up with. She traced the herringbone patterns of the poles supporting the roof. She shifted her gaze to look through the open window high on the outside wall. On a ledge under the eave of the roof was a tiny wren's nest made of grass and the soft fuzz of seed heads. The three eggs had hatched and the heads of the infants turned this way and that, the liquid brown eyes watching for the mother bird to return. The wrens had built a nest in that very spot every year for as long as she could remember. How many generations of birds had that been?

She tried not to think of what she planned to do. Instead she concentrated on the young wrens in their cozy nest. They were safe there. Yet in a few days, the mother would push them out from the nest, out from under the protective eave of the house and into the world. There the wrens would kill to survive.

Celeste must also kill or she would lose everything. Dokken would not give up simply because she now had some money. No, he would increase his efforts, choosing his time to strike. She was so awfully vulnerable. And her property even more so. She knew of a man who had burned his enemy's fields of wheat just as it became ripe but before it had been harvested. Dokken could do the same, wait, allowing her to expend her money and then destroy her crop, as easily as dropping a match.

She began to move more purposefully. She completed her bath, put on a robe and went into the main house.

"Elosia, bring your scissors. My hair must be cut short."

The old woman came with her sewing basket. "You should not fight that man," she said. "You'll be killed."

"Don't say that. Have faith in me."

Tears came into Elosia's eyes. "Celeste, I love you and don't want you hurt."

Celeste put her arms around the old woman. "I know you do. But I must keep my oath to Ernesto. It is even more than that. This man Dokken will destroy us unless I can stop him. Now cut my hair quite short."

Elosia wiped at her tears. She opened her sewing basket and took out her scissors.

"Oh, how I hate to do this," Elosia said, as a long strand of hair black as a slice of midnight fell to the floor.

An hour later Celeste stood in front of her mirror. She had bound her breasts tightly to her body with a broad strip of cloth. Then she had dressed in the clothing of a *caballero*, gray trousers, shirt and vest. The vest was decorated with heavy silver stitching along the front. She left it unbuttoned to hide the swell of her bosom that still showed even with the tight binding. A gray *sombrero* with a flat crown sat squarely upon her head. Heeled boots were on her feet.

She stared into the mirror and evaluated herself from several angles. She looked like a very young man. At least she hoped she would be taken for one.

Ernesto's Colt revolver was belted around her lean waist. She slid the black iron weapon from the holster. She had continued to practice with it every day and it felt light and comfortable in her hand. She extended the gun and sighted down the barrel. The weapon was rock steady.

With a hiss of steel on leather, the Colt slipped back into the holster. In San Francisco, she would carry the pistol in her belt under her vest where it would not be so conspicuous.

Celeste was ready to find Dokken and challenge him to a duel. She had seen how easily he had beaten Ernesto. Could she aim her weapon and shoot Dokken before he killed her?

* * *

Levi and Errin raised their mugs of beer, grinned at each other across the table, and took long pulls of the cold brews.

"Damn good of you Americans to bring ice from Alaska just to cool my beer," Errin said.

"What do you mean, you Americans?" Levi replied. "I thought you were an American now."

"I guess I really am. And I like my beer cold."

They sat in the Miner's Billiard Palace, a place where the more wealthy Americans of the City came to shoot billiards, drink and talk business. The large hall was full of the click of ivory balls at a dozen tables, and the drone of voices from half a hundred men seated at tables and standing at the bar.

Levi caught the eye of the bartender. He held up his empty mug and two fingers.

"Damn fine celebration," Errin said.

"That last group of men you signed up gives us two hundred and sixty working for us. We're on the way to getting rich."

"The men who can speak English keep quitting us and taking off on their own once they get to know the city."

"There's still plenty of men who can't speak English, and also new men coming off the ships," Levi said. "And the blacks don't leave us. We've got a permanent business going."

The bartender sat two beers on the table, took Levi's money and left.

Levi sat facing the entrance. As he lifted his drink, he saw a slender, young Mexican dressed in gray clothing come into the billiard hall. The Mexican halted just inside the door and his black eyes swept the patrons.

"Errin, look, it's one of those Mexican cowboys," Levi said. "You don't see many of them around."

Errin turned. "Not just a cowboy. Looks more like one of the high-born Mexicans. Strange he's in a place like the Miner's Billiard Palace."

They watched the *caballero* examine the men standing and drinking at the long bar. He shifted his scrutiny to the players at the billiard tables along the opposite wall. Then he scanned the men seated at the tables in the center of the hall.

"The fellow's looking for somebody," Errin said.

More and more of the men in the hall noted the presence of the Mexican and conversations began to die.

The Mexican ignored the stares. He thrust his head forward in a defiant attitude and his jaw tightened. With a slight swagger, he moved away from the entrance and deeper into the hall for a closer look at the many patrons, some of whom had their backs to him.

Errin heard the thud of the Mexican's boots as he drew nearer. The flaps of his vest were unbuttoned and the butt of a revolver was visible stuck under the belt of his trousers. The dark eyes of the fellow caught Errin's, and held them for a moment before ranging on. Errin thought the eyes were familiar, but how could that be?

As the Mexican went past, Errin's pulse jumped with a sudden realization. The Mexican was a female and he was certain of that. Errin had been forced to live in close confinement with male convicts in the barracks and on the floating prison hulks of Australia for years and he knew men's odors, how they moved, their facial characteristics, expressions. More than that, more than thought and logic, he could sense this person's inner difference, the female aura. The ancient instinct of the male for the female could not be deceived by the man's garb she wore.

"It's a woman," Errin whispered.

"What?" Levi asked. "A woman?"

Errin twisted in his chair and watched the woman walk on, her back straight and head swinging to see the face of each man she passed. She was indeed searching for someone. He would be an enemy for why else would that grim expression be on her face and the pistol in her belt.

Celeste stopped abruptly, every strand of her senses focused upon one of the men seated at a table near the rear wall. Her hand went into the front of her vest. She drew her pistol, cocked it as it swung down to point at the floor.

She placed her feet firmly and lowering her voice from its natural pitch, called out sharply. "Dokken, you bastard, stand up."

The room fell silent at the challenging command. Then there was a scrape of chairs and feet as everyone not already watching, turned to look at the youthful Mexican holding a pistol.

Dokken looked over his shoulder and saw the Mexican. A surprised expression ran over his face, then swiftly vanished. He pushed back from the table and rose to his feet.

His eyes dropped to the pistol in Celeste's hand, and then lifted to bore directly into her. He began to smile thin-lipped.

"Those are strong words coming from a Mexican, and a young one," Dokken said. "Who the hell are you and what do you want?"

"I'm Carlos Beremendes from Santa Fe. You killed my cousin Ernesto. Now I've come to kill you."

Dokken laughed. "No kid such as you could kill me. Now go away before I get mad and shoot you."

As Celeste looked into the confident eyes of the killer, she had her first glimpse of real fear, felt its cold, numbing fingers paralyzing her brain. The danger was terrible, and absolute. And she had sought it out.

Afraid or not, she must not fail to carry out her oath to Ernesto. She let her hot hate boil up, using it to combat her fear.

"You're a coward," Celeste said. "If not, then you will fight me."

Errin watched in awe at the woman's unexpected bravery in challenging the man to fight her. But how did she expect to beat a man who must be an expert with a gun for he had killed her cousin.

"Suppose I won't fight you?" Dokken suggested with mock gravity.

Celeste had not anticipated that her challenge might not be accepted. Dokken must be made to fight her. "Then I'll shoot you where you stand," she said.

"You leave me no choice then." Dokken seemed pleased at Celeste's answer. "I must protect myself."

He gestured at her pistol. "How do you propose we fight?"

She had thought of that and knew what she must say. "We will stand at opposite ends of the room. Someone will give the signal to shoot." Celeste's eyes became hooded, implacable. "Then I will kill you."

"You can't beat me," Dokken said.

"Yes I can," Celeste stated simply. She began to back away from her foe.

The two men at Dokken's table quickly stood up and fanned out, one going a few steps left and the other to the right.

Errin studied the woman's finely chiseled features, that now rigid with determination, seemed made of stone. God! How he admired her. But she could soon be dead. He rose to his feet and shoved his hand inside his jacket and gripped his Colt.

Catching movement in the periphery of her vision, Celeste turned quickly toward Errin. She tried to read the man's intent in his cold gray eyes.

"I'll see that none of Dokken's friends tries to take a part in this," Errin said to the unasked question.

Celeste nodded, the barest tilt of her head. The thought that someone might aid Dokken had entered her calculations but she had not arrived at a solution to the problem. She had an answer now. She once again riveted her attention on her enemy and resumed backing up.

Celeste stopped a step from the front wall of the billiard hall. She pivoted a quarter turn to put the thin side of her body toward Dokken. She reseated the pistol in her hand. Her thumb checked the cock of the hammer. She held the weapon pointing at the floor.

A tremble started in the core of her. Death from a bullet through the heart, the same as Ernesto, could be only a few seconds away. She caught the tremble, stifled it before it could reach her gun hand. Her shot must go true to the mark.

Dokken took off his coat and tossed it with a nonchalant air onto the table beside him. He drew his pistol from a shoulder holster, rotated the cylinders examining the firing caps. The gun was lowered to hang beside his leg.

Dokken called out across the billiard hall in a loud voice. "All of you heard this Mexican threaten to kill me. Don't forget that." He turned to the bartender. "Give the signal to fire. Make it loud and clear."

"I don't want that job," the bartender replied.

"Do it!" Dokken ordered harshly.

"All right then," the bartender said hastily. He looked at Celeste. "Both of you stand ready."

Celeste's eyes were locked on Dokken as she listened intently for the bartender's signal to shoot. Was she truly swift enough to beat Dokken, to kill him before he could kill her? *Madre de Dios, ayúdame.* Mother of God, help me.

"Fire!" cried the bartender and slapped the bar with the flat of his hand.

Celeste snapped up her pistol. Shoot! Shoot! Don't hesitate. She pressed the trigger.

A thunderbolt exploded in her chest. The intensity of the pain seemed to fry her mind. She was hurled backward. Oh God! Dokken had shot her.

As Celeste fell, she saw Dokken standing with a smoking gun. Had her gun not fired? What had gone wrong? She crashed against the wall.

She stiffened her legs to stay erect. She tried to aim her pistol to shoot. Her arm strained, but the gun weighed a ton and would not hold steady. She crumpled, sliding down the wall to lie on the floor.

Dokken must not be allowed to live. Celeste struggled to rise, her body quivering with the effort. She only managed to turn her face toward her enemy. Her hate-filled eyes cut across the room.

Errin moved quickly toward the woman. He was angry at her. When the bartender had shouted his command to fire, she had lifted her pistol with amazing swiftness, beating Dokken to the shooting position. But then she had paused, a tiny length of time before she fired. Dokken's pistol had exploded in that brief delay. Damn her, why start a fight unless you were going to kill. But she had grand courage.

He knelt beside the woman. Her eyes were open and staring, her breathing shallow. Gently he rolled her from her side to her back.

She was much thinner than he had first thought. The loosely fitting shirt and the open flaps of the vest had given her a fuller appearance. He grabbed the bloody shirt and ripped it open, popping the buttons.

The woman's breasts were tightly bound to her chest with a band of cloth. Immediately below that was a ragged wound where Dokken's bullet had skittered across her ribs, tearing the flesh open in a long, deep groove. Blood flowed in a steady stream.

The woman's eyes, black pools of pain, shifted to Errin. She blinked, focusing. "Errin Scanlan?"

"Yes." He understood how she knew his name, for this was Celeste Beremendes.

"I failed and he's still alive," Celeste said over the searing pain in her chest.

"You shot too late. His bullet hit you and made you miss."

Celeste was quiet for a short moment, then her hand rose to weakly clasp Errin's. "Please don't let me die in here. Carry me outside."

"All right. But I don't think you'll die. Levi, get her pistol." Errin tenderly gathered Celeste up in his arms.

Celeste turned her head back to look at Dokken smiling a small, deadly smile at her. Then she groaned as a drum began to beat inside her temples, and it grew louder, the percussion beats jarring and thunderous. Images went out of focus. The world spun around her. Total darkness engulfed her.

Errin cast one last look around the Miner's Billiard Palace and then, followed by Levi, carried Celeste outside.

"Señorita Beremendes!" Ignacio cried, springing down from the buggy parked on the edge of the street. He hurried toward Errin. "Is she dead?" he fearfully asked.

Errin recognized the man as being with the Beremendes

woman at the auction. "No, but she's badly wounded. Why in hell was she fighting Dokken? Where's her menfolk?"

"She has no men left in her family."

Errin looked down at Celeste. "Then I see why she tried to do it herself. Where's the nearest doctor?"

"There's a medico a few blocks from here," Ignacio replied, pointing up the street. "Lay her on the seat and I'll drive her there."

"You drive, and I'll hold her," Errin said. He stepped up in the buggy and sat down. He cradled Celeste against his chest and bent to listen to her breathing. It was still shallow, but steady. He had helped her in the sale of her land, and now he had participated in the duel by offering his aid to prevent Dokken's cohorts from taking up the fight. Now Errin felt responsible, no more than that, protective of the gravely wounded and unconscious young Mexican woman.

Ignacio lashed the team of horses, and the buggy sped along the street. Four blocks fell away behind and he pulled the horse to a halt in front of a two-story house. "El Medico Carrington has his office here," Ignacio said.

Errin stepped down from the vehicle and carrying Celeste, followed Ignacio up the walk to the house. As the door of the doctor's office opened, a bell tinkled somewhere deeper in the house. Half a minute later, a small, white-headed man came in the outer office.

The doctor took one short glance at Celeste's bloody body in Errin's arms. "Follow me," he directed, and led back through the door by which he had entered.

"Place him there," the doctor said, gesturing to an operating table. "We must stop the bleeding."

"He's a she," Errin said as he carefully lay Celeste down. He straightened her body and stepped back.

"How long ago did this happen?" asked Dr. Carrington. He took hold of Celeste's wrist and began to count her pulse.

"Less than ten minutes," Errin replied.

"It's good that you brought her straight here." He began to probe at the wound on Celeste's chest. "Why is her breast bound?" Without waiting for an answer, he continued to speak.

"There's no broken ribs, but some are chipped. I'll take out the bone fragments and cleanse the wound. It'll require several stitches to close it."

Carrington looked at Errin and Ignacio. "You two wait outside. You're of no use to her, or to me."

"Will she be all right?" Errin asked.

"She's young and seems in remarkable physical condition. It's a serious wound, but I believe she'll be well in a few days. The flesh has been badly torn, and she'll have a scar. But it'll only show to her lover."

Chapter 21

Celeste struggled mightily to pull herself from the cold pit of unconsciousness. Her head was full of a loud roaring and all was darkness around her except for a tiny glimmer of light faint and far away. The light beckoned, drawing her, and it radiated a frail but wonderful warmth. She strained, clawing her way in the direction of the only source of light in all the black universe.

For a span of time that seemed immensely long, she made almost no progress. Then her ascent abruptly increased and she was hurled forward. She burst into the light, suddenly conscious and all her senses strumming with fear. Dokken stood on the far side of the room wherein she lay. He held a smoking pistol and smiled a deadly smile at her.

Celeste's hand jumped to her waist and grabbed for the pistol that should be in her belt. The sudden lifting of her arm wrenched at the bullet-torn muscles of the wound in her chest. She cried out at the piercing stab of pain.

The pain swept Dokken from her vision. He was not there by the wall after all. The man had been conjured up from her memory of the last terrible sight she had before falling unconscious. She was alone and lying on her own feather-tick bed with her old and familiar belongings about her. Oh, how grand to be alive and safely home.

Her servant Elosia hurried in through the open door of the bedroom. To Celeste's surprise, Errin Scanlan came swiftly behind Elosia. She was astonished at the worry so evident on his face. Her heart lifted at his presence.

"We are here, Celeste," Elosia said reassuringly.

"How do you feel?" Errin asked, his eyes intense and questioning.

"I failed to kill Dokken," Celeste said dejectedly and looking up at Errin. Her throat was dry and raspy. "I didn't keep my promise to Ernesto."

"It's not an easy thing to kill a man," Errin said. "You hesitated a fraction of a second to shoot."

"And he shot me while I wasted time." She touched the bandage on her chest. "My ribs ache. How badly am I injured?"

"You will live," Errin said with a glad voice. "But the doctor said you must take it easy for a few days."

He seems genuinely pleased that I'm not badly hurt, Celeste thought. She owed him for his offer in the billiard parlor to keep Dokken's cohorts from helping him in the duel. After the shooting, she had passed out, and he must have carried her outside and then taken her to a doctor and following that brought her home.

Celeste held out her hand. "May I properly introduce myself? I'm Celeste Beremendes."

Errin stepped close to the bed and clasped the extended hand. "And you know I'm Errin Scanlan."

Celeste gripped Errin's hand. "Yes I know, and I'm very fortunate you were there when I foolishly challenged Dokken."

"It seems to me you had reason enough to try to shoot him. Elosia told me about your oath to your brother."

"Dokken killed him," Celeste said, feeling the raw sense of loss.

"I never had a brother," Errin said. "But it must be awful to lose one."

He felt the fine bones of Celeste's hand inside its covering of soft flesh and skin. Even with the serious wound she had received, her handshake was firm. That was not unexpected for he knew she was strong from the ease with which she had lifted her pistol in the duel. He sensed the instinct for survival she possessed, the will to do what must be done to face a dangerous world, one often ruled by uncaring fate. Though the fact that she had not killed greatly bothered her, that failure somehow pleased him.

He continued to hold Celeste's hand and stare down marveling at her beauty. He saw a hint of a smile as if she had some secret and pleasant thought.

Celeste make a slight tug to withdraw her hand from his. However he retained his hold on the warm hand. The pleasure of touching her was too great to surrender it so soon.

Celeste relented and allowed her hand to remain in Errin's. "How long have I been unconscious?" she asked.

"Through the night and now it is almost noon."

The raspiness had left Celeste's voice and the tone of her words was gentle, pleasant as little tinkling bells. He suppressed the sudden urge to grab her up and hug her to him. Never had he felt such a yearning for a woman. He saw Celeste's full lips curve upward in a full smile. Had she read his thoughts? He hoped she had.

Celeste studied the man who had appeared so unexpectedly in her life. He was an explosive man quick to anger and violence, that she knew. There was no violence in him now as he gazed down at her. There was only a man's look at a woman so obvious in his gray eyes. His desire for her was evident in every fiber of him.

"Who are you, Errin?"

"An Englishman who has come a very long distance. Perhaps a man who has found what he has always wanted, but did not really know what that was until now."

"And what do you want?" Celeste asked. Surely it could not be what he implied, still it would be interesting to hear the answer.

Errin smiled at Celeste's direct question. He stared into the woman's eyes, beautiful dark pools full of the promise of the pleasures she could give a man. "Some day I may tell you," he said.

Celeste laughed outright. "All right. But there's something that can't wait, and that's my deepest thanks for bidding on my land at the auction. Those men surely intended to cheat me on the price. Then you helped me at the duel with Dokken. I might have died in that billiard parlor for I had no friends there. Except as it turned out, for you."

Errin looked at Celeste in a reflective way then added, "Our fates do seem to be tied together."

"Do you believe in fate?"

"Any man who has been where I have been, and now lucky enough to be where I am now, can't deny the fact that it plays a big part in every man's life." Surely my discovery of you must be fate.

"You must tell me of the places you have been and of the things you have done."

Errin released Celeste's hand and stepped back. She saw the wave of remembrance that threw a troubled shadow over his face. What horrible places had he been?

"Who taught you how to use a pistol?" Errin asked.

"The best *pistolero* in all California." She knew he had deliberately changed the subject.

Elosia spoke. *"Señorita,* are you hungry? I have food ready to serve."

"I'm more thirsty. Please, bring me a glass of water. I will eat in a little while."

"Yes, *señorita,"* Elosia said and left.

"I should be going," Errin said. "But may I come again this evening? Maybe we could have dinner together at dark. That is if you feel well enough."

"Please do come. I'm feeling better every minute." And I believe much of the reason is because of you. "Is there anything special you would like to eat? Elosia is an excellent cook."

"You choose for us. I like all kinds of food."

"Very well."

Errin looked steadily at Celeste for a moment feeling reluctant to leave, then he turned and walked from the room.

He moved thoughtfully through the house with its pegged wooden floor. The house and furnishing were very old with everything about it solid and comfortable. Celeste had grown up here, Elosia had told him, and at a *rancho* on Mount Mocho. Her family must have been wealthy at one time, before the Americans conquered California.

He opened the front door and stepped out onto the covered stoop of the house. A cold, drizzly rain fell, blowing in long, slanting streamers on a stiff wind. The huge trees and the shrubbery in the yard were wet and dripping, and the lane leading out to the street ran with water.

Errin moved out from the protection of the stoop. The day was wet and dismal. Still he began to hum happily to himself as he contemplated the evening with the lovely Celeste. He walked through the rain in the direction of his office.

Errin had crossed Sansome and Battery Streets and was within half a block of his office when he saw George Louden stop his buggy opposite the Scanlan and Coffin office. The man sat under the waterproof top of the vehicle and looked at the entryway for half a minute. Then he stepped down and hurried across the rainy sidewalk and into the building. Errin continued on along the street.

Levi and Louden were seated and talking when Errin pushed open the door of the office and entered. Both turned to look at him.

"Errin, you're wet and the rain's cold," Levi said. "Why didn't you catch a hackney?"

"I felt like walking," Errin replied as he shook his hat to remove part of the water it had soaked up. "And the rain's not that cold."

He perched on the corner of Levi's desk and faced the Wells Fargo man. "Hello, Mr. Louden," he said.

"Hello, Errin."

"What brings you out on a day like this?" Errin asked.

Louden regarded Errin with a kindly air. "I consider you and Levi my friends. I was just about to tell Levi something the Pinkerton detectives that I hire discovered and reported to me."

"Is it about our business?" Errin asked.

"No, something entirely different. I believe you two fellows are in danger if what I'm thinking is correct." He paused and looked from Errin to Levi. "My detectives heard that a Chinese girl escaped from her owners while she was being transported across town. This happened a few nights ago. Two young white men, one speaking with an English accent, helped her. The story goes that these two men beat the hell out of the men chasing her and took the girl off with them. From the description the men gave, it fits you two." Louden ceased speaking and watched the faces of the two young men.

"What's so bad about helping a girl to escape from her captors?" Levi asked.

"Levi's not saying it was us," Errin said quickly. "That description could fit any number of men." Levi should not be so quick to talk. Not all men who said they were friends truly were, though he believed Louden was. Yet it was Levi's openess and honesty that made him so likable, and so valuable as a partner.

"Yes, it could be two other men." Louden was satisfied Levi and Errin were the ones. "But whoever they are, they're in danger. A reward of a thousand dollars has been posted by the owner of the girl for the identification of those two young men. And further, the girl was one of those brought from China for Scom Lip the leader of the Chee Kong Tong. He has posted a reward for her on several bulletin boards scattered around Chinatown. She's marked for death and it is stated publicly. Professional assassins, both Americans and Chinese are searching for her to take her head. All the tongs want her killed as an example to the many hundreds, probably thousands, of other girls held in bondage in the city. Those poor creatures must be kept frightened nearly to death to prevent them from running away."

"It's not right that young girls should be treated like that, bought and sold like pieces of furniture for a man's use," Levi said.

"I couldn't agree more. But whoever has her should know that a pretty Chinese girl can't be hidden for long in this city with all its informants."

"Thanks for telling us about the girl and the rewards," Errin said.

"It's an interesting event," Louden said. "However unless one is directly involved with the Chinese girl's escape, there are more important matters happening in our growing city. If you are to succeed in your new business, then you must know as much as possible about what is going on in the mayor's office, the actions of the tongs, and the protective associations."

"How do we do that?" Levi asked.

"We find men within those camps who can be bought and pay them very well to keep us informed," Errin answered. "And we make friends among the important men who really run the city, like Mr. Louden."

"Well I don't know how important I am," Louden said. The two fellows might make their business survive and grow. Levi was young and inexperienced. Errin, on the other hand, was quick to grasp the crux of a situation and to act. Louden judged Errin would be a dangerous enemy to anyone who threatened them.

"Both of you heed what I've told you and be on your guard," Louden said.

"We will," Levi replied.

"So long," Louden said and climbed to his feet.

Errin shook Louden's hand. "Thanks for taking an interest in us," he said sincerely, his eyes meeting Louden's with understanding.

Errin waited for Louden to be well clear of the office and then spoke to Levi. "Chun can't stay at our house now that our descriptions are out."

"I know. You warned me she would cause trouble for us."

"She could get you killed."

"I'll not throw her out on the street, regardless of the danger to me. Really to both of us."

"I'm not saying you should, Levi. But you've only known her for a few days and she can't mean that much to you."

"Well she does. Hasn't any girl ever got to you in just a short time?"

Errin thought of the lovely Celeste and his feeling for her and understood Levi's emotions. "If you're going to keep her, then find a safe place to hide her, or send her out of the city. For all our sakes, don't let anyone see her. And start wearing a gun at all times."

"All right." Levi felt the revulsion rise in him at the thought of fighting and killing. The specter of the battle at Boatswain Swamp came full blown to him. He could again see the faces of the charging men, and them falling into the muddy water of the swamp at the crack of his rifle. His lungs began to burn as if he was again breathing the acrid smoke of burnt gunpowder as he had those weeks ago during the battle.

But he would fight and kill again if it became necessary to keep Chun safe.

"It's Dokken," Errin growled to Levi and stopped dead on the sidewalk.

The two men were walking to their rented house after meeting with Louden. Dokken had just emerged from the entrance of the bank on Stockton Street. He stood under the awning of the bank out of the drizzling rain.

"He hasn't seen us yet," Levi said and halted at Errin's side. "He'll be mad at you for helping that Mexican woman and may want to fight."

"I hope he does start something," Errin replied flat and ugly. He set his feet and slid his hand in under his jacket and took hold of his pistol.

Dokken looked expectantly to the side at the carriageway that led past the bank to the stables at the rear. Then he glanced in the opposite direction and saw Errin and Levi. He pivoted swiftly to face the two men and his hand disappeared in under the front of his coat.

"He's trying to decide whether to shoot you or not," Levi said.

"Quiet!" Errin commanded.

Levi saw Errin was taut, his eyes locked on Dokken. He was coiled, prepared to fight. More than that, from his expression, he wanted to fight. Levi then understood the sharp order to be silent. It had been dangerously foolish to have spoken and thus break Errin's concentration on Dokken and lessen his chance to live through this hazardous confrontation with the expert pistolman.

"Who are you?" Dokken called in a rough voice. "Why have you twice butted into my affairs?"

"My name's Scanlan. The Beremendes woman is a friend of mine and I don't like the way you treat her."

Dokken thrust a glance at Levi, checked him, and then back to Errin. "Get in my way one more time and I'll shoot you," Dokken threatened.

"Stay away from Celeste Beremendes," Errin retorted.

Brol Mattoon came out of the bank and onto the sidewalk. He looked at Dokken and then along the street at Errin and Levi. He said something to Dokken in a low voice that Errin could not hear. Dokken replied in the same muted tone.

"Mattoon's even better with a pistol than Dokken," Levi said, daring to speak. "For God's sake, don't fight both of them."

"Are they that good of friends that he would help him?" Errin asked. He didn't want Levi shot. Should a gunfight start, he would surely be one of the targets. Errin must end this before it got out of control. But how?

A horse-drawn buggy, the top raised and a young Chinaman driving, wheeled out of the carriageway and stopped on the street near Mattoon and Dokken. Mattoon said something to Dokken. The man shook his head. Mattoon spoke forcibly to

Dokken and then climbed into the buggy. Dokken grudgingly turned away from Errin and Levi and followed after Mattoon.

The Chinaman tapped the reins upon the rump of the horse and the vehicle pulled into the street. As it passed, Dokken was speaking to Mattoon and both were watching the two men on the sidewalk.

"You probably just escaped getting killed," Levi said.

"Maybe. And maybe someone else would've got himself killed."

"You'd fight for the Mexican woman?"

"Yes. And stop calling her the Mexican woman. Her name's Celeste Beremendes."

"All right. Celeste Beremendes. But now you know how I feel about Chun."

"I know. Those two women can get us into a hell of a lot of trouble. But what's a man without a woman?"

Chun bowed low to the two Americans as they entered the door. She was freshly bathed and her dark hair glistened. She wore a new dress, a dark blue one she had purchased with money Levi had given her. She raised her head and looked at Levi with bright eyes. He had left the house early in the morning without waking her and she was glad to see him.

"Good day, Mr. Coffin," she said.

"Good day to you, Chun, and call me Levi."

The Chinese girl turned to Errin. "Good day to you, Mr. Scanlan."

"Hello, Chun." Errin felt the girl's dislike for him. It was deserved for she had heard him tell Levi that she would be trouble for them. Further, he had not been friendly toward her.

"What smells so delicious?" Levi asked.

"I have prepared food," Chun said, pleased. "Is that agreeable to you?"

"It surely is, for I'm hungry," Levi replied. "What did you cook?"

"You will see. If you both will be seated, I shall serve you."

Levi watched Chun as she placed the food on the table. Her movements were fluid and graceful. He caught her casting glances at him. The expression in her eyes mesmerized him. He wanted to reach out and caress her ivory skin, to do more than that, something that made him blush. He looked away.

Levi saw Errin looking at him. He grinned at Errin and began to eat the food Chun had prepared.

Errin had observed how the China girl often looked at Levi, her almond eyes lingering upon him. Levi was embarrassed by her attention. That young fellow would soon have to do something about Chun. The first thing he should do was to make love to her and satisfy her obvious yearning.

Levi liked the food, fresh oysters in a mixture of vegetables, millet soup with noodles, bamboo shoots, warm bread, and strong black tea. It was a strange combination of ingredients but quite tasty. "Where did you get the food for the meal?" he asked.

"There is a store that sells these things only a few blocks away in a place called Portsmouth Square," Chun said. "They also sell clothing," she added and hoped Levi would notice her new dress.

"You shouldn't have gone out of the house. It was risky because the men could still be looking for you." He would not tell her of the reward.

"I thought I would be safe in the daytime."

"You're not safe in the daylight or in the night," Errin interjected bluntly. "Levi should tell you that there are assassins searching for you to take your head. And there's a reward for Levi for helping you to escape."

Chun staggered back a step. "Take my head? Reward for Levi? Is that so, Levi?"

"And a reward for Errin too since he helped me."

"Oh, Levi, I'm so sorry that I may have brought more danger to you and Mr. Scanlan. I will be much more careful in the future. But how am I to learn the city and find employment?"

"Don't be in a hurry about that. You're welcome to stay with us. Isn't that right, Errin?"

"Whatever you want, Levi. But now for certain, she can't stay in this house any longer. Wait until it's late night, then take her to Isaiah Green's house. Be sure you're not seen or followed."

"That's a good idea," Levi said. "No one will think to look for her in a black man's house."

"I'm not that sure," Errin said worriedly for he believed the assassins would be very thorough in their search for Chun.

Chapter 22

"Goddamn heathen Chinamen!" a man shouted fiercely.

"Bastard coolies!" a second man bellowed.

Errin heard a hundred voices take up the call, a bedlam of angry curses and threats. The cries came from the throng of white men completely blocking The Embarcadero at the shoreward end of a long pier extending into San Francisco Bay. The mob seemed ready to pounce upon somebody that he couldn't see. He hastened his step toward the crowd, mostly men wearing the coarse clothing of laborers.

Errin had come to the waterfront to contract newly arriving immigrants for his pool of skilled workers. He had heard of two ships arriving and wanted to catch the men coming directly off them so that he had his choice of those who were true journeyman level craftsmen. This tactic had proved very successful and he was pleased with the caliber of workmen on the roster for his hiring hall.

He pushed through the press of men to the front. Hundreds of Chinese men, carrying their skimpy possessions in their arms, were filing down the gangway of a steamship and hurrying on along the pier toward the shore. The Chinamen were small men, gaunt and bony. They appeared quite alien with their foreheads shaved for a third of the distance back across the tops of their heads and long queues hanging down their backs. Their eyes rolled with apprehension as they watched the large white men shouting and cursing them.

"Send the heathens back to China," a man near Errin shouted. "Cut off their pigtails for a starter." He pulled his jackknife and ran forward and grabbed the queue of one of the Chinamen trotting past. Before the white man could wield his knife, the frightened Chinaman tore free and darted ahead out of reach.

At the shoreward end of the pier, two American port officials sat at a table under a portable shelter. A Chinaman, an interpreter, and a pair of policemen stood beside the officials. The policemen uneasily eyed the noisy, threatening swarm of white men.

The interpreter called to the arriving Chinamen and they formed up in two lines in front of the table and facing the port officials. The small men answered a series of questions put to each of them through the interpreter. Then the policemen searched them with rough hands.

"What are they looking for?" Errin asked a man standing beside him.

"Opium," answered the man. "The heathens are all dope addicts."

The man turned back to the Chinamen and yelled out, "Send all the yellow bastards back to China so they won't take American jobs." He lifted a half brick he had hidden beside his leg, cocked his arm and hurled the missile at the Chinamen.

As the man heaved the brick, Errin struck his arm and the object flew wild, sailing over the heads of the Chinamen. The brick struck the wooden decking of the street and bounced into the crowd on the far side. A man, hit by the brick, cursed and shook his fist across the street.

The man who had thrown the brick wheeled around on Errin. "What the hell are you doing? You made me miss."

"You could kill a man with something like that," Errin replied.

"Then you did it on purpose. Why you damn, Chinaman lover, I'll smash your face."

Errin didn't want a fistfight with one of the swarm of white men. He moved swiftly upon the angry man and caught him by the points of his shoulders, and dug his fingers viciously into the muscles. The man winced.

"You're not man enough to smash my face," Errin said in a flinty voice.

The man swallowed and his Adam's apple pumped up and down. He pulled back trying to break free. Errin let him go.

"You're still a Goddamned Chinaman lover," yelled the man as he retreated hurriedly into the crowd.

Errin pushed his way closer to the inspection station and listened to the questions and watched the prying hands of the lawmen check the bodies and clothing of the Chinamen. The small, brown men answered the queries in the briefest of words. They remained stoic and unmoving to the prodding fingers. Yet Errin saw the doubt and uncertainty in their eyes. They were brave men to have undertaken such a dangerous journey across the stormy ocean. Many would die in the Sierra Nevada Mountains, called the Gum Shan—the Golden Hills—by the Chinamen.

Errin walked away along the docks. He had gone but a short distance when an uproar of shouts erupted behind him. He twisted to look. The first of the Chinamen had left the inspection station and were moving up the hill street toward Portsmouth Square where most of their countrymen lived on eight or ten blocks straddling Dupont Street. They were now out from under the protective eyes of the policemen. With nothing to curb them, the white men had given vent to their anger and were hurling horse turds and pieces of wood they had scooped up from the street at the foreign men.

One of the flying objects struck a Chinaman in the head with a sodden crunch. He fell to his knees. Two of his comrades quickly grabbed him by the arms and carried him onward with them.

The local guide, a Chinaman in white men's clothing, began to shout and motion with his arms for the new arrivals to move more swiftly after him. The Chinamen broke into a trot and drew away from the abusive Americans.

Errin gave no sign that he was aware of being followed. A young Chinaman wearing a black brocaded jacket and black pants and hat had sauntered along trailing Errin for the past half hour as he went about the city bidding on jobs for his workmen. However the sun was down now with the streets full of shadows and the Chinaman was closing the distance that separated them.

Errin continued on toward an alley between tall brick buildings. Reaching the alley, he stepped quickly into the opening, halted, and pulled his pistol. The Chinaman's presence meant trouble. The tongs must have discovered that Chun was with Levi and Errin.

The seconds dragged by as Errin waited. Yet the Chinaman did not appear in the mouth of the alley. Errin waited patiently, holding his weapon.

"Mr. Scanlan, my name is Ke," a voice sounded from a location just out of sight around the corner of the building on the street. "I mean you no harm. I simply want to talk with you. Do you hear me?"

"I hear you. Come out where I can see you."

Ke stepped into the alley. His hands were open with the palms showing. He glanced down at the pistol Errin held.

"You don't need your barking dog."

"Barking dog?"

"Your pistol."

"Maybe I do. Why in hell are you following me?"

"Honorable Lip wishes to speak with you. He has asked me to extend his humble invitation to come and talk with him about things that are important to both of you. You have heard of Scom Lip?"

Errin examined Ke closely. He would be one of the tong fighters, a *boo hao doy,* or hatchetmen as Louden had called them. He seemed very young. His eyes were steady and sure, a man who knew his own strength.

"Yes, I've heard of him. Why doesn't he come and see me? He must know where my office is."

"He knows. But Honorable Scom Lip believes it would be so much wiser if you and he hold this conversation in some private place where there are no other white men to see or hear."

"What would this talk be about?"

"I don't know. Honorable Scom Lip will inform you himself."

"And if I don't want to talk with your Honorable boss, what then?"

Ke shrugged his shoulders. "You may decide not to speak with my boss." Ke's eyes narrowed as he said the word *boss*. "But I think that would be stupid."

Errin did not let the use of the word "stupid" bother him. He watched the tong warrior, trying to read him. This was the second day since Celeste had been shot and he had planned to have dinner with her. But that would have to be delayed for he had no choice except to go with Ke. He must find out how much danger Chun and Levi and even he himself were in.

"I'll go with you," Errin said and shoved the pistol back into its holster. "How is it that you speak English so well?"

Ke was silent for several seconds as if in doubt whether or not to answer Errin's question. "I came to California several years ago as a boy, a stowaway. I studied your language, for I knew it was important to be able to talk with Americans. Because I can, now I have a treasured position with a very important man. Are you ready to go now?"

"Sure. Why not?"

"It's best that we're not seen together. Follow me some distance behind. It's not very far."

Ke left the alley. Errin waited a half minute and then went out to the street. He saw Ke was heading for Dupont Street.

On Beale Street they came to a huge, high-roofed building, a factory of some sort Errin thought. He saw not one sign of activity, not a crack of light in any of the windows. Midway the length of the structure, Ke descended a flight of steps leading down from the sidewalk and did not re-emerge.

Errin reached the stairwell and looked into the murky pit. It was empty so he went down. He put his hand on his pistol and knocked on the wooden door in the sunken wall of the building.

The door jerked open. A man stood framed by a weak light emanating from some distant source behind him. He held a big-bore shotgun pointed at Errin's stomach.

"You're Scanlan?" the man asked.

"Yes." Errin didn't like the gun pointed at him and he shoved the barrel aside.

"The Chinaman Ke said to let you in. Go straight ahead to the auction room." The man stepped aside.

Errin moved down a stone-walled passageway. The overhead was the floor of the building above. He could smell the sour dampness of the subterranean depths of the building. From ahead came voices distorted and undecipherable by their journey along the passageway. He came out into a lighted room of a very large size.

The floor of the room was of wood and the walls and ceiling paneled with the same material. Four chandeliers with several gaslights on each brightly illuminated the space. A low, half circular stage took up one end of the room. A black curtain was drawn closed, hiding whatever might be on the stage behind. Two dozen or so chairs were arranged facing and close to the stage. Nearly every chair was occupied by a well-dressed man. Ke sat on the extreme left side.

Errin continued on into the room just as the black curtain swept open. A young Chinese girl, thin and delicate and very beautiful stood with downcast eyes on a raised dais in the center of the stage. She was clothed in a sleeveless, green gown that clung to the young female contours of her body. Her pale ivory skin, contrasted against the green of the gown, seemed almost luminescent.

An older Chinaman with a sparse goatee was at the girl's side. He bowed to the seated men below the stage. With their eyes locked on the girl, not one of them saw his bow.

"I am Quan Ing, gentlemen," said the Chinaman. "You know the rules of the sale, but I will repeat them. There should be no noise or signals except from those men bidding. The initial bid must be at least one thousand dollars. The minimum bid thereafter is one hundred dollars. Of course, there is no upper limit.'' He smiled.

''Now look closely at this lovely girl. She is fifteen years old and perfect in every way. She is a virgin. I have a doctor's statement to that effect.'' The auctioneer extended his hand and raised the chin of the girl. The light played upon the exquisite curves and planes of her beautiful face, the flawless skin, the lustrous, long black hair.

The girl cast one swift glance out over the assemblage of men. Her eyes touched Errin's for a brief moment. He felt the fear that she tried to hide behind her innocent face, and sensed her drawing away from the lusting men and deeply within herself. He was sad for the little slave girl. How had she come to this secret auction ground in faraway America? Had she been taken by force or trickery and transported to this place with all the rewards for her sale going to her abductors? He hoped whoever bought her, would treat her gently.

''Who will begin the bidding at one thousand?'' said the Chinaman.

A hand rose.

''I have a bid,'' said the auctioneer. ''Do I have one for eleven hundred?''

''Fifteen hundred,'' a second man called.

The bidding went swiftly. The girl sold for thirty-three hundred dollars. The purchaser, a big, burly white man, climbed upon the stage and took the girl by the arm in a possessive manner. With Quan Ing leading, the white man took the girl out through a door on the side of the stage.

Errin looked at Ke. The Chinaman nodded with the barest of movement of his head and climbed to his feet. Errin followed slowly after the tong fighter through some curtains on the side of the room. Ke waited for him out of sight of the men in the auction room.

''Why did you bring me here?'' Errin asked.

''In case someone saw us, he would think I was merely guiding you to the auction. Now we shall hurry to our true destination?''

You lie, Errin thought. You wanted me to know what was in store for Chun should you take her from Levi.

The two men walked along Market Street for a few minutes and then veered right onto Dupont Street. Shortly they came to a two-story building occupying half a square block. A sign, extending out over the sidewalk from the building, read Chinese Foods, Scom Lip, Proprietor.

The structure was surrounded by buildings of like age and character. All were badly in need of paint. Errin had heard the exteriors of Chinese-owned buildings were deliberately left in a run-down condition so that the white people of the city would not become jealous of the foreigner's growing wealth. A bell tinkled as Ke and Errin entered the door.

A young Chinaman was behind a counter that ran nearly across the room. A second Chinaman seated at a table on the right near the wall, sprang to his feet as Ke and Errin entered. He was dressed in black clothing similar to Ke's. A clerk and a hatchetman, Errin judged. Behind them was a series of shelving extending rearward into the dark recesses of the building. Every square inch of the shelves was chock-full of a wide variety of drygoods and foodstuffs.

"Hello, Ke," the hatchetman said.

Ke nodded a return greeting and continued along one of the aisles between the shelving and out a door in the rear. The new room was very deep. Four men were at desks and transferring numbers from sheets of paper onto abacus boards and recording sums in ledgers. Beyond them three men were unpacking mining tools from large wooden crates and repackaging various portions of the contents into heavy burlap bags of a size a man could carry.

"Honorable Scom Lip outfits our newly arriving countrymen for their journey into the mountains to search for gold," Ke explained and gestured at the burlap sacks.

Two men in the customary black clothing of the tong sat at a table near a door and played dominoes. They immediately came to their feet when they saw Ke.

More tong fighters, thought Errin. By the way they had acted toward Ke, he must be their superior, probably a lieutenant of Scom Lip. But why so many guards?

He followed Ke through the door and into a room splendidly decorated with long silk drapes on the walls. Thick mohair carpets covered the floor. The finest wooden furniture, delicately and ornately carved was arranged in a most pleasing pattern.

A middle-aged Chinaman, thick chested and with a deep scar across his right cheek, rose from an overstuffed chair. He wore a richly embroidered black silk Mandarin pants and blouse. His step was strong and elastic as he came forward.

"Welcome, Mr. Scanlan, I am Scom Lip," the man said. He watched Errin with quick, alert eyes sunk deeply under a broad forehead.

"Hello, Scom Lip," Errin replied. He measured the leader of the most vicious tong in San Francisco. The man stood half a head shorter than Errin. Yet there was something about him that made him appear a big man. Errin decided he was a fighting leader. The scar must be a souvenir of some tong battle.

"Please be seated." Scom lip indicated a chair. "Ke, have some hot tea brought for Mr. Scanlan."

Ke hesitated, frowning, glancing at Errin.

"I know, Ke, Mr. Scanlan will be armed. But he and I have no arguments. This is a business discussion. Now see to the tea. And bring something sweet. Have Ging serve us."

"Yes, Honorable sir."

"What do you want to talk to me about?" Errin asked.

Lip reseated himself. His eyes swung to again fix on Errin. "You and your friend Mr. Coffin came to my attention a few days past and I've been watching the growth of your business. It is unique, this contracting of skilled workmen and I think it would be very profitable."

"We're making an honest living."

"Part of your workmen are black. Does their color create a problem for you?"

"Only a little. They're good workers and earn their pay."

"I'm sure they do."

Ke came into the room with a hurried step. He glanced at

Errin and Scom Lip. Satisfied with the situation, he backed away against the wall and became motionless.

A young, very beautiful Chinese girl came into view with a whisper of felt slippers. She carried a tray holding a pot of tea, two small cups, and a plate of rice cookies which she placed on a low table before the men.

"This is Ging Ti," Lip said, inclining his head at the girl. "She has only recently arrived in San Francisco from Canton. She came on the same ship as Chun Quang. You know Chun, don't you?"

Errin kept his eyes upon the girl. She had been tense before, but now at the mentioning of Chun, she started, almost spilling the tea that she was pouring.

"Yes," Errin replied, glad the real reason for him being here was out in the open. "And I imagine you have known of her whereabouts since she bought food in Portsmouth Square," he countered.

Lip smiled, the scar pulling his face into a menacing scowl. "Exactly so. And since then, I've been wondering what to do with the knowledge. I would judge that she is no longer a virgin and thus she would only have value as a whore. That is not much as compared to her worth before you took her. In fact, Mr. Scanlan, there are some associates of mine who believe her head should be severed from her body as a warning to other young women who may think of running away instead of honoring their contracts."

Errin took the cup of tea Ging handed to him. "Chun had no contract to break," he said. "She was on the waterfront in Canton when a buyer of girls was loading several aboard ship to bring to California. Some of the girls tried to run away. Those girls were caught, but the man also caught Chun and forced her aboard the ship too."

For a moment Scom Lip silently considered what Errin had said. "That may be true. However she would then owe me for passage to California since I am the actual owner of the ship that brought her to America. That is the same as a contract."

"That's not the same at all for she was forced to come here. But I don't want to fight with you so I'll pay for her passage."

Errin wouldn't allow Lip to kill Chun without a fight. He was deep within this tong chief's stronghold and the man could but raise his hand and the hatchetman, Ke, would try to kill Errin. Still Errin thought Scom Lip would appreciate bravery and not attack after inviting him to come.

"Would you fight me?" The scar on the Chinaman's face turned red with a rush of blood, then a thin smile stretched his mouth. "Your suggestion to pay would be one solution, or I could forget her passage fee and give her to you."

So this is only partly about Chun. Scom Lip was after something more valuable. "What do you want from me?" Errin asked. He must be very wary for the tong chief would prove to be a trickster, and a deadly foe.

"You have shown skill at contracting employment for workmen. I want you to put some of my countrymen to work for wages, two hundred, three hundred if possible. These are men who have failed to find golden riches in the mountains and now want to return to China. They need to earn the passage money."

"I don't think that would be possible. Just a few hours ago, I saw a group of your people cursed and hit by a mob of white men afraid of losing their jobs to Chinamen."

"I know my people are not liked by the white workers of the city. However if anybody can find them employment, that person is you."

"Simply trying to do that could hurt my business."

"They will work for a dollar a day," Scom Lip pressed on. "You could get a dollar and a half a day. Thus one-half dollar for each man would be yours. You could earn much money in a short time. When someone questioned you about why you worked Chinamen, you could tell them they worked only long enough to earn the passage to leave America and go home to China. Please do not reject my request until you have given it full thought."

Lip was asking too much. White businessmen would be afraid to employ the Chinamen even if they believed the foreigners would shortly leave California, yet Errin dared not flatly refuse the tong leader. Chun's life might then be forfeit, for no matter how diligently Levi and he guarded her, she could still be killed.

"Maybe there is some type of work that your people could do and the white men would not cause trouble because of it. I'll think on it."

"I knew we could reach an understanding. If we succeed, Chun may stay with you without fear of harm from any Chinaman." Scom Lip pointed at Ging. "In addition, I will give you pretty Ging. Until then I shall keep her pure for you."

Errin saw that the girl seemed to understand Lip's words. She peered at Errin from under her bowed head. She didn't appear displeased at the proposition.

"You're generous," Errin said. Ging was indeed beautiful. He would accept her if it came to that. Or maybe he would win the lovely Celeste. He laughed behind his face. His sights were high for a highwayman. But a troubling thought worried him, for Scom Lip to give such a valuable property, he must intend to take a major portion of the dollar-a-day wage remaining to each Chinaman after Errin took his cut. Even that would not pay for the girl. Scom Lip was after something even more important to him. At the moment, Errin could not fathom what that was.

"Have another rice cake and some more tea, Mr. Scanlan," Scom Lip said and smiled his crooked smile.

"I must go," Errin said and climbed to his feet.

"There is one more thing that I wish to say, something of importance to you."

"What's that?"

"Someone else searches for Chun. A white man named Mattoon."

"Brol Mattoon, the banker?"

"A banker among other things. It was his men who were guarding the girls when Chun escaped. Because of her, he has lost face. He is powerful on the waterfront, and has many men to obey his orders. Should he find the girl, he would surely kill her, and your friend Mr. Coffin. And even you, Mr. Scanlan, for hiding her. Watch carefully for him."

Chapter 23

Celeste clenched her teeth as the wheels of the surrey struck a rut in the road and pain rose in her wounded chest. She lay upon a thick pallet of blankets on the floor of the vehicle. Though it was mounted on leaf springs, it still bounced and jarred on the primitive dirt way.

"Can you see the *hacienda* yet?" she said to Ignacio who drove the surrey.

"Yes, *señorita,* it is not more than three miles ahead. We shall soon be there."

"That's good." She smelled the dust stirred up from the surface of the road by the rolling wheels. She felt the gritty particles of earth settling upon her. But the discomfort was easy to bear for the dust that fell upon her was soil of her own land. That was a very pleasant thought.

She looked from under the canvas top of the surrey and up at Errin. He was watching her from the back of his horse.

"Are you all right?" he asked.

"I've never felt better in my life."

"I think that might be a fib."

"Maybe a little one," Celeste smiled at him.

Celeste, Errin and Ignacio were traveling across the San

Joaquin Valley. Celeste, on the third day after the duel, prepared to go to her *rancho*. She insisted that in the dry air of Mount Mocho, she would heal more rapidly than in damp, foggy San Francisco. Errin had agreed and, finding great pleasure in her presence, quickly volunteered to accompany her and Ignacio. Taking a surrey and a pair of trotters and Levi's saddle mount, they caught a steamboat up river to a farmer's cooperative grain landing some thirty miles downstream from Sacramento. There Ignacio and he had unloaded the surrey and horses from the boat and the overland portion of the journey began.

Errin looked ahead from the back of his horse to where dense clouds of dust moved under the burning sun. Within the thick dust, men drove mules pulling land levelers, harrows and plows. The hazy forms of the men and their animals and machines seemed to be only particles of the floating dust.

"Ignacio, stop," Celeste called when the surrey drew abreast of the men nearest the road.

Ignacio pulled the horses to a halt. "What is it that you need, *señorita?*" he asked.

"I want to speak to the men."

Errin dismounted and came to the side of the vehicle. "Do you want help to get down?" he said.

"No. The men must see that I'm not badly hurt and can still fight to hold the *rancho.*" She stood erect on the ground and lifted her arm. She waved to the men, hiding the pain that came from the torn flesh of her wound.

Two men who had been working a land leveler, had stopped and come out of the dust. They shouted their greeting to Celeste. Men at the other machines heard the calls and halted. They saw Celeste and added their happy voices to the welcome. Celeste laughed as the voices rolled across the valley bottom.

"There, see, Errin, they feel better and so do I," Celeste said in a pleased voice. "I have thousands of acres suited for growing wheat. But I need many more men to help prepare the land and plant the seed. Wheat can be the salvation of my *rancho.*"

She climbed gingerly back into the surrey and lay down. "Take me home, Ignacio."

"With pleasure, *señorita.*"

They journeyed on under the blazing sun. Celeste watched the newly spun dust rise up from the surrey, and from the scrapers and other machines. The yellow clouds represented gold for it meant she could grow wheat. She did not mind the heat at all.

Errin glanced backward at the toiling men. He had the answer to finding work for Scom Lip's Chinamen. He would bring them far away from San Francisco to this inland valley. Here there were tens of thousands of acres of land to be prepared for farming. With no angry white men to cause trouble.

The surrey and lone rider left the valley bottom and climbed the road winding up the side of Mount Mocho. With the sun nearly to its zenith, they entered the courtyard of the *hacienda*.

The wives of the *vaqueros* rushed to greet Celeste and help her from the carriage. Errin drew back from the bevy of chattering women and looked around.

The *hacienda* was huge with thick adobe walls and a veranda extending the entire length of the front. Tall cottonwoods and oaks shaded the house. Errin knew the structure must contain many rooms. There were outbuildings and a blacksmith shop and a stone and log corral, and down the slope were several small residences. A ditch running with water led to a garden. He turned back and saw Celeste's happy face. Being home in such a place was a perfect reason to be happy.

When the noisy welcome had quieted, Celeste slipped away from the women. She breathed deeply of the warm, sweet wind of the mountain. It had been right to come here. Soon she would be completely healed.

She turned to Errin standing off to the side and watching her. She felt her heart do a little tattoo of beats against her ribs as their eyes met. How natural it was for him to be here.

"Errin, this is my home. Please treat it as if it was yours. Let us wash away the dust and then have something to eat."

"I am hungry."

"Ignacio will show you to the men's bath house. Come into the *hacienda* when you are finished."

"I won't be long," Errin said.

"Come this way, *señor*," Ignacio said.

Errin removed his pack from where it was tied behind the saddle on his horse and followed after Ignacio into the *hacienda*. He noted the worn concave shape of the threshold stone. How many feet, bare and booted had trod upon the stone?

Ignacio led along a high ceiling passageway that stretched away into the interior of the house. Errin felt the coolness of the structure and smelled the odor of the earth with which it was built.

Ignacio stopped and pointed ahead. "At the end of the hall and just outside is the bath house. There are several tubs. The water in all of them will be fresh. It is the duty of the bigger boys to see to that. After you have finished bathing, follow your nose to the kitchen. The dining room is next to it."

Errin bathed quickly and was soon seated with Celeste alone at a table in the big dining room. He ate with high relish, but slowly, savoring his food, concentrating upon the flavor. The food was spicy, aromatic, and delicious.

Celeste ate slowly matching Errin's leisurely pace, and slyly watching him. She did not understand his obvious delight in the simple food that had been served to him.

Errin looked at Celeste sitting so peaceably in her home. As she ate, her expression frequently changed, flashing across her face like rainbows with each new thought. Her eyes touching his from time to time were almost as pleasant as kisses. He knew how painful her wound must be, and yet she gave no sign of it. There was a splendor in her, in the union of gentleness, will, and courage. He could not get enough of her.

A brilliance came into Celeste's face, a brash sparkling light. She smiled mischievously at him. Had she again read his desires. If so, she did not seem to mind them.

Celeste's eyes lost their sparkle and she climbed to her feet. "I'm tired from the trip, Errin. I think I will rest for a while."

Errin immediately rose to his feet to help her.

"I can walk well enough," Celeste said. "Finish your meal and then take a *siesta*. Everyone else will."

Errin gazed after Celeste as she walked away over the earthen floor and vanished through a doorway. He looked down at his food. Without the presence of the woman, it was not so appetizing.

He left the dining room and went out into the patio, with its wide overhanging roof. He leaned against the wall in the shade and let his view drift out over the mountain and the great valley lying a thousand feet below him. As he looked at the ancient land created in an age long-lost in antiquity, he sensed a deep, gentle peace. He could be happy living the rest of his life here with Celeste.

The hum of honeybees reached him and he walked about the patio until he found them searching for nectar in the hollyhocks growing in a large flower bed. There was no other sound. How restful the moment was with the sun hanging in midheaven, casting no shadows, and the women and children dozing.

Lulled by the food in his stomach, he felt his own sleepiness putting weights on his eyelids. He took a wool blanket, hand-woven perhaps by Celeste herself, from where it covered a wicker chair and spread it on the ground in the shade. With the peacefulness of the old house surrounding him, he went to sleep.

Celeste awoke and lay listening to the quiet of the *hacienda*. Usually there were the cries and shouts of the children at play at the *vaqueros'* homes. But for the moment, a deep hush held sway over everything.

It was comforting to know Errin was in her home. She was pleased that he had accompanied her and Ignacio when she decided to come to the *rancho*.

She rose from her bed and walked quietly through the house. She found Errin sleeping in the shade of the patio. For a time she gazed down at him, looking at his face and watching the rise and fall of his chest.

She moved on to the front veranda. A summer storm was brewing. She could see it rising like an enormous bird, with its large head showing above the mountains that rimmed the south end of the valley. She sat down on a padded swing and gazed at the growing cloud mass. At the *vaqueros'* homes,

children began to play, chasing each other and laughing happily
Two women went into the weaving hut.

"Will it rain?" Errin asked behind her.

Celeste turned to look at him. "Yes, in a couple of hours.'

"You seem very sure of that."

"I've spent nearly every summer of my life here on the
mountain. I know how the storms come. Sit down with me and
watch and see that I'm right."

"I'd like that."

They sat together in the swing without speaking, comfortable
in each other's company. A breeze came alive and drifted past
making pleasant sounds in the leaves of the tall trees in the
yard. The storm grew, its head rising high in the sky and its
broad wings spreading to cover the entire end of the valley
Distant lightning flashed and thunder muttered.

Ignacio approached from inside the house. "*Señorita,* you
have a visitor," he said.

"I saw no one arrive. Who is it?"

"I think it best if you come and see for yourself," Ignacio
said with a glance at Errin.

"Very well, Ignacio. Errin, watch the storm and see if I'm
not correct about it raining very soon."

"I've already decided you're right about that."

"I'll be back in a few minutes," Celeste said. She motioned
for Ignacio to lead the way and followed. Errin wondered about
the new arrival and the unwillingness of Ignacio to speak the
person's name. Then he let the matter go and lazily gazed at
the growing thunderheads.

A short time later, Errin heard footsteps approaching from
inside the *hacienda.* Celeste spoke. "Errin, I would like for
you to meet a good friend of mine."

Errin stood up and turned. An old, gray headed Mexican
was beside Celeste.

"Vicaro Zaragoza, I want you to know another good friend
of mine, Errin Scanlan."

"I am pleased to make your acquaintance, Señor Scanlan."

The man's words did not agree with his expression. Errin
thought him quite reluctant to meet him.

"Glad to know you," Errin said.

Celeste had also noted Vicaro's reluctance. "Be at ease, Vicaro," she said with a laugh. She looked at Errin. "He has had trouble with *gringos* and is cautious. I had to plead with him to come out here."

"Being cautious is why I'm still alive," Vicaro said. He fastened a foxy look of his black eyes on Errin. "They call me a bandit and would hang me if they could catch me."

"Anyone who is a friend of Celeste, has nothing to fear from me," Errin said.

"I wouldn't fear you even if you were not a friend of Celeste," Vicaro replied with heat.

Testy old fart, Errin thought.

"Vicaro, is that a way to talk?" Celeste said in a rebuking tone. "I want you and Errin to be friends."

Vicaro's expression instantly filled with remorse at what he had said. He bowed quite low to Celeste. "Please accept my apology, *señorita*. I forgot myself. That comes from a long life always full of enemies." He straightened and turned to Errin. "My apology to you also, Señor Scanlan."

"I took no offense for I've had enemies myself."

"Than all is right," Celeste said.

"Certainly," Errin said. "Now I know the answer to something else that I've been wondering about."

"What is that?" Celeste asked.

"That this is the man who taught you to use a pistol. The man you called the best *pistolero* in all California."

The old bandit grinned broadly. "I taught her what I know. But the sharpest edge of her accuracy and quickness, she taught herself."

"I saw a sample of her courage. Without courage, skill means nothing."

"Without the will to kill, neither skill nor courage has value against an enemy," Celeste said disparagingly. She did not want more talk of enemies and guns. "Vicaro, a storm is coming so please stay the night here in the *hacienda*. I do not like to think of you sleeping in the rain."

"That is kind of you. I accept."

"Good. Find Ignacio and tell him to give you one of the guest rooms."

"Very well, Celeste. Good day to you, Señor Scanlan."

The thunderheads strode like giants up the San Joaquin Valley. Lightning flared brightly, trapped within the towering cloud masses and lighting them with a smoldering, infernal glow. Distant thunder rumbled like advancing artillery.

The lightning broke free of the clouds and speared down to wound the earth. The rains came driving hard, wetting quickly.

"See, I was correct," Celeste said. "It's raining."

"I never doubted you," Errin replied with a gentle chuckle. He stopped the slight movement of the swing upon which Celeste and he sat. He lifted his head to draw in a deep breath of the rain filled air. He heard the pleasant drumbeat of the drops on the roof of the *hacienda* and in the yard.

Lightning struck the side of the mountain a short distance above them. The *hacienda* shook. The bright flash blinded him, the thunder deafened him.

He felt Celeste move against him and he put his arm around her shoulders. The touch of her body sent a thrill through him.

"Errin?"

He barely heard her above the turmoil of the storm. He looked down at her.

She reached up with both hands and cupped his face, and her fingers gently caressed his cheeks, his eyelids, his temples. Her dark eyes were wide, and full of the most wonderous expression. Errin gazed at her with surprise and awe. Was this real?

He bent and kissed her, a soft touch of his lips on hers. Then again, hungrily.

Her mouth opened inviting him inside. He tasted the warm sweetness of her. What a truly lovely creature she was. Could he totally win her?

Celeste leaned away and looked up at him. Her eyes searched his as if looking for the answer to an unasked question. Then she clasped him by the hand.

"Come with me. I know a private place where we can talk."

She led him along shadow filled passageways to a far corner of the *hacienda*. They entered a room containing a large blanket draped couch, a chair, and a desk with papers and pens upon it, and several flowers in pots. She closed the door.

"No one ever comes into this room except me," Celeste said, drawing Errin down beside her on the couch.

Her mouth curved into a happy smile, and her black eyes filled with a mischievous light. "Kiss me."

Errin leaned and kissed Celeste.

Errin lay on the couch and held the sleeping Celeste. The rain still fell, now a slow, gentle patter on the rooftop. He let his mind bask and revel in this moment lying with the woman and the music of the falling raindrops.

They had made love. And he had told her all, of being a child slave, a highwayman, and shooting the two "thief-takers" who had tried to kill him. He had described the cruelty of the penal colony in Australia, of being flogged with the cat-o'-nine-tails. She had felt the scars on his back and a sob escaped her. Then he told her of his escape in the small boat, the death of Swallow, and being picked up from the sea by the American ship hunting seals and brought to San Francisco.

She had listened silently to the very end. "I'll never give you scars," she had said, and kissed him. "Hold me." She went to sleep in his arms.

Quietly he rose from the couch and left the room. The storm was ending as he came out onto the veranda, and the last of the clouds were hurrying off to the north. He squatted down with his back against the adobe wall and looked out over the broad lands of the *rancho*. Far away and below him, the dark shadows cast by the clouds were uncovering the rain-drenched valley.

A gloomy melancholy fell upon Errin. He was in reality an intruder into this grand place. What right did a thief and escaped murderer have to lay claim to such a beautiful woman as Celeste, who owned such extensive land holdings? Maybe he should leave before Celeste awoke. He rose to his feet with that thought hard in mind.

The *hacienda* came out of the shadows of the rain clouds and into the full light of day. The rays of the sun struck the last remaining water crystals hanging in the air and sundogs began to flash their tiny, incomplete rainbows of dazzling colors. Errin felt his mood brighten. Once he had told Celeste that perhaps he had found what he had been searching for. He was certain now that she was the goal of his long journey. He would not voluntarily give her up. He reseated himself firmly on the floor of the veranda. The only way he would leave would be for Celeste to drive him away herself.

Chapter 24

Chun went swiftly along the fog-filled San Francisco street. She fervently hoped Levi wouldn't be angry at her. He had warned her not to leave the home of Isaiah Green. But he had not come to see her the evening before as he had every other day. He might not come again this evening and she couldn't wait one hour longer to see him. What had kept him away? Was he tired of her companionship? Was he sick? She had to know.

She thought no one would recognize her and she would be safe for she wore a coat that hung to her knees and a scarf wound around her head and across the lower portion of her face. Both garments had been borrowed from Ruth, Isaiah's wife. The attire was not out of place and would not draw attention to her. A dense, chilling fog blanketed the city. Ruth had tried to convince her not to go onto the street; however, she would not listen to the black woman's pleas.

She lowered her face and hastened past the two Chinamen standing on the street corner. She did not see them turn and watch after her through the fog.

* * *

"No blade work," Ingram told Turk. The man was too quick to use his big knife. "Remember what the boss said."

"Unless somebody doesn't pay up, then I'll do some carving on him," Turk replied.

Kass, the third man spoke. "One of these days, the boss is going to take that blade away and carve on you."

"I wouldn't let him do that," Turk said and his swarthy skin became even darker with the thought.

"Not much you could do about it, if he decided to do it," Kass said.

"Both of you shut up," Ingram said. "We've got a job to do so let's get on with it. Turk, you come with me. Kass, you stay out here on the sidewalk and watch for anything that might cause us trouble."

Levi watched the three men standing in the fog in front of his office window and talking. When two of them moved toward the office door, he felt a premonition of danger and a chill went through him. He reached for his rifle, standing propped against the wall near him, and laid it across his knees below the edge of the desk behind which he sat.

The day was Friday and he was preparing the payroll for his workers for they would want their wages on Saturday. With Errin away to the Beremendes's *rancho,* Levi had taken on additional tasks and had to stay late in the day to accomplish the chore. He raked the nearly one thousand dollars of gold and paper money from the desk top into a drawer. Damnit, why wasn't Errin here?

The first man through the door was a redhead with rusty splotches on his face that looked like rotting flesh. The second man was rail-thin and dark as a Spaniard. Both stopped just inside the entryway and their eyes swept the room.

The redhead pointed at the closed door that led into the room where Levi's workers assembled before going out on a job. "Check that," he ordered the dark man.

"Right."

Ingram stalked forward until only the desk separated him

from Levi. He stared down at the tense, young man. "You the owner of this here business?" he asked.

"Half owner," Levi replied not liking the prying question.

"What kind of business do you run here?"

"We contract out skilled workers," Levi said. "We've the best carpenters, bricklayers and metalworkers in the city. What kind of job do you need men for?"

"We don't want any damn men," Turk said sarcastically coming up beside Ingram.

"I wouldn't think there's much cost to finding men and sending them out on jobs," Ingram said. "This must be a real money-making business."

"It's not as good as you might think," Levi said and then fell silent waiting to hear the reason the two men had come. It would not be one he would like.

"So you say," Turk replied in a disbelieving tone.

"We can help you be more profitable," Ingram said with a knowing look. "That's why we're here."

"How would you do that?" Levi asked, and immediately wished he hadn't.

"By warning you about the terrible mean things that can happen to businesses near the waterfront. There are many troublemakers here. They get drunk and wreck and burn buildings, just for the plain hell of it. We think you need some protection against that happening to you."

"Yeah, and we are just the men to see to it that nothing bad happens to your business," Turk added.

"Once we put the word out that we're watching over your place, no one will dare cause you any problems," Ingram said.

Levi understood the threat. He needed time to think and to talk the situation over with Errin. He didn't think Errin would ever pay any man for protection. He gestured around at the scant furnishing of the office, a desk and three chairs. "I've nothing much to wreck or burn," he said.

Ingram smiled crookedly. "You're not as dumb as you act."

"How much will this insurance cost to keep me safe from all those bad men you mentioned?"

"We'll see that you're kept safe for thirty dollars a week," Ingram said.

"That's steep, a man's wages for two weeks of work," Levi said. He gripped the rifle lying across his legs. "I have a partner and I'll have to talk it over with him."

"We want an answer now," Turk said. He hooked a thumb in his belt near the knife and stepped threateningly forward.

Levi started to bring up his rifle, but halted the movement before the weapon came into view when Ingram caught Turk by the arm and stopped him. "Now hold up, Turk. This fellow has the right to talk this over with his partner." Ingram spoke to Levi. "But because we got to wait for your answer and come again, the price of the insurance goes up. Tomorrow the price will be forty dollars a week."

"Ingram, I like that, make him pay extra for us havin' to wait," Turk said.

"Tomorrow we'll be back," Ingram told Levi. "Make the right decision. The smart one."

Chun slowed as she drew near the door of Levi's office and unwound the scarf from her face and head. A bright smile of anticipation at seeing Levi broke through her worry at disobeying him. She smoothed her hair, stepped quickly past the man looking the opposite way along the street, and entered the office.

Two men were standing and talking with Levi. Both turned and looked at Chun.

She gave the redhead and dark man a quick glance and stopped in her tracks, her breath catching and her heart almost stopping. Oh! what a dreadful mistake she had made. She recognized the men. She put her head down and without a word to Levi continued straight across the room and into Errin's office at the rear.

Ingram and Turk stared after Chun until the door closed behind her. Then Ingram turned to Turk. "Let's go."

"Ingram, that was . . ."

Ingram shook his head and spoke quickly to cut Turk off.

"He has until tomorrow, so come on now." He went out through the door with Turk following. The third man joined them on the sidewalk.

With heavy dread, Levi watched the men vanish into the fog. There had been a knowing look in the men's eyes, and Chun's fright upon seeing them told him something very dangerous had occurred.

The men had hardly disappeared when the door opened from the rear office and Chun came hesitatingly across the room to Levi. He climbed to his feet and caught her by the shoulders. "Why in the devil . . . ?" he started to scold her and then saw the terrified expression on her face.

"Levi, those men were two of those that were taking the girls from the waterfront to Chinatown," Chun said, her voice quivering. "And they recognized me."

"Are you sure?" He knew Chun was correct but wanted to hear it.

"I could never forget such strange faces. They will come back and force me to go away with them. I don't want to leave you. What shall we do?"

Levi knew the danger was far greater than just taking her away. The men would kill Chun, and sever her head from her body to prove she was dead. He pulled her shaking body against him and held her. She had made a grievous error in coming out onto the street against his orders. But what was done was done. What to do now?

Levi stopped pacing back and forth across the office and picked up his rifle from the desk. "We can't stay here," he said to Chun who was anxiously watching him. "From the way those men acted they must not know you've been staying with Isaiah so we'll go there. After that, we'll figure out a safer place to hide you."

He went to the window and pressed his face to the glass to look both directions along the street. The fog was thick and he could see only a short distance. He turned back to Chun.

"We've got to leave. Maybe we can slip away in the fog before the men block all the ways. Stay close to me."

"I will," Chun replied. The scar on Levi's forehead made him appear fierce, but she knew he was a caring, gentle man. She had put him in danger and now she must not allow anyone to harm him. "I have my knife," she said. "If the white men try to hurt us, I will fight them."

"I hope we don't have to," Levi said. Chun's dark, worried eyes held him, and he wanted to caress her, to take away the haunted expression. At that moment, he decided he would make love with her this very night, if they survived, and she was willing. First he had to find them safety from their enemies.

Levi went to the front door and cautiously checked outside. "I don't see anybody," he said. He took Chun by the hand and they stole off along the street.

They reached the first cross street and Levi looked both directions. His eyes wrestled with the fog and the dusk deepening to night. He started to move ahead, then halted, pulling Chun against him. He sensed an unseen menace and an icy shaft grew in his stomach. Men were there in the fog, men who would kill beautiful Chun. They would also try to kill him, but that had less importance.

A shrill whistle sounded ahead of them. An answering whistle came from behind.

"They've found us," Levi whispered and lifted his rifle. Chun and he were trapped between two groups of foes. He would need all his skill with the rifle if he was to keep her alive.

"What will we do?" Chun whispered.

"Try to find a place to hide. We'll check every door we pass. Pray hard that we find one that's not locked."

Hugging the wall, they slipped along the street. Levi's eyes drilled into the deeper shadows that appeared out of the murk before them. Any one of them could be the hiding place of a gunman.

He slowed when the mouth of an alley took shape. As he reached to take hold of Chun to stop her, a pistol exploded from the gloom of the alley. Instantly Levi jerked up his rifle and fired a shot a foot to the right of the red flash. A groan reached him followed by the thump of a body falling. One man was down, at least wounded. But how many more were there? While he had spent time planning his move, had other men joined in with the first three to capture Chun?

A gun crashed twice behind them. Bullets spanged from the bricks of the building beside them, ricocheting away with the snarl of small, deadly animals.

Levi hurled himself down, yanking Chun with him onto the wooden planks of the street. A third bullet whizzed by over their heads.

The firing ceased as Levi rolled to his knees and brought his rifle up. His eyes probed the fog and the growing darkness trying to see an enemy. But there was no target, only the mist-laden night.

He heard the swift, scared breathing of Chun beside him. He caught her by the hand and drew her erect. He pressed her against the wall of the building and stood protectively in front. His nerves tingled with the seething, primal urge to kill as he stared into the blinding fog. But how could he kill his assailants when he couldn't see them?

His attackers had the same problem, except they had only to wait, wait until daylight, if necessary, and then they would win.

However they wouldn't have to wait because the night was brightening. Through the fog, Levi saw the faint outline of the top curve of the full moon just poking above the buildings lining the street. Adding to the danger, a slow wind had come alive and was sliding down the hill toward the bay. The cold fog brushed Levi's face as it was carried along on the wind. In a few minutes, the protective covering of the fog would be gone and Chun and he would be naked before the guns of the hunters.

Even as Levi watched, the fog began to roll up into drifting ground clouds with clear zones forming in between. The sharp edge of panic stabbed him.

"Let us run, Levi," Chun whispered.

"No, for then they would hear us and maybe see us."

In the wall of the building by their side was a shallow
recessed alcove with a double-wide door set in its rear. An
entrance to some type of factory, Levi thought. He tried the
doors. Both were locked.

He pushed Chun into the alcove. "Stay there and don't
move," Levi said. "I'll draw them away before the fog lifts
any further and they can see I'm alone."

"Please don't leave me," Chun pleaded.

"I'll be back for you soon. Now wait here for me." He
pressed her shoulders for encouragement. Levi raced across the
street where the fog was thickest. A bullet zipped past, pulling
at the waist of his coat. He bent low and bolted steeply right.
God, how he wished he knew how many men were after Chun
and him, and where they were hidden?

A shaft of moonlight angled down on the street. At the
sudden brightening of the night, Levi saw a man duck into a
doorway ahead. The opening was not deep and the shoulder
of the man protruded. Then his head appeared as he peered
along the street.

Levi raised his rifle and fired. The man stumbled out into
the street and fell.

Chun crouched in the darkness of the doorway and listened
to Levi's pounding feet fade away. A gun exploded and her
heart cramped with fear for him. Had he been wounded, killed?
She strained to see.

Something moved there in the street. It couldn't be Levi
returning. His footsteps had been much farther away. To her
growing fright, the figure of a tall man materialized out of the
fog in front of her. He stepped close and towered over her.

"So there you are, China Girl," Turk said with a savage
chuckle.

The man was a giant to Chun and she cringed back from his
huge size. Then she steeled herself knowing she would have
to fight the man, giant or not. She sprang to the far side of the
building's alcove. As she moved, she swiftly pulled her knife
from its sheath inside her clothing.

Turk saw Chun's hand appear clutching a knife. He laughed outright and thrust out a hand holding his long-bladed knife. A ray of moonlight glinted off the honed steel.

"Why you little, Moon-eyed Celestial, you have no chance in hell of beating old Turk in a knife fight. I'm the best Frisco has. There are at least ten men that'd swear to that, if dead men could talk."

Chapter 25

"Levi, help!" Chun screamed and held her knife ready to fend off the enemy poised to kill her.

She didn't believe Levi could return in time to protect her even if he should hear her cry. She must save herself, and knew that to have any chance to survive, she must get out of the small, recessed space of the double doorway in the side of the building, and into the street where perhaps her quickness might shield her from the reach of the man's long arms. She sprang to the opposite end of the confining alcove with the intent then to dart past the man.

Turk anticipated Chun's strategy of breaking clear of the alcove. With one long stride, he blocked her path.

The man had moved much more quickly than Chun had thought possible and now she must fight her way clear. "Aii!" she cried fiercely and struck at the man with her knife.

Turk moved agilely to the side. Chun's thrust missed.

Turk extended his arm and pointed the keen blade of his knife at Chun's throat. There was no way the small woman could reach him with her knife. The dice had been rolled. She had lost and would die.

"Aiii!" Chun screamed wild and fear-filled and again

tabbed at Turk. Then swiftly again. But each time her reach vas short of its mark.

Turk laughed blackly, then stopped. "Enough," he said. "It's time you lost your pretty head."

As Chun swung yet again, the man slashed out and the razor sharp edge of his blade cut deeply into her extended arm. Her hand went numb. She lost the grip on her knife and it clattered down on the street.

Turk stepped in. Chun tried to dodge to the side, away from the giant. She slammed into the brick wall of the alcove. Turk stabbed viciously with his long-bladed weapon. The knife penetrated Chun through the lower ribs, drove onward and tore free at her back. He grabbed his knife with both hands, and hoisting powerfully upward, lifted Chun's body off the ground and over his head.

He looked up at Chun impaled on his steel blade. "That's right, China Girl, kick your life away up there on old Turk's knife. In a second, I'll take your head and trade it for gold."

Levi heard Chun cry his name in a voice so full of fear that he trembled. She screamed again, a shrill, harrowing pitch slicing the night. Then abruptly her cry ceased.

Caring nothing for the danger to himself, Levi raced toward Chun. She must not be hurt. No! No!

The fog before Levi thinned and a man became visible in the moonlit street. A man who held something aloft, a slight body that kicked and struggled in the air above his head. The small body was Chun, and her long hair whipped about with the intensity of her battle to break free.

The man flung Chun down on the street and bent over her.

Levi slid to a stop and snapped up his rifle and fired. Turk's crouching body jerked under the impact of the driving bullet. He fell away from Chun.

Levi sprinted on and knelt by the girl's side. Gently he straightened her limp body. He saw the heavy stream of blood flowing from the knife wound in her chest.

"Oh, my God! Chun, speak to me!"

Chun stirred. Her eyes opened, black pools of pain in th
night. "Levi, I'm terribly hurt," she whispered.

"Hold on. I'll take you to a doctor." Tenderly he took he
into his arms and rose to his feet.

Chun moaned with excruciating pain, a sobbing echo in th
shadowy mist. "I think I will die."

"No you won't." Levi's throat was so constricted with hi
sorrow that he could barely speak.

For the very first time he kissed her soft lips. He tasted th
salt of her tears.

"Levi, why didn't we make love?" Chun said, her voic
thin as a ghost's. "If we had, then my death wouldn't be s
awful."

Levi drew her more closely to him. "You won't die. W
will yet make love."

"We are too late," Chun said in a sobbing, weakening voic

Chun exhaled a fragile breath against Levi's cheek. H
waited, hoping desperately for another. None came.

"Don't die," Levi whispered. "Dear God, don't let her die."
He placed his cheek to Chun's. Her flesh was cold, and dam
with the mist of the fog. He knew he had lost her. He held he
tightly to him with the pain of his loss cascading through him

Levi roused himself and glanced hastily around. He mus
get away from this place for the shots would have been hear
by other enemies and they would be coming. With his visio
blurred by tears, he staggered off along the dark street wit
Chun in his arms.

Levi did not know how long he carried Chun. Sometim
later, he found himself leaning on the door of the house wher
he and Errin lived. He entered and lay Chun tenderly on hi
bed.

He sank weakly down on the bed beside the body of th
girl. Chun had captured his heart, and yet he hadn't made lov
to her. He would always regret that. She had been right i
scolding him. Now there would only be memories of her. The
would be memories that he would always cherish. He place
his arm lovingly over her.

* * *

Errin awoke in the Beremendes *hacienda* constructed decades before on the high flank of Mount Mocho. He lay breathing the cool mountain air that held the odor of the good earth with which the walls of the *hacienda* were built. And he smelled the sweet aroma of the yellow flowers Celeste had placed in a blue vase on a table when she had shown him where to sleep. He climbed out of bed, and humming as he relived the evening before with Celeste, dressed in the light of a tallow candle.

He grinned ruefully as he compared his life today with those when he had been a highwayman in England, and a prisoner in Australia. Though the dangerous game of highwayman was gone forever, he had to admit to himself that he would miss the exhilaration that always came during the robberies. He laughed out loud as remembrance came of the expressions on the faces of the rich men when he took their gold and jewels. For a moment he wondered what was in him that called so loudly for action.

He left the bedroom and went along the dark passageway to the front entrance of the *hacienda*. He stopped in the doorway and looked at Celeste who stood in the courtyard in the night's silver moon-glow and silently stared out over the San Joaquin Valley. He still found it hard to believe that this beautiful woman had given him her love.

Errin watched Celeste for a few seconds longer and then went to her. "So you're a person who also rises early," he said.

Celeste caught his hand and held it. "I like to stand here and think of what my grandfather built so long ago and to see the morning sun come up over the Sierra Nevadas. To me this land must be the most beautiful place in all the universe."

"I think so too." Errin looked at her in the soft splendor of the setting moon. And you are the most lovely woman in all the universe.

They were quiet, holding hands and feeling the pleasant nearness of each other as the yellow moon fell behind Mount

Mocho. To the east the sky gradually brightened as the dawn came gliding in. The chatter and chirrup of the night creatures slowed and stilled. There was total silence in that short span of time when the night creatures were going to sleep and the daytime ones were not yet fully awake.

The sun lifted its stunning head above the Sierra Nevadas. Bright rays slanted down into the valley and extinguished the lingering shadows of the night. The morning sky was a brilliant blue, swept clean by the storm of yesterday.

"There go your men to work," Errin said, watching her *vaqueros* come out of the cabins, and other men, recent hires, come from tents erected farther down the side of the mountain.

"I need many more men."

"I'll get them for you," Errin said. "One of the Chinese tong leaders in San Francisco has asked me to find jobs for two hundred of his people. They're hard workers and will get your land ready."

"I can't pay their wages this year."

"I can. I'll have them here in two or three days."

Celeste looked at Errin. He saw her considering how to answer. Both of them knew how very important her answer was to their lives. Was she going to let him help her?

"All right," she said. Her gaze again went to the men and mules winding down the road leading into the valley.

Errin saw the dimple that was part of a smile form in Celeste's cheek that was turned toward him. By accepting his help, she had acknowledged their relationship as permanent. He was barely able to contain the shout of pleasure that rose in his throat.

Errin too focused on the men and mules. Celeste had established a camp of tents for the workers from Sacramento on a bench below the cottages of her *vaqueros*. The wives of the *vaqueros* prepared morning and evening meals for their husbands, and also for the new workers. Errin knew he would have to set up a separate camp and kitchen for the Chinamen when they arrived.

"Come with me and I'll cook your breakfast," Celeste said. "Do you feel well enough for that?"

Celeste laughed and squeezed his hand. "I did something more strenuous than that last evening. And here at home on the mountain, I am healing swiftly."

"All right, but you must let me help you."

"I would like that. First go and wake Vicaro so he can eat with us."

"I hope the old bandit doesn't shoot me when he wakes."

"He has indeed shot men. Several of them. I believe he now wants only to live out the rest of his life in peace."

"So do I," Errin said.

Ignacio reined his running horse into the stone paved courtyard of the *hacienda*. He dragged the mount to a clattering halt near the patio where Celeste sat talking with Errin and Vicaro.

"Señorita Celeste," he shouted. "Come quickly. They are in danger."

"Who's in danger?" Celeste asked, hurrying out into the courtyard.

"Our *vaqueros*. Men with guns have beaten Mavro Carmillo, maybe to death, and are driving all the other workers from your land."

"Who's doing this?"

"Three Spaniards. They say they will shoot any man who works for you."

"Go saddle my mare," Celeste exclaimed, her fury rising. "I'll get my pistol and go back with you and stop them."

"No, *señorita*," Vicaro said, coming up beside Celeste. "This is something that I'll do. You must allow me for my debt to your father is not yet paid in full."

"Then we'll both go. Two guns are better than one."

"You're not strong enough," Errin said. "But you're right about two guns being better than one. I'll go with Vicaro and help him deal with those men."

"I'll go and that will make three guns," she said.

"But we can . . . ," Errin started to speak.

"I'm going," Celeste said with finality. "Ignacio, saddle my horse."

The three men hastened to the corral. Shortly they returned mounted, and leading the gray mare. Celeste stood waiting, Ernesto's pistol belted around her waist.

Errin sat his horse and watched Celeste. He hoped that she would change her mind about going with them. Perhaps mounting without help would convince her she was not in condition to fight a pistol duel. Then Ignacio sprang down to help his mistress.

She motioned him back. "I can do it myself."

Celeste's face blanched with the sharp lance of pain as she pulled herself into the saddle. She wiped at the sweat that had suddenly popped out on her forehead. She was not as well or strong as she thought.

She looked at Errin. "You and Vicaro had better hurry on ahead. Ignacio and I will come as fast as we can."

"Are you ready, Vicaro?" Errin said.

The old bandit nodded and spurred his horse. The two men left the courtyard running their horses at the top of their speed.

As the horses raced down the winding road toward the valley, Errin looked to the side at Vicaro. The man sat very erect in his saddle. His hat had blown from his head and hung down his back by its cord. His hair streamed out behind in a long white mane in the wind. There was an expression of pleased anticipation on his face. The old bandit wanted to fight. Errin hoped Vicaro was as good with a gun as Celeste had said.

They came off the mountain road and sped north over the valley bottom. Ahead the machines could be seen sitting idle, and the mules, still hitched to them, standing slumped shouldered and resting.

Three armed men were confronting Celeste's group of workers. A man lay unmoving on the ground. That must be Mavro, thought Errin.

He and Vicaro reined their mounts down to a walk. Both men, acting on one thought, drew their pistols.

"Señor Scanlan, have you ever been in a fight with pistols?" Vicaro asked.

"Yes."

"Then you know that if a fight begins, you shoot until all

your enemies are down and dead. Wounded men are very troublesome. They can still kill you, and if they live, they can testify against you at a trial.''

''None of these will leave here alive.''

Vicaro saw Scanlan's eyes were hard, and alert like an eagle watching a coiled rattlesnake. Vicaro had never seen an eagle lose a fight with a snake.

''I think you would make a very good bandit,'' Vicaro said. ''Now let us go talk to these men who are already dead, but don't know it.''

Errin studied the gathering of men. All were silent and watching Vicaro and him approach.

One of the Spaniards, a thin, hatchet-faced man, said something in a low voice to the other two with him. Errin knew that man was the leader and would give the signal to start the fight. He must be the first one to die.

Celeste's workers were tense. They shuffled their feet nervously as Errin and Vicaro dismounted and walked toward the Spaniards.

''Why are you three on the land of Celeste Beremendes and threatening her *vaqueros?*'' Vicaro called.

''Who are you, old man, that you question us?'' the thin Spaniard replied in a rough voice.

''I am Vicaro Zaragoza. Who are you?''

''I am Gomez.'' The Spaniard leader focused on Scanlan for a moment, then back to Vicaro. He had heard of the bandit, but surely he was too old to be much of a fighter. The American now, he should be watched.

Gomez spoke. ''I'm here to tell these men that it is dangerous to work for the Beremendes. That they must leave here and now.''

''You're wrong,'' Vicaro said. ''I will keep them safe and Scanlan will help me. But you are trespassing and therefore you're not safe.''

Gomez laughed. ''We're in no danger.''

''You're very wrong,'' Vicaro said in an ugly voice. He swung his pistol up from beside his leg and fired into the center of Gomez's chest.

Errin, taken by surprise by Vicaro's abrupt attack on the Spaniards, jerked his pistol up. Gomez was falling. The two men with him were reacting swiftly, their weapons rising to point at Vicaro. By starting the fight, Vicaro would draw the fire of both men. Errin must try to protect the old man. He shot the Spaniard on the left.

Errin's target twisted to the side and fell. The third Spaniard and Vicaro fired at the same instant. The Spaniard collapsed and lay prone on the ground.

Errin heard a choked cry beside him. He turned to find Vicaro on his knees, his head sagging and his white hair cascading down like a snowfall to cover his face.

With a mighty effort, Vicaro raised his head and shoved the hair out of his eyes. He put a hand over the hole in his chest where the blood poured out. He stared at his dead enemies.

"We killed them all," he said.

"You're one hell of a fighting man," Errin said, kneeling beside Vicaro.

"But a dying one." Vicaro pressed harder on the wound in his chest and blood ran out between his fingers. "The *gringos* won't get to hang me now." He held himself rigidly erect on his knees. His eyes were full of the animal ferocity that refused to die until the last drop of blood had drained from his body.

He began to shiver as if freezing. His head gradually sank. He crumpled to the side. With a supreme effort, he rolled onto his back. His eyes stared up at the blue sky. His stare became fixed.

"Yes, you are now safe from all your enemies," Errin said.

He speedily checked the Spaniards. Two were dead. He squatted by Gomez who still breathed, but barely.

Gomez struggled to focus on Errin. "Damn that old bandit, and damn you too. What part did you have in this fight?"

The man was dying and his voice came weakly. Errin bent close to hold the man's eyes with his own. "Who sent you to stop the Beremendes workers?" he asked.

Gomez did not answer. His eyes were glazing. Errin held the man's thoughts by only a little spider's thread. He slapped him savagely. "Who paid you to hurt the Beremendes?" he shouted down at the man. "Tell me, damn you." He slapped the man again.

Gomez's eyes fluttered. "Mattoon will kill you." Gomez's voice broke and bloody bubbles burst on his mouth. He shuddered and died.

"Mattoon," Errin repeated and stood up. The man was offering a reward for Chun's capture and this Errin understood, but why was he ordering men to attack Celeste?

Celeste and Ignacio came up running their horses. They halted their mounts with tight reins.

"You're not hurt?" Celeste asked Errin.

"No."

"Vicaro?" she said, jumping down from the back of her mount.

"He's dead. A damn brave man."

"I always knew that," she said as she knelt beside Vicaro and put a tender hand on his gray head. Her tears came and streamed down her face. "My old friend, your debt is more than paid in full."

As Errin watched Celeste, a chilling fear for her safety washed over him. Mattoon had tried to drive off her workers, or kill them. He had failed. Now he would attack Celeste directly.

He went to his horse and took powder and shot from a saddlebag. As he reloaded the spent chambers of his Colt, he saw Celeste go to Mavro and examine him.

Celeste told two men to carry Mavro to the *casa* where he could be treated for his injuries, and to take Vicaro there also until his family could claim his body. Ignacio was directed to get a wagon at the *hacienda* and transport the three dead Spaniards to the law officials in Sacramento. The other men were sent back to work.

Celeste came to Errin's side. He was looking westward in the direction of San Francisco. His eyes were remote and seemed to have lost their color.

"What is it Errin?"

"A man named Mattoon sent those men to drive away your

workers. One of the Spaniards told me that before he died. You'll not be safe as long as Mattoon lives.''

"Do you think Mattoon and Dokken are partners against me? Is he hiding behind Dokken?''

"They must be working together. I'll find out for sure and stop both of them." He stepped to his horse and yanked himself astride.

"Can't you wait just for a little while?" Celeste was afraid for Errin.

"No. I must get to San Francisco and find Mattoon and Dokken before they learn about the deaths of these men. I'm certain others will be sent and they'll come to kill you.''

Celeste's fear for Errin was growing rapidly. She knew of Mattoon's skill with a gun, she had seen him shoot. Dokken was also an expert with a pistol. She wanted to tell Errin not to leave her. Yet hadn't she sought out Dokken with only one purpose in mind, to kill him? Errin and she were very much alike. She could say nothing more to stop him.

With her men watching, Celeste stepped close to Errin and turned up her face. He leaned down and kissed her on the lips.

"Come back," she said.

"All the hounds of hell couldn't stop me.''

Chapter 26

Errin ran the black horse north on the road lying between the San Joaquin River and the base of the rugged Diablo Mountains. The straining horse glistened with sweat but sped on its long legs, devouring the miles and the morning. Now and again Errin called encouragement to the animal and petted the sleek, muscular neck. He must reach San Francisco and track Mattoon down before any word could reach and warn him his attack on Celeste's men had failed.

As the miles fell away behind, the San Joaquin River veered off to the north and the Diablo Mountains dropped away behind Errin. The horse rushed onward and descended onto the broad flood plain of the Sacramento River.

Errin checked the Sacramento some two miles distant and flowing west toward the ocean. A riverboat that could carry him to San Francisco was approaching from upriver. The boat was riding the current, and with its boilers hot and big rear paddle wheel spinning, was approaching rapidly. Before the boat passed, he must reach the farmers' landing on the river bank and signal it to stop.

He shouted a shrill, keening cry into the ear of the horse and slapped it smartly on the side of the neck. The willing beast responded to the primal call, its nostrils flaring, and its hard hooves pounding the earth, stretching for every inch of distance.

They tore through the willows lining the road and thundered up to the riverbank where Errin pulled the horse to a sliding stop. He sprang down and ran to the dock and hoisted the white flag high on its wooden staff. The wind caught the cloth and sent it flapping.

A moment later, the riverboat gave a blast of its steam whistle in acknowledgment that it had seen the signal, and angled across the brown current toward the landing. The boat reversed the spin of the paddle wheel, and pressed its side to the dock.

Errin led his tired horse aboard among the other passengers and their animals and vehicles. The people moved aside to give him space on the crowded deck. The riverboat pulled back onto the breast of the river, added its speed to that of the current and bore on toward the coast.

Errin draped his arm over the neck of the horse and turned his face in the direction of San Francisco. A fierce violence seethed and boiled within him. The urge, the burning need to strike at Celeste's enemies sent a prickle up his spine.

In late afternoon, the riverboat carrying Errin docked at San Francisco. He hastened ashore, and after leaving the horse at a livery, headed immediately for his office. He had to see Levi at once.

He slowed his pace and became wary when he came within sight of the office. The white man in the vehicle on the street paid him no attention. The two white men on the sidewalk nodded a greeting and walked on. A lone Chinaman was leaning against the corner of a building a half block from the office idly watching the traffic go by on the street.

Errin passed under the Scanlan and Coffin sign and entered the office. Levi and George Louden stood talking in the center of the room.

"How did you get here so fast?" Levi asked. "I just sent the messenger for you this morning."

"I saw no messenger. Why did you send for me?"

"Chun's dead," Levi said, his voice breaking. "And they tried to kill me."

"Are you hurt?" Errin asked.

"No, I'm all right. Errin, the bastard stabbed Chun to death."

"How did it happen? Who were they? Tell me all—right from the beginning." An attack on Levi and Chun had occurred almost at the same time as the one on Celeste. Was there a connection? How could there be?

Levi swiftly told how Turk and Ingram and a third man had come to the office demanding protection money, threatening to burn them out if they didn't pay. They had seen Chun, who against his wishes, had come to the office. "They caught us on the street and killed Chun before I could stop all of them," Levi ended.

Louden spoke. "The chief of police is a friend of mine and he told me the bodies of three men were found just a few blocks from your office. Also they found a Spencer rifle. Since I knew Levi owned one, I thought you fellows might've been involved in the shooting, so I came to tell you what I've learned."

"Were the police able to identify the men?" Errin asked. His rage at the murderers of Chun and the attempt to kill Levi was growing like some great snake uncoiling in his stomach. Someone would pay dearly for that.

"They knew them," Louden said. "They were waterfront thugs. Further he said they often hung around the saloon owned by Brol Mattoon."

"Brol Mattoon, eh? I heard that name this morning. A man spoke it just before he died from a bullet."

"Your bullet?" Louden asked.

"Whose bullet isn't important. But the man said Mattoon had sent him and other men to run Celeste Beremendes's workers off so she couldn't grow wheat. Do you know what interest Mattoon has in the claim on her land?"

"I know the Beremendeses. I wouldn't think Mattoon would have any interest in their land. Dokken is the man who is contesting her land grant."

"Mattoon's your friend and yet you don't seem to know much about him. Besides causing Celeste trouble about the title for her land, he might be the man who sent those three water front rats here to force protection money from us. Those men killed Chun and could have done the same to Levi. I thought your detectives would have told you all about the important men of the city.''

''Several of us have been curious about Mattoon for we know he has business interests on the waterfront. Besides the saloon, he owns at least one factory that I know about. But many other people have legitimate business interests there. My detectives have reported certain things about him that I don't like. Still no one has gathered sufficient evidence to bring him to trial on a charge.''

''I'm beginning to think the honest men of the city haven't tried very hard. Perhaps he's too big a man for that. Or since Mattoon is such a famous pistol shot, perhaps everybody is afraid he might call them out for a duel on Angel Island and shoot the hell out of them.'' Angel Island was the favorite location for duels and many disagreements had been settled there in blood.

''I'm no coward and don't you think it,'' Louden said, bristling with anger.

''Errin, Mr. Louden is our friend,'' Levi interjected.

''I believe that too,'' Errin said and meant it. The man had simply not checked his associate closely enough. There had been no justification for Errin's insult. ''Mr. Louden, please accept my apology for I overstepped myself and was unfair to you.''

''All right then, apology accepted,'' Louden said. He was silent for a few seconds, obviously considering whether or not to speak. ''I know what you and Levi plan to do,'' Louden said. ''But be warned, Mattoon is tough just as you said. Further if it's true those thugs work for him, then he'll be hard to get to.''

''Nothing can protect him,'' Errin said.

Louden saw the implacable hatred on the faces of the two young men. ''I may have made a mistake in not investigating Mattoon more thoroughly,'' he said. ''His bank handles much

nminted gold and the gold that has been stolen from Wells
Fargo could be easily hidden there.''

"Then come with us and help us," Levi said.

"There isn't any evidence at this time that he has done
nything illegal against Wells Fargo. I'll start an intensive
nvestigation. Of course if I find evidence, I would first turn it
over to the law and see what they do with it.''

Errin shrugged his shoulders. "I have evidence enough, and
don't have to let the law do anything. Levi and I can handle
t by ourselves. It's getting dark, where would Mattoon be this
ime of day?''

"He would've left the bank by now, if he had been there,''
Louden replied. "So he could be home. But like I said, he has
other businesses and could be at one of them. Also he is often
nvited out to parties and card games with other businessmen
of the city. He could be at any one of a number of places.''

"Where does he live?" Levi asked.

"He has a beautiful home up high on the hill, on Larkin
Street just south of Clay," Louden replied. He told the two
young men how to find the residence.

"Levi, let's go hunting," Errin said.

"I've just been waiting for you," Levi said.

"Do you have a gun?"

Levi opened his coat to show a holstered pistol. "I'll never
again go out on the street without this.''

"Then let's go do it." Errin led out through the door and
onto the street. They turned up the hill.

Ahead of them, a large covered buggy pulled by a team of
horses drew away from the curb of the street and came toward
them. A Chinaman clothed in a black liveryman's outfit drove
from the open front seat. The rear of the buggy was enclosed
by leather curtains that hid the occupants.

"Watch it, Levi," Errin said as the driver reined his team
in close to the sidewalk.

Both men moved back from the street and reached inside
their coats to clutch their weapons. At that moment, the side
curtain of the buggy was shoved aside and the face of the Scom
Lip, the tong chieftain, appeared.

"Mr. Scanlan, and you Mr. Coffin, may I speak with you?" Scom Lip said.

"It was the Chinaman's Goddamn reward that got Chun killed," Levi said in a low, angry voice to Errin.

"Maybe, and maybe not. Now take it easy for we don't want to fight the Chinaman and Mattoon both at the same time."

"We have no time to spend now," Errin called to Scom Lip. He walked on with Levi matching strides with him. "See us later," he said over his shoulder.

"This is not about business," Scom Lip called after them. "It's about revenge and taking it without dying."

Errin and Levi halted abruptly and turned back to the Chinaman. "You know what happened to Chun?" Levi's voice was sharp.

"Of course. I've had my men watching and waiting since daylight for Scanlan to arrive. I have information for both of you. Come ride with me."

Errin's ire rose at the thought of Scom Lip spying on Levi and him. Still, the Chinaman didn't act guilty of having a hand in the killing of Chun. He might know something that could be useful, but he wasn't to be trusted.

"I think we should listen to what he has to say," Errin said to Levi.

Errin and Levi climbed into the carriage and took a seat. Ke, the tong chieftain's bodyguard, sat tense and watchful beside his leader. Scom Lip closed the curtain, and at a command from him, the buggy moved off.

"What do you want to tell us?" Errin said.

"I think you and your partner will soon go to take vengeance on Mattoon for killing Chun Quang."

"So you know who killed Chun, and that it was Mattoon's men?" Levi said.

"His men killed her, and I know that for a fact."

"You had a reward out for her," Levi said accusingly.

"Yes, for I had bought her."

"That's not what she told us."

Scom Lip moved his hand in a deprecating gesture and his voice became hard. "I've gone through all this with your friend

ere. I removed my reward from Chun while I waited for him
find work for some of my people. Now let's get down to
e immediate problem.'' Scom Lip put an end to the discussion
ith Levi by turning to Errin.

"I know much about Mattoon that the Americans don't.
hey see him as a banker, a rich man, and he is all that, so he
highly regarded by many influential people. However they
e blind to the many crimes he has committed. He is the boss
f the thugs who rule the underworld of the waterfront and
rey upon the ship owners and the honest businessmen there.''

"Tell us all you know,'' Errin said.

"You are friendly with the Beremendes woman. Well, Mat-
on works with Dokken to steal her land.''

"How would you know that?''

"Nobody pays much attention to a Chinaman sweeping the
oor of a bank, or working as a servant in a rich man's house, or
imply standing on the sidewalk and quietly watching. Further,
hite people don't think many Chinese understand English.
ou'd be surprised how many do. From them I learn many
ings, for I must as you and I have discussed before.''

"And one of these things is that Mattoon and Dokken are
artners.''

"Not partners!'' Scom Lip scoffed. "Mattoon would never
ave a partner. Dokken merely takes Mattoon's orders. But I
ould think, Dokken should be killed also.''

"So now, for your own reasons, you give us information
hat will help us kill Mattoon,'' Errin said. "Why didn't you
ell me about him before so we could be prepared? Or why
idn't you destroy him yourself? There are many ways to do
hat and the other white men would never know who did it.''

"Would you have believed me earlier? And as I told you,
could never risk attacking a white man. I want to inform you
f what I know, and to warn you that Mattoon will not be easy
o punish for what he has done.''

Errin waited for Scom Lip to continue. The man's enmity
or Mattoon showed in his hooded black eyes. It was obvious
Mattoon was the personal foe of the Chinaman. The tong leader
was doing his best to persuade Errin and Levi to kill the man.

"Errin, why should we trust him?" Levi asked.

Scom Lip looked sharply at Levi. "You don't believe me?"

Errin saw Levi was going to reply angrily, and spoke quick
to prevent it. "I believe him, Levi. Mattoon sent men to driv
Celeste's workers away. That much of what he says is tru
Mattoon deserves to be punished for that alone."

"What is your plan?" Scom Lip asked.

"Just a plan," Errin said.

"I see you don't trust me."

"Would you help us kill him if I told you?"

"No. But I can tell you where he sometimes is at nigh
That's at the Porpoise Saloon on The Embarcadero."

Errin laughed harshly. Levi and he were all alone in the fig
with Mattoon and his thugs. "Stop and let us out. Levi an
I've wasted enough time."

Chapter 27

The sailors wearing their dress-blue uniforms came off the Union battleship with lively steps. Laughing and joking and looking expectantly toward the shore, they went down the pier to The Embarcadero. The whores knew of the ship's arrival and waited bedecked in brightly colored clothing. The women went forward to meet the sailors and worked through them like a fish seiner. Few sailors escaped the women's perfumed mesh.

Errin and Levi halted and backed against the front of a building to let the throng of seamen and whores pass. When the last pair had disappeared into the night, the two men moved on.

"That fellow can tell us where Mattoon's saloon is," Errin said. He gestured at a spindly, dapperly dressed man watching with a pleased expression after the whores and their catches. The man was a pimp, of that he was certain for he had seen a thousand of them on the streets of London and Liverpool and knew their distinctive manners. The pimp would know every inhabitant of the street and most everything that happened on the waterfront.

They crossed the street and stepped upon the sidewalk beside the pimp. Errin caught the man by the shoulder with an easy grasp. "Friend, where can I find Brol Mattoon's Porpoise Saloon?"

The man looked Errin and Levi up and down evaluating their clothing, and then cocked his thin face to regard them. "No need to go there for women," the pimp said. "I can help you find the prettiest ones, any color, black, brown, red, or white and each one willing to satisfy two men about the city that I can see you both are."

"We're not looking for women," Levi said. He wanted to find Mattoon quickly.

"But I can get . . ."

Errin clamped hard on the man's shoulder, digging in with the bony ends of his fingers and thumb. The man winced with pain. "Listen, pimp, we're in a hurry," Errin growled and leaned close. "I asked you a simple question, now where's Mattoon's Porpoise Saloon? Answer quick or I'll break your head against the wall of this building." He dug deeper into the man's shoulder.

The pimp shrank under Errin's hurtful grip. "Down that direction five, maybe six blocks," he said and pointed with his free arm along the street weakly lit by gaslights. "Just beyond Vallejo Street."

"Have you seen Mattoon tonight?" Errin asked in the off chance the man had.

"Not tonight."

"All right. Now get on your way." Errin released the man. The pimp hastened off.

Levi and Errin checked the Porpoise Saloon through the door that opened out onto The Embarcadero. The saloon was huge and jam-packed with patrons. Large chandeliers, each holding several lighted oil lamps, hung from the ceiling and cast a yellow illumination down on the drinking, gambling throng. The broad center of the place held many tables, every one full. A bar crowded with men standing elbow to elbow lay on the right. At the far end of the saloon was a raised platform where a band consisting of a drummer, a fiddler, and a man pumping an accordion played for half a score of dancing, promenading couples. Several men and saloon girls were on the upstairs balcony and watching down at the main floor.

"I hope the bastard's here," Levi said.

"We'll soon know," Errin said and moved through the door.

They made their way across the room and shoved up to the bar. One of the men pushed aside, turned and glared at them. When he saw their taut, angry faces, he looked away.

"A cold beer," Errin told the bartender. "And one for my partner."

"Have you seen Mattoon?" Levi asked the man as he turned away.

"No. Sometimes he don't come, and when he does it's always late. But if he comes, he'll sit at that big table over there near the wall." The man made a halfhearted gesture with his hand.

The table was at least twice as large as any of the others and set off by itself. Three men with mugs of beer in front of them sat talking among themselves. All were dressed in the clothing of waterfront workers with billed seamen caps. A saloon girl came past and spoke and smiled at one of the men. He said something in reply. The woman laughed and walked off swinging her hips.

The bartender returned with the beer. Errin handed him some coins. "I reckon those fellows at the table keep order in the saloon?" he said.

"They do the bouncing, except when Mattoon's here. He's a brawler and likes to use his fists. And he's good with them." The bartender moved away in response to a call from down the bar.

"Didn't you tell me Mattoon's men threatened to burn us out if we didn't pay?" Errin asked Levi.

"Among other ways to hurt us."

"Men who own things that'll burn shouldn't threaten others with fire. This place is made of wood. Let's look around back there in the rear."

Carrying their beers, Levi and Errin moved slowly away from the bar and made their way past the card tables to a partially open doorway in the rear wall of the saloon. They glanced about at the patrons and found none were paying them any attention. At the big table, Mattoon's men were talking to a woman.

Errin looked through the door and saw a stairway leading down, to a basement storeroom he judged. "I've got an idea," Errin said to Levi. "Stop anyone who tries to come down after me." He thrust his mug of beer into Levi's hand.

"How?" Levi asked.

"You'll think of a way."

Errin stepped to the door and shoved it wide. He started cautiously down, his path lighted by a lantern hanging from one of the joists of the main floor above. He reached the bottom and peered around. Numerous bottles of whiskey were stored on shelves along three walls. Kegs of beer were stacked along the fourth wall.

In the center of the basement, four pairs of wooden posts spaced some eight feet apart were set solidly in the hard dirt floor. Wrist manacles were fastened to one post of each pair, and leg manacles to the opposite posts. Between the posts, the dirt floor was worn and scuffed. Errin knew the posts for what they were, prisons for men. The seaports of England had their share of shanghaiers. Many of the shanghaiers there, like Mattoon obviously was here, chained their victims between posts and in this manner held them captive until they were forced onto some outgoing ship. Damn foul business.

He began to grab bottles of whiskey, and breaking off their necks by smashing one against another, poured the highly flammable contents on the remaining bottles stored in the basement. Then from a bottle, he dripped a stream of the liquid to the bottom of the steps leading up to the main floor of the saloon. To lengthen the time period of his fuse, he took a sheet of newspaper found in a corner on the floor and twisted it tightly lengthwise. He placed one end on the whiskey-soaked earth. The other end was lighted with a match. He hustled up from the basement.

He slowed at the top of the stairs, and leaving the door open, stepped out into the saloon. He took his beer from Levi.

"What'd you do down there?"

"Started a fire."

"What's there that'll burn?"

"Gallons upon gallons of whiskey."

"That damn stuff'll explode when it gets hot," Levi said anxiously. "Best we get out of here."

"Don't be in a hurry. We've got too be sure the fire happens. We want Mattoon to know we were here."

"How're we going to let him know that?"

"Why we'll tell the bartender as we leave," Errin said with a chuckle.

Levi looked to see if Errin was joking, and saw he was deadly serious. He went with his wild friend as they wound their course slowly back to the bar.

"Another pair of cold beers," Errin told the bartender.

"Right."

The beer came and Errin paid. He lifted his mug to Levi and winked. "Here's to a hot time in the old town tonight."

They watched across the milling crowd of men and women to the doorway leading to the basement storeroom.

"Soon now," Errin said in a voice that only Levi could hear. "I think it'll take about two or three minutes for the unopened bottles to get hot enough to explode."

A tendril of gray smoke drifted out of the basement door in the rear wall. It stretched and floated up toward the saloon's high ceiling. More smoke poured into the saloon until there was a small cloud near the door. The fire was now burning too strongly to be put out. The real inferno should soon erupt.

"Bartender," Errin called along the bar, "I think something is burning there in the back of the saloon."

The bartender hastily looked. "Sure as hell 'ppears so," he said. He hurried out from behind the bar and roughly shoved a path to the back of the saloon. He disappeared into the smoke now spewing strongly from the doorway. An instant later he plunged back into view. "Get over here," he shouted at the men at the big table and motioned frantically for them to come. Several patrons had noted the bartender's actions and had followed him with inquisitive eyes. Now they saw the smoke streaming into the saloon.

"Fire!" a woman screamed in a high, scared voice.

The shock of the call rippled through the crowd. All voices died. The music ceased. Silence fell everywhere, and held for a stunned second. Then a mighty roar of shouts of "FIRE" rang against the rafters. A stampede started for the front entrance.

"What now?" Levi asked.

"We should roust out all the lovers upstairs that didn't hear the alarm," Errin said, nodding at the second floor where the women had bedrooms. "We don't want to let anyone get hurt except Mattoon, or his men."

They mounted the stairs to the balcony and moved along flinging open the doors to the saloon girls' rooms. Three were locked and these they kicked open. "Get out," they told the startled, naked occupants. "The saloon's on fire." The men and women snatched up their clothing and fled.

Levi and Errin followed the fleeing people down from the balcony. As they reached the main floor, the building shook with a violent explosion. The chandeliers jumped on their chains and swung violently. A fraction of time later, an even larger explosion crashed and the floor buckled and heaved upward. Errin and Levi were flung roughly against the wall.

Errin straightened and looked at Levi. His comrade was getting to his feet. He seemed to be unhurt. "Run for it!" he shouted.

The two men darted from the building. The roof collapsed with a crash at their heels. They pulled up quickly in the edge of the throng of people who had escaped the saloon before them.

"So much for a job well done," Errin said to Levi.

"So good that it almost got us," Levi said.

Errin looked around at the crowd that was shocked to silence by the suddenness of the fire and explosions. Where was the bartender? He saw the man standing with two of Mattoon's other men and staring woefully at the demolished building. As they watched, flames broke into view licking up through the jumble of beams and boards and broken furniture. Smoke and sparks spiraled skyward.

Errin moved to stand beside the bartender. "Exploding whiskey makes a hell of a fire," Errin said.

"Yeh," said the bartender. Then he quickly looked at Errin. "What do you know about the fire? Who are you?"

"Tell Mattoon that Scanlan and Coffin were here." Errin pivoted about and followed by Levi, went into the crowd.

Chapter 28

"Let's burn Mattoon's fancy house like we did his saloon," Levi said fiercely as he looked about in the light cast by the candelabra Errin held aloft. "There's no one here inside to get hurt, and the servants' quarters are far enough away the fire couldn't reach them." His pain at the murder of Chun made him ill. Only the death of Mattoon would heal him.

"Best we take time to think this through," Errin said. "We've got Mattoon chasing us so our ambush must be damn well laid." He could feel his partner's sorrow, at least part of it, for he had his own deep worry about Mattoon harming Celeste.

He turned, sweeping the light around to better see the wide, cavernous main room of Mattoon's home. "I want to make him pay for what he's done to you, and to Celeste, but let's not destroy this beautiful place just yet. If Mattoon escapes from us, then we'll burn it."

Levi and he had gone straight from the waterfront to Mattoon's huge three-story mansion located high on the hill above San Francisco. Stealing onto the grounds, they had discovered the small bungalow of the servants set some one hundred yards back from the main house. Through a lighted window, they saw the servants were Chinese, a man and a woman.

Searching around the main house they found a window on the side that they could force open and had climbed into the dark interior. Not certain whether or not the house was occupied, they had crept from room to room. They discovered no one, and then Errin had lighted the candelabra. He had expected Mattoon's home to be grand in size and richly furnished, still he was amazed at the number of rooms, eighteen in number, and astounded by the amount of wealth the man had poured into its decoration. There was walnut and cherry paneling, opulent furnishings of thick wool carpets, overstuffed couches and chairs covered with velvet, and crystal and silver, and original paintings. A fortune had been spent to create the man's home.

"It's time to plan our ambush on Mattoon." Errin said.

"And a clever one he won't see until it's too late," Levi added.

Mattoon stopped with Dokken on the street and scanned the broad grounds surrounding his home. He paid special attention to the carriageway that led to the side of the house, passed under a covered walkway leading directly to the entrance, and continued on to the stables in the rear. That portion of the carriageway between the street and the house was flanked by shoulder high shrubbery and large, tall trees that were ideal for hiding an enemy.

He focused on his home, rising serene in the moonlight, a beautiful white jewel in the center of the dark grounds. Life here was so very different from the sensual, and violent life he lived on the waterfront. Here in this house he entertained San Francisco's elite people, the rich and the powerful, in lavish parties. Since he was a bachelor, lovely daughters were trotted out for his inspection. Young widows made their coy overtures to show they were available. Ah, what a great life. He hoped Scanlan and Coffin, two nobodies, were indeed hiding somewhere near thinking to pounce on him? He would shoot them all to hell before they could spoil the life he had built for himself.

Mattoon knew of the death of the Chinese girl, and the killing of the three men he had sent to collect protection money from the pair of young businessmen. The death of the girl pleased him, a just reward for daring to escape from his custody. The slaying of his men did not bother him at all for there were others to take their places. But the skill Coffin had shown in the killing of the men did make him cautious. It seemed that winning the rifle shooting contest in Sacramento had not been a fluke for Coffin. Then he had been joined by Scanlan returning from the Beremendes *rancho* where he had prevented Mattoon's men from driving off her workers. Mattoon would like to know exactly what had happened there. Then the two men had burned the Porpoise Saloon. Mattoon had not expected that, and surely not the action the men took to identify themselves to the bartender. They had obviously calculated that the saloon was valuable to Mattoon and had destroyed it in an attempt to bring him chasing angrily after them. Others on the waterfront knew about the challenge to Mattoon, and for him to maintain supremacy in his domain, he had to take up the challenge. He had done just that, but warily and with plenty of tough fighters backing him. He had survived many battles and knew there were times for boldness, but when your opponent started the game, that was a time for caution.

With Dokken and five tough fighters, Mattoon had led in a search for Scanlan and Coffin, checking their office, their home and the home of their foreman, Isaiah Green. A damn foolish name for a black man. He had been tempted to give Green a hellish beating and then run him out of town, but had constrained himself, and instead put a man to watch him in the chance he would lead them to his employers. He had dismissed the remainder of his men, except for Dokken, and then made his way through the night to his home.

Mattoon had been surprised when the two partners hadn't been found. He had had trouble with other men who had resisted his efforts to collect protection money from them, or had other grievances against him. Those men had either forted up in their places of business, or at home. Mattoon had patiently waited. Until the day they came outside, thinking the battle was over when Mattoon's men had not again approached them. Once on the street, they were easily taken prisoner, never to be seen again. He had thought Scanlan and Coffin would have acted the same.

"We'll check the entire grounds and then inside," Mattoon said.

"It's damn strange we haven't been able to find them. Do you think they would be so dumb as to come here?"

"I don't think they're here. But it wouldn't be so dumb for most men would drop their guard when they reached home. We'll stay together as we look for them so we don't shoot each other."

Mattoon moved out. Dokken took a parallel course on the right. They went warily through the broad grounds landscaped with stone walls, flower beds and tall trees towering over everything. Mattoon noted Dokken was tense, his eyes constantly probing the night shadows. Dokken, like Mattoon, had seen Coffin shoot. Scanlan could be equally skilled with a gun.

"What's that?" Dokken asked. "There ahead in those trees."

Mattoon swiftly looked at the copse of trees faintly illuminated by moonlight. The light was not good, still he could see the dark, vertical outlines of the boles of the trees. He minutely examined the open space among the half-dozen trees, and found nothing that resembled the body of a man. "Do you still see something?" he asked.

"Not now. I thought I saw movement, but I must have been mistaken."

"Keep alert," Mattoon said.

Levi waited in the darkness that gripped the house. His eyes searched for movement and his ears reached out for the slightest sound. He held his pistol, a weapon with which he was not handy, and wished he had his familiar Spencer rifle instead. The police had it now and he would never again have possession.

He believed Errin and he had been here for hours, but his only measurement of the passage of time was by the size of the cold knot that was growing in his stomach. Why didn't Mattoon come? Then this waiting could end.

He could see nothing directly ahead where he knew the stairway rose to the upper two floors. To the side he could make out the barest of the dim outline that marked a window on the far side of the wide room. Errin sat in the gloom a few feet in the opposite direction. He had made not one sound since they had carried two chairs into the hallway and seated themselves. Levi envied him his self-control. They had chosen this location in the center of the house, for as Errin had said, there was no way to guess which way Mattoon would enter. From here they could move swiftly to intercept the man at either the rear, side, or front entrance. In fact, Mattoon might appear any place in the house for he could have a secret entrance to use when he felt threatened, and he must feel threatened after the burning of the Porpoise Saloon.

"Why doesn't he come?" Levi whispered.

"Patience, pardner," Errin replied. He had heard Levi moving fretfully in his chair. "He'll come and when he does, we'll do what has to be done." The darkness and the waiting wasn't too awfully difficult for him and he realized his tolerance had come from the countless days he had spent in the total darkness below deck in the prison hulk ships in Botany Bay, Australia. Strange that something so horrible as the hulks had helped prepare him for this fight against Mattoon. His young comrade without doubt had lived an entirely different life.

A loud crashing sound of the heavy front door slamming into a wall reverberated through the house. A pistol exploded. A shout erupted, quickly cut off.

"What the hell!" exclaimed Levi.

"At the front," Errin shouted. "Come on let's see what's happening."

Levi moved hastily toward the door. Errin caught him by the shoulder as he passed and slowed his reckless pace. "Careful now, this might be a trick to make us show ourselves."

"How'd Mattoon know we'd be here?"

"He'd figure it out if anybody could."

"But we've got to see."

"Right. But slow and easy does it."

In a few steps they were close enough to see the door standing wide open and could hear the stomp of feet and thud of fists striking flesh and bone and the strained breathing of men in fierce combat. Mystified by who the fighters might be and why they fought, Errin stole up to the door and looked out into the night. Levi came up beside him and stood in the doorway.

The dark form of a man lay motionless on the three steps rising up to the entrance. Just beyond that, a tangle of four men rolled and thrashed on the stone paved walk leading from the carriageway. The men grappled and struck swiftly and in the murk Errin could not make out who they were. Close by, four men surrounded a man much larger than they, and were attacking him from all sides. Errin thought the man, from the size and shape of his body, was Mattoon. The man pounded his assailants and seemed for the moment to be holding them at bay. Then one of the attackers ran forward and launched himself through the air at Mattoon. Despite the big man's effort to dodge the flying body, it struck him solidly in the side, and he went down. The smaller men swarmed upon him, hammering him with their fists, stomping him with their feet.

Not a word escaped the attacked or attackers. Their harsh breathing rent the air and the thud of striking fists and feet.

Abruptly from beside the wall on Levi's side of the door, shapes took form, black from black. Men, seemingly having cat's eyes in the darkness, leapt upon him. One man swung a blackjack, a twisted leather club a foot in length with a lead weight in one end, and brought it down on Levi's extended gun hand. His weapon went flying. The men jerked him from the doorway and fell upon him, hitting him savagely with their fists on the head and body.

Errin pointed his pistol at the mass of men, trying to find one of Levi's foes to shoot. But the bodies of the men moved too swiftly and Errin held his fire for he didn't want to hit Levi. He jumped forward swinging his pistol at the head of the nearest man. As he cleared the doorway and before he could

reach his target, a man came out of the darkness on the side
and caught his arm in a vise-like hold. A second man grabbed
the pistol, and twisting mightily, wrenched it from Errin's grasp.
Errin thought his trigger finger was broken. A third man dove
in low and encircled Errin's legs with his arms and clamped
them tightly. The first two men sprang upon Errin, and, with
his legs pinioned so he couldn't hold his balance, drove him
to the ground. A bony fist landed a head-jarring wallop to his
jaw.

Errin struck upward with his fist into the man's face above
him and knocked him away. He swiftly hit a second man, but
it was a glancing blow. The man, little hurt, bore in and hit
Errin powerfully in the ribs. The man holding Errin's legs,
released them, and rising quickly to his knees, rifled a flurry
of hard strikes into his stomach. The man Errin had knocked
away came in swinging. Yet a fourth man entered the fray,
coming up behind him. He landed two savage blows in Errin's
back.

Time jumped backward for Errin, and once again he was in
the black hold of a prison hulk and fighting for his very life
against men who would kill for a worn pair of shoes or a torn
shirt. He fought with all the tricks he had learned in that hard
school. He grabbed the man in front of him and flung him
away. He whirled on the man behind. The man bravely closed
with Errin and they fell locked together. The two remaining
men jumped upon Errin. Errin rolled, and bucked, and hurled
himself and his clinging foes against the wall of the house. As
they careened off the wall, a shoulder came in contact with
Errin's mouth and he bit down savagely, twisted his head and
ripped loose a large piece of flesh. His thumb found an eye he
could not see and he gouged without mercy. He found himself
face to face with a man, and he butted him savagely, feeling
the man's teeth break, and pain shoot through his own head.

The sheer number of Errin's opponents caused them to be
often in each other's way and this hindered their efforts to
overpower him. He tore free of their strong hands and fought
to his feet. He lambasted his foes fiercely with both fists. They

grunted with pain as his blows landed. He laughed wildly at their cries, and struck them with every ounce of his strength.

One of the attackers shouted something Errin could not make out. Until that moment, though the men had grappled fiercely with Errin, they had hit him only with their fists. They had seemed intent only in subduing him. Now a vicious blow of some weapon thudded into Errin's head. Stars exploded behind his eyes. Total blackness took him like a thunderclap.

Chapter 29

Levi lay silent and unmoving striving to quiet the splitting pain behind his left temple. He had been conscious for seconds. He remembered the battle with the men in the yard of Mattoon's home and the terrible blow to the side of his head by some hard object. The last thing he had heard was Errin's shout of defiance, and then there was only blackness. How long had he been unconscious? Where were the men who had attacked Errin and him? Where was Errin?

His fear for Errin overrode the pain and he rolled his head to look around. He found he was on the floor of the foyer of Mattoon's home. The feeble dusk of morning was seeping in through the open doorway. He could see into the yard and nothing stirred within the range of his vision. Through the murk in the room, he saw Errin on the floor near the far wall.

"Errin, are you alive?" Levi whispered.

Errin, only partially conscious, heard the taunting whisper of someone asking him if he was alive. Hell yes, I'm alive and will prove it. He flung himself to the side intending to roll, to make a moving target for the fists and blackjacks that could come striking out of the darkness at any instance. The violent spasm of his muscles barely turned him onto his side. To hi

alarm, he discovered his hands and feet were tightly tied. He
flopped back onto his back.

"Errin, it's me Levi. Are you hurt bad?"

"Good to hear your voice, pardner," Errin replied. "I'm
damned bruised, but alive."

"I'm tied up, hands and feet."

"Same here. Those little bastard Chinamen did a fine job
on us."

"Who do you think they were?"

"Scom Lip's hatchetmen is my guess. Couldn't be anybody
else."

"I don't understand why they jumped us," Levi said. "I
thought we were on the same side."

"Since we're still alive, my best guess is that we got in the
way when they came for Mattoon."

"Mattoon was ours. I wonder what Scom Lip did with him."

"Let's go ask the Chinaman. He tied our hands in front so
he meant for us to get free without too much work. Roll over
here so I can untie you."

Errin kicked the entry door of Scom Lip's big store with his
booted foot and the strong wooden panel rattled with a harsh
sound on its iron hinges. "Open up in there," he shouted.

But a few seconds passed before the door slowly swung wide
and two tong warriors with pistols in their hands stepped into
the opening. Their wary black eyes checked Levi and Errin,
swiftly and then ranged both ways along the street.

"I'm Scanlan and this is Coffin. Take us to Scom Lip."
Errin's voice was hard and he would fight his way inside if
the men tried to deny him entrance.

The tong men spoke together rapidly in their tongue. Then
one hurried away into the rear of the store.

Errin would be damned if he was going to wait for an invitation. He stepped forward to enter. The tong man lifted his
empty hand in a signal to stop and shook his head rapidly back
and forth.

"Stand out of the way," Errin growled. Ignoring the pistol but closely watching the man, Errin advanced.

The eyes of the tong fighter narrowed and his finger tightened on the trigger of his pistol that was aimed straight at Errin's stomach. Errin knew that if he proceeded further, there was a strong probability the man would shoot.

Errin halted just as the first man returned at a trot. The man bowed to Errin and Levi. "It is very early, but Honorable Scom Lip welcomes you to his place of business. Come this way."

Errin and Levi followed the tong man back past the loaded shelves and through the rooms behind where men were already working at there ledgers and sorting and packaging supplies. They came to the door of the office of the tong chieftain.

"Honorable Scom Lip waits for you in this room," the guide said. He gestured for Errin and Levi to enter.

Scom Lip came to his feet as the two white men came into the room. A smile that held no welcome spread grudgingly across his lips. Ke, taut and watchful, stood a few feet to Scom Lip's left. Several large, purplish bruises marred his face.

Neither Levi nor Errin smiled. Their bodies still ached from the beating they had received at the hands of the Chinaman's fighters.

"I have been expecting you to come," Scom Lip said.

"We have a good reason," Errin replied in a brittle tone. "Why did your men jump Levi and me?" He stabbed a finger at Ke. "And he must have been part of it from the looks of him."

At Errin's harsh tone, Scom Lip's smile vanished and a menacing scowl appeared. Ke started to advance upon Errin.

Errin pivoted to face Ke. "Come on. Try it alone."

"Stop," Scom Lip commanded Ke. "We must not fight with our friends."

Ke halted. "But he insulted you," Ke said, trembling with the effort to control himself.

Scom Lip stepped to a nearby table and took up two pistols that lay there. He turned and pointed the weapons at Errin and

Levi. With a face that seemed carved from stone, he stared at the men for several seconds. Then he held out the weapons. "I believe these are yours."

Both Errin and Levi knew the cost to Scom Lip not to retaliate in some manner, but instead he gave them their pistols. Errin spoke in a flat, neutral tone. "Why did you prevent us from shooting Mattoon? Did he escape?"

"Mattoon did not escape. Nor did Dokken, your other enemy."

"Then what happened to them?" Levi asked. "Are they dead?"

"Oh, no. At least not yet."

"They were ours to kill," Levi said. He couldn't keep all his disappointment from his voice.

"But you would have killed them quickly, much too quickly. Or have been killed by them. So I decided to arrange their punishment. It was not difficult to reason out what you planned to do, after you burned the Porpoise Saloon. I regret that you were hurt. Ke had very strict orders to not harm you. But you both are fierce fighters and he had to use more force than we had thought would be necessary to subdue you. We meant only to quiet you until we had captured Mattoon. Dokken being there was an unexpected bonus."

Scom Lip looked closely at Levi and Errin. "Neither of you seem to have been badly hurt."

"We're all right," Errin said. "What happened to Mattoon and Dokken?"

"They are bound to the Antarctic on my ship that left at daylight this morning to hunt seals."

"What kind of punishment is that?" Levi exclaimed. "I wanted the pleasure of shooting them, to see them die."

"I assure you the voyage will be the most severe punishment. Mattoon and Dokken have shanghaied many of my countrymen for the ships that go south for seals and whales. The shanghaied Chinamen are sold to the most ruthless of the cruel, renegade captains. They are worked like slaves for two or three years before the ships return. Some of the Chinamen die in those cold waters. When the ships have almost reached San Francisco again, the remaining Chinamen are thrown overboard. All the profit from the skins and whale oil taken during all that long voyage goes to the white captain and the few white seamen aboard. Now Mattoon and Dokken go into the storms of the cold seas on that same journey.''

''You run too big a risk,'' Errin said. ''Those two will live and return to San Francisco to take revenge on us. Now we must always be on guard against them.'' Scom Lip could have also sent Levi and him on that some voyage.

''I agree they are strong, tough men. Though both were wounded by Ke during their capture, I expect, I want them to survive the hard, never-ending labor and the cold storms.''

Scom Lip leaned tensely forward, his eyes glistening. ''Can' you imagine Mattoon's and Dokken's dreams of revenge as their ship once again draws close to San Francisco? For three years they will have waited for this one moment, the moment when they can come ashore and wreak vengeance on you two and me. But before the ship sails through the Golden Gate to San Francisco, the captain and the other crewmen will set upon those two and throw them into the sea to drown.''

''You have badly underestimated Mattoon,'' Errin said. ''He will have convinced the crew long before that time to mutiny and take over your ship. He will promise them a fortune from his own money when they arrive back here, and they would also have your ship and the sealskins.''

''There is no chance of that happening,'' Scom Lip said with a wave of his hand. ''The captain is my brother, and the crewmen are all Chinese, many of them my relatives. No, Mattoon and Dokken are doomed men. Their deaths will be slow and lingering. Three years will seem like a lifetime to them. Making an enemy suffer is like making love to a woman, it should be extended for the longest possible time.''

''Our way would have been more certain,'' Levi said.

''But you would not have made them bear the full measure of pain.''

"The thing is done," Errin said. "But I'm surprised at what you did. You told me that a Chinaman shouldn't raise his hand against a white man."

"If there is danger of being caught, that is true. However when you burned the saloon and told the bartender you, a white man did it, that made it safe for me to act."

Scom Lip looked at Errin and Levi with an amused expression. "I knew you would want Mattoon to know that you were indeed the ones who burned his saloon, and further that you had arranged for my help in shanghaiing him to sea on a Chinese ship, so I told him that. He seemed quite angry at you two."

Scom Lip was indeed a trickster, thought Errin. He looked at Levi, who only shrugged.

"I have sent our mutual enemies off to certain death," Scom Lip said. "Now please know that I want only to be your friend. In San Francisco friends are very important. Doubly so to businessmen such as you and I here on the waterfront."

"It's over, finished," Errin said to Levi.

Levi nodded in agreement as he studied the tong chieftain. Scom Lip would be a very dangerous friend, one who could turn against them at any moment. They would have to watch him carefully. "Friends are always valuable," he said.

"To show you that we've no hard feelings, we'll work some of your countrymen," Errin said. "Have two hundred of your strongest men meet me at the docks in Sacramento tomorrow. I have thousands of acres of land to clear of brush and to level for farming."

"They will be there as you ask, and you have my deep thanks."

In the breaking dawn, the crippled clipper ship fought its way eastward through the huge, white-capped waves. The fierce winds of the past two days had blown themselves away to other regions of the world. Behind it, the winds had left a shattered, splintered stub of the tall mainmast. The shorter foremast and aftmast carried every sail that the crew could crowd on. Below decks, men labored without end at the two pumps fighting the cold sea water pouring in through the cracked hull of the ship. They were losing to the sea.

"Goddamned heathens," Dokken cursed as he helped Mattoon tighten the downhaul of the foresail. "They should learn how to sail a ship. They almost sunk us. Maybe they still will."

"You're a fool," Mattoon said disgustedly. He also hated the Chinamen, but he admitted they were fine sailors. Nobody could have forecast the storm that came out of the night. Nor the giant rogue wave, towering tall as the foremast, that knocked them on their beam end and cracked the hull. As the ship had rolled back onto keel, the mast had snapped under the combined stress of the powerful wind and the weight of the wet sails. Part of the crew had manned the pumps. The others had chopped loose the broken strays, shrouds and wood of the mainmast and had thrown them all over the side into the sea.

Mattoon looked to the east. This was the beginning of the fourth day on the ship. The storm had struck in the dark of the first night. After the loss of the mast and the leak that poured hundreds of gallons of water into the ship's hold each hour, the captain had reversed course and made way as best he could for San Francisco. With the loss of the mainmast, the ship could carry but a fraction of the sails she normally raised. The race between sinking under the flood of water and reaching the safety of land was swiftly becoming a very close thing.

There was no sign of land, not yet. Still, California could not be far beyond the horizon. There he would escape, he somehow knew it. Then he would make Scanlan and Coffin and the Chinaman suffer as no man had ever suffered before.

The Chinese captain, from his station near the helmsman, saw Mattoon look in the direction that land should soon appear. He put his hand on the butts of the two pistols in his belt. Scom Lip had warned him about the prowess of Mattoon. And the second white man was not to be underestimated. What should be done with them now that the ship was being forced back to San Francisco? Should they be thrown overboard? He considered the plan Scom Lip had described for the deaths of the two men.

The captain shouted at two of his strongest men, both armed with sharp knives, and motioned for them to come with him. He pulled his two pistols, cocked both weapons, and moved upon Mattoon and Dokken.

Chapter 30

Mattoon stood in the center of the sail locker in the bottom of the ship. He swayed to the pitch and roll of the vessel. The expression on his injured face was fixed, his concentration intense.

Dokken sat on the big bolts of sailcloth piled against a bulkhead. He watched Mattoon by the small amount of light that came in through the tiny porthole set in the hull of the ship. The man had been in that position for more than three hours. Dokken had tried to question Mattoon about the plan he had briefly outlined and had received a snarled curse and told to shut up.

Dokken ached in a hundred places from the brutal blows he had received when he was captured. His face felt mangled. Fortunately none of the blows had crippled him. Mattoon was in even worse condition. His face was a gruesome, bloody mask. His right ear had been nearly torn from his head and the tattered remnant was a mass of dried blood. Many lesser wounds were purple and swollen. Through the wounds, the man's eyes glared out with a ferocious, predatory animal expression. Dokken was glad he was not the enemy of the man.

Mattoon's senses were riveted upon the motion of the ship.

He had determined the rhythm of her pitch and roll to the wind and the waves running under her keel. Now he had to wait.

He cursed himself for having been taken prisoner by Scom Lip's club-swinging tong fighters outside his home. They had poured down from their hiding place on the roof of the covered walkway like a dark waterfall. The battle had been close in and fierce. He had shot one man before his pistol had been knocked from his hand. Then the tong men had swarmed over him, beating him savagely. They had carried him nearly unconscious from his yard and dumped him into the bed of a wagon waiting in an alley a short distance away. Dokken was thrown in beside him, and the wagon hauled them away along the foggy streets to the waterfront. Scom Lip and Captain Chou of the sailing ship were at the top of the gangway when the two white men were dragged aboard. The captain called his crew of Chinamen near while Scom Lip taunted Mattoon with what would happen to white men shanghaied aboard a Chinese ship. Then four seamen forced Mattoon and Dokken below deck and locked them in one of the ship's holds.

Matton felt the incipient change in the motion of the ship. Mainly the pitch, the alternating rise and fall of the ship's bow and stern, was growing less pronounced. Then shortly came the weaking of the roll. The ship must be approaching the entrance to San Francisco Bay and its protected waters.

"We've just entered the Golden Gate," Mattoon said.

"I can feel the difference too," Dokken replied.

"Get ready to go ashore."

"I'm going to kill that little yellow heathen Scom Lip."

"Scom Lip has maybe two hundred men who take his orders and we don't know what they'd do if he was killed. So we've got to plan very carefully. No one will care if Scanlan and Coffin die. You and I will see that they die in the worst possible way."

"It's going to be a damn cold swim to shore," Dokken said.

"And a long one. In about five minutes we'll be directly off North Point. We must get off the ship when she's closest to land. When you reach the main deck, head straight for the starboard rail and go over the side."

Mattoon knew North Point well, the head of the long penin-sula that enclosed the southern portion of San Francisco Bay. Captain Chou would hold as near the center of the bay inlet as possible and that would mean a swim of about half a mile to reach land.

"Get that yardarm out from under the sail canvas," Mattoon said. His captors had unknowingly made a major mistake when they had locked Mattoon and Dokken in the hold with the bolts of canvas, replacement cloth for the ship's sails that would be blown away by storms during the long voyage. They had overlooked, buried beneath the canvas, the half-dozen extra yardarms, fifteen-foot lengths of tough oak wood designed to be attached to a mast to carry a sail. No better battering ram than the yardarms could be found.

"Right," Dokken replied. He dragged a yardarm from under the mound of sailcloth. He hoisted one end and held it.

Mattoon picked up the opposite end of the yardarm. "The crew will be scattered around the ship with several of them aloft working sail. So there should be only a few to get in our way and try to stop us. Now let's break that hatch and get out of here."

"Call it."

"Back up against the far bulkhead," Mattoon said. "We'll make a run and hit the hatch with everything we've got. Don't let anything or anybody stop you.

"Now!" Mattoon cried.

They charged forward, legs thrusting. The thick end of the yardarm struck the hatch near the latch with a thunderous boom. The iron locking bolt on the outside of the hatch ripped loose from its rivets and flew across the passageway. The hatch popped open and slammed back against the bulkhead.

Mattoon dropped his end of the yardarm and leapt ahead the few paces to the ladder that led up to the main deck. He mounted the ladder in three long steps and jumped out onto the main deck of the ship.

To Mattoon's surprise, fog drifted aft over the ship. Both bow and stern were almost invisible in the mist. Men hung in the rigging awaiting orders to change sail once the quiet water of the bay was reached and the open ocean was behind them. Two seamen were coiling line off to Mattoon's right. Both wheeled around and looked at him with startled expressions.

Mattoon sprang across the deck toward the ship's railing. He saw the two seamen quickly pull long-bladed knives from scabbards on their belts and fearlessly spring to intercept him.

Mattoon laughed at the men, hardly more than half his size. He could break their necks and be over the side before others could arrive to assist them in stopping him. Still the two would have to be prevented from cutting and laming him with their knives. He must be able to swim ashore.

Moving swiftly, Mattoon passed in front of the nearer seaman. He thrust out his long right arm to fend off the second man. The heel of his hand caught the small sailor in the forehead. The man's charge was stopped abruptly and he was rammed backward.

Mattoon sprang onto the combing of the railing and instantly kicked off into space. He plunged down feet first to the sea. The cold water engulfed him. He spread his arms, caught the slippery water, and stopped his descent. Swimming powerfully, he stroked away from the ship and up at an angle. He surfaced half a ship's length away. Shivering he treaded water and waited for Dokken.

From the hatchway, Dokken saw the Chinese seamen rush at Mattoon, the first one missing his knife strike, and Mattoon stiff-arming the second. Then the men turned to Dokken and crouched poised to go either left or right to block his escape. One shouted a loud warning to alert the ship's captain and other crewmen.

Dokken snatched up a thick coil of rope from the deck and lunged for the ship's side. He hurled the rope out ahead of him. Uncoiling as it sailed through the air, the rope went straight at the seamen's faces. One man's hands flashed up to ward off the rope.

The second man nimbly dodged aside and avoided the rope. Then he immediately reversed directions and leapt back valiantly trying to reach Dokken. He slashed with his knife as

Dokken went past him. The keen-edged blade sliced into Dokken's forearm.

Dokken felt the sharp pain but did not slow. The damn heathen had gotten lucky. Without touching the railing, he launched himself head first up and over the ship's side.

He hit the sea and arrowed downward. His arms flared and he began to pull himself upward. His head popped into the daylight and he cast a look around for Mattoon.

"This way," Mattoon called. "Over here." He saw the ship gliding past in the fog. Orders were being shouted on board, however there would be no time for the captain to put gunners on the deck to fire down on them before the ship was past and out of sight in the fog. Further, with his ship rapidly taking on water, the captain wouldn't halt her and lower small boats with armed crewmen.

Dokken swam up near Mattoon. "My arm's cut and bleeding."

"The cold water will slow it. Follow me to land."

"Do you know which direction to go in this fog?"

Mattoon treaded the heaving, bone-chilling waves and stared into the gray, impenetrable fog. North Point lay hidden someplace south of them. At this moment he knew south should be at a right angle to the ship's course. However the evening tide would be running seaward with a speed of three to four knots. In the long swim to the point, the tide, though it could not be felt, would carry them a long distance off course and they could miss land entirely and end up in the open sea. He looked at the wind riffling the water. It was slow and steady and blowing toward the sea. It could be seen and felt and would help guide them.

"This way," Mattoon called over the water to Dokken.

He swam off bucking the waves with strong strokes. To compensate for the tide carrying them out to sea, Mattoon swam at an angle into it, maintaining his course by holding the wind in his left eye.

* * *

"It's time to have Chun's casket sealed for shipping," Levi said, struggling to prevent his voice from breaking. God! how he hated those words for they meant that never again would he see that lovely face.

"Levi, do you want me to go to the mortuary and have it done?" Errin asked.

"No, but would you go with me and help take the casket to the dock? The ship leaves on the morning tide."

"Glad to. Are you sure you want to send her back to China?"

"She'll rest more peacefully there in the same soil as her ancestors."

"All right, if you say so. I'm ready when you are."

Levi opened the office door and went out onto the sidewalk. Errin blew out the lamp and followed. They halted while Errin locked the door behind them, and waited a few seconds longer to let their eyes adjust to the darkness of the falling night.

"It's a black one," Errin said. They should have left earlier, but business matters had prevented that. He led to the small spring mounted wagon parked on the street. He didn't think Levi felt like driving, so he took up the reins of the horse himself. He clucked the animal into motion.

At the first cross street, Errin stopped the horse to allow a surrey loaded with prostitutes heading for whorehouses on The Embarcadero go by. The two oil-burning lanterns hanging on the front of the vehicle glowed like giant yellow eyes in the gloomy night. In the light cast by the lanterns, Errin noted a buggy had halted behind his wagon. There were several other vehicles on the street so he thought nothing more about the buggy as it followed along at their rear. A few blocks later Levi and Errin arrived at the mortuary.

Levi stepped down from the wagon and, slump shouldered and silent, looked in through the window of the mortuary. A lamp sat on a table near the far wall and cast a frail light over the undertaker's parlor. Chun's casket rested upon a satin covered table in the center of the parlor. The lid was open and he could see the pale cameo of her face. Errin came up beside him. It was good to have a friend near you in such a time of loss and sorrow.

Errin caught Levi by the shoulder. In all his life, Errin had had only two friends. The first was little crippled Swallow, whom he had come to know aboard the English prison ship and who had died in their effort to escape. To his great good fortune, when he had first stepped upon the beach of his new country, he had encountered Levi who had taught him the value of having a truly honest man for a friend. Brave Swallow and brave Levi, what a fine pair of men. Errin was the better for knowing them.

Errin felt the wooden sidewalk beneath his feet move as a weight was put upon it. As he turned to see who it was, a brutal blow struck him in the back of the neck. He was catapulted head first into the window. Sash and panes of glass broke against his head and shoulders. He crashed down on the floor of the undertaker's parlor among the debris of the window.

He rolled to his knees, shook his head to clear it as he reached inside his jacket for his pistol. Where was his assailant? Who was he? He glimpsed a huge figure springing through the broken window. A heavy-booted foot smashed into his ribs. Errin was lifted off the floor by the impact and sent rolling, his pistol flying from his hand.

"I'm going to beat you to a bloody corpse," Mattoon shouted down at Errin.

Errin scrambled away on hands and knees, feeling the shards of glass from the broken window puncture his flesh in a score of places. He jumped to his feet and raised his clenched fist to protect himself.

Errin saw, through the window, Levi locked in combat with a man who must be Dokken. But he couldn't help Levi now. Mattoon was advancing swiftly upon him. How in hell had the man escaped from Scom Lip's ship?

Mattoon lunged, his big body bearing down on Errin. He expected the smaller man to retreat. To his surprise, Errin leapt to meet him. Each lashed out with his fist.

Errin's fist struck Mattoon square in the chest. The man's body felt as solid as a tree trunk. Errin had ducked as he struck and Mattoon's swinging fist was slightly high and hit him a glancing blow on the top of the head.

Errin came out of his crouch and drove his right hand into Mattoon's stomach. His left fist landed a hard blow to the man's ribs.

Mattoon was driven back a step by Errin's powerful wallops. Then he came back and planted his feet.

Errin and Mattoon, blocking each other's blows as best they could, stood toe to toe slugging each other in the body and face with a flurry of blows. They grunted and sucked air between their teeth. Their flailing fists landed with sodden thuds.

Never had Errin fought a man with such hard strength, so tough. Mattoon gave no ground at all. His large head was turtled down between his shoulders and the merciless eyes glaring out at Errin showed not one sign any blow caused him pain.

Errin stopped trying to fend off Mattoon's blows and launched an all-out assault on the man by pounding him savagely with both fists. If he could fend off the man for a moment, perhaps he could find his pistol. Mattoon wavered at Errin's onslaught, then steadied and lashed back fiercely swatting Errin with a left and right. The blows landed on Errin's face and a black film fell over his eyes, and stars whirled and exploded in the blackness. He fell to his knees, and caught himself there with his hands in the broken glass on the floor. Mattoon was too strong for him.

Mattoon chortled with a guttural, animal sound. "You're beat, Scanlan," he said. "Now I'm going to skin you alive." He jerked a knife from a sheath on his belt.

Errin felt the shards of glass jabbing into the palms of his hands. Was there a weapon here? He looked down, saw a narrow, jagged piece of windowpane nearly a foot long and snatched it up. He scrambled to his feet, held the piece of glass out in front of him, and waited for Mattoon's attack with the knife.

Mattoon smiled and scornfully shook his head at Errin's fragile weapon. Then he struck, a flick of his arm. The steel blade of his knife hit the glass and half of it broke away and fell to the floor.

Errin firmly gripped the slender, stiletto-like sliver of glass left to him. He felt it cutting into his flesh. But that was of no consequence now. Mattoon's movement had shifted his knife a few inches to the side and exposed a small opening. Errin, thrusting his pointed piece of glass out in front of him, sprang in past Mattoon's knife.

As Errin went by the blade, Mattoon slashed sideways and ripped a deep wound across Errin's ribs. Errin felt the searing weight of the knife, but continued on. He must strike now or die, for there would be no second chance at his opponent.

He was now within striking distance. He stabbed out full arm's length and rammed the fragile stiletto of glass into Mattoon's throat.

Immediately Errin leapt backward. Mattoon grabbed for him as he retreated, but Errin spun and tore loose from the bigger man. Mattoon followed.

Mattoon took one step and then stopped frozen in place. A stream of blood spurted from the punctured jugular in his neck. In the lamplight, the blood glistened like a jet of quicksilver. He put out his hand and caught some of the arcing stream. He looked at the blood in a disbelieving manner.

"You're a dead man, Mattoon, for your jugular's cut" Errin said, in a matter-of-fact voice.

For a few seconds, Mattoon continued to stare at his hand, turning it first one way and then another looking at the blood in the lamplight. Then he reached up and shoved his finger into the hole in his neck. But the wound was wider than his finger, and the heart pumping wildly, sent the blood spraying out around the finger.

"Don't die too quickly," Errin said.

Mattoon, straining with the effort, focused on Errin. His eyes glittered with fear. He tried to speak, but his voice came garbled through the blood gurgling in his throat. He dropped his knife and reached for the pistol on his belt.

Errin moved swiftly forward and wrenched the weapon from the man's feeble grasp. "You should've used that the very first thing. Now it's too late."

Mattoon fell back against the wall. He braced himself to keep from falling and fastened his eyes on Errin. His hand dropped from the wound in his throat. The jet of blood came weakly now. He slid down to sit on the floor. Slowly his large head sank to rest on his chest.

Errin turned hurriedly to go to the aid of Levi. To his surprise, Levi, Scom Lip and Ke were entering the undertaker's parlor by the door. Levi was safe. Now, suddenly, with the easing of tension, Errin could feel the wound on his ribs and the deep cut on the palm of his hand received from driving the glass into Mattoon's throat.

"Mr. Scanlan, I . . ." Scom Lip started to speak.

Errin was within a step of the tong chieftain and his lieutenant. He clenched his fists tightly and hit Ke savagely in the face. The man crashed backward to the floor unconscious.

Errin swung at Scom Lip. The man jumped away. Errin missed, but moved swiftly onward. He swung again and caught the Chinaman on the side of the head with his fist.

Scom Lip staggered under the blow. He retreated, his hand darting inside his clothing and coming out gripping a pistol.

"I don't want to shoot you," Scom Lip growled as he felt his face. "But if you try to hit me again . . ." He pointed his pistol threateningly.

"You should've warned us that Mattoon and Dokken had escaped." Errin raged at the tong leader. "Levi and I could've been killed."

"Captain Chou came at once after docking and told me they had jumped ship. This was only a short time ago. I didn't know if they were able to swim to shore or were drowned. Still Ke and I began searching for you to tell you to be on guard. We did arrive in time to help Levi slay Dokken."

"Errin, they probably saved my life," Levi said. "Dokken was getting the best of me."

"Mattoon and Dokken are dead, isn't that what you wanted?" Scom Lip said.

Errin measured the Chinaman, poised on the balls of his feet and prepared to fight him. You are a cunning fellow and I don't want you as my enemy, he thought. "Since you may have saved Levi's life, we aren't enemies," he said aloud to Scom Lip.

Scom Lip steadily watched Errin as if to be certain he meant what he said. Then he spoke as he reholstered his pistol. "Help me get Ke to his feet for we mustn't be found here when the police come. I don't want them to ever know we helped to kill white men."

"We won't mention you," Errin said. "I'm sure George Louden will have found out what a bastard Mattoon is by now. He'll believe our story that Mattoon and Dokken tried to kill us and we only defended ourselves."

Levi stood on the end of the pier and looked across San Francisco Bay toward the Golden Gate. The big clipper ship had caught the wind and was racing for the open sea. Though miles away, the ship's tall sails were visible, a narrow pyramid of white against the blue morning sky. The ship carried Chun away from him.

He wiped at his tears as the ship vanished behind the headland. The loss of Chun tore at his heart. With the memory of her beautiful face sharp in his mind, he remained staring at the empty bay. He heard her sad, gentle voice repeating the words that they had never made love.

Trying to subdue his sorrow, he turned and walked gloomily along the pier. He raised his eyes and looked at the waterfront and the warehouses there and higher still up at the main part of San Francisco where the white houses stair-stepped up the sand hills. It was now a lonely city.

He crossed the quay and climbed the sloping street toward the company office. There was only work for him now. The city was rich, and Errin and he could become wealthy here, if they remained strong.

Two horses were tied in front of the office. One was his and a second was strange to him. Errin came out of the office as Levi drew close.

"I've been waiting for you," Errin said.

"What's the horses for?" Levi asked.

"I'm riding over the mountain to the Beremendes *rancho.*

'm going to ask Celeste to marry me. If she'll have me, I want
you to stand up with me at the ceremony. Will you do that?''

Levi's face brightened. ''Nothing would please me more.
One of us can't get married without the other being best man.''

''Then climb on that horse and let's get on our way.''

Author's Note

The United States invaded Mexico in 1846, and captured Mexico City, the capitol, in 1847. Under the terms of the Treaty of Guadalupe Hidalgo of 1848, the Mexican government surrendered claim to New Mexico and California and all the vast wilderness from the Rocky Mountains to the Pacific, an area larger than France and Germany combined. The treaty bound the U.S. to honor all valid Spanish and Mexican Land Grants on the ceded land. In 1851 the Land Grant Commission was established by the American Government to examine documents and hear testimony to determine the validity of the grants. California contained the largest number of grants, therefore the commission was set up in San Francisco.

Eight hundred and thirteen grants, covering thirteen million acres, some of the most valuable land in California, were subject to examination and a ruling by the Land Grant Commission. Of this huge number of acres, nine million acres were eventually confirmed by the Commission.

The average length of confirmation was seventeen years. Some cases were fought in the courts for up to thirty years.

Villainous Americans destroyed government records, forged documents, and bribed congressmen to influence the Land Com

nission. One ploy used by the Americans to win was to appeal
o ever higher courts, and thus through the cost of litigation,
o force the Mexicans into bankruptcy.

Australia was colonized by English convicts. During the
ighty years from 1788 to 1868, eight hundred and twenty-five
hips transported 160,000 convicted criminals to that island-
ontinent prison. Sentences were either seven years, fourteen
ears, or life.

Male convicts outnumbered women six to one. Children con-
icts numbered a few thousand. The youngest male transported
vas nine years old. The youngest female was thirteen. Each
ad been sentenced to seven years for stealing minor objects.

Life was hell for the convicts, male or female. They worked
rom daylight to dark and were whipped unmercifully with the
at-o'-nine-tails for the smallest offense. The worst hell of all
vas under the sadistic government officials on Van Diemen's
Land and Norfolk Island. Male convicts were given one hundred
ashes for accidentally breaking a flagstone in the quarry, or
inging a song, and fifty lashes for getting a light to smoke.
Female convicts were usually given twenty-five lashes. Some-
imes a woman could reduce her punishment if she would expose
her nakedness to the male convicts and the Marine guards.

Prisoners could become free upon completion of their sentences. Of course this did not include "lifers." Most of the
freed convicts remained in Australia. A few built great fortunes
in sheep, shipbuilding, and land speculation.

The American Civil War was the most bloody war ever fought
by the United States. The Union Army contained two million
and eight hundred thousand soldiers. Three hundred and sixty
thousand died, three-fifths from disease. The Confederate Army
contained one million one hundred thousand soldiers. Two
hundred and sixty thousand died, two-thirds from disease.

The Battle of Gaine's Mill was the high point of the Seven
Days' Peninsular Campaign wherein the Union Army under

*the command of General McClellan attempted to capture Rich-
mond, the capitol of the Confederate South. General Lee savagely counterattacked and began to repel the Union forces.*

*On the third day, the main Union force holding firm agains.
Lee was General Porter's Army. His position was very stron
with lines of infantry ranged across a long slope, artiller
massed on a plateau behind, and the large Boatswain's Swam,
forming a nearly vertical waterfilled moat between him an
the Rebels.*

*Lee directed General A. H. Hill to break through Porter'
defense. Hill ordered a charge across Boatswain's Swamp. .
failed with men dying by the hundreds. Another charge followe
with the same results. Only on the twelfth deadly charge di
the Rebels break through the Union lines. A. H. Hill's Arm
was nearly destroyed in this ruthless loss of men. His arm
was not an effective fighting force for months afterwards, unt.
the depleted ranks could be filled with recruits.*

BOOK YOUR PLACE ON OUR WEBSITE
AND MAKE THE
READING CONNECTION!

We've created a customized website just for our very special readers, where you can get the inside scoop on everything that's going on with Zebra, Pinnacle and Kensington books.

When you come online, you'll have the exciting opportunity to:

- View covers of upcoming books
- Read sample chapters
- Learn about our future publishing schedule (listed by publication month *and author*)
- Find out when your favorite authors will be visiting a city near you
- Search for and order backlist books from our online catalog
- Check out author bios and background information
- Send e-mail to your favorite authors
- Meet the Kensington staff online
- Join us in weekly chats with authors, readers and other guests
- Get writing guidelines
- AND MUCH MORE!

Visit our website at
http://www.pinnaclebooks.com

THE ONLY ALTERNATIVE IS ANNIHILATION ..
RICHARD P. HENRICK

SILENT WARRIORS (8217-3026-6, $4.50/$5.5(
The Red Star, Russia's newest, most technologically advanced sul
marine, outclasses anything in the U.S. fleet. But when the capta
opens his sealed orders 24 hours early, he's staggered to read th
he's to spearhead a massive nuclear first strike against the American

THE PHOENIX ODYSSEY (0-8217-5016-X, $4.99/$5.99
All communications to the *USS Phoenix* suddenly and myster
ously vanish. Even the urgent message from the president cance
ing the War Alert is not received, and in six short hours th
Phoenix will unleash its nuclear arsenal against the Russian mai
land. . . .

COUNTERFORCE (0-8217-5116-6, $5.99/$6.99
In the silent deep, the chase is on to save a world from destructio
A single Russian submarine moves on a silent and sinister cours
for the American shores. The men aboard the U.S.S. *Triton* mu
search for and destroy the Soviet killer submarine as an unsus
pecting world race for the apocalypse.

CRY OF THE DEEP (0-8217-5200-6, $5.99/$6.99
With the Supreme leader of the Soviet Union dead the Kremli
is pointing a collective accusing finger towards the United States
The motherland wants revenge and unless the USS *Swordfish* ca
stop the Russian *Caspian,* the salvoes of World War Three are
mere heartbeat away!

BENEATH THE SILENT SEA (0-8217-3167X, $4.50/$5.50
The Red Dragon, Communist China's advanced ballistic missile
carrying submarine embarks on the most sinister mission in hu
man history: to attack the U.S. and Soviet Union simultaneously
Soon, the Russian *Barkal,* with its planned attack on a single U.S
submarine, is about unwittingly to aid in the destruction of al
mankind!

*Available wherever paperbacks are sold, or order direct from th
Publisher. Send cover price plus 50¢ per copy for mailing an
handling to Kensington Publishing Corp., Consumer Orders
or call (toll free) 888-345-BOOK, to place your order usin
Mastercard or Visa. Residents of New York and Tennessee mus
include sales tax. DO NOT SEND CASH.*